TEAR DOWN
THE
THRONE

Also by Jennifer Estep

THE GARGOYLE QUEEN SERIES
Capture the Crown
Tear Down the Throne

THE CROWN OF SHARDS SERIES
Kill the Queen
Protect the Prince
Crush the King

THE ELEMENTAL ASSASSIN SERIES

BOOKS

Spider's Bite	*Poison Promise*
Web of Lies	*Black Widow*
Venom	*Spider's Trap*
Tangled Threads	*Bitter Bite*
Spider's Revenge	*Unraveled*
By a Thread	*Snared*
Widow's Web	*Venom in the Veins*
Deadly Sting	*Sharpest Sting*
Heart of Venom	*Last Strand*
The Spider	

E-NOVELLAS

Haints and Hobwebs
Thread of Death
Parlor Tricks (from the *Carniepunk* anthology)
Kiss of Venom
Unwanted
Nice Guys Bite
Winter's Web

TEAR DOWN THE THRONE

THE THRONE

A GARGOYLE QUEEN NOVEL

JENNIFER ESTEP

HARPER Voyager

An Imprint of HarperCollins*Publishers*

TEAR DOWN THE THRONE. Copyright © 2022 by Jennifer Estep. Excerpt from CONQUER THE KINGDOM © 2022 by Jennifer Estep. All rights reserved. Printed in the United States of America. No part of this book may be used or reproduced in any manner whatsoever without written permission except in the case of brief quotations embodied in critical articles and reviews. For information, address HarperCollins Publishers, 195 Broadway, New York, NY 10007.

HarperCollins books may be purchased for educational, business, or sales promotional use. For information, please email the Special Markets Department at SPsales@harpercollins.com.

Harper Voyager and design are trademarks of HarperCollins Publishers LLC.

FIRST EDITION

Designed by Angela Boutin
Maps designed by Virginia Norey
Title page and chapter opener art by Angela Boutin

Library of Congress Cataloging-in-Publication Data has been applied for.

ISBN 978-0-06-302309-3

22 23 24 25 26 LSC 10 9 8 7 6 5 4 3 2 1

To my mom and my grandma—for your love,

your patience, and everything else that you've given

to me over the years.

To readers who wanted more stories in my Crown

of Shards world—this one is for you.

And to my teenage self, who devoured every single

epic fantasy book that she could get her hands on—

for writing your very own epic fantasy books.

Andvarians and Mortans are like gargoyles and strixes—they invariably try to kill each other.
—ARMINA RIPLEY, FIRST QUEEN OF ANDVARI

Trusting a Morricone is like trying to grab a lightning bolt. Even if you manage to latch onto it, you're still going to get burned.
—DOMINIC RIPLEY, CURRENT CROWN PRINCE OF ANDVARI

Any fool can tear down a throne. Keeping a crown on your own head is far more difficult.
—MAEVEN MORRICONE, CURRENT QUEEN OF MORTA

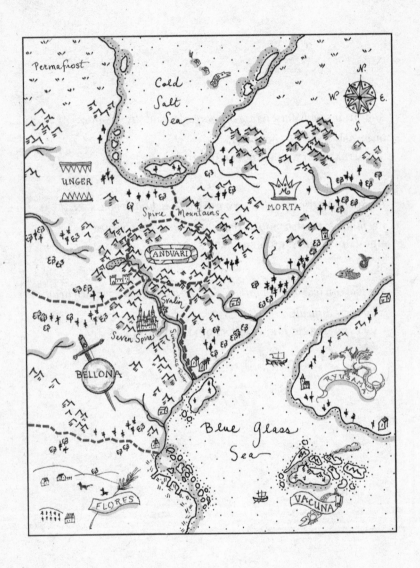

CALDWELL CASTLE

Caldwell Lake

Antheia Island

Amphitheater

Merilde's memorial bench

Arena

PART ONE

WORTH THE RISK

CHAPTER ONE

Sometimes, I despise being a princess.

Don't get me wrong. I know how fortunate I am. As Gemma Armina Merilde Ripley, the crown princess of Andvari, I have everything I could ever want, from beautiful gowns to sparkling tiaras to scrumptious foods. And I do those fine things proud. I am an excellent dancer, a moderately talented jewelry maker, and an enthusiastic connoisseur of toasted cheese-and-jam sandwiches.

I want for nothing, smile at everything, and can converse on a plethora of benign topics, from the mercurial Andvarian fall weather to the most famous Bellonan gladiator troupes to the unusual intricate patterns of Ungerian competitive ballroom dances.

Oh, yes. I bloody *excel* at playing the part of a pampered princess. Most of the time, I even enjoy it.

But this was not one of those occasions.

"...don't you think, Your Highness?"

The deep, booming voice jarred me out of my snide reverie. Several lords and ladies were staring at me, as though I were a caladrius in a menagerie they had gathered around to gawk at. At times like these, being a princess was definitely its own sort of prison.

Today my gilded cage was a dining hall lined with white stone planters boasting evergreen shrubs. To my left, servants were clearing away plates from the table in the center of the room. To my right, musicians were performing beneath a white wicker arbor draped with green vines. Clusters of pink wisteria bobbed above the musicians' heads, as if the flowers were dancing along to the low, soft tunes, including "The Bluest Crown," my own cursed, unwanted personal anthem.

A dark gray banner featuring a black snarling gargoyle face—the Ripley royal crest—hung on one of the walls next to a forest-green banner with a gold oak tree with gold acorns dripping from its branches. The crest of Lord Eichen, the luncheon host.

"Don't you think, Your Highness?" Eichen repeated, his trumpet of a voice much louder than before, as though I hadn't heard him.

With his silver-rimmed glasses, dark brown eyes, wrinkled dark brown skin, and cropped iron-gray hair and mustache, Eichen looked like a kindly grandfather, and he was a longtime friend of my own grandfather, King Heinrich Ripley. The sixty-something Eichen was also a wealthy plant magier whose estate was within spitting distance of the Mortan border.

His booming voice drowned out all the other conversations, and this time, everyone in the dining hall looked at me. The musicians paused their playing, and even the pink wisteria seemed to peer in my direction.

The weight of everyone's stares pressed against my chest like an anvil, but I smiled as though my ears weren't still ringing from Eichen's sonorous voice. With that ability to bellow, he should have been a gladiator ringmaster.

"You're right," I replied. "The Black Swan troupe will be the main rivals to our Andvarian gladiators heading into the winter season. Why, it wouldn't surprise me if the Black Swan troupe once again won a championship or two."

"They've won almost every bloody championship for the last sixteen years. Ever since Serilda Swanson returned to Svalin." Eichen spat out the famed warrior's name like it was the vilest curse. Several of his grandchildren competed for the Andvarian troupes, so he took the gladiator rankings, victories, and defeats much more seriously than most folks did.

"Serilda is a fine warrior," I murmured, not wanting to further incite Eichen.

"That she is." A smile split his face, and his mustache bristled with a happier mood. "Did I ever tell you that I once saw Serilda herself compete? I did! It was against a Mortan troupe, and she wiped the floor with every gladiator they set against her..."

Eichen launched into a long-winded tale about Serilda's tournament. I kept smiling, although I once again tuned out his words.

As Princess Gemma, I was a traveling ambassador for the Ripley royal family, responsible for maintaining good relationships with wealthy nobles, especially those like Eichen with strategic holdings near the Mortan border. For the last three days, I had been visiting with Eichen and his family at Oakton Manor, oohing and aahing over his impressive gardens, and charming and ingratiating myself with everyone, from the wealthiest lady to the newest servant.

Today was the grand finale of my visit and included a luncheon with dozens of nobles, merchants, and guilders from the nearby city of Haverton. The actual luncheon had ended thirty minutes ago, and now the guests were indulging in some more wine before taking their leave to get ready for the ball tonight.

A few weeks ago, I would have enjoyed whiling away the afternoon with idle gossip, picking up information, and seeing who I could convince to keep me abreast of the goings-on in Haverton so I could expand my network of unofficial spies into this corner of Andvari.

Not anymore. Now every hour that passed increased the threat to my kingdom—

I still can't believe she *defeated a group of Mortan soldiers.*

The stories must be lies. She's a princess, not a warrior.

She can't possibly *be a mind magier. Otherwise, she would know exactly how ugly I think her dress is* . . .

I kept my smile fixed on my face, as though nothing were wrong and I couldn't hear what everyone truly thought about me.

The nobles were right—and wrong. I might be a princess, but a few weeks ago, I had defeated a group of Mortan soldiers. As for my being a warrior, well, that was debatable, but I was most definitely a mind magier who could hear each and every one of their deepest, darkest secrets.

Unfortunately.

People thought *all the bloody time*, and their mental musings constantly buzzed around me, like bees droning on and on in my ears.

Not only could I hear the nobles' not-so-kind thoughts, but I could also feel their emotions, from the slightest bit of dull boredom to the sharp pricks of curiosity to the petty jealousy that scraped against my skin like sandpaper. Lady Kendra really did *not* like my dress, and the disgust rolling off her was strong enough to make my own stomach churn.

I drew in a deep breath and focused on myself, on my tiny internal ship that constantly sailed around on the sea of other people's emotions. Slowly, that choppy sea smoothed out, Lady Kendra's disgust faded away, and my ship righted itself.

Normally, I would have ignored people's thoughts and feelings as best I could. But given the danger I planned on putting myself in later, I actually needed to hear people's silent musings to make sure I could pull off my scheme—and that no one was spying on me the way I planned to spy on my enemies.

So I waited until Eichen launched into another story, then reached out with my magic. In an instant, I was leaning over the deck of my internal ship, dipping my fingers into that sea of emotions, and skimming the thoughts of everyone in the dining hall, from the nobles clustered around Eichen to the servants still clearing the table to the guards stationed in the corners.

This wine is awful . . .

Wish I could get closer to the princess . . .

Glitzma's hands are ruined now . . .

That last snide, mocking thought, also by the dress-hating Lady Kendra, made my hands clench into fists. *Glitzma* was my unofficial nickname, and one I had thoroughly embraced for years, since the pampered princess persona had been the perfect cover for my secret missions. But as more time had passed, the nickname had started to annoy me, and now I utterly despised it, especially given the brutal torture I had suffered a few weeks ago.

Rage bubbled up inside me, and dull aches rippled through my clenched fists, while my fingertips tingled with hot sparks of remembered pain. Despite several rounds of healing, bright red scars still adorned my hands, front and back, as though someone had painted scarlet starbursts on my skin.

The sight of the ugly marks made more rage bubble up inside me, along with my magic, both of them burning even hotter and fiercer than the phantom sparks of pain still twinging my fingertips. I blinked, and from one instant to the next, the dining hall vanished, and I was staring down at my own body chained to a table. Ribbons of fire rippled through my back, while white-hot agony throbbed in my hands and blood dripped out of the gruesome wounds in my palms—

"What do you say, Your Highness?" Eichen's voice blasted over me yet again, shattering my memory and snapping me back to the here and now.

All eyes turned toward me. I loosened my fists, flexed my fingers, and picked an imaginary piece of lint off my skirt, even as I rewound Eichen's words in my mind. Princesses learned at an early age to always listen with half an ear.

"Oh, yes," I replied. "The Haverton troupe does have a good chance of advancing to the championships, especially given the impressive performance your grandchildren treated us to earlier."

Several gladiators had sparred in an outdoor fighting ring before the luncheon. The warriors had been skilled enough, but I had seen far better. Serilda Swanson, Paloma, and of course Queen Everleigh Blair. Still, it would be rude to insult my host.

Eichen's chest puffed up with pride. "Thank you, Your Highness! I appreciate the vote of confidence. Perhaps King Heinrich will allow some of our more accomplished gladiators to serve as your guards and escort you to the upcoming Summit. After all, we wouldn't want the Morricones to get their hands on you again."

All around us, the other nobles froze, and Lady Adora, Eichen's gladiator granddaughter, sucked in a strangled breath. I kept my smile fixed on my face through years of practice and sheer force of will.

A few weeks ago, I had been undercover, trying to figure out who was stealing tearstone from a mine in the Andvarian city of Blauberg, when I had encountered Prince Leonidas Morricone. Even though Leonidas was a childhood enemy, I had still saved him from being murdered by Wexel, a Mortan captain. Later on, Leonidas had saved my life when Conley, the

Blauberg mine foreman, had shoved me into a chasm and left me for dead.

Leonidas had taken me to Myrkvior, the Mortan royal palace, to be healed, and I'd stayed there under an assumed name in hopes of figuring out who had stolen the Andvarian tearstone—and what they planned to do with it. While at the palace, I'd had a series of dangerous, disastrous encounters with both Queen Maeven Morricone and her firstborn son, Crown Prince Milo Morricone.

Maeven had assassinated Emperia Dumond, one of her bitter rivals for the throne, and blamed me for the noble lady's murder. After I'd discovered Milo was making barbed arrows out of the stolen tearstone, he had taken great pleasure in torturing me. First, he had lashed my back with a whip made of coral-viper skin. Then, he'd driven his cursed arrows through my hands.

And Leonidas . . . Well, his betrayal had been the cruelest, most calculated one of all.

He had made me believe he actually cared about me.

Eventually, I had escaped from Myrkvior and returned to Blauberg, where I had faced off against Milo, along with Captain Wexel and numerous guards. Using my mind magier magic, I had driven the Mortans out of the city and warned Milo that I would kill him if he set foot on Andvarian soil ever again.

Tales of my supposed heroism during the Battle of Blauberg, as it had been dubbed, had quickly spread through Andvari. Rumors abounded about exactly what had happened, but my family and I had taken control of the story as best we could and had (mostly) told the truth. Officially, I had tracked some stolen tearstone to Myrkvior, where I had been held as a political prisoner by the Morricones, before escaping, returning to Blauberg, and driving some rogue Mortan soldiers out of the city. Despite my obvious scars, we'd downplayed my suffering and the conflict with the Morricones, so as not to appear weak to our nobles or worry our citizens.

The curiosity of Eichen and his friends didn't surprise me, as I'd heard more than one silent speculation about my part in the battle, but so far, no one had been brave, bold, or stupid enough to mention the Morricones—and my ordeal at their hands—out loud to me.

Adora rammed her elbow into Eichen's side. His eyes bulged, and his mouth gaped as he realized his mistake.

"Your—Your Highness!" Eichen sputtered. "Please forgive me! I meant no offense!"

His apology blasted through the dining hall, drawing even more unwanted attention. Everyone stared at me again, and their thoughts slapped up against my mind, threatening to capsize my internal ship and render me frozen and useless.

I gritted my teeth, glanced down, and focused on the pendant that lay against my blue dress. The silver base featured small pieces of black jet that formed the Ripley snarling gargoyle crest. Tiny, midnight-blue tearstone shards made up the gargoyle's horns, eyes, nose, and teeth, turning the crest into the face of Grimley, my own beloved gargoyle. Alvis, the Andvarian royal jeweler, had made the necklace for me when I was younger and first learning how to control my power.

Everyone in Andvari and beyond knew that Princess Gemma always wore her famed gargoyle pendant, but it was far more than just a pretty bauble. The pieces of black jet helped to block people's mundane thoughts, while the blue tearstone shards would either store my own magic or deflect an enemy's power.

Dozens of thoughts crowded into my mind, causing the bits of black jet to heat up. I grabbed the pendant and rubbed it between my fingers, concentrating on the sharp pricks of the hot jewels against my skin instead of the snide, sympathetic, and speculative musings buzzing in my ears.

I used to be almost totally reliant on my pendant to block other people's musings and keep their feelings from overwhelming me. But ever since the Battle of Blauberg, I had been relying more on my own skill and willpower to control my mind magier magic, rather than shoving my power down as I had for so many years. Now I could usually keep my internal ship from capsizing in the sea of thoughts and emotions that constantly roiled around me. As for controlling and using the storm of my *own* thoughts, emotions, and magic that continuously churned inside me . . . Well, that was still a work in progress.

But there was no hiding from the nobles still silently wondering how I would react to Eichen's words, so I released my pendant and lifted my head. The lord's face was pinched tight with worry, and I decided to put him out of his misery.

"No offense taken," I replied. "Your offer of gladiators is quite kind, but Grandfather Heinrich, Prince Dominic, and Captain Rhea have already seen to our security needs for the Summit."

Rhea had done most of the planning, since my stepmother was the leader of the royal guards, but I didn't remind Eichen of that fact. It would be lost in the red-hot embarrassment pounding through his body and burning in my own cheeks.

"I'm relieved to hear that," Eichen replied, his voice softer and more subdued than before.

Eichen cast a desperate glance at Adora, as if hoping she would introduce a new topic of conversation to break the awkward silence.

"Princess Gemma! There you are!" a light, feminine voice sounded.

Heels clattered on the flagstones, and a woman glided forward, her quick, purposeful strides easily cutting a swath through the nobles as she stepped up beside me. She was a couple of inches shorter than I was, with a lean, strong, muscled body. Her long black hair had been curled into fat ringlets that danced around her head, while gold shadow and liner brought out her vivid emerald-green eyes. Dark red berry balm stained her lips, further enhancing her golden skin and pretty features.

The woman was wearing a long formfitting green jacket covered with flying dragons done in gold thread. A gold pendant, also shaped like a dragon, dangled from the gold chain around her neck. Emeralds glittered as the dragon's eyes, while jet and ruby shards spewed out of its mouth, as though it were exhaling jeweled fire.

Lady Reiko Yamato, my friend and fellow spy, smoothly threaded her arm through mine. I glanced down at the dragon face with green scales and black eyes that adorned her right hand. The dragon gave me a mischievous wink, although Reiko's features remained schooled in a polite mask. All morphs had some sort of tattoo-like mark on their bodies that indicated what larger, stronger creature they could shift into. My friend had transformed into her dragon during the Battle of Blauberg, and she had been a fearsome sight to behold.

I just hoped she wouldn't have to do it again before the end of our mission.

"Are you ready to stroll through the gardens?" Reiko asked. "You've been spouting the benefits of long, contemplative walks for *weeks* now."

The same mischief that her inner dragon had shown me filled her green eyes. I resisted the urge to stick my tongue out at both of them.

Eichen frowned. "But I showed you both the gardens when you first arrived. Princess Gemma sneezed quite violently throughout the tour."

Reiko's lips twitched, as if she was holding back a grin, and she arched an eyebrow, indicating that I would have to lie my way out of this. My friend had a very large competitive streak when it came to our spy games, and she was always giving me little tests just to see if I could keep up with her quick wits.

"Oh, yes," I purred, rising to her challenge, since I too had a very large competitive streak. "I did promise Lady Reiko that we would stroll through the gardens."

I glanced around, as though making sure no one was listening, even though everyone was clearly straining to hear what I would say next. Then I leaned a little closer to Eichen and dropped my voice to a conspiratorial whisper. "Lady Reiko has a personal . . . *affliction*, and I thought some herbs in your gardens might prove useful. You don't mind if we pick a few, do you?"

Reiko stiffened. This time I was the one who had to hold back a grin.

Eichen eyed Reiko like she'd suddenly grown another head and not-so-subtly sidled away, lest he catch the dragon morph's mysterious affliction just by standing next to her. "Of course not. Take whatever you need."

Reiko smiled at him, but magic swirled around her body, and long black talons sprouted on her fingertips. She curled her hand a little tighter around my arm, her talons digging into my skin, even as her inner dragon glared at me.

What's the matter? I sent the thought to her. *Is your affliction flaring up again?*

Reiko winced, still not used to me mentally communicating with her, but she muttered in her mind. *The only* affliction *I have is you and your bloody lame excuses.*

I winked at her before turning back to Eichen.

"Thank you ever so much for the delicious luncheon," I purred again. "But Lady Reiko's condition needs *immediate* attention, so please excuse us."

Eichen's eyebrows drew together in confusion, but he shot Reiko a wary look and scuttled back a few more steps, clearly not wanting to be exposed to whatever was wrong with her.

Reiko's talons dug a little deeper into my arm, but I was grinning as we left the dining hall.

Reiko and I strolled through the manor house. All the noise, commotion, and conversation in the dining hall quickly faded away, leaving us in both physical and mental silence.

Reiko dropped my arm and slapped her hands on her hips. "Affliction? Condition? You made it sound like I had the clap!"

"You're the one who suddenly wanted to stroll through the gardens. Don't blame me for arranging it the quickest and easiest way I could think of. Besides, Eichen won't try to follow us now. Neither will any of the other nobles once word of your *condition* spreads."

Reiko harrumphed, spun around on her heel, and stalked away. I grinned again and fell in step behind her. Still, my merriment quickly faded away. As much as I enjoyed teasing my friend, we had come to Oakton to do a job, and it was time to get on with it.

Reiko and I returned to my chambers. The servants were still cleaning up the dining hall, so no one saw us slip inside, strip off our luncheon garb, and don more practical clothes.

"Did you find out anything new?" I asked, stuffing the bottoms of my black leggings into the sides of my matching boots.

"Unfortunately not." Reiko's voice floated out of her room, which adjoined mine. "I talked to every noble at the luncheon, along with several servants and guards, but no one has heard anything about Mortans being in Haverton."

I ground my teeth in frustration. Ostensibly, I had come to Oakton Manor to visit Lord Eichen, but really, I was here because my network of spies had passed along some rumors that

Mortan guards had been spotted near an abandoned tearstone mine in the area.

Over the past several weeks, Milo Morricone had engineered the murders of dozens of my countrymen and -women so he could steal thousands of pounds of tearstone from places all along the Andvari-Morta border. Then, more recently in Blauberg, I'd seen Captain Wexel buy tearstone ore from Conley, the treacherous mine foreman.

Grandfather Heinrich had increased the guards and security on all the active tearstone mines, especially those near Morta, but dozens of abandoned, unguarded mines dotted the Spire Mountains—like the one close to Haverton. I still didn't know exactly what Milo wanted to do with the magical ore, but I didn't want to let him steal another bloody shard of it.

Reiko strode into my room. She had donned dark gray leggings and boots, along with an emerald-green tunic and matching cloak. She leaned against the wall while I laced up my boots.

"This could be another one of Milo's schemes," Reiko pointed out. "He could have ordered Wexel to spread those rumors just to lure you here, Gemma."

"I know, but I have to check them out anyway. Especially since Alvis still hasn't figured out what Milo is planning to do with all the tearstone arrows he's made. Seeing if the Mortans are lurking around the old mine and potentially picking up new information about Milo's plans is worth the risk."

Reiko eyed me. "You've been saying that more and more. *Risking* more and more."

I sighed. "That's because I keep getting more and more desperate, especially with the Summit coming up."

The Summit was a yearly meeting where royals, nobles, merchants, and guilders from the various kingdoms came together to hammer out trade agreements for goods, services, and the like. Everything from coal to lumber to wheat would be discussed, bartered for, and sold to whomever could pay the asking prices.

"You don't have to attend," Reiko replied. "Prince Dominic and Captain Rhea can handle things."

I shook my head. "No, I have to go, just like I usually do. Andvari cannot afford to appear weak right now, especially not during something as important as the Summit. Rumors are still flying fast and furious about my trip to Myrkvior. I have to show everyone that I survived my time in the Morricone palace relatively unscathed."

Reiko's gaze dropped to my scarred hands. Her face remained expressionless, but her inner dragon winced, as if it hurt them both just to look at the red marks.

My hands clenched into fists, strangling my bootlaces and making the tight scars stand out that much more vividly, like volcanoes of blood about to erupt out of my pale skin. The sudden angry motions caused those dull aches to ripple through my hands again and reignited the hot sparks in my fingertips. People often experienced phantom pain from old injuries, but thanks to my magic, the sensations were as intense and as vivid as when my wounds were first inflicted. I had never particularly enjoyed being a mind magier, but at times like these, I cursed my magic and all the bloody misery it caused me.

Reiko remained silent, although her dragon's wince melted into a sympathetic look. I ground my teeth again and finished tying my bootlaces. Then I straightened up, spun away from her, and tied a dark gray cloak on over my matching tunic.

Reiko had already cinched a sword and dagger around her waist, and I grabbed my own weapons belt, which also featured a dagger. My dagger was made of pale gray tearstone, which was surprisingly lightweight, and the hilt bore the same snarling gargoyle crest made of black jet and blue tearstone that my pendant did.

I buckled the weapons belt around my waist, then picked up two other items from a nearby table—the tearstone arrows Milo had used to torture me.

The shorter-than-normal projectiles stretched only from my wrist up to my fingertips, but the pointed tips were razor-sharp, and the two arrowheads themselves were unusually large and lined with curved barbs that looked like fishing hooks. Milo had driven the arrows through my hands, then used them like lightning rods to conduct his hot, electric magic throughout my body. And then, for a final cruel touch, he had ripped the arrows out of my hands, causing the hooked barbs to tear through even more of my flesh.

For the second time in the past hour, the room around me flickered and vanished, and I saw my own body stretched out on a table, blood pooling under my damaged hands. My muscles tensed with brutal remembered pain, even as my heart pounded and sweat pricked the back of my neck—

"Gemma?" Reiko's voice dragged me back into the present. "Are you okay?"

"Fine," I lied, struggling to make my voice light, although it still came out as a harsh rasp. "Just thinking."

"About what?"

"Why the arrows changed color."

It was the first thing that popped into my mind and a question that had been nagging at me for weeks now. I held the two arrows up to the light streaming in through the glass doors. In addition to absorbing and deflecting magic, tearstone had another dual nature—it could change color, shifting from bright starry gray to dark midnight-blue and back again.

Before Milo had used the arrows on me, they had been a light gray, just like the tearstone dagger on my belt. But after he'd punched the weapons through my hands, they had turned—and still remained—a dark blue, as though Milo's lightning magic had somehow changed the innate properties of the tear-stone itself. There had to be some clue in that about Milo's ulti-mate plan for his wicked weapons, but so far, I hadn't been able to puzzle it out.

Perhaps I would ask Milo—before I killed him.

Back in Blauberg, I'd warned the crown prince that I would kill him if he ever set foot on Andvarian soil again, but that was a lie. I was going to murder the bastard anyway. Something else I needed to figure out how to do, along with sussing out his true plans for the stolen tearstone.

But pondering the elusive, frustrating secrets of Milo's ar-rows wasn't helping anything, so I returned the weapons to the table, then strode over to the glass doors in the back of the room, opened them, and let out a soft, low whistle.

Several seconds later, a shadow zipped through the air, briefly blotting out the afternoon sun, before landing on the stone bal-cony outside and taking on the familiar shape of a gargoyle.

Gargoyles were as common in Andvari as wild horses were in Flores, and the creatures often roosted on the roofs of homes and shops, both in the cities and out in the countryside. Sev-eral gargoyles nested on the towers that topped Eichen's manor house, but this creature had come with me all the way from Glit-nir, the royal palace in the capital city of Glanzen.

This gargoyle was roughly the size of a horse, although his body was much thicker and stronger, and his powerful, muscled legs were set much lower to the ground. His eyes burned a bright sapphire blue in his dark gray stone face, and tiny bits of blue also shimmered throughout the rest of his body, like pinprick stars embedded in his skin. Two curved horns jutted up from his head, while broad wings fanned out from his shoulders. Black talons protruded from his large wolflike paws, and an ar-rowlike point tipped his long tail.

The gargoyle yawned, revealing his razor-sharp teeth, then

blinked sleepily. "I don't see why we have to do this in the middle of the afternoon," Grimley grumbled, his voice sounding like bits of gravel crunching together. "I was just about to catch a whole warren of rabbits in my nap."

"Because I want to be able to actually *see* what the Mortans are doing. Not trip over them in the woods in the middle of the night."

"Which we could have easily done this morning, without spoiling my afternoon nap," he grumbled again.

"You should know by now that my spy work is never done, and neither is yours."

Grimley shot me a sour look. I grinned and scratched his head right in between his horns, just where he liked.

He sighed and leaned into my touch. "Very well. Let me summon Fern—"

Thump.

Another shadow swooped down from the sky and landed next to Grimley. The shadow popped up, also morphing into a gargoyle, although this creature's face was more rounded, and her jade-green eyes matched the tiny veins of green running through her light gray skin. She too had come here all the way from Glitnir.

"Hello!" Fern chirped in a much lighter, feminine voice than Grimley's low, gravelly grumble. "Ready to fly, Princess Gemma?"

I grinned again, then scratched Fern's head as well. She also had two horns, although hers were a bit smaller, since she was younger than my Grims and not yet fully grown like he was.

"Almost, Fern. And I've told you countless times to call me Gemma."

The female gargoyle reared back, a horrified look on her face. "But you are a *princess*—our *beloved* princess—and you should *always* be addressed as such."

Grimley rolled his eyes. Fern kept smiling at me, even as she lashed out with her tail and snapped the flat edge of the arrow on the end against Grimley's shoulder. He glowered at her, but Fern merely sniffed in return and sat upright, perching on her paws as prettily as a cat.

Reiko stepped out onto the balcony and closed the doors behind her. "This is a bad idea," she muttered.

I arched an eyebrow. "Don't tell me that Reiko Yamato, skilled warrior, fierce dragon morph, and accomplished spymaster, is afraid of flying on a gargoyle?"

She huffed. "Of course I'm not afraid of flying. I flew on a strix when I followed you and the Mortans back to Blauberg, remember?"

"But?"

"But the strix had a saddle and reins and harness straps." Reiko eyed Fern with wariness. "This gargoyle has none of those things, which exponentially increases the odds of me falling to my death."

"Don't worry. I've ridden on Fern plenty of times, and she is an excellent flier. Saddle or no saddle, she won't let you fall off. Besides, this is the quickest, easiest way to reach the mine."

"Very well." Reiko stabbed a finger at me. "But if I die, then I'm coming back to haunt you. Dragons are good at that."

I grinned again. "I would be delighted to be haunted by the great Reiko Yamato. Now, let's go see if the rumors are true. If any Mortans are lurking around Haverton, then I want to thoroughly fuck up whatever they're doing here."

eiko grumbled some more, but she climbed onto Fern's back. I did the same with Grimley. Then, with a whisper of wings, the gargoyles took off.

I leaned over Grimley's side, admiring the gardens below. White crushed-shell paths shimmered like opalescent ribbons twining around the lush green lawns, while gray stone arbors draped with pink, purple, and blue wisteria stood next to the enormous oaks that gave Oakton Manor its name. The wind whistled through my hair, bringing with it the delicate scents of the ice violets, frost pansies, and other blossoms, as well as that crisp earthy tang that was uniquely fall. The cerulean sky was clear of clouds, and the late October sun added some pleasant warmth to the brisk day.

I was never happier than when I was on Grimley's back, sailing through the sky, the landscape laid out before me like a carpet at a queen's feet. And perhaps best of all, way up here, there was no dining hall full of condescending nobles, gossipy servants, and bored guards silently judging me in their minds, where they thought I couldn't hear them. These days I appreciated the quiet more than ever, especially given all the unquiet in my own mind. So I tilted my face into the wind, breathed in deeply, and enjoyed every moment of our flight.

The gargoyles swiftly zoomed past the stone walls that bordered Eichen's estate, along with the nearby city of Haverton. People were walking and shopping in the plazas below, and no one seemed to notice us pass by overhead. Then again, they had no real reason to, since gargoyles flew over the city all the time to hunt for rats, rabbits, and more in the countryside.

We left the city behind, and Grimley and Fern flew for about thirty more minutes before I spotted an odd shape on the forest floor. The remains of a campfire stood in a stone pit in the middle of a clearing, like a black bull's-eye on an archery target.

I pointed out the spot to Grimley. *Over there. That might be what we're looking for.*

Grimley flexed his wings and veered in that direction. But instead of landing in the clearing, he flew past it. I might be taking a risk by investigating the rumors, but I wasn't about to land right beside the fire pit. That was just asking for trouble, especially since I didn't know how many Mortans might be nearby.

Grimley spiraled down and landed in another, smaller clearing. Fern and Reiko glided to a stop beside us.

I slid off Grimley's back and pulled my dagger out of its scabbard. Beyond the clearing, the woods stretched out as far as I could see, and my breath steamed faintly in the chilly air. Given the high elevation of the Spire Mountains, fall was rapidly waning here. Many of the trees were already bare, although a few were still swathed in brilliant garnet and citrine leaves like ladies draped in colorful ball gowns.

No one was moving through the trees, converging on our position, so I glanced over at Reiko, who was still sitting atop Fern.

"You can let go now," Fern chirped in a helpful voice.

Reiko flinched at the gargoyle's bright tone, but she released her white-knuckle grip on the bases of Fern's wings and slid to the ground.

"Problems?" I drawled.

Reiko shook her head, and some of the sickly green tinge faded from her face. "Nope." She shook her head again, as if pushing away the rest of her nausea, then drew her sword. "Let's go find the Mortans."

We left Grimley and Fern in the clearing to hunt and headed deeper into the woods.

Reiko and I moved from one tree to another, careful to step on as few dried leaves and dead twigs as possible. We were still making far too much noise, but we didn't encounter anyone, and we quickly reached the clearing I'd glimpsed earlier.

The fire pit was much larger than it had appeared from above, and the scent of charred wood hung in the air like an invisible smoky cloud. I reached out with my magic, searching for whispers of thoughts and flickers of feelings, but the surrounding area was silent and still. I nodded at Reiko. Together, we moved into the clearing.

I strode over, crouched down, and studied the blackened detritus of the fire. The gray ash was still wet, indicating that someone had been here recently. I glanced around, looking for crusts of bread, stray buttons, loose coins, or anything else someone might have accidentally dropped, but nothing had been left behind—except bootprints.

Several bootprints grooved into the soft, muddy ground around the fire pit. At least half a dozen people, maybe more, had recently tromped through here. My heart picked up speed. This *had* to be a Mortan campsite. No one in Haverton would have any reason to be this far out in the woods, especially not this many people at once.

Reiko also eyed the bootprints. "Whoever was here cleaned

up after themselves. The next hard rain would have washed away all traces of them."

I got to my feet. "Let's track them and see if the rats lead us back to their nest."

Together, weapons in hand, we headed out the far side of the clearing and even deeper into the woods.

The Mortans might have doused their campfire and picked up their trash, but they hadn't bothered to hide their trail, and Reiko and I easily followed the bootprints, broken branches, and scuffed leaves over the hilly, rocky terrain.

I was about to crest yet another ridge when Reiko lifted her hand, stopping me. She held her finger up to her lips, then pointed at her ear. Most morphs had heightened senses, including hearing.

I reached out with my magic, and a couple of presences sputtered to life in my mind, like matches flaring in a dark room.

"We've caught up to them," I whispered.

Reiko nodded. We stepped off the trail we'd been following, then crept forward and climbed to the top of the ridge.

This ridge made a wide, sweeping curve to the left before sloping down into another, much larger clearing. At the base of the ridge, an opening had been carved into the rocks and shored up with wooden beams. No light spilled out of the black hole, but it was clearly man-made.

"That must be the old tearstone mine," I murmured.

Reiko pointed at the ground. "And judging by how thoroughly the grass has been trampled, several people have been here recently."

She had barely finished speaking when two men stepped out of the mine entrance. We fell silent, watching them.

The men strode through the clearing and stopped next to a couple of flat waist-high boulders that looked like table leaves pushed together. The men were both wearing black tunics, leggings, and boots. No crests or symbols adorned their clothes, but their purple cloaks marked them as Mortans.

My heart quickened with equal parts worry and excitement. The rumors were true. The Mortans *were* here.

Each man slung a black leather satchel down onto a boulder and riffled through the contents, causing several soft but distinctive *tink-tink-tinks* to ring out. I might be a pampered princess, but mining was one of Andvari's main industries, and I recognized the sound of rocks—ore—rattling together.

"You're sure this is all of it?" one of the men asked, his voice floating up the ridge to Reiko and me.

The second man nodded. "Yep. We got every last piece."

The first man hoisted his satchel onto his shoulder and headed toward the far side of the clearing. The second man hurried to do the same, but he didn't close his satchel all the way, and something slid out of the top and dropped to the ground. Another distinctive *tink* rang out, but the second man rushed after his friend, and they both disappeared into the trees.

Reiko scanned the woods, while I reached out with my magic. Other than the two men, I didn't sense anyone else in the immediate vicinity. I nodded at Reiko, and we followed the curve of the ridge down to the clearing.

I stepped inside the mine opening, scanning the ground, just in case the Mortans had strung up some trip wires. But the area was clean, so I ventured in a little deeper. Rough-hewn rock walls stretched out several feet before the mine's yawning darkness swallowed up the sunlight, but the smell of freshly dug earth filled the air, indicating that someone had been working in here recently.

My gaze landed on a pile of rubble close to the entrance. I crouched down for a better look, but it was just a mound of gray rocks, many with jagged, blackened edges, like they were shards of burned glass rather than solid stone. Odd. Perhaps Milo had used his lightning magic to blast the tearstone out of the mine, although no scorch marks marred the walls. Either way, something about the burnt stones made me extremely uneasy. I slid one into my pocket to study later, then got to my feet.

The last time I'd been in a mine was a few weeks ago in Blauberg, when Conley, the corrupt foreman, had shoved me into a chasm and left me for dead. I stared into the darkness in the back of the mine, but instead of seeing total, absolute blackness, memories flooded my mind.

The cool air rushing over my face as I fell. My body slamming into a ledge jutting out from the side of the chasm. The bones shattering in my left arm and leg. White-hot agony exploding in my wounds. The chill of death slowly sinking into my body. And then a shadow looming over me, slowly morphing into a man with dark amethyst eyes—

"Gemma," Reiko called out. "Come look at this."

Her voice jolted me out of my memories, although all that remembered pain kept pounding through my body, hammering right alongside my racing heart. Perhaps it was all the trauma I had endured in Myrkvior, but ever since I had returned home, my magic had been flaring up in new, unexpected ways, including all these unwanted glimpses of the recent past that kept intruding on my present.

I wiped the cold sweat off my forehead with a shaking hand, then exhaled and strode back out into the clearing.

Reiko was standing by the flat rocks the Mortans had used as a table earlier. She plucked something out of the grass and handed it to me.

The jagged shard was about the size of a small dagger. I rolled it back and forth in my fingers, watching as the rock, the ore, shifted from light gray to dark blue and back again.

"It's definitely tearstone. The mine must not have been as played out as Lord Eichen claimed during the luncheon."

"Either that or Eichen is working with the Mortans," Reiko suggested.

Surprise shot through me, and I opened my mouth to vehemently defend my countryman, but Reiko stared me down.

"First rule of being a spy—anyone can betray you at any time. Even someone you think is a staunch ally."

She was talking about Eichen, but another man's face filled my mind—the same handsome face with the same dark amethyst eyes I'd seen in my vision a few moments ago. In some ways, Leonidas Morricone haunted me far more than any injuries I'd received in the Blauberg mine.

I shoved those memories away and considered Reiko's point. "Eichen *could* be working with the Mortans, but it's highly unlikely. He has plenty of power and money, and he's never shown any interest in trying to wrest the throne away from my grandfather. Plus, Eichen's wife was killed by Mortan bandits a few years ago. He has no love for them."

Reiko nodded, accepting my conclusion.

I rolled the tearstone shard back and forth in my fingers again. "We should follow the Mortans. They might have a camp set up nearby. Maybe that's where Milo is storing all the arrows he's made with the stolen tearstone."

Reiko's eyebrows shot up. "It could still be a trap. Us just *happening* to see two Mortans outside an old mine and one of them just *happening* to drop a piece of tearstone is highly suspicious."

"I know, but it's—"

"Worth the risk," she finished.

I gave her a sour look. Reiko grinned back at me, as did her inner dragon, then jerked her head. "Let's go, princess."

She headed toward the far side of the clearing. I nestled the tearstone shard in the side of my boot so that I wouldn't lose it, then pictured Grimley in my mind.

We've found the Mortans. We might need you and Fern.

Grimley quickly answered me. *We're done hunting. We'll be there soon.*

Quietly, please. We don't want to alert the Mortans.

You might like sneaking around, but I prefer a more direct approach.

Really? Is that what you told the Glitnir glass masters last week when you and Fern were flying around doing barrel rolls and you accidentally smashed through the windows in Alvis's workshop?

Grimley huffed. *Glass shouldn't be so bloody fragile.*

I grinned, released my magic, and headed after Reiko to keep tracking our enemies.

Reiko and I crept through the woods. We didn't speak, but she clutched her sword a little more firmly than before, and her worry throbbed like a splinter embedded deep in my own heart. I tightened my grip on my dagger and tried to ignore her concern, along with my own.

Another faint trail ran through this section of the woods, although the dirt was so hard-packed I couldn't see any boot-prints or tell how many people might have passed this way. Reiko and I stayed within sight of the trail, moving from one tree to the next.

We walked for the better part of a mile before the trail led into another clearing that was even larger than the one in front of the old mine. Wide, flat rocks jutted out from the surrounding ridges like stone bleachers, making the whole area look like a rough, unfinished gladiator arena.

I didn't see the two Mortans, although the trail led through the center of the grassy clearing before winding its way past the rocks and up the opposite ridge. The surrounding ridges were too steep to climb without a rope, so the men still had to be following the trail.

"How close are we to the Mortan border?" Reiko asked.

I pointed to the opposite ridge, where a four-foot gray obelisk had been driven into the ground beside the trail. I couldn't see it from this distance, but I knew the Ripley snarling gargoyle crest was carved into the top of the obelisk. "See that stone?"

Reiko squinted in that direction. "Is that a trail marker?"

"Yes. It's also a warning that we are exactly one mile from Morta. The obelisks along the actual Mortan border are painted purple and have the Morricone royal crest carved into them, so people know when they cross from one kingdom into the other."

"We're too close," Reiko muttered. "Especially if this is a trap."

Given my recent disastrous trip to Myrkvior, I would have been ecstatic to never set foot in Morta ever again. But finding where Milo Morricone was storing the stolen tearstone might help us stop his plot before more lives were lost.

"What about your magic?" Reiko asked. "Picking up any thoughts?"

I concentrated, scanning the clearing again, but I didn't hear so much as a whisper of thought, and I didn't sense anticipation or any other strong emotions. "No one's hiding in the grass to stab us in the back, but I can't tell what's on the other side of the ridge without getting closer. Sometimes, large solid objects can dilute or even block my power, especially if the ground here is full of tearstone."

Reiko twirled her sword around in her hand. "Then let's get closer." She grinned. "After all, it's worth the risk."

I rolled my eyes. "Are you going to mention that every time I want to do something dangerous?"

Her grin widened. "Absolutely."

I huffed with annoyance, but we entered the clearing. We moved through the knee-high wild grass as quickly and quietly as possible, but the longer we walked, the greater the unease that filled me. I still didn't sense anyone nearby, but the clearing and surrounding woods were unnaturally still and quiet. No birds twittered in the trees, no chipmunks rustled through the underbrush, even the breeze had stopped blowing.

A shadow flitted by overhead, momentarily blotting out the sun. I glanced up, thinking it was Grimley or Fern, but the shadow's shape was sleeker and more streamlined than those of the blocky gargoyles. The shadow vanished over a ridge before I could get a good look at it, but a presence flickered through my mind, as soft and light as a feather tickling my skin. I frowned. That felt like—

A faint *creak* of leather sounded, and a man stepped into view beside the trail marker at the top of the ridge. I froze, as did Reiko, who let out a soft, muttered curse. The two of us were completely exposed in the clearing, and there was no way he didn't see us.

The man was more than six feet tall, with short black hair, hazel eyes, and bronze skin. His body was thick and muscled, and he clutched a sword with the easy familiarity of a seasoned soldier. Even though it was only midafternoon, heavy stubble had already darkened his square jaw. Most people probably would have thought the man handsome. I might have too, if I didn't know how cruel, petty, vindictive, and vicious he was.

Just like the two Mortans we had seen earlier, this man was also wearing a purple cloak over a black tunic, leggings, and boots. A fancy cursive *M* surrounded by a ring of strix feathers— the Morricone royal crest—was stitched in gold thread over this man's heart, marking his importance and position.

Wexel, the captain of the Mortan royal guards, who was loyal to Milo Morricone.

Wexel sneered at me, then lifted his sword and brought it down in a sharp motion. Several more *creaks* sounded, and more than a dozen men clutching crossbows appeared along the top of the ridge.

My heart sank, and I cursed my own foolishness. Reiko had been right.

It was a trap.

CHAPTER THREE

eside me, Reiko let out another muttered curse. Magic rippled off her, turning her fingernails into long black talons as she partially shifted into her larger, stronger morph form.

"Well, well, well, look who we have here," Wexel called out in a loud, mocking voice. "Little Princess Glitzma and her pet dragon Reiko."

My gaze darted from one man to the next, but I didn't see the face I was looking for. "Tell me, Wexel, where is your master? Or did Milo let you off your leash for an afternoon stroll?"

Anger stained the captain's cheeks a dark mottled red. He stepped forward as though he wanted to charge down the ridge and attack me, but he reined in his rage and stopped at the edge of the incline. The Mortans had the high ground, and thus, the advantage.

"Milo said you would come investigate the rumors I spread," Wexel said. "I'm surprised it took you this long. We've been waiting in the woods for two days."

Once again, I cursed my own foolishness. Part of me had

been hoping the rumors were true—and that I could finally find some clue as to what Milo's ultimate plot was against Andvari. But I'd let my ambition overpower my common sense, and I had plowed straight into another Morricone trap. Even worse, this time I'd dragged Reiko into the deadly snare with me.

But I wasn't about to let Wexel see my worry. "How *is* Milo? I've been wondering about your poor crown prince. Are his hands still horribly scorched? Or did the Myrkvior bone masters manage to heal the burns?"

More anger stained Wexel's cheeks, although a bit of fear also flickered off him, tickling my spine like a cold finger. Wexel had seen me toss Milo's own lightning right back at the crown prince, and the captain was smart enough to be wary of me. Good. Because right now, I wanted to hurt Wexel for leading me on this fool's errand even worse than I had hurt Milo in Blauberg.

So much *worse*.

That familiar storm churned and crackled inside me, and ice-cold viciousness filled my body. Before the Battle of Blauberg, I would have shoved that viciousness down as deep as it would go and tried to ignore the emotion and magic raging through me. But when I'd killed the Mortan guards and driven Milo and Wexel out of the city, I'd realized my feelings weren't a weakness or a detriment or something to be avoided. They were a strength, *my* strength, one that let me wield my magic to its fullest potential. Something I was going to enjoy showing Wexel in painful, bloody detail—

"Gemma," Reiko said in a warning voice.

I blinked. I'd been so caught up in my vengeful thoughts that I'd taken several steps forward, putting myself that much closer to the Mortans. As much as I longed to charge up the ridge and ram my dagger into Wexel's chest, the archers would cut me down before I even got to take a swing at their captain. My revenge would have to wait for another day.

I glanced at Reiko. "Thanks."

"You're welcome. Now let's get out of here."

Reiko started creeping backward through the grass. Still keeping an eye on Wexel, I did the same. Our best bet was to retreat into the woods—

Loud, heavy footsteps thumped behind us. I glanced over my shoulder. A dozen men, all wearing purple cloaks and carrying swords, stepped out of the woods and into the clearing, blocking our escape.

If the archers on the ridge didn't kill us, then these soldiers would. Milo had planned his trap well, and Wexel and his men had us surrounded and outnumbered.

Grimley. I sent the thought out. *Be careful. Wexel is here, along with dozens of Mortan soldiers armed with swords and crossbows. More of them might be hiding in the woods, just waiting to shoot you and Fern out of the sky.*

Hang on, Gemma! His voice filled my mind. *We're almost there!*

I could feel Grimley getting closer, along with Fern, as though they were two threads I was looping back up onto their respective spools. But the gargoyles wouldn't arrive before the fighting started, so I pushed them to the back of my mind.

"Any last words before my men cut you to pieces?" Wexel asked.

Instead of responding to his taunt, I reached out with my magic. In an instant, I could feel the energy surrounding everything in the clearing, from the burliest guard to the sharpest sword to the smallest rock buried in the dull brown grass. Not only could I feel all that energy, but as a mind magier, I could also manipulate all those layers of power, as though I were a puppeteer with strings attached to my fingertips connecting me to every single person and thing in the clearing.

"Well, Glitzma?" Wexel sneered down at me again.

I grabbed hold of one of those strings and curled the fingers on my left hand into a tight fist. Up on the ridge, a tree branch slowly drew back in commensurate measure, although none of the Mortans seemed to notice the movement.

"Oh, come on," Wexel said. "Surely you have *something* to say before my men kill you—"

I opened my fist and released my grip on that string of energy, and the tree branch snapped forward and slapped Wexel across the face.

Thwack!

The sharp, jolting motion surprised the captain, who staggered to the side. Wexel's feet flew out from under him, and he fell down on his ass and started sliding forward. At the last moment, he dug his sword into the ground and stopped his skid before he slipped off the edge of the ridge. Pity. I'd been hoping he would topple off the side and hit each and every rock on the way down.

Wexel's head snapped up. Hate glittered in his hazel eyes, and his left cheek was an angry red from where the branch had slapped him. I smirked at the captain, who scrambled back up onto his feet.

"Kill them!" he roared.

Up on the ridge, the archers aimed their crossbows at Reiko and me, the arrows in the weapons glinting a bright starry gray. Milo had equipped his men with his cursed tearstone arrows to attack us. Wonderful.

"You stop the archers!" Reiko yelled. "I'll handle the soldiers!"

More magic blasted off her, making my fingertips tingle. Reiko grew several inches taller, and her body bulged with thick, hard muscle. Her black hair flickered around her head like curls of ebony fire, while razor-sharp teeth sprouted in her mouth. A few hot green sparks also shot off her fingertips, although they quickly winked out.

Reiko snarled, lifted her sword, and charged forward, taking the fight to the soldiers down here in the clearing. As much as I wanted to wade into the fray, Reiko was right. I had to stop the archers. Wexel would have no compunction about firing on his own men as long as Reiko and I were killed.

So I shoved my dagger back into the scabbard on my belt and faced the ridge where Wexel and the archers were.

"Fire!" the captain screamed.

The archers pulled the triggers on their crossbows, and arrows streaked in this direction. I snapped up my hands and reached for my magic.

One, two, three . . . four, five, six . . .

Seven, eight, nine . . . ten, eleven, twelve . . .

I grabbed hold of all those arrows, all those strings of energy zooming through the air. I waved one hand, then the other, scooping them all up into my fingers like I was gathering twigs to light a fire. My hands snapped into tight fists, and the arrows froze, hanging in midair like wind chimes waiting to clang together.

A relieved breath hissed out of my lips. It was always harder to grab multiple objects at once, and I hadn't been sure I could do it, especially given how fast the arrows had been moving.

"Fire another round! Quick! Quick!" Wexel screamed.

I tightened my grip on all those strings of energy until the arrows were quivering in front of me like an army of angry, silent bees. I rotated my wrists, spinning the arrows around in midair, then flexed my fingers and hurled them all right back at my enemies.

Thwack. Thwack. Thwack.

The arrows zipped upward and slammed into the necks,

arms, chests, and legs of the archers who had fired them. Blood sprayed, howls of pain rang out, and the Mortans dropped like dead flies. In an instant, I had cut down half of the archers on the ridge.

"Shoot that bitch!" Wexel screamed again. "Right fucking now!"

The remaining archers scrambled to reload their crossbows, so this time, I grabbed hold of *them*. One after another, I snapped my hands left, then right, up, then down, like a music master conducting an orchestra through a lively tune.

People flew through the air, just like the arrows had before. Some men slammed face-first into the ground, while others thumped into trees and bounced off, moaning and groaning from broken bones and other injuries. In addition to the archers' audible cries, their silent pleas also flooded my mind.

I'm bleeding...

Hurts to move...

Can't catch my breath...

The last thought made me grimace, and my chest constricted, as the pain of that man's injury invaded my own body. My gargoyle pendant heated up against my heart, reminding me that I controlled my magic, not the other way around, so I gritted my teeth and shoved away the man's pleas and pain. My chest loosened, and I could breathe again—

"Gemma!" Reiko yelled. "Behind you!"

I whirled around. Several guards sprawled on the ground around Reiko. Some had died from the stab wounds she'd inflicted on them, while others were choking on their own blood and clutching their throats, which she'd torn open with her talons.

But one man had slipped past Reiko and was charging at me. He must have been a mutt with some speed magic because he closed the distance between us in the blink of an eye. I ducked his deadly swing and grabbed my dagger.

The man growled and charged at me again, but I stepped up, dodged his defenses, and buried my dagger in his stomach. He screamed, and I ripped the blade free, tearing out a good portion of his guts.

I started to shove him away, but he put his shoulder down and barreled into me. The attack took me by surprise, my feet flew out from under me, and I landed flat on my back, my head bouncing off the ground. Pain spiked through my skull, and I accidentally bit down on my tongue, hard enough to draw blood.

"Gemma!" Reiko screamed again. "Get up!"

Another guard rushed at her, and she lashed out with her sword, driving him back.

I planted my hand on the ground and sat up. The guard that I'd gutted was looming over me, his face twisting with pain and anger.

My head was throbbing from my hard fall, and I couldn't get a grip on my magic, so I dug my heels into the dirt, trying to scuttle backward. But I was moving too slowly, and he still had too much speed, despite his gruesome injury. The guard lurched forward, raised his sword high, and swung it down. I lifted my hand and grabbed onto the string of energy attached to his blade—

The sword stopped inches from my heart.

He growled and surged forward, trying to shove his sword past the invisible barrier of my magic, but I gritted my teeth, clenched my hand into a fist, and tightened my grip on his weapon. Pain pounded through my body, sweat dripped down my face, and blood filled my mouth, but I held on, my arm shaking from the effort.

"Give me that!" I heard Wexel yell.

Up on the ridge, the captain wrested a crossbow away from one of the injured archers. And that was all I saw before the man in front of me churned his feet again, still trying to force his way past my magic.

The guard must have had some strength power to go along with his speed because his sword lunged another inch closer to my heart.

Then another inch. Then another inch.

I snarled with anger and frustration, but try as I might, I couldn't hold him back, and it was only a matter of seconds before he punched his blade into my chest and killed me—

The guard flew across the clearing and slammed into the base of the ridge. Rocks tumbled to the ground, and so did the man, his spine snapped like a toothpick and his legs no longer lined up with the rest of his body.

My eyes widened in surprise. I hadn't done that. A shadow fell over me, blotting out the sun, and my head snapped up.

A man was standing on top of the ridge to my right.

He looked to be a year or two older than me, thirty or so. His longish black hair was as shiny as polished onyx, the wavy layers ending in tips that reminded me of the sharp points on a strix's feathers. His skin was tan, and he had a straight nose and sharp, angular cheekbones, along with those dark amethyst eyes that had haunted my dreams for weeks, months, years.

His black cloak fluttered around his tall, muscled body, pushed back and forth by the chilly breeze, and snapped around his legs like a coral viper lashing out at its prey. He was wearing a long black riding coat over a black tunic, leggings, and boots, and a tearstone sword and dagger dangled from his black leather belt. Silver buttons marched down the front of his coat, and the Morricone royal crest—that fancy cursive *M* surrounded by a ring of strix feathers—was done in silver thread over his heart, if he even had such a weak, treacherous organ.

As for my own heart, well, it quickened at the sight of him, betraying me yet again—just like he had.

Prince Leonidas Luther Andor Morricone, my childhood nemesis and mortal enemy.

CHAPTER FOUR

eonidas stared down at me, his face calm and blank, as if killing his own countryman to save my life was of no consequence. Perhaps it wasn't. He had cut down Mortan guards before, when Wexel had attacked us in King Maximus's old workshop in Myrkvior.

Leonidas was a mind magier, just like I was, and despite the distance between us, his magic—that light, feathery, electric presence that was uniquely his—brushed up against my own storm of power. My fingertips tingled in anticipation, and my traitorous heart picked up its pace, hammering like a drum against my ribs.

"Gemma!" Reiko yelled.

I dragged my gaze away from Leonidas's hypnotic stare and scrambled to my feet, still clutching my dagger.

"Wexel has reinforcements!" Reiko stabbed her sword up at the ridge.

I might have gotten rid of the first wave of archers, but several more had stepped into view. The way my head was aching, I wasn't sure if I could stop their arrows like I had before—

Out of the corner of my eye, I spotted Wexel sneaking through the trees and creeping up on Leonidas. An evil grin split the captain's face, and he stopped, aimed the crossbow, and pulled the trigger, shooting an arrow at the Morricone prince.

I didn't think about the awful ache in my head. Or how shaky my body was. Or how this was the very last thing I should be doing.

No, my focus narrowed to that gray jeweled arrow zipping through the air, and I stretched my hand out and lunged forward, as though the extra bits of motion would help me grab that one invisible string of energy. My magic tried to squirt out of my grasp, along with the arrow, but I ground my teeth, concentrated, and yanked on that string hard, hard, hard—

The arrow stopped a foot away from Leonidas's back.

Surprised, he spun around toward Wexel. Leonidas took hold of the arrow with his own magic, flicked his wrist, and sent the projectile shooting right back at the captain.

Wexel ducked behind a tree, and the arrow thunked harmlessly into the wood.

"Gemma!" Reiko yelled again. "Let's go!"

She cut down the last guard in the clearing with her sword, then started running toward the woods.

I glanced up at the ridge again. Wexel had vanished, along with the remaining archers. My gaze zoomed back over to Leonidas, who was once again staring down at me with that infuriatingly calm expression.

My hand curled even tighter around my dagger, and rage flooded my body, drowning out my pain. Any . . . *softness* I had felt for Leonidas Morricone had been destroyed the night he had handed me over to Queen Maeven and played me for a fool in front of the Myrkvior court. I didn't know what Leonidas was doing here, or why he had saved my life yet again, but knowing the duplicitous prince, it was probably part of some Bellonan long game to worm his way back into my good graces so he could use and humiliate me again.

Even more rage flooded my body, and I had the sudden urge to charge up the ridge and cut Leonidas to pieces with my dagger. A smirk curved his lips, and he arched an eyebrow, as if sensing my boiling emotions with his own mind magier magic. Smug, arrogant bastard.

"Gemma!" Reiko yelled. "Come on!"

I glared at the Morricone prince a moment longer, then spun around and ran out of the clearing.

Reiko plunged back into the woods. I sprinted to keep up with her smooth strides, even as I reached out with my magic.

Grimley! Where are you?

Right above you! His voice rumbled through my mind. *Fern and I just circled around the ridge where the archers were. We'll meet you on the other side of the woods!*

"Grimley's going to meet us in the clearing in front of the mine!" I yelled to Reiko. "Go! Go! Go!"

She picked up her pace, and I followed her lead.

Even though we were on the trail, we still had to be careful of the woodsy detritus littering the ground. Reiko easily sailed over every obstacle, but more than once, my boots snagged on an upraised root or scraped against a rock, throwing me off balance and costing us precious seconds. My head was still aching from my hard fall, and a stitch throbbed like a red-hot needle in my side, but I sucked in as much air as I could and kept going.

Several minutes later, just when I thought my heart was going to explode, we sprinted out into the clearing in front of the old mine. Reiko skidded to a stop, and I had to lurch to the side to keep from plowing into her.

A dozen guards were lined up in this clearing, right in front of the mine entrance.

I muttered a curse. Wexel had been far cleverer than I'd expected and had planned not one, but two traps.

"Bloody Mortans don't know when to quit," Reiko snarled.

She twirled her sword around in her hand, and I stepped up beside her, still clutching my dagger—

A couple of low, ominous growls rumbled through the air like thunder, and two shadows dropped down from the sky.

Grimley and Fern landed right on top of the guards, smashing two men to death under their heavy stone bodies. The gargoyles growled again and tore into the rest of the Mortans with their horns, teeth, talons, and long arrow-tipped tails. Flesh ripped, men screamed, and blood flew through the air like scarlet rain.

None of the guards escaped the gargoyles' wrath. In less than two minutes, it was over, and all the Mortans were dead.

Grimley pivoted to me, his sapphire eyes bright, and his horns, teeth, and talons covered with blood. "Let's go!"

I shoved my dagger into its scabbard, then hurried over and climbed onto his back, while Reiko scrambled up onto Fern.

More Mortans charged into the clearing, led by Wexel.

"Shoot them!" he screamed. "Don't let them escape!"

"Up! Up! Up!" I yelled at Grimley.

The gargoyle pumped his wings and shot up into the sky. Fern did the same thing, causing Reiko to shriek in surprise.

Go. I sent the thought to Fern. *Get Reiko out of here. Grimley and I will hold them off.*

Yes, my princess.

Fern flapped her wings and veered away, heading back toward Haverton. Reiko let out another shriek at the sudden change in direction, but I knew Fern wouldn't let her fall, so I turned my attention back to the Mortans below.

There weren't nearly as many archers as before, but one arrow could send Grimley and me plummeting to our deaths. The Mortans had spread out, taking cover behind large rocks and fallen logs, so I searched for something that would let me kill as many of them at once as possible.

There. That would do.

I raised my right arm high and curled my fingers into a tight fist. This time, instead of grabbing hold of the arrows or the archers, I concentrated on a towering maple with brilliant garnet leaves that was standing atop a small hill at the edge of the woods, close to where Wexel was still screaming at his men to shoot Grimley and me out of the sky.

I grabbed hold of all the strings of energy surrounding that maple and pulled on them as hard as I could.

I yanked and yanked and yanked on the tree, trying to tear it out of the hillside. Catching all those arrows earlier had been hard, but this was harder still, especially given the pain and exhaustion rippling through my body. Plus, the maple was enormous, more than a hundred feet tall with thousands of leaves, dozens of branches, a thick trunk, and deep, strong roots. It was by far the biggest, heaviest, most difficult thing I had ever attempted to move with my magic.

I tightened my grip on all those strings of energy, my knuckles reduced to white dots on my clenched fist, even as my red starburst scar bulged up, as though it were about to start weeping blood.

"Shoot her!" Wexel screamed again.

The archers lifted their crossbows.

If I didn't do something right now, then I was going to wind up dead, and Grimley along with me. So I dove into that storm of emotion churning inside me and reached for even more magic. Sweat poured down my face, the salty drops stinging my eyes, and my body shook so badly I almost toppled off Grimley's back.

Curses, growls, and snarls spewed out of my lips, but the longer and louder I muttered, the more easily my power came to me. The curses, growls, and snarls merged into one sound that quickly rose in pitch and volume.

With a violent scream, I yanked on all those strings of energy again, harder than before, and I finally ripped the tree out of the hillside.

For a moment, the maple hung in midair, like a drunkard trying to keep from toppling over. Then, with a shower of dirt, it plummeted into the clearing.

The Mortans never had a chance.

Too late, the guards realized something was wrong. Several men stared up in frozen horror at the tree rushing toward them. A few tried to run, but the maple was far too large, wide, and heavy to escape.

THUMP!

The tree landed with a crashing roar, its sturdy branches snapping like matchsticks from the force of it hitting the ground. Dirt, wood, and garnet leaves flew in every direction, and the smell of churned earth flooded the air, tickling my nose with its rich, dark scent.

Grimley pumped his wings, holding us steady in the air, while I squinted through the clouds of dirt. The dust slowly settled, revealing that I had killed most of the Mortans—but not all of them.

Oh, the tree had flattened several men, but a few were still standing. Unfortunately, Wexel was one of them, along with a couple of archers, who aimed their crossbows at Grimley and me again. Exhaustion filled my body, and I didn't know if I had enough magic left to stop another hail of arrows—

A purple blur dropped down into the clearing and plowed into the remaining archers, scattering them like balls in a child's game. The archers screamed, and many of them flew through the air and landed with loud, wet *thwacks* on the broken branches jutting up from the shattered maple.

Wexel shot the blur a hate-filled glare, then sprinted into the woods. The few men who were able hobbled after him.

The purple blur zipped back and forth through the air a few more times before landing in the clearing next to the uprooted tree.

It was a strix.

The large hawklike bird was about the same size as Grimley, although its body was a bit taller, narrower, and sleeker than the gargoyle's shorter, broader, and stockier form. The strix's eyes were a dark vibrant amethyst, as were its feathers, which were tipped with hard, sharp onyx points that looked like arrows. The creature's pointed beak and curved talons were also the same shiny black.

The strix fluffed out its feathers and winked at me. Lyra was bonded with Leonidas the same way Grimley was bonded with me. And once again, Lyra had saved Grimley and me, just as her prince had done earlier.

Lyra winked at me again, then shot up into the sky, disappearing from sight.

Do you want me to chase after her? Grimley asked, still flapping his wings and hovering in midair.

No. It's too risky. More archers could be waiting to shoot us. Land in the clearing, please.

Grimley eased down to the ground. "What are you going to do?"

"See if anyone is still alive. Maybe one of the guards can tell me more about Wexel or Milo."

I slid off his back, grabbed my dagger off my belt, and crept through the clearing. Now that the battle was over, the only noise was the clumps of dirt dropping off the maple's roots and *plop-plop-plopping* against the ground like dusty raindrops.

I moved from one body to the next, staring down at all the people I'd killed. Most had been crushed by the tree, with only their arms and legs sticking out from beneath the massive trunk, but a few had been impaled on the broken branches, and their dead, sightless eyes seemed to follow me as I tiptoed past them. I shivered, glad I couldn't hear the thoughts of the dead, although their earlier screams kept echoing in my ears like a song from a music box that just kept playing and playing—

A low moan of pain rang out.

I looked to my right. A guard was sprawled across the ground, his arms and legs weakly thrashing, despite the large branch sticking out of his chest like a crooked spear.

No one else was still alive, so I hurried over and dropped to my knees beside the guard. Grimley followed me.

The guard was much younger than I expected, fifteen, maybe sixteen, and covered with blood, dirt, and grime. Guilt churned in my stomach, but this was the cost of war. Today, I had forced the Mortans to pay that awful toll, and I would do so again in a heartbeat, as many times as was necessary to stop Milo from slaughtering any more of my people.

"Help . . . me . . ." the boy rasped.

Even if I'd been a bone master, I doubted I could have saved him from that gruesome wound. But just because he was my enemy didn't mean I couldn't have some compassion, so I set my dagger down, reached out, and gripped the boy's left hand, trying to comfort him in some small way.

And then I questioned him.

"What did Wexel say about me? Do you know anything about Milo Morricone? And what he plans to do with his tearstone arrows?"

The boy slowly dipped his right hand into a pocket on his leggings and drew out a small black leather pouch, which slid out of his fingers and dropped to the ground. He opened his mouth, but only a thin trickle of blood emerged. The boy's breathing became much more labored, and I didn't think he was going to say anything else before he died—

"Experiments . . . here . . ." he rasped. "And . . . at the Summit . . ."

I frowned. What did that mean? Before I could ask, the boy shuddered out a final breath, then his head lolled to the side, and his hand slipped free of mine.

Wexel had said he'd spread rumors to lure me into Milo's trap, but the boy's dying words made it sound as though Milo had been doing something *else* here. The crown prince was known to tinker with creatures, magic, and more, and I'd seen his grotesque projects firsthand in his Myrkvior workshop.

So what had Milo been experimenting with here in the woods? His barbed arrows? The tearstone shards from the old mine? Something else? And how did the upcoming Summit play into Milo's plans? Everything I learned led only to more troubling questions.

My gaze dropped to the black pouch the boy had pulled out of his pocket. I opened the strings and tipped it over.

A small dried flower fluttered out of the pouch and landed on the ground.

My eyebrows shot up. Not what I'd expected. I picked up the flower and twirled it back and forth in my fingers. The tiny blossom had three light purple petals that reminded me of clover, along with a green stem covered with prickly, sticky fuzz. I didn't know what kind of flower it was, but it didn't seem particularly sinister or important. Perhaps it had simply been a gift from the boy's mother, sister, or sweetheart.

I dropped the flower back down into the pouch and stuffed the whole thing into my own pocket, next to the scorched rock I'd picked up earlier in the mine. I searched the boy's other pockets, but they were empty, so I scanned the clearing, wondering if I should search the rest of the dead Mortans. The ones I could reach anyway, since so many of the bodies were trapped beneath the fallen tree—

"Gemma," Grimley growled out a warning.

Once again, a shadow fell over me, and two familiar, feathery presences tickled my mind. I plucked my dagger off the ground and got to my feet.

Lyra landed in the clearing, with Leonidas perched on her back. The Morricone prince smoothly dismounted the strix and strode toward me. Once again, his black cloak fluttered around his tall, strong body, adding to his commanding presence and making him look like a shadow knight, some dark, deadly, unstoppable force capable of destroying everything in his path, including me.

Especially me.

I tightened my grip on my dagger and stalked toward him. We met in the middle of the clearing, facing off in front of the ruined tree, with the dead Mortans gathered around to witness the spectacle like a silent crowd in a gladiator arena.

Lyra lurked behind Leonidas, her amethyst eyes bright and watchful, while Grimley stood close to me, his long tail lashing from side to side, the arrow on the end aimed at the prince.

Up close, Leonidas was even more handsome than I remembered, his features sharp, angular, and beautiful, even with his face schooled into its usual icy mask. I drew in a breath, and his honeysuckle soap wafted over to me, the soft scent utterly masculine and completely intoxicating.

My heart skipped an unwanted beat, even as disgust curdled my stomach. I'd hoped I would be completely unaffected if I ever saw him in person again. But despite my best intentions and simmering ire, I was just as attracted to Leonidas Morricone now as I had been in Myrkvior, despite how badly he had fooled, used, and betrayed me.

Leonidas's gaze lingered on the dagger in my hand, but he didn't reach for the sword belted to his waist. Maybe he thought I wouldn't attack him, that I wouldn't kill him.

Well, he was wrong. My fingers clenched around my dagger even more tightly than before. So very, very wrong.

Leonidas eyed me, as if making sure I wasn't going to charge at him, then glanced over at the tree I'd ripped out of the hillside. "An impressive display, Gemma. You're getting stronger in your magic."

His gaze flicked back over to me and slid down my chest, making heat ripple through my body. "Even if you are still foolishly wearing that gargoyle pendant to try to contain your power."

I lifted my hand and touched the pendant, which had gone cold against my heart. The pieces of black jet heated up as they blocked out other people's thoughts and emotions, but the blue tearstone shards frosted over like bits of ice as they soaked up my own feelings—like the anger currently crashing through me. But even stronger than my anger at Leonidas was my rage at *myself*, for standing here, for talking to him, for still foolishly wanting to be near him, when all I should be doing was getting away from him as fast as possible.

I curled my fingers around the pendant, focusing on the chilly pricks of the tearstone shards against my skin, then released it. The silver disc swung back and forth like a clock pendulum, the same way my own emotions were veering wildly from attraction to disgust and back again. I held on to my rage, though, and wrapped it around me like a cold cloak, dousing all the warmth and softness in my heart. It was the only armor I had against him.

"I wear my gargoyle pendant because it's *mine*. No other reason."

That wasn't quite true, but he didn't need to know that. Just as he didn't need to know that every time I touched the pendant

I thought of how he had fished it out of the rubble after Milo had torn it off my neck during the Battle of Blauberg. Leonidas had repaired the broken chain and handed the pendant to me through our respective Cardea mirrors, when he had been in Myrkvior and I was back home in Glitnir. Even now, I could still feel his fingers wrapping around mine, still feel the imprint of his skin against mine, still hear the low, husky promise in his voice as he confessed he was as drawn to me as I was to him.

No, Leonidas Morricone didn't need to know *any* of those things. And he especially didn't need to know that part of me longed to pick up where we had left off on the dance floor in the Myrkvior throne room. To see what might happen when there were only thoughts and feelings and heat between us, and none of the messy history involving our warring families and how many times we had hurt each other in the past.

Leonidas arched an eyebrow. "So you're not trying to hide from your magic any longer? I find that hard to believe."

He reached out with his own magic, trying to read my mind, although I easily swatted his power away. I didn't bother trying to read his mind in turn, since he would just block my magic the same way I had his.

"I'm not hiding from anything. Although I see you're still as arrogant as ever, thinking that your words, opinion, or approval matter to me. They do not."

Not a flicker of emotion crossed Leonidas's face at my harsh words, but I hadn't really expected to see any. We might both be mind magiers, but I seemed to feel far more than he did, especially when it came to sensing other people's thoughts, along with my own stormy emotions.

Leonidas gestured at the boy I'd questioned. "Did he say anything before he died?"

He stared at me, his face still blank, but worry filled his eyes.

My own eyes narrowed. "Wait. Why are *you* here?"

"Leo heard you might be in trouble," Lyra chirped in her high singsong voice.

The prince grimaced, as though he'd just been caught doing something he shouldn't, like a child gobbling down sweet cakes before dinner.

"I don't need *rescuing*," I said in an icy tone.

"I never said you did," Leonidas snapped back.

"So why are you here?"

His jaw clenched, and he fell silent. A bitter taste filled my mouth, and a surprising amount of disappointment washed over me. After everything that had happened in Blauberg and Myrkvior, and all the times we had saved each other's lives, I'd thought we could at least be honest with each other. But apparently, I had only been fooling myself yet again.

I shook my head in disgust and stepped back to leave, but he eased forward. I stopped, watchful and wary.

"I heard some rumors that Milo had moved his weapons to this area," Leonidas said. "That he had set up a workshop here and was conducting experiments while he pried the last few scraps of tearstone out of an old abandoned mine."

Once again, I got the distinct impression he was telling me only the part of the truth he wanted me to hear, just as he had at Myrkvior. Frustration boiled up in my veins, along with a burning need to hurt him as badly as he had hurt me, to punch through his icy armor and make him bloody *feel* something, make him feel just a fraction of the irritation and attraction and all the other unwanted emotions I felt when it came to him.

"You open your mouth, and all I hear are lies, lies, and more lies. At least you're predictable and consistent that way."

Instead of anger, sorrow filled his amethyst eyes, and that same emotion surged off him, softening the sharpest edges of my own rage.

"I am so deeply sorry for everything that happened to you in Myrkvior, Gemma. For all the horrors you suffered because of me," Leonidas said in a raspy voice, pain rippling through each and every one of his words. "If I could go back and undo it all, I would—in a heartbeat."

This wasn't the first time he had apologized. Leonidas had voiced similar sentiments the night of Maeven's birthday ball, after Milo had tortured me. I knew he was sincere, that he really did regret what had happened, something he had proven by helping me escape from the Mortan palace, even though he'd been brutally tortured himself.

In some ways, Leonidas had been wounded even more badly than I had been. Not only had Maeven manipulated her son, but she'd also threatened Delmira, his sister, to force Leonidas to go along with a scheme to expose my real identity. Maeven had also allowed Wexel and Milo to beat and whip Leonidas when he had tried to keep me out of the crown prince's workshop. We had both been victims of the Morricone queen's scheming, and we were both still hurting as a result.

Part of me wanted to forgive Leonidas, if only so I could move past what had happened, so I could finally move past *him*. But the other part of me wanted to hold on to my hurt, and especially my rage, since it was the only defense I had against him. I feared that if I ever gave in to our mutual attraction, and especially to my own feelings, then I would be thoroughly crushed when he inevitably betrayed me yet again, just as I had crushed the Mortan guards with that tree.

"I know you're sorry," I replied, my voice losing some of its previous venom. "And I'm sorry too, for everything you suffered because of me. I never wanted you to be wounded."

"But?"

I blew out a breath. "But it doesn't change the fact that you're a Morricone and I'm a Ripley. Or that your mother used me to keep her crown and your brother tortured me just for fun. And it especially doesn't change the fact that I can never, ever trust you."

Hurt flickered across his face before he could hide it. A treacherous needle of sympathy pricked my heart, but I ignored the sharp, troublesome sting. I was getting better at that, thanks to my time at Myrkvior.

"Why do you say that?" he asked.

"Because you will always choose your family, your kingdom over me, just as I will always choose my family and kingdom over you. It's what Morricones and Ripleys and Blairs and all the other kings and queens do. It's the royal trap we all fall into. It's who we *are*, for better or worse."

I stared at Leonidas, committing his face to memory, even as I breathed in his honeysuckle scent. Then I spun around, strode over to Grimley, and climbed onto the gargoyle's back. I slid my dagger into its scabbard and fussed around, as though I were settling myself into place, but really, I was trying to arrange my emotions in some semblance of order.

Lyra nuzzled up beside Leonidas, and he smoothed his fingers down her feathers, the motion eerily similar to how I stroked Grimley's stone skin. Not for the first time, I cursed how alike Leonidas and I were.

"Most of our enemies are dead," I told Grimley. "Let's go."

He flapped his wings and shot up into the sky. Leonidas's face was the last thing I saw before the gargoyle crested the ridge, flying me away from the dark, dangerous prince.

CHAPTER FIVE

Grimley quickly returned to Lord Eichen's estate and landed on the balcony outside my chambers, where Fern and Reiko were waiting.

When she saw we were in one piece, Fern stretched out in a sunny spot on the stone and closed her eyes to take a nap. Grimley trotted over to her. Without opening her eyes, Fern poked her arrow-tipped tail into his side, shoving him out of her spot. Grimley grumbled, but he too settled down to take a nap.

Reiko stopped her pacing. "Gemma! What happened?"

I opened my arms to hug her, but she stabbed her finger into my chest, knocking me back with her morph strength.

"Why didn't you fly away on Grimley? It was stupid to stay behind and put yourself in even more danger!" Reiko glared at me, as did her inner dragon.

I grinned in the face of their collective anger. "Well, it's nice to know you were worried about me."

Reiko kept glaring at me. "Topacia warned me that you would give me gray hair."

Topacia was my longtime personal guard, and she had often

helped with my missions. After the Battle of Blauberg, she had resigned, claiming she didn't want to worry about me anymore. She had also been longing to spend more time with her family, especially since her daughter was going to have a baby soon.

With Topacia's resignation, Reiko had become my partner in spycraft, reporting about the Mortans to her cousin, Queen Ruri Yamato of Ryusama.

I slung my arm around Reiko's shoulders. "You're only twenty-nine. That's far too young to have gray hair, even for a spy."

Reiko glowered at me again, but she leaned into my hug a moment before pulling back. "Why were you gone so long? I was about to get Fern to fly me back to that old mine."

Fern opened her eyes and lifted her head. "Which I would *not* have done. Once I have an order from my princess, I obey it to the very end."

I bent down and scratched the gargoyle's head. "Thank you, Fern."

She preened at me, then shot Grimley a smug look. Grimley snorted and rolled away from her.

Reiko and I left the gargoyles to their naps and stepped inside. We checked to make sure no one was eavesdropping outside our chamber doors, then met in my sitting room.

While we'd been gone, the servants had laid out some refreshments, and Reiko piled several bite-size cakes onto a napkin. Like her cousin Cho Yamato, Reiko had a massive sweet tooth.

"Well?" she asked, nibbling on one of the cakes. "What happened?"

I sprawled across a settee and told her about my ripping the tree out of the hillside, Wexel retreating, and the dying boy's mysterious words. I also showed her the dried flower from the boy's pouch, although she didn't know what kind of blossom it was either.

Reiko popped another cake into her mouth, but the sweet treat didn't lessen her deep frown. "Do you think Milo is going to try to assassinate Maeven again? The Summit would be an excellent place to kill the queen and blame it on someone else."

A few weeks ago, Milo had staged a coup at Myrkvior and tried to tear his mother down from her throne. He had wanted to kill Maeven, along with Leonidas, and marry off Delmira to some lord who would support his kingly ambitions. But Maeven had thwarted Milo's plot by exposing my real identity to everyone during her own birthday ball, and thus showing the Mortan nobles that she was still completely in control of her kingdom.

Later, Maeven had murdered Emperia Dumond, Milo's lover and co-conspirator, who had financed his theft of the Andvarian tearstone. Emperia had thought to capture the Mortan crown for herself, but Maeven had stabbed the noble lady with my gargoyle dagger and blamed her death on me. From the rumors I'd heard, Corvina Dumond, Emperia's daughter, had vowed to avenge her mother's murder, adding yet another powerful Mortan to my growing list of enemies.

"I'm sure Milo still wants Maeven dead, or at least deposed, so that he can be king," I said.

"But?" Reiko asked.

"But he wasn't planning to kill Maeven with his tearstone arrows at Myrkvior. He was going to let Wexel and the other guards murder her. Besides, from the few of Milo's thoughts I overheard at Myrkvior, I got the impression he wants to use his weapons against the *other* kingdoms. That he specifically *needs* the arrows to try to conquer all the kingdoms, starting with Andvari, so he can steal even more of our tearstone and add it to his arsenal."

I kept turning Reiko's words over in my mind. "Still, you might be right. Maybe Milo *is* going to kill Maeven during the

Summit and blame it on someone else. Avenging his mother and their queen would be one way for Milo to justify attacking And-vari to the Mortan nobles."

"I'll send word to Queen Ruri." Reiko eyed me. "Now, let's talk about the most interesting thing—what you said to Leonidas after the battle was over."

I tensed. "How did you know I spoke to him?"

"I saw him save you from that guard in the clearing, and then you save him from Wexel's arrow. I figured he would track you down eventually." Her lips curved up into a sly smile. "What did he say? Tell me *everything*."

I snorted. "You make it sound like he's some noble suitor instead of my mortal enemy."

"Sometimes, enemies make the most interesting suitors—and *especially* the best lovers."

The knowing tone in her voice caught my attention. "Are you speaking from personal experience?"

Reiko didn't answer, but her green eyes sparkled, and her inner dragon winked at me. I couldn't tell if they were toying with me or not. My friend was much better at hiding her true feelings and intentions than I was.

"You could always take Prince Leo as a lover," Reiko suggested. "Fuck him and forget him."

"Is that more of your personal experience speaking?"

She shrugged. "Sometimes, the wanting, longing, and anticipation are far better than the real thing. Once you've tasted the forbidden fruit, it often loses its appeal altogether."

I thought of the hard, defined muscles lurking beneath Leonidas's many layers of clothing. The intense focus in his amethyst eyes. His honeysuckle scent. His lips scorching my skin as he pressed a courtly kiss to my hand. And especially the gentle yet firm way he had held me on the dance floor at Myrkvior, as though he never wanted to let me go.

I highly doubted climbing into the prince's bed would lessen his appeal. Probably just the opposite.

"So what *did* you and Prince Leo talk about?" Reiko asked.

"We both wanted to know what the other was doing there, and we both skirted around the truth and kept our secrets as best as we could."

"Secrets that you are now going to share with *me*."

Reiko speared me with a hard look, so I gave in and told her about my conversation with the prince.

"Leonidas Morricone is certainly complicated," she said. "Then again, how could he not be growing up in Myrkvior with Maeven as a mother?"

"He's a Morricone, and I'm a Ripley. Our families have been enemies for generations on end, and we are more of the same. There is nothing *complicated* about that."

Not only had Maeven orchestrated my uncle Frederich's murder during the Seven Spire massacre, but the bitch had also tried to kill me with her lightning magic that awful day, even though I'd only been twelve at the time. Later on, Maeven had sent assassins to Glitnir to try to eliminate my father and had ordered Dahlia Sullivan, Grandfather Heinrich's mistress, to poison him as part of a plot to put Dahlia's son, Lucas Sullivan, on the Andvarian throne.

If the opportunity ever presented itself, I would happily murder Maeven for her attacks against my family. Leonidas would probably feel honor-bound to retaliate, and thus the cycle of violence would continue through our generation.

"Oh, no. There's nothing *complicated* about you and Prince Leo—except how you feel about each other," Reiko purred.

I waved away her words, although I couldn't deny the longing they stirred in my heart. "I'll admit I'm attracted to him, far more than I should be, especially given everything that's happened between us."

"But?"

"But I'll tell you the same thing I told him—I can never, ever trust Leonidas Morricone."

"Why not?" Reiko asked, seeming truly puzzled.

"Because Leonidas has always chosen his family above everything else, including me, even when we were children."

I had first met Leonidas in the Spire Mountains when I had been fleeing from Bellona after the Seven Spire massacre. He had been helping a group of turncoat guards track me down so they could capture and deliver me to King Maximus in Morta. One moment, Leonidas had been telling me to run, to escape. The next, he'd handed me over to a guard. Even though I had tried to murder Leonidas for that betrayal, he had later used his magic to kill a guard who was attacking me. He had claimed Maeven had already hurt me enough and that no one deserved to be tortured by his uncle Maximus the way he had been.

Reiko was right. Leonidas Morricone was most definitely *complicated*.

And that wasn't the only time I'd run into him in the Spire Mountains. We'd had another encounter that had been even more dangerous. Memories flickered in my mind, and my own screams rang in my ears, but I gritted my teeth and willed them away.

Reiko kept staring at me, clearly wanting more of an explanation, so I shrugged, trying to hide how important this was to me—and how hurt and disappointed I had always been by the inescapable, unchanging truth.

"Leonidas Morricone always puts his own survival first. The sad thing is that I can't blame him for it. Survival is probably all he's ever known at Myrkvior. But Leonidas can't change that about himself any more than a strix can change its feathers from purple to green."

I paused, struggling to put my feelings into words. "In some ways, I'm just like him. I've put my own survival first plenty of times, like I did today when I killed all those Mortans. And I will *always* put the survival of Andvari, of my people and gargoyles, above everything else."

"Even the feelings between you and Leonidas?" Reiko asked in a soft voice.

"Even above them."

Doubt filled Reiko's face, but I had spoken the absolute truth, and for once, my mind was clear, even if my heart was a bit bruised.

I stood up and gestured at my grimy clothes. "We should get cleaned up for the ball before Lord Eichen realizes we weren't strolling through his gardens, attending to your *condition*."

Reiko had been about to pop another cake into her mouth, and her hand drew back, as though she were thinking about tossing the treat at me. She huffed, then ate the cake and licked the sugar glaze off her fingers.

"As I said before, the only *affliction* I have is you, princess." She looked regretfully at the empty tray. "Along with an alarming lack of sweet cakes. Something that can be easily fixed at the ball."

Reiko rose to her feet and disappeared into her room, leaving me to contemplate the crumbs she'd left on the platter. If only I could make my attraction to Leonidas disappear as quickly as she'd gobbled down those cakes, I would be much happier—and in far less danger from the duplicitous prince.

The ball was a long, tedious affair, and Eichen's booming voice gave me a headache, but this was the final night of our visit, so I stayed to the bitter end, chatting and dancing with the nobles and merchants. Eichen would have stayed up talking well past midnight, but Adora, his gladiator granddaughter, announced that it was time for bed, and I was finally able to retire to my chambers.

Reiko had grown annoyed by all the speculative whispers about her supposed *affliction*, so she had left the ball early. Her door was closed, so I went into my own room, shed my gown, and took a hot bath.

The oversize porcelain tub had a built-in seat, so I rested my head on a pillow, while I swept my hand back and forth through the water.

Slap. Slap-slap. Slap-slap-slap.

The water sloshed up against the side of the tub, but the soft sounds echoed in my mind, growing louder and louder. Recognition and dread filled me. I might be getting better at keeping other people's thoughts and feelings from overwhelming my mind and freezing my body, but that didn't stop *other* things from triggering my magic.

Words, colors, tastes, scents. Sometimes, the faintest whisper of sound was enough to make my magic veer wildly out of control—like the sloshing water that was swiftly morphing into a dull, steady, ominous roar . . .

I jerked upright to climb out of the tub, but the bathroom around me melted away, and suddenly, I was standing in my usual clothes at the edge of a rushing river, listening to the water slap-slap-slap *against the rocks—*

"Damn it!" a voice snarled.

I turned around. A few feet away, a girl with brown hair, blue eyes, and pale skin was glaring at the river. The girl was wearing a gray cloak over a gray tunic, along with black leggings and boots, although the stolen clothes were all far too big and covered with dirt and grime.

I sighed, knowing the girl couldn't see or hear me. In addition to my mind magier magic, I had also inherited a bit of power from my mother, Merilde Ripley, who had been a time magier. My mother had usually gotten glimpses of the future, but more often than not, my magic shoved me back into the past, making me relive all the horrible things that had happened during and after the Seven Spire massacre.

Earlier today in the dining hall and at the mine, I'd seen brief flickering images of my tortured body at Myrkvior, but now I was fully immersed in my magic, my mind, my past. In a way, it was like being trapped inside a memory stone. I could see and hear everything that was happening, everything I had thought, felt, and experienced back then, but I couldn't do anything to alter the outcome.

This particular ability was called ghosting, and I thoroughly despised it. If I could have managed it, I would never have thought about the massacre again, or my frantic journey through the Spire Mountains with Alvis and Xenia, and all the weeks we'd spent running from the turncoat guards. But all I could do now was wait for my magic to calm down and for the memory to spit me back out into the present. So I sighed and sat down on a boulder to watch the show, as it were.

"A river?" the girl muttered to herself. "You've got to be kidding me."

I mouthed the words along with her. After all, she was me, or rather Gems, as I thought of this twelve-year-old version of myself.

Gems paced back and forth, searching for bootprints in the mud that oozed between the boulders, but she didn't find any. Frustration pinched her face, and she kicked a rock, making it skip into the water. Gems glared at the river again, then let out a breath and closed her eyes.

"Alvis, Xenia," Gems muttered. *"Where are you?"*

Her magic curled around her body, gathering strength, then streaked outward, like tiny spools of thread unwinding into the woods.

I eyed Gems, the river, and the trees, trying to place exactly where and when I was. Ah, yes, this was the morning when some turncoat guards had rushed into our camp. Xenia had told me to run while she and Alvis battled the men, and I had darted into the woods like a deer fleeing from a pack of hungry greywolves.

I sighed, wishing my magic wouldn't constantly remind me what a bloody coward I had been. During the Seven Spire massacre, I'd hidden under a table, instead of warning Uncle Frederich that something was wrong, and this time, I'd abandoned my friends to save myself.

Gems strained with all her might and magic, but she didn't sense Alvis's and Xenia's familiar presences. No signs of life. No whispers of thought. Only thin fragments of sounds. Nothing that would tell her how or where to find her friends.

"Please," Gems whispered, a desperate note in her voice. "Please, please, please be alive."

She tried again and again, but she still couldn't find her friends—

Crack.

Someone stepped on a twig. Gems's eyes snapped open, and she spun around.

A boy stood in front of her.

He looked to be about thirteen, fourteen at the most, with black hair and dark amethyst eyes that gleamed in the morning sunlight. He was wearing a black cloak over a light purple tunic and black leggings and boots, although his clothes were as torn and dirty as Gems's were. Dirt also covered his face, which was pale and painfully thin. The *only clean thing on his entire body was the cloak pin at his neck—a silver strix with shiny amethyst eyes.*

"You!" Gems growled, her hands balling into fists. "What are you doing here? Come to try to kill me again, Morricone?"

Young Leo's eyebrows creased together in confusion, as though her words puzzled him. "I never wanted to kill you or your friends."

"Really?" Gems growled again. "Because it didn't seem that way when you were handing me over to your guards a few days ago."

Leo shook his head. "Those weren't my guards. They work for Uncle Maximus."

Gems flinched at the mention of the cruel Mortan king, then lurched forward, reached down, and pried a large stick out of the mud.

Leo held out his hands and crept toward her, as though he were trying to tame a skittish strix. "I don't want to hurt you. I promise."

She brandished the stick at him like a spear. "I don't believe you. I know better than to trust a Morricone."

"Just because I'm a Morricone doesn't mean I'm inherently evil," Leo snapped back, as though this were an argument he'd had more than once.

A bitter laugh tumbled out of Gems's lips. "A Morricone? Not evil? Please. King Maximus won't be satisfied until he's conquered us all."

Leo kept creeping toward her. "Forget about my uncle. You need to get out of here. The guards told me that bandits like to hide along the river and rob people who stop for water."

"Where are Alvis and Xenia?" Gems demanded. "Where are your guards?"

Leo shook his head again. "I don't know where your

friends are, or the guards either. They rushed out of our camp first thing this morning. I tried to follow them, but they were moving too quickly, and I ended up out here all alone." He paused. "Until I found you."

"And how did you do that?"

"I felt your magic." Leo smiled, and his entire face brightened. "You're going to be very strong in your power someday."

Gems snorted. "You say that like it's a good thing."

"Of course it's a good thing. You'll be able to do wonderful things with your magic. You'll be able to help people with it."

Her eyes narrowed. "Like you're helping Maximus's guards track me with your own magic?"

Leo grimaced. "I don't have a choice. There are . . . consequences if I don't help them."

"What consequences?"

"You don't want to know."

His weary, resigned tone made my own heart twinge with sympathy. I'd seen those consequences—the layers and layers of scars that covered Leonidas's back from where Maximus had repeatedly whipped, burned, and otherwise tortured him.

Gems hoisted her stick a little higher. "I'm going to find my friends. Stay away from me, or I'll kill you."

Frustration pinched Leo's face. Then he tilted his head to the side, as though he'd heard something. His eyes widened, and he lunged forward. "No! Wait! Stop!"

Gems tried to jerk away, but Leo grabbed her arm. The two of them seesawed back and forth, with her still trying to jerk away and him trying to drag her toward the trees.

Finally, Gems managed to wrest herself free. Leo staggered back a few steps, then found his balance and charged at her again. This time Gems was ready, and she slammed her stick into his stomach.

"Oof!" He tumbled to the ground.

Gems started to run away, but Leonidas reached out and latched onto her ankle. "Stop!" he rasped. "Don't go that way!"

Gems yanked her ankle free and turned toward him. "I told you that I would kill you!"

Anger stained her cheeks, and she raised her stick high. Leonidas snapped his hand up, magic flaring in his eyes and swirling around his body—

"I do so love a good brawl," a feminine voice drawled.

Gems froze, then whirled around, the stick still clutched in her hands. I also looked around for the source of the voice.

A woman and two men now stood on the riverbank. They were all short and stocky, with black hair, dark brown eyes, and ruddy skin. Siblings, most likely. They were all dressed in dark green tunics, gray leggings, and black boots, and each one was clutching a sword.

"Who are you?" Gems asked.

The woman smiled, but it was a sharp, hungry expression. "My name is Farena, and I'm the . . . tax collector for this section of the river."

Leo scrambled to his feet and stepped up beside Gems. "I told you there were bandits," he muttered. "You should have listened to me."

Gems grimaced, and she and Leo watched while Farena and her two brothers advanced on them . . .

Water splashed on my face, breaking the unwanted spell of my magic. The riverbank vanished, and I was back in the bathtub in my chambers at Lord Eichen's estate.

I hoisted myself up and out of the tub, not wanting another *slap* of water to trigger my magic again. I dried off and donned my nightclothes, still thinking about that long-ago encounter with Leonidas.

Even back then, I'd let my emotions get the better of me when it came to him, and I'd fallen into the same trap in the clearing again today. Despite all the awful things we'd done to each other, both as children and as adults, I couldn't stop thinking about Leonidas. My heart betrayed me far too easily where he was concerned.

Perhaps that was what truly made me a fool, instead of any duplicity on Leonidas's part.

I pushed aside my troubling thoughts, threw on a robe, and sat down at the writing desk in the sitting room. Eichen had been kind enough to let me ransack his library, and more than a dozen books were piled up on the desk.

I'd told Eichen that I wanted to learn more about the flowers in his gardens, but really, I'd been looking for clues about tear-stone and its magical properties in hopes of figuring out Milo's plot. So far, I hadn't discovered anything new, but I hadn't been through all the books, so I opened the closest one and started skimming through it.

Since Eichen was a plant magier, most of the titles were about flowers, fruits, and vegetables, although a few dealt with different kinds of soils, rocks, and the like. I had leafed through the remaining books and was just about to admit defeat when a small drawing at the bottom of a page caught my eye—a black vine with long, sharp thorns, some of which had bloomed into spikes of purple lilac.

Liladorn, which could be found throughout Buchovia, but was especially prevalent in Morta.

Seeing the odd, beautiful liladorn snaking around fountains and twining through the walls was one of the few things I had enjoyed about my time in the Morricone palace. The thorny vines seemed to guard Myrkvior the same way the gargoyles did Glitnir, and the liladorn contained some sort of sentient presence that had spoken to me more than once. The vines had also closed doors and barred Wexel and his men from chasing after me when I had been escaping from the palace.

Curious, I started reading.

Liladorn might not be the prettiest plant, but it is one of the strongest, hardiest, and most stubborn. It can grow practically anywhere, and once it takes over a garden, it is extremely difficult to cut back, given its rock-hard yet strangely flexible vines. Even fire is not enough to destroy it.

Liladorn also has powerful healing properties. A variety of potions and salves can be made from it, and legend has it the sap from a single vine is enough to counteract the effects of coral-viper venom, along with amethyst-eye and other deadly poisons . . .

Back at Myrkvior, Delmira Morricone had used a liladorn salve on me when I'd been chained in Milo's horrid workshop. The lilac-scented ointment had completely healed the wounds Milo had lashed into my back with his gruesome coral-viper-skin whip. It had also repaired much of the damage he'd done to my hands with his barbed arrows, although the salve hadn't managed to get rid of the red scars that still marred my skin.

Thinking about the liladorn sparked an idea, and I pulled out the dried purple flower that had been in the Mortan boy's pouch. I compared the blossom to the drawing in the book, but it didn't match the liladorn.

Frustrated, I shut the book, set the dried flower aside, and leaned back in my chair.

Not for the first time, I wished I could be more like the queens on the Buchovian continent. Everleigh Blair of Bellona and Zariza Rubin of Unger never seemed to let their emotions get the better of them. Neither did Ruri Yamato, from what Reiko had told me about the Ryusaman queen. And Maeven Morricone was perhaps the coldest queen of all.

Fresh humiliation, embarrassment, and shame burned in my heart at how Maeven had used me to hang on to her crown and at how easily and skillfully she had manipulated me, Leonidas, Delmira, Milo, and everyone else at Myrkvior. Still, over the past few weeks, I had forced myself to examine and dissect all the steps Maeven had taken to remain on her throne. Like it or not, there were lessons to be learned from the Morricone queen, especially when it came to playing the Bellonan long game and getting other people to do exactly what you wanted them to.

A few weeks ago, when we had spoken through our respective Cardea mirrors, Leonidas had told me that Maeven was already plotting something else and that she had been researching courtly etiquette, of all things. No doubt she would unveil her next scheme, whatever it was, during the upcoming Summit, in order to inflict maximum damage on Andvari and the other kingdoms. But I couldn't do anything about Maeven tonight, so I grabbed the book with the information about the liladorn and stacked it atop the other volumes so the servants could return them to the library tomorrow.

An ebony jewelry box adorned with flying silver gargoyles was also sitting on the desk. Yaleen, my thread master, always packed the box full of rings, bracelets, and necklaces to complement my clothes, although I rarely wore any of them. I traced a finger over a silver gargoyle on the side of the box. A quick tap on this creature would pop open the secret compartment where I stored my gargoyle pendant—along with another special keepsake.

I thought about opening the compartment, but there was no point in looking at the item inside. I'd already spent far too much time staring at it recently—and thinking about Leonidas.

My mind drifted back to how he had looked standing atop the ridge earlier. Strong, powerful, cold, distant, handsome, dangerous. My heart clenched, and I snatched my hand away from the jewelry box. One day I was going to rip open that secret drawer, grab the item inside, and toss it into the nearest fireplace. Perhaps that would also be the day when I finally shoved my emotions down into the dungeon of my heart and locked them up so tightly they would *never* escape again.

But sadly, tonight was not that night.

Still, I was bloody tired of thinking about the Morricones, especially Leonidas, so I got up from the desk, stalked into the adjoining room, and slid into bed.

Try as I might, though, it was a long, long time before I went to sleep, and my last thought before my eyes drifted shut was of Leonidas standing in the clearing across from me, so close, yet so far away.

CHAPTER SIX

Early the next morning, Reiko and I boarded a train to return to Glanzen. Lord Eichen and Lady Adora insisted on accompanying us to the station and making sure we were settled in a private car before they finally left.

As soon as the lord, his granddaughter, and their entourage departed, Reiko and I slipped off the train and into the nearby woods where Grimley and Fern were waiting. I had been planning on taking the train home, but given Wexel's attack yesterday, I was wary of more traps. So Reiko and I climbed onto the gargoyles and flew back to the capital. When Glitnir, the royal palace, came into view a few hours later, my mood lifted.

It was always so wonderful to come home.

Glitnir's pale grayish marble walls gleamed with an opalescent sheen in the midday sun, as did the palace's centerpiece—a tall, wide wing topped with an elevated dome that boasted several spiked towers, making it look like a crown resting on a king's head. A plethora of precious metals and gems, all from Andvarian mines, adorned the outside of the palace. Bits of hammered gold framed the windows, while ribbons of silver snaked over the archways, and bronze weathervanes shaped like flying gargoyles spun around on the tower rooftops. Sapphires, amethysts, emeralds, rubies, and diamonds were embedded in many of the walls, and the mosaic patterns twinkled like merry eyes that were happy I was home.

But the jewels weren't the only things that greeted me—so did the gargoyles.

Several creatures were lounging on the rooftops, soaking up the sun. The gargoyles came in all shapes and sizes, from those barely bigger than tiny, owlish caladriuses to enormous behemoths larger than Floresian stallions. Their bodies also ranged in shade from the palest white to the darkest gray to the deepest black, with blue, purple, green, red, white, and other undertones, while their bright jewel-colored eyes matched the gems glittering in the palace walls.

Grimley buzzed low over the rooftops, and the lazing gargoyles let out gruff, grumbling, but welcoming cries. The creatures' presences also filled my mind, their warm, drowsy contentment a soothing balm to my heart. Lucky, Boodle, Pansy, Iris . . . All the palace gargoyles had names, either ones they had chosen or ones I had given them.

I silently called out their names, although most merely grunted in response, their voices dim and dull in my mind. Despite my mind magier power, I had never been able to communicate easily with all the gargoyles or even with more than a few at a time. Not like Armina Ripley, the first queen of Andvari, who had led legions of gargoyles into battle against the Morricones and their strixes.

The human guards patrolling the walls lifted their hands in greeting, and I waved back at them.

"Isn't this great!" I yelled to Reiko.

My friend was flying on Fern, and she shook her head, her face taking on the same green tint as the dragon on her hand.

Grimley swooped lower, as did Fern, and the gargoyles landed on a terrace that jutted out from the side of the palace. I slid off Grimley's back. Reiko dismounted Fern much more slowly, and her legs shook when they hit the flagstones. Reiko kept one hand on Fern's side, as if she was having trouble finding her balance.

"Problems?" I drawled.

Reiko scowled at me, but I jerked my head at Fern, who had plopped down on her hind legs and was looking up at the dragon morph with a hopeful expression.

Reiko's left eye twitched, but she scratched the gargoyle's head. "Thank you, Fern. That was a very . . . safe ride."

Fern leaned into Reiko's touch, and the arrow on the end of her tail enthusiastically *thump-thump-thumped* against the flagstones. "Any time, Lady Reiko! You're my new favorite!"

Grimley rolled his eyes. "Everyone is your new favorite as long as they pet you. Let's go hunting. I am in desperate need of a tasty rabbit or three before my afternoon nap."

Grimley nuzzled up against my legs, then flapped his wings and took off. Fern followed him up into the sky.

"Are you okay?" I asked.

Reiko's eye stopped twitching, and some of the green tinge faded from her face. The dragon on her hand also unclenched its jaw. "I will *never* get used to that."

I grinned. "I still can't believe a spymaster such as yourself is laid low by a little pleasure ride on a gargoyle."

Reiko shuddered. "There was nothing *pleasurable* about it, except for putting my feet on the ground again. Besides, if the gods had wanted me to fly, then they would have given me wings, like some of the other dragon morphs have. Instead, all I got was a bit of fire."

She shot a few green sparks off her fingertips. I laughed and threaded my arm through hers. Together, we went into the palace.

Walking through the Glitnir hallways was like strolling through a life-size jewelry box. Gray crushed velvet drapes adorned the windows, while gold, silver, and bronze leaf formed intricate patterns on the walls before climbing onto the ceilings and swirling around the chandeliers encrusted with white and gray diamonds. Glass cases glinted in various alcoves, each one housing a sword, shield, statue, pickaxe, or some other piece of Andvarian history.

Nobles, merchants, guilders, palace stewards, and servants were moving through the hallways, going about their business, while the guards were stationed in their usual spots. Everyone stopped and bowed to me, and I smiled and nodded, even as I skimmed their thoughts.

Princess Gemma is back already? That was a short trip. Perhaps Eichen's hospitality wasn't up to its usual standards . . .

She's tromping around in a common tunic, and her hair is a rat's nest of snarls. Glitzma is looking rather ragged today . . .

I wonder how she'll react to seeing the Morricones during the Summit . . .

The regular sort of chatter whispered through my mind, although the last thought made me grimace. I would have been quite happy never to set eyes on Milo again, but I couldn't kill the crown prince if I didn't see him, so it was a necessary evil. The same thing went for Maeven.

I wasn't sure how I felt about coming face-to-face with Delmira again, and of course I'd already had my disastrous encounter with Leonidas yesterday. Our mutually harsh words still troubled me, like a tangle of thorns scratching up against my heart. Perhaps that's how I should think of the Morricone prince. Like a thorn on a liladorn vine—pretty to look at, but dangerous to touch.

Reiko and I reached a set of double doors bearing the Ripley gargoyle crest, and I knocked three times.

"Enter!" a familiar voice barked out.

I opened one of the doors, and Reiko and I stepped into a study filled with ebony tables and gray velvet settees. Flames crackled in the large fireplace, adding some welcome warmth to the cool, drafty room, while white fluorestones blazed in the diamond-crusted chandelier overhead, throwing slivers of prismed rainbow colors onto the gold-framed paintings of famous Andvarian battles that adorned the walls.

Three desks were clustered together in the back of the room—two set at angles and flanking the third in the center.

King Heinrich Aldric Magnus Ripley, my grandfather, was sorting through a stack of papers at the center desk. He was in his seventies, with wavy hair that was more silver than dark brown. Wrinkles grooved into his tan skin, but his blue eyes were sharp and clear behind his silver reading glasses. He was wearing a dark gray jacket, with our gargoyle crest done in black thread over his heart.

To his right, Crown Prince Dominic Heinrich Ferdinand Ripley, my father, was ensconced at a slightly smaller desk and reading through his own papers. He had the same tan skin and blue eyes as my grandfather, although his brown hair contained only a few strands of silver, since he was in his fifties. He too was wearing a dark gray jacket bearing the gargoyle crest.

Rhea Hans, my forty-something stepmother and the captain of the royal guard, was perched at the desk to Grandfather Heinrich's left. She was wearing her usual dark gray gargoyle-crested tunic, and a sword with three rubies embedded in its hilt was resting on top of the desk. In addition to being an excellent fighter, Rhea also had strength magic, although no one dared to call the future queen consort a mutt, a somewhat derogatory term for those with strength, speed, enhanced senses, and other common powers.

Several gray crystal pins held Rhea's black curls back from

her face, showing off her pretty features and ebony skin. Her topaz eyes were narrowed in concentration as she stared down at an enormous diorama of a castle. She picked up a figurine, painted gray to represent an Andvarian soldier, and positioned it at different points. Purple, red, and other colored figurines also populated the diorama. Rhea had been planning our security for the Summit for weeks now.

The sight of my family going about the common everyday business of running our kingdom warmed my heart. Before my trip to Myrkvior, I had taken such things for granted, but not anymore. Not with Milo Morricone and the threat of war hanging over us like a sword poised to lop off our heads.

"Gemma!" Father got to his feet. "You're back!"

"Safe and sound."

Father grimaced. He and Grandfather Heinrich had never approved of my secret missions, but after the Blauberg battle, they had been much more supportive and understanding, especially of my desire to get to the bottom of Milo's plot.

After a round of hugs, Grandfather Heinrich called for some refreshments, which were laid out by the fireplace. Reiko immediately reached for the platter of sweet cakes. Rhea also nibbled on several sweet cakes, along with fresh fruit and crackers, while Father and Grandfather Heinrich downed mugs of spiced orange cider.

Me? Well, I focused on the tray that featured toasted triangles of sourdough bread stuffed with thick slices of melted gruyère cheese and slathered with different flavors of jam, including apricot, my personal favorite. Golden bread, gooey cheese, warm jam. It was the perfect combination of crunchy, salty, and sweet. I ate the whole platter of sandwiches all by myself, washing them down with some cider.

When we were all comfortably stuffed, Father leaned forward in his chair. "What did you discover?"

Reiko and I recounted everything that had happened in Haverton, including Wexel's ambush in the woods.

"So Milo set a trap to kill you. Sneaky bastard," Grandfather Heinrich growled. "Then again, I suppose we can expect nothing less from the Morricones—"

A cough erupted from his lips, one that rattled out of the deepest part of his chest. A few weeks ago, Grandfather Heinrich had developed a cough he couldn't quite seem to shake. The bone masters theorized that the recent unusually cold and damp weather had taken a toll on him and that he would be fine with some rest.

I shot Father a worried look, but he shook his head, indicating that we would talk about it later.

"I'm sorry we didn't learn more," I continued. "I was hoping Milo might be storing his tearstone weapons in the mine outside Haverton. It would be a natural place for the Mortans to launch an attack."

Grandfather Heinrich waved his hand. "It's fine, Gemma. I didn't expect it to be easy to find out what Milo is plotting."

"We have outfitted the palace guards with more armor and warned everyone to be wary of archers," Rhea chimed in. "We've prepared as much as we can against Milo's arrows, although I do wish we knew what he thinks is so special about them."

"Has Alvis found out anything else about the tearstone?" I asked.

"Unfortunately not," a familiar voice murmured.

Alvis, the Andvarian royal jeweler, strode into the study, drew a chair over to the fireplace, and sat down with us. Gray canvas gloves covered his hands, while a wide gray leather strap studded with fluorestones and adorned with a few small tools circled his head, making his wavy hair stick out in odd directions. One of the fluorestones was still turned on, highlighting his hazel eyes and ebony skin, along with the gray strands in his black hair.

I grinned. The eighty-something metalstone master often forgot to remove his headlamp when he left his workshop. "How are the tearstone experiments going?"

"Not well," he grumbled. "So far I've exposed Milo's arrows to coral-viper venom, along with amethyst-eye and several other poisons, but the tearstone hasn't reacted to any of them."

Well, that explained the gloves, although I still frowned in confusion. "Why are you experimenting with poisons?"

Alvis shrugged. "I'm trying to figure out how Milo got his arrows to conduct his lightning magic when he tortured you with them. I thought he might have coated the arrows with something. You know how much the Morricones love their potions and poisons."

Yes, I did. Roughly sixteen years ago, Dahlia Sullivan, Uncle Lucas's mother, had given Grandfather Heinrich small doses of amethyst-eye poison in hopes of eventually killing him, although Everleigh Blair had thwarted the plot. Remembering how sick my grandfather had been made my stomach churn, but I considered Alvis's theory. I had been concentrating so much on just finding the stolen tearstone I hadn't considered that Milo might be augmenting his arrows with *other* things.

Like flowers.

I reached into my pocket, drew out the black pouch the Mortan boy had been carrying, and showed the dried purple flower to Alvis. "Do you recognize this?"

Everyone stared at the flower, while I related the dying boy's mysterious talk of experiments.

Alvis flipped the magnifying lens attached to his headlamp down over his right eye and studied the blossom. "No, but I'm no plant magier. It could be anything from a common wildflower to a hothouse blossom. Let me try something."

He pulled a small shard of light gray tearstone from one of

his pockets and rubbed the purple petals back and forth over it. I held my breath, hoping we had found the answer . . .

Nothing happened. The shard didn't change color, and the flower remained just a flower.

Alvis sighed and handed the dried blossom back to me. "Sorry, Gemma."

"It's not your fault."

"I'll keep experimenting," he promised, getting to his feet. "Perhaps you're right, and some sort of plant is the answer, rather than a poison. If anyone could make a pretty little purple flower deadly, then it's the Morricones."

"I'll come help you later. Together we'll figure it out." I forced myself to smile with a confidence that I didn't feel.

Alvis returned my smile with one of his own, but the expression didn't quite reach his eyes, and the same worry rippled off him that was beating in my own heart. He nodded to the others, then left the study.

"Regardless of what Milo might be using on his arrows, our plans for the Summit remain the same," Father said. "We will negotiate with the other kingdoms and spy on our enemies, just as we always do. And they will do the same to us."

"Perhaps Milo will make a mistake during the Summit, and we'll be able to figure out his scheme that way," Rhea suggested.

Reiko popped another sweet cake into her mouth. "Perhaps. Although Milo only seems to make mistakes when it comes to Queen Maeven. He severely underestimated her at Myrkvior. He's a fool if he makes the same error again during the Summit."

"Milo is certainly arrogant, but he is definitely not a fool," I replied. "No doubt he has his own plans for the Summit, perhaps something to do with the mysterious experiments the dead Mortan boy mentioned."

Talk turned to other things, and soon our break was over,

and Grandfather Heinrich announced he had to get back to work. I kissed his wrinkled cheek, then watched while he settled himself behind his desk. He seemed okay, if a bit tired. Then again, he had been king for more than forty years. That responsibility would weigh heavily on anyone, especially given Andvari's recent renewed hostilities with Morta.

Reiko left to update Queen Ruri through the Cardea mirror in her chambers, while Rhea went to check in with the guards. Father jerked his head at me, and we exited the study together. My father and I often strolled through the palace while we discussed various affairs of state.

"How is Grandfather?" I asked as soon as we stepped into a deserted corridor. "His cough doesn't seem any better."

Father shrugged. "It's no better, but no worse either. The bone masters still think he needs rest more than anything else, but you know your grandfather. He doesn't like to slow down for anything, not even to help himself."

A smile tugged at my lips. Grandfather Heinrich wasn't the kind to sit still, and he wasn't happy unless he was doing *something*, whether it was running our kingdom, reading a book, or tending to his stands of bees, his latest hobby. "Perhaps he needs a lesson from Grimley about the benefits of morning, afternoon, and evening naps."

Father chuckled. "Perhaps. But I've finally gotten him to agree to stay here at Glitnir, rather than attending the Summit."

That was some welcome news. Father, Rhea, and I had all thought it best if Grandfather Heinrich remained at home, where it was safe, especially given Milo's brewing plot against Andvari.

Father cleared his throat, indicating that he needed to address a less pleasant matter. "How was it seeing Leonidas Morricone again?"

His question, and especially the soft, warm concern radiating off him, made me grind my teeth, but I answered him. "It was fine. We exchanged a few taunts and insults, then went our separate ways."

I had downplayed my relationship—or whatever I truly had—with Leonidas, although I got the sense my father knew I hadn't told him everything that had happened in Myrkvior between the Morricone prince and me.

"Why do you think he was in the woods?" Father asked.

Leo heard you might be in trouble, Lyra's voice whispered through my mind.

"Leonidas claimed to be chasing the same rumors Reiko and I were following."

That much was true, although I didn't mention Lyra's confession. Part of me was pleased Leonidas had been worried about me, but the other, larger part of me was angry and insulted. I could take care of myself, something I'd demonstrated by killing all those Mortans in the woods yesterday. I didn't need—or bloody *want*—the prince to hover over me like I was some fairy-tale damsel constantly in distress.

"Do you think Leonidas will attend the Summit?" Father asked.

"I don't know. Even if he does, we probably won't have any dealings with him. Maeven will be the one in charge. She always is."

Father snorted. "You're right about that. No matter how much I personally loathe her, even I have to admit Maeven is a clever queen. All things considered, she has done far more good than harm for Morta during her reign."

Surprise shot through me. "That's the nicest thing I've ever heard you say about her."

It was certainly far nicer than anything *I* had ever thought about her. Even now, some sixteen years later, I could still see the shocked, pained look on Uncle Frederich's face when Crown Princess Vasilia Blair had driven her dagger into his heart during the Seven Spire massacre. I could still smell the burned skin of Lord Hans, Rhea's father, after Vasilia had blasted him with her lightning, and I could still hear the screams of everyone else who'd died that awful day—

My magic bubbled up in my chest like a geyser about to erupt. The hallway flickered, and the gray carpet transformed into a green lawn soaked with scarlet blood . . .

I dug my nails into my palms. The dull aches in my hands helped me shove my magic down. The grass and blood vanished, and the hallway was just a hallway again.

Father didn't seem to notice my turmoil. "Maeven might be a dangerous enemy, but she has at least done some good things for her people. Abolishing Maximus's labor camps, protecting the strixes, keeping a tenuous peace with the other kingdoms."

His face darkened like a storm cloud, and magic flared in his eyes, making them burn a bright, fierce blue. "But if Maeven attacks our family again, especially during the Summit, then I will do everything in my power to destroy her. I promise you that, Gemma."

Father put his arm around me and hugged me close. Sorrow surged off him, and Uncle Frederich's smiling face filled his mind, as well as my own. Sometimes, I got so caught up in my own painful memories of the massacre I forgot my father had lost his brother that terrible day.

I hugged him back. "And I promise you the same thing. If Maeven, Milo, Leonidas, or any of the other Mortans make trouble for us, then I will do my best to destroy them."

Father wrapped his other arm around me and hugged me even more tightly than before, so he didn't see the grimace that twisted my face, and he especially didn't sense the doubt that twinged my heart when I said Leonidas's name.

Father returned to the study, while I headed to Alvis's workshop. The metalstone master and I conducted experiments the rest of the afternoon, but we didn't discover anything new about the tearstone or the dried flower.

Eventually we stopped working for the day and had an early dinner with Reiko and my family. We talked some more about what Milo might be plotting, but no one had any new theories, so we all went our separate ways for the evening.

I couldn't sleep, not with thoughts of Milo and mystery experiments churning in my mind, so I decided to walk through the Edelstein Gardens, the gleaming green heart of Glitnir.

The gardens were famous for their mix of real live trees, flowers, and plants, along with those made of gold, silver, and colorful gemstones. Something beautiful glittered around every corner, from blue striped orchids standing tall in white marble pots to peridot pansies peeking up out of beds of emeralds and topazes. Hummingbirds and butterflies fluttered around stained-glass bowls filled with sugar water, and the beating of their tiny jewel-toned wings further spread lilac, honeysuckle, and other floral scents through the cool evening air.

But my favorite part of the gardens was the massive evergreen hedge maze, which was almost always shaped like the Ripley gargoyle crest. The palace plant magiers changed the paths every year to make the maze seem fresh and new, but I knew every pattern, and I easily made it to the gargoyle's nose in the middle.

The hedges fell away, revealing an enormous gazebo overlooking a pond. Tall cattails lined the bank like soldiers standing guard, while black, gray, and white water lilies twirled around like dancers constantly in motion atop the rippling water. In the gazebo, silver gargoyle faces with jeweled eyes glimmered in the white marble columns, while white and gray diamonds arranged to look like water lilies sparkled on the ceiling, along with jet cattails, in an artistic mirror of the real pond in the distance.

I stepped into the gazebo and ran my hand along the ebony railing. No nicks or scratches marred the smooth, shiny wood, but my mind still wandered back to the night when Dahlia Sullivan, Maeven, and other members of the Bastard Brigade—a group of bastard-born Morricone royals who carried out murders and other plots—had tried to kill Everleigh Blair here.

At the time, I was thirteen and had snuck out of a royal ball to climb onto one of the palace roofs. I'd been petting Grimley when I saw Mortan assassins creeping through the gardens. I'd been so ashamed by my cowardly inaction during the Seven Spire massacre that I'd scrambled onto Grimley's back and begged him to fly me down into the thick of the fight.

Grimley and I had helped Everleigh drive back some of the assassins before going to the throne room to sound the alarm. Evie and Uncle Lucas had eventually killed the Mortans, and Dahlia Sullivan had also died by deliberately drinking the amethyst-eye poison she'd planned to use on Evie. Maeven had escaped, though, the way she always did.

Bitterness washed through me, and suddenly, I couldn't stand to be in the same spot where Maeven had almost succeeded in killing Aunt Evie and Uncle Lucas. So I stormed out of the gazebo, plunged back into the hedge maze, and took the path that led to the corner of the gargoyle's right eye. This part of the design never changed, and the space was always shaped like a teardrop, although few people came here.

Most folks didn't like to visit the dead.

A dark gray granite mausoleum curved around the bottom of the teardrop, following the sweeping arc of the maze, and the Ripley gargoyle crest stretched across the closed doors. Inside, stairs plunged down into the old mining tunnels where my ancestors were laid to rest. Ripley tradition decreed that the royals give our bodies back to the earth as repayment for all the ores, stones, and gems that Andvarians mined out of the Spire Mountains.

I stalked past the mausoleum and headed over to a bench made of tendrils of silver twisted together to look like delicate vines. The bench was tucked under a large pear tree, and I had to brush away several scarlet leaves so I could sit down. I ran my fingers over the words etched into the silver plaque embedded in the center of the backrest.

Merilde Edelle Irma Ripley, Beloved Mother, Daughter, and Wife

My mother was buried in the mausoleum with the other royals, but the two of us used to sneak out here and spend hours sitting in the shade, laughing, talking, and reading stories. After Mother had died, Father had erected this bench in her honor, and I often came here whenever I needed to escape the thoughts and feelings of everyone in the palace. A long, weary sigh dropped from my lips like another leaf plummeting from the pear tree. Too bad I couldn't escape my own worries—

Hello, a soft voice whispered in my mind.

I jumped to my feet, my hand dropping to my dagger. My gaze snapped back and forth, but I didn't see anyone lurking in the shadows. So who—or what—had spoken to me?

Over here, the voice whispered again.

A flutter of movement caught my eye, and I eased back over to the bench. Several black vines with long thorns had twined through the silver slats and curled around my mother's plaque, looking like an ebony frame holding a pretty portrait.

Strange. I had never noticed any liladorn in the gardens before, and it had certainly never spoken to me before. But this plant had to have been here for quite some time, given how large it was. Curious, I reached out to touch it—

One of the vines whipped out, and a thorn gouged my skin, leaving a long scratch on my right hand. Blood welled up out of the wound, which cut through the center of my starburst scar.

I hissed at the sharp sting and wrenched my hand back. *Ouch! Why did you do that?*

The presence in the liladorn sniffed. *We are not to be petted like a common gargoyle, Not-Our-Princess.*

Not-Our-Princess? What did that mean? Before I could ask, the vines uncurled from around the plaque, slithered down to the ground, and melted into the shadows.

I glared at the spot where the liladorn had been for the better part of a minute before I realized how ridiculous I was being. Ever since my mind magier magic had first manifested, I had always worried it would someday drive me mad, and now here I was, standing in the chilly dark, trying to figure out how to murder a sentient plant.

I sighed again, my breath frosting in the air. Yesterday I'd foolishly walked into Wexel's trap, and tonight I'd been reprimanded by the liladorn. Plus, I still didn't know what horrible thing Milo was planning to do with his arrows, what new scheme Maeven might spring at the Summit, or whether I could control my emotions the next time I saw Leonidas.

Everything was going wrong, and if I didn't find a way to fix it, then a scratched hand would be the least of my problems. More than likely I would suffer a terrible death and doom my family and Andvari along with me. Oh, yes. I was tightly snared in this royal trap, and right now I didn't see a way to escape it—or save my kingdom.

PART TWO

THE ROYAL TRAP

CHAPTER SEVEN

Three days later, we left Glitnir for the Summit.

This time, we did take the train, due to the enormous entourage of servants, courtiers, and guards who always traveled with Father and Rhea. Since everyone's attention was on Crown Prince Dominic Ripley, Reiko and I were able to stay in the background, which was a relief. But in public, I still had to play the part of Princess Gemma, smiling, laughing, and pretending everything was fine and that I wasn't deeply worried we wouldn't survive the Summit.

We arrived at the city of Caldwell early the next morning. The train pulled into the station, where my father was greeted by trumpets blaring out the Ripley royal march. Father smiled and waved to the cheering crowd, shook hands with the rail guilder and other workers, and then climbed into a carriage surrounded by Rhea and several guards. Reiko and I got into a different carriage, and our entourage rolled through the streets.

Caldwell was one of the most unusual cities on the Buchovian continent, since it was located in not one, not two, but three kingdoms. The majority of the city was in Andvari, although homes and shops had spilled over into both Unger and Morta long ago. For centuries, an uneasy truce had existed in Caldwell between the three kingdoms and their respective peoples, although tensions had eased a bit ever since Maeven had become queen. As much as I hated to admit it, Father was right. Some things *had* changed for the better under her rule.

Reiko peered out the carriage window, curiosity creasing her face.

"You've never been here before?" I asked.

"No, but it looks very similar to Glanzen. Gray cobblestone streets, plazas with pretty fountains, little bits of gold and silver adorning all the homes and shops. It's quite charming, like something out of a storybook."

"Caldwell has always been one of my favorite cities. Of course the Summit is usually held here, but Caldwell was also my mother's hometown, so we would visit at other times as well."

Fond memories filled my mind, everything from summer picnics, swimming, and sailing to winter sledding, skating, and snowball fights. Through them all, my mother's smile warmed my heart, and her soft laughter echoed in my ears.

Even though we had spent most of our time at Glitnir, I had always felt much more connected to Merilde in Caldwell, as if my mother was hiding around a corner, waiting for me to come find her, just as she had when we would play hide-and-seek when I was a child.

The carriage crested a hill, and Reiko leaned forward. "So that's the lake I've been hearing so much about."

All three kingdoms and sections of the city bordered Caldwell Lake, which stretched out for miles before giving way to the snowcapped peaks of the Spire Mountains. Many of the homes and shops had been built into the surrounding hillsides so that they overlooked the picturesque lake, along with Caldwell Castle, which dominated much of the steep, rocky shoreline.

Our carriage crossed the bridge that led from the city into the castle and stopped in a courtyard. Reiko and I got out and walked over to where Father and Rhea were climbing out of their own carriage. The servants, courtiers, and guards also hopped down from their own vehicles.

Unlike Glitnir, with its dazzling displays of precious metals and gems, no such adornments brightened the dark gray stone walls of Caldwell Castle. I'd always thought my Ripley ancestors had deliberately left the castle facade plain so as not to remind the neighboring Ungers and Mortans of Andvari's massive wealth. Better not to tempt fate, with friends and enemies alike lurking so close by.

But one thing was the same here as at Glitnir—the gargoyles.

Images of flying gargoyles were carved into the walls, as well as into the wooden shutters that flanked the stained-glass windows. Bronze gargoyle weathervanes topped many of the towers, at least here in the Andvarian section of the castle, along with gray flags bearing the Ripley snarling gargoyle crest done in black thread. And of course a few real live gargoyles were napping on the roofs, basking in the morning sunlight.

A lone gargoyle was perched on the tower closest to the castle entrance, staring down at our procession as though he were a gatekeeper deciding whether to grant us entrance. He was a little bigger than Grimley, with a thick, wide body and large paws that boasted long black talons. His light gray eyes gleamed like moonstones, while opalescent veins gave his dark gray skin a pearlesque shimmer. The gargoyle looked strong and healthy, although the top half of his left horn was broken off into a jagged stump. Curious. Few things were hard, strong, or sharp enough to damage a gargoyle's stone skin.

I knew many of the creatures who roosted at the castle, although I didn't remember seeing this one before.

Hello. I gently sent the thought to him. *What's your name?*

Otto, he grumbled. *Not that you or anyone else here truly cares, princess.*

He spread his wings and took off toward the lake. I frowned. Grimley could sometimes be grumpy, but that gargoyle had been downright rude. Still, he was gone, so I pushed him out of my mind.

As with the city, all three kingdoms had their own section of Caldwell Castle, while a fourth section was devoted to housing people from other kingdoms. I glanced up at the towers on the other wings. To my left, the flags featured a snarling red ogre face with gold eyes on a gold background—the Ungerian contingent was already here. No surprise. The Ungers loved punctuality almost as much as they loved dancing, so they were almost always the first ones to arrive for the Summit.

To my right, on the Mortan side of the castle, the towers were free of flags, indicating that Queen Maeven wasn't here yet. Again, no surprise. The Mortans cared little for others' schedules, and they never appeared at the Summit until they were good and ready.

My thoughts drifted to Leonidas. Ever since I'd returned from Haverton, I'd felt his presence lingering in the back of my mind, like an itch I couldn't quite scratch. My magic surged up, and an image of him popped into my head—Leonidas standing at attention, with his hands clasped behind him, wearing his usual black riding coat. Somehow I knew this wasn't a memory, that I was seeing him as he was right now, in real life.

Once again, I cursed my magic. Instead of ghosting back into the past, I was now *seeking*, or casting my mind about to find a particular person. And just like with my ghosting power, I didn't seem to have any control over this ability either.

Leonidas frowned and turned his head, as if something had caught his attention. His eyes locked with mine, and his frown deepened. Despite the distance between us, I knew he was seeing me, just as I was seeing him.

Gemma . . .

His voice whispered in my mind, a low, husky rasp that made my stomach clench. Suddenly, *all* I could see was him and the hot, intense emotions flaring in his gaze—

"Gemma? Gemma!" Reiko snapped her fingers in front of my face. "Are you okay?"

I blinked. Leonidas's face vanished, although his presence still lingered in my mind, the itch of him stronger and more irritating than before.

Get out of my head, I snarled.

But there was no reply, no voice, no flicker of emotion. It was as though I could feel him, but he couldn't feel me. But how was that even possible? He had always wielded his mind magier magic much more skillfully than I ever had mine.

I waited, but his presence didn't vanish or fade away. It just stayed there, as steady and annoying as a mosquito's hum. For better or worse, Leonidas Morricone was stuck in my head, and I had no idea how to remove him from my mind—or especially my heart.

"Gemma?" Reiko asked again. "What are you looking at?"

"Nothing," I lied. "Nothing at all."

I led Reiko to my chambers at the top of one of the Andvarian towers. She took the bedroom closest to mine, which was on the opposite side of a sitting room that connected both areas.

Servants set out trays of sweet cakes and stoked the flames in the fireplaces. When the chambers were suitably warm and the servants had departed, I opened one of the glass balcony doors in the sitting room and let out a low whistle. A few seconds later, Grimley flew through the opening and landed inside.

"Finally!" he grumbled. "I thought you were going to make me stay outside in the cold all morning."

"You've already been out in the cold all morning," I pointed out. "And last night too."

Grimley had ridden—napped—on top of the train from Glanzen to Caldwell, since he didn't like being cooped up in the car with so many people.

"Plus, I saw you sneak off to go hunting with Fern while Father was greeting everyone at the train station. How many rabbits have you eaten today?"

Grimley sniffed. "Only three. That's hardly enough for a *proper* snack. I'll have to go hunting again later—*after* my morning nap."

The gargoyle trotted over and lay down in front of the fireplace. Less than a minute later, low gravelly snores started rumbling out of his mouth.

"After spending the past few weeks at Glitnir with all its gold and jewels, Caldwell Castle and its furnishings seem rather . . . plain." Reiko trailed her fingers along an ebony writing desk. "Why, there's nary a gem in sight."

"Has the fearsome dragon morph spy gotten used to the finer things at the royal palace?" I drawled. "If that's the case, we might have to give you a nickname. You can be Reiko the Resplendent to my Glitzma."

Reiko rolled her eyes. "That is a *horrible* nickname. And for the record, I like pretty things just as much as you do. The Ryusaman royal palace has its fair share of gold and jewels, as does my family's home."

A wistful note filled her voice, and the dragon on her hand sighed, a puff of black smoke drifting out of its mouth and wisping across her skin.

"Are you looking forward to seeing Queen Ruri at dinner?" I asked.

Reiko's face twisted into a grimace, as did the one of her inner dragon. "It depends."

"On what?"

"Whether my father is with her."

Despite all the time we'd spent together over the past few weeks, Reiko hadn't talked much about her father or the rest of her family, except for Queen Ruri. I had been most curious about the other Yamatos, but I hadn't wanted to pry. But now that we were at the Summit, politics would be front and center, and I needed to know as much about the Ryusamans as possible.

"Your father's name is Tatsuo, right?"

I already knew it was, since I had long ago memorized the names and ranks of every member of every royal family in Buchovia, from the youngest infant lord to the oldest dowager lady.

Reiko nodded. "Tatsuo Akio Bunta Yamato, the famous former gladiator who is now the chief advisor to Queen Ruri."

"He sounds like a very important, powerful man."

"Oh, yes, my father *is* very important and powerful. So are my two older sisters. Me, much less so." Her face remained blank, but hurt rippled through her voice.

"What do you mean?"

Reiko fell silent and stared down at the desk again. My friend could be exceptionally stubborn, especially when it came to keeping her own secrets, so I glanced around, searching for a way to reach her. My gaze landed on the tray of sweet cakes on the table in front of the fireplace. That should do the trick.

"You might as well tell me," I replied, sitting down in a chair by the table. "Lest I be forced to eat this entire platter of sweet cakes whilst you brood in silence."

Reiko snorted. "You like those weird cheese-and-jam sandwiches much more than you like sweet cakes."

I popped a cake into my mouth. "Mmm-mmm-mmm. This one tastes just like cranberry-apple pie, one of my favorites."

I popped another cake into my mouth and poured myself a glass of cranberry cider. Reiko arched an eyebrow at me in a clear challenge.

I downed a third cake, then a fourth, then a fifth. The cakes were tiny, no more than two bites each, but they were rapidly filling up my stomach. Still, I was determined to win this game, and if I had to eat every single cake on this platter, then I would do it and cough up the crumbs later—

Reiko huffed, marched over, and flopped down into the chair across from mine. "Fine. You win. Give me the bloody cakes."

I nudged the platter over to her side of the table. Reiko ate three cakes in quick succession and washed them down with some cider.

"My father has never been happy about my being a spy," she finally confessed.

"Why not?"

Reiko took her time chewing and swallowing another cake before answering. "Because I used to be a gladiator."

"*What?*" I screeched in surprise. "You never told me that!"

"That's because I wasn't very good at it."

"But you're an excellent warrior. Smart, strong, disciplined. I would have died half a dozen times in Blauberg and then again in the woods outside Haverton if you hadn't saved me."

A harsh, bitter laugh erupted out of Reiko's mouth. "According to my father, being excellent is not good enough. I must be the absolute *best*—like he was. Tatsuo won the Tournament of Champions during the Regalia Games when he was about my age—*twice.*"

I opened my mouth to ask another question, but I thought better of it and kept silent. This was Reiko's story to tell, in her own way and time.

"Most of the Yamatos are dragon morphs. Sakura, my eldest sister, is a talented music master who will eventually take over my father's estate, while Akari, my other sister, is a captain in the Ryusaman navy. So my father pinned his gladiator glory hopes on me." Reiko blew out a breath. "Tatsuo was bitterly disappointed when I did not do nearly as well as he had, especially when I got knocked out in the fourth round during the most recent Tournament of Champions last year."

She tossed back the rest of her cider and turned the empty mug around in her hands. "Tatsuo told me that I needed to train harder, but my heart wasn't in it."

A rueful smile flitted across her face. "I told you once that you'd read too many storybooks about being a hero and saving people. Well, I heard too many stories from Cho as a child." Reiko waved her hand over the tray of cakes. "He would swipe sweet cakes and lemonade from the palace kitchen, take me on picnics, and tell me about all the sneaky things he did, along with Xenia Rubin, Serilda Swanson, and his other friends."

Cho Yamato was the ringmaster of the Black Swan gladiator troupe and famous for helping Everleigh Blair infiltrate Seven Spire palace and take the Bellonan throne from her murderous cousin, Vasilia. Cho had visited Glitnir many times, and I'd also heard his wonderful stories, tales filled with action, adventure, danger, and intrigue. No wonder Reiko had longed to be a spy, rather than a gladiator.

"I had studied with the Ryusaman spymasters on and off over the years, as all royals do, but after my disastrous Regalia tournament, I began training with them in earnest," Reiko continued. "Eventually I started going on missions with them, something Tatsuo did *not* approve of. When Queen Ruri needed someone to investigate the rumors about Milo Morricone stockpiling Andvarian tearstone, I volunteered for the mission."

"Because you wanted to get away from your father?" I asked.

Reiko sighed. "More like I wanted to get away from our fights. I love my father, but Sakura and Akari have flourished in the paths he set for them, and he's never understood why I didn't want to do the same, why I *couldn't* do the same."

"Because being a gladiator is not who you are," I murmured.

She nodded, then dropped her gaze to her empty mug again. The dragon on her hand also lowered its eyes. Pain rippled off both of them, squeezing my own heart tight.

I thought of how Reiko had so seamlessly blended in with the other miners in Blauberg, as though she'd been doing the job for years. How she'd smiled, laughed, and joked with Queen Maeven at Myrkvior, despite the fact that discovery would have meant her death. How she'd disguised herself as a Mortan guard, flown on a strix, and fought with me during the Battle of Blauberg. How she could change her whole walk, talk, posture, and persona, going from an arrogant noble to an ordinary servant in an instant.

No, Reiko Yamato was not a gladiator—she was a spy through and through.

"Maybe Tatsuo is just worried about the danger that comes with being a spy," I said, trying to be diplomatic. "You know how my own father hates it when I go off on a mission."

"You're the crown princess, the heir," Reiko replied. "You're too valuable to keep risking your life as a spy."

"But your life is okay to risk because you *aren't* the heir?" I shook my head. "That's ridiculous."

Reiko gave me a pitying look. "Oh, Gemma. You know as well as I do some lives are far more important than others. You just haven't had to make those choices yet—to decide who you want to save and who it's okay to let die and why. Well, Tatsuo decided long ago that if I didn't live the life *he* chose for me, then my life simply wasn't worth as much as those of my sisters."

She drew in a deep breath, then let it out, along with a rush of words. "I hoped that if I unraveled Milo's plot and protected Ryusama, I might finally be able to convince my father that I was a far better spy than I ever was a gladiator."

"That you were the best," I murmured, echoing her earlier words.

Reiko had expressed that sentiment many times before. When I'd first met her, I'd thought it was pure arrogance, but she must have been trying to convince herself as much as anyone else. Just like I was still trying to convince myself that I could fully control my magic, as well as my feelings for Leonidas, when the opposite seemed to be true.

I stretched my hand out across the table to grasp hers, to tell her that I understood, but Reiko shot to her feet.

"Grimley has the right idea about taking a nap. Tonight's dinner will be long and tedious, but I should strive to stay awake through it." She paused, then plucked the tray of sweet cakes off the table. "And I'm taking these with me."

Reiko marched out of the sitting room, went into her adjoining chambers, and closed the door behind her.

In front of the fireplace, Grimley grumbled something in his sleep and rolled onto his other side. The gargoyle hadn't woken up, despite my conversation with Reiko.

I slumped back in my chair and rubbed my head, which was suddenly aching. Plots and politics between the kingdoms were treacherous enough, but sometimes I thought nothing was more dangerous than trying to navigate familial feelings and duties.

It was going to be a long Summit—in more ways than one.

CHAPTER EIGHT

Reiko wasn't the only one who needed some rest, so I also took a nap. My sleep was deep, dreamless, and refreshing, and I woke up feeling ready to face whatever treachery might be in store tonight.

Grimley went out hunting for an evening snack, so I summoned Yaleen, my thread master, and got ready for dinner.

Tonight's event was just an opening salvo in the intense high-stakes negotiations that would be taking place between the royals, nobles, merchants, and guilders over the next few days, so I dressed in a simple gown of light gray velvet with sleeves trimmed with glittering black thread, along with flat black shoes. My gargoyle pendant hung from the silver chain around my neck as usual, and I slid my dagger into the scabbard on the black velvet belt cinched around my waist.

Herra, my paint master, dusted my face with almond powder, used smoky gray shadow and liner to emphasize my blue eyes, and stained my lips with a dark plum berry balm. For the finishing touch, Jacha, Herra's daughter, used a hot iron to add loose waves to my shoulder-length brown hair.

I thanked everyone for their time and skill, then knocked on Reiko's open door and stepped into her chambers. A thread and paint master had worked on her as well, and she was wearing a long, tight gown that looked like it was made of spun gold. Her gold dragon pendant hung around her neck, and a matching ring stretched across all four fingers on her left hand, as was the popular Ryusaman style. Her long black hair had been pulled back into a fashionable fishtail braid, while gold shadow and liner brought out her green eyes, and dark red berry balm emphasized her lips.

"You look amazing," I said.

Reiko grinned, seeming more like her usual confident self than she had earlier. "You too. Why, you'll be certain to turn Prince Leo's head tonight."

I rolled my eyes at her teasing. "Let's concentrate on keeping our heads attached to our shoulders."

She smirked. "Whatever you say, princess."

I threaded my arm through hers. "Come along then, spy."

A shadow passed over Reiko's face, and I wondered if I'd said the wrong thing, but then she grinned at me again, as did her inner dragon.

We left my chambers and walked down to the ground level. In addition to the royals and their entourages, scores of nobles, merchants, and guilders from across Buchovia had also flocked to the Summit, so throngs of people were crowding the corridors.

Several folks smiled, nodded, and bowed when they saw me, but no one stopped moving. Everyone wanted to get the best seat possible for tonight's festivities, which trumped taking the time to ingratiate themselves with me. Besides, I was still only a princess, and thus not nearly as important as the senior royals in attendance.

Reiko and I stepped outside into a courtyard. The sun was

setting, bathing the sky in a soft golden glow, and the gargoyles had returned from their day's hunting and were now relaxing on the rooftops. All the creatures had their faces tilted toward the sun, trying to soak up a few more warm rays—except for Otto.

Unlike the other lounging creatures, the grumpy gargoyle was perched on the edge of a roof, sitting up tall, as though he was once again standing guard. His face was creased into a frown, and his gray eyes were narrowed to slits as he glared down at the people moving below. Perhaps he didn't like so many humans invading the castle for the Summit.

I scanned the other rooftops, but I didn't see the gargoyle I was looking for. *Grimley, are you back at the castle? Any sign of the Mortans yet?*

He answered me. *I'm up on one of the Andvarian towers, along with Fern. Servants and guards are scurrying around the Mortan wing, and the flags have been hoisted, but I haven't seen any of the Morricones yet. No strixes either.*

I pushed our connection to the back of my mind. "The Mortans have arrived, but Grimley hasn't spotted the Morricones yet."

Reiko snorted. "Of course not. They won't show themselves until the last possible minute. Maeven loves to make an entrance, just like King Maximus did."

We left the courtyard, walked through an archway, and emerged in the enormous plaza at the center of the castle. Freestanding wooden carts draped with colorful banners ringed the area, while tables and chairs clustered together in the open spaces between several bubbling fountains. Starting tomorrow morning, the plaza would transform into an open-air marketplace, where merchants would show off everything from handmade wooden crafts to bolts of fine cloth to rare spices for the nobles, guilders, and others looking to buy their wares.

Several merchants were unpacking their goods, while some

of the food carts were already serving customers. My mouth watered as the sweet and savory scents of fudge, funnel cakes, and cornucopia wafted through the air. A few folks stopped to buy treats, but most people were heading toward the arena that dominated the center of the plaza.

Compared to the Black Swan and other gladiator arenas, the Caldwell one was relatively small, seating only a few thousand people. Still, the stone structure soared several stories into the air and boasted three towers, one each for Andvari, Unger, and Morta.

Reiko and I walked past the Andvarian guards flanking the main entrance, strode down a long tunnel, and emerged onto the arena floor. This main, bottom level was a large circle, ringed by a four-foot stone wall. Outside the wall, steps climbed to the upper levels, which featured audience boxes filled with tables and chairs.

Even though I had been coming to the Summit for years and had been in the arena countless times before, I always found a new bit of artistry to admire. Andvarian gargoyles, Ungerian ogres, and Mortan strixes were carved into the thick gray stone columns that supported the upper levels, while the roof was made of clear panes of glass etched with even more gargoyles, ogres, and strixes. Much like the center wing at Glitnir, the Caldwell arena always reminded me of a crown with a round base, with the various boxes and levels climbing higher and higher, like square jewels and spikes of metal spiraling upward and outward on a queen's head.

Down here on the main floor, four long rectangular tables draped with crested banners were perched on raised stone daises arranged in a loose semicircle. The Andvarian table with its gray-and-black gargoyle banner was first; then came the Ungerians, with their red ogre on a gold backdrop. Beyond them was the Ryusaman table with its banner of a green dragon on a gold background. The final spot belonged to the Mortans, with their stylized silver *M* on a purple banner, which was directly opposite the Andvarian table. Naturally.

Only four senior royals were attending the Summit this year. Queen Everleigh Blair was dealing with a problem in Bellona, so she wasn't here. King Cisco Castillo of Flores and King Eon Umbele of Vacuna were also absent, which wasn't unusual.

In recent years, Aunt Evie had started holding her own Summit at Seven Spire palace, which was easier for Cisco and Eon to attend, since their kingdoms were closer to Bellona than they were to Andvari. She had even invited some of the DiLucris, the wealthy family who ran the Fortuna Mint and made their home on Fortuna Island, to her Summits. Then again, Aunt Evie was all about keeping an eye on her enemies.

Dozens of the wealthiest, most important nobles, merchants, and guilders had already gathered on the arena floor. Servants were offering drinks to the crowd, while guards from the various kingdoms were spaced around the wall. The excited atmosphere was that of a royal ball, despite the lack of music and dancing. The opening night of the Summit was always a way for everyone to mingle and take stock of one another before the more serious negotiations about trade, goods, and the like began the next morning.

I fixed a smile on my face and stepped into the crowd, with Reiko gliding along beside me. Several folks eyed me, and whispers sprang up in my wake. The audible chatter was loud enough, but people's silent thoughts rang in my ears like bells that wouldn't stop chiming out the hour.

Princess Gemma looks well, all things considered . . .

Except for the scars on her hands . . .

Why doesn't she hide those ugly marks with gloves?

My gargoyle pendant heated up as it strained to hold back the silent musings, and I focused on its warmth, rather than the voices echoing in my head. Slowly the pendant cooled, and the choppy sea of emotion churning inside me smoothed out. Leonidas had been right about one thing. I was getting stronger in my magic, or at least better able to control it in simple situations like this.

Still, I had no desire to be in the thick of things, so Reiko and I took up a position by one of the iron gates in the wall. I looked out over the crowd, searching for the biggest throngs of people.

That's where the royals always were.

Father was already here, wearing a short formal gray jacket, while Rhea was dressed in a lovely scarlet gown, although a brace of ruby-studded daggers circled her waist. She might be the future queen consort, but she would always be the captain of the royal guard first and foremost.

Father and Rhea were talking to a fifty-something woman with amber eyes, bronze skin, and a long mane of red hair that cascaded down her back like a river of fire. Her gown was the same glorious red as her hair, and a morph mark with matching red hair and amber eyes was visible on her neck.

Queen Zariza Rubin toasted me with her goblet, and I dipped into a curtsy. The ogre on Zariza's neck winked at me. Then she returned to her conversation with Father and Rhea.

My gaze skipped over to the people clustered around a slender seventy-something woman with green eyes, golden skin, and black hair shot through with thick seams of silver. The woman was wearing a long, formal green coat patterned with tiny gold-thread dragons, and a morph mark of a green dragon with black eyes adorned her left hand.

Queen Ruri Yamato of Ryusama turned in this direction, and I curtsied to her as well, while Reiko dropped into a traditional Ryusaman bow. Ruri smiled at us in return.

The crowd parted, revealing a man standing next to Queen Ruri. He too had golden skin and black hair sprinkled with silver, although he looked to be in his fifties. He was also wearing a long coat, although his was a light sandy brown. His dark brown eyes glinted in the light, as did the dragon on his neck, which had gold scales and black eyes.

The man stared at me, neither friendly nor hostile, before his gaze slid over to Reiko, who stiffened. The man's face remained neutral, although his inner dragon frowned.

"Your father?" I asked.

"The great Tatsuo Yamato himself," Reiko muttered.

She bowed to her father, while I curtsied. Tatsuo tilted his head to us, then focused on Queen Ruri again.

From what Reiko had told me, she had left Ryusama months ago. If I hadn't seen my father in all that time, I would have hurried over to greet him, but the two of them remained distant, their relationship even chillier and more strained than I'd imagined.

Tatsuo gestured with his hand, and another man strode into view. This man was younger, in his thirties, with a tall, muscled body, black hair, and golden eyes and skin. A dragon with red scales and black eyes was visible on his neck, and his fingers rested on the hilt of the sword belted to his waist.

"Who's that?" I asked.

Reiko's mouth flattened out into a thin line. "Kai Nakamura. He was a gladiator in the Crimson Dragons, the same troupe I was in. He was the best fighter in the troupe and won several bouts. He also defeated me on his way to winning the Tournament of Champions at the Regalia Games last year."

Kai tipped his head respectfully to me, then winked at Reiko. Merriment sparked in his eyes, and a sly smile curved his lips. Reiko shot him an icy stare in return, which made Kai smile even wider.

Sometimes, enemies make the most interesting suitors—and especially the best lovers. Reiko's voice floated through my mind.

"So *he's* the one you were talking about back in Haverton," I murmured. "The enemy turned lover. He looks beautiful and dangerous."

"Something like that," Reiko muttered. "And he is both beautiful and dangerous, and the arrogant bastard knows it."

She grabbed a goblet of raspberry sangria from a passing servant and downed it in one long gulp. She obviously didn't want to talk about Tatsuo or Kai, so I didn't press the issues.

I scanned the rest of the arena floor. I didn't see any of the Morricones, although a few servants wearing Mortan purple were scurrying around. Reiko was right. Maeven was probably waiting to make a grand entrance at the last minute.

Reiko turned this way and that, eyeing the clusters of people. I did the same, seeing who was talking to whom and trying to make new friends in order to undercut old rivals.

So far Crown Prince Dominic, Queen Zariza, Queen Ruri, and their entourages seemed to be mingling well. Father was now talking to Ruri and Tatsuo, while Zariza was admiring one of Rhea's daggers. The nobles, merchants, and guilders also looked relaxed, although a faint undercurrent of tension hummed through the air, as everyone waited for the Mortans to arrive—

A loud, familiar *tap-tap-tap* sounded on the flagstones, and a warm, welcome presence brushed up against my mind.

"Stand up straight, Gemma," a feminine voice growled. "I taught you better posture than that."

I grinned. "Only on the dance floor."

A woman stepped up beside me. She was in her seventies, tall and strong, and she didn't need the silver cane she was leaning on. She never had, as far as I knew. Streaks of white snaked through her wavy, shoulder-length coppery hair, and a few more wrinkles had grooved into her bronze skin since the last time I had seen her, but her golden amber eyes were as bright and sharp as ever. She was wearing a dark green tunic patterned with snarling ogre faces done in gold thread, along with flowing black pants and flat black shoes.

Lady Xenia Rubin looked me over from head to toe, her lips puckering, as did the ones of the ogre on her neck, which had a lock of red hair curling around its face and the same amber eyes Xenia herself did. She lifted her cane, which was topped with a silver ogre head, as if to prod me into standing up straight, but I moved forward and wrapped my arms around her.

Xenia sighed, but her free arm came up, and she hugged me back. "You always were too quick for me, Gemma."

I drew back and grinned at her again. "I saw how many times you poked Everleigh with your cane over the years, and I decided long ago I wasn't going to fall into the same trap. How are you?"

Xenia shrugged. "The same as always. Chasing down whispers and rumors and trying to ensure we all don't end up killing each other." Her gaze skipped past me to Reiko, and she smiled at the younger woman. "Hello, Lady Reiko. It's a pleasure to make your acquaintance."

Reiko's mouth gaped, as if she couldn't believe Xenia was standing in front of her, that she was finally meeting the famed spymaster, and that said spymaster actually knew her name. I hadn't told Reiko that Xenia would be attending the Summit because I'd wanted the ogre morph's appearance to be a surprise. I hadn't expected my friend to be quite this stunned, though.

"Reiko helped me greatly during my time in Blauberg and Myrkvior," I said. "She's also a big admirer of yours, Xenia. Why, she's told me more than once she's just as good a spymaster as you are. Maybe even better."

My words finally penetrated Reiko's daze. Color stained her cheeks, and her fingers twitched as though she wanted to throttle me for revealing her boasts.

Xenia arched an eyebrow. "Better than me? That's a very

lofty claim." Her gaze flicked to Reiko's hand. "Especially for a dragon."

Reiko lifted her chin. "Dragons make excellent spies."

"So Gemma has told me," Xenia replied. "She has sung your praises quite loudly in recent weeks."

Reiko blinked again, as if my actions had surprised her as much as this meeting had.

"I told Xenia the same thing I told you earlier—that I would have been dead countless times over if not for your help." I pitched my voice a little lower. "You *are* the best, and never let anyone convince you otherwise."

Reiko grimaced, knowing I was talking about her strained relationship with her father, but her inner dragon smiled at me. I winked back at both of them.

Xenia threaded her arm through Reiko's. "Gemma has been quite complimentary about your skills. So much so that I'm tempted to lure you to Bellona. I have some pressing issues that could use a delicate touch . . ."

She drew Reiko aside and started whispering about those pressing issues. At first, Reiko looked stunned, then thrilled, but her face quickly turned serious, and soon she was nodding, completely absorbed in whatever skulduggery Xenia was trying to engage her in.

Father gestured at me, and I approached him. He was now speaking with Zariza and Ruri, and I curtsied to both queens again.

"Your Majesties, you're both looking lovely this evening."

Zariza tossed her long red hair over her shoulder. "I always do."

Ruri rolled her eyes at the other queen's boast. "Thank you, Gemma. Allow me to introduce my advisor, Tatsuo Yamato."

She waved her hand, and the lord stepped forward. He had the same high cheekbones as Reiko, and he carried himself with the alert but easy grace of a seasoned fighter, ready to spring into action at any moment.

I curtsied to him as well. "It's wonderful to meet you, Lord Yamato. Your daughter has told me so many things about you."

"I'm sure she has." Tatsuo's voice and words were benign, but his lips turned down, and the gold dragon on his neck frowned at me.

I would have dearly loved to know what he was thinking, but morph musings were often difficult to hear, since there were two creatures in one body. Still, I could clearly sense his emotions, and disapproval blasted off him like heat from the summer sun. Despite his polite mask, Tatsuo was no fan of mine.

"And this is one of my most trusted guards, Kai Nakamura." Ruri gestured, and he stepped forward.

I tilted my head to Kai, who gave me a low, formal bow.

"Princess Gemma," he said in a deep, silky voice. "So wonderful to meet you. I've heard a great many things about you."

"And I look forward to learning a great deal more about you."

Kai grinned, and the red dragon on his neck winked at me. I found myself smiling back at both of them. Reiko was right. Kai was arrogant but with a healthy amount of charm.

"How are you, Gemma?" Zariza asked. "No ill effects from your time in Myrkvior?"

She kept her eyes focused on mine, but the ogre on her neck peered down at the scars on my hands. Ruri, Tatsuo, and Kai also focused on my scars, not even bothering to hide their curiosity. My fingers flexed under their silent scrutiny, which caused those dull aches to ripple through my hands again.

Even though I'd been bracing myself for these questions, my teeth still ground together, and I had to unclench my jaw so I could answer Zariza. "No ill effects. Just some bad memories."

Ruri let out a very unqueenly snort. "If bad memories are all you have when it comes to the Morricones, then consider your-self lucky."

I started to respond, but my fingertips tingled in warning, and a familiar presence lashed up against my mind, one that was all hot, electric magic.

Spy the storm brewing, and you won't get struck by lightning. Ignore the clouds, and you'll get burned to a crisp. Xenia had said those words to me years ago in the Spire Mountains when we'd been fleeing from the turncoat guards.

I didn't hear any rumblings of thunder, but I could definitely feel this bitch of a storm approaching. Too bad I couldn't escape from it, from *her.*

Mortan guards wearing purple cloaks streamed into the arena, and all conversation ceased. Several sets of footsteps sounded, although I could easily pick out the *snap-snap-snap-snap* of heels striking the flagstones, the noise a bit higher and sharper than all the others. Even her stride was powerful and distinctive.

A glimmer of purple flared in the black depths of the main tunnel, like a match sparking to life in the darkness, and swiftly morphed into a teardrop amethyst in the middle of a stunning silver choker. Despite the crowd of people separating us, I knew exactly who was wearing that bauble, especially since her cursed lightning magic washed over me with every step she took.

Queen Maeven had finally arrived.

CHAPTER NINE

The Mortan guards parted, stepping back into two lines, and a woman strode forward through their ranks. People fell back at her approach, and she finally stopped in an open space near the center of the arena.

Queen Maeven Aella Toril Morricone lifted her head high and regarded the royals, nobles, and others with a calm expression, as though she were the ruler of everyone she surveyed, not just the people from her own kingdom.

A few weeks ago, Maeven had turned sixty, and I had been unfortunate enough to attend her birthday ball at Myrkvior. More than a few locks of silver glinted in her golden hair, which was sleeked back into a high bun. Wrinkles grooved into her pale skin, especially around her lips, which were often puckered in displeasure, and she had the dark amethyst eyes that marked her as a Morricone.

Maeven was wearing a beautiful gown of plum-colored velvet, along with matching heels. In addition to her choker, silver bangles studded with amethysts were stacked up on her wrists, and matching rings adorned her fingers. Each one of the amethysts practically dripped with Maeven's magic, but they were nothing compared to the lightning the queen herself possessed, which was still making my fingertips tingle.

Maeven turned back toward the archway and tilted her head. Three more people strode out of the blackness.

The first was a woman in her mid-twenties, a few years younger than me. She too had dark amethyst eyes and pale skin, but her ebony-black hair was woven into an intricate braid that arched over her head like a crown. Her lilac-colored gown was similar to Maeven's, although a short velvet cape covered her shoulders. Her only jewelry was a silver ring featuring onyx and amethyst shards that looked like three liladorn vines twining up her finger. I'd made that ring for her a few weeks ago in Myrkvior.

Princess Delmira Myrina Cahira Morricone stopped a few steps behind her mother, a calm expression on her face, although wariness surged off her and prickled my own skin. Curious. Back at Myrkvior, I had rarely been able to feel Delmira's emotions, but she seemed far less protected here. I wondered how much the liladorn at Myrkvior had to do with that.

Leonidas flanked his sister. Instead of his usual long riding coat, he was wearing a short, formal light purple jacket, and his black hair gleamed like polished onyx. I had been bracing myself for this too, and I forced myself to meet his gaze. Leonidas's face remained in its usual icy mask, but heat sparked in his amethyst eyes. Answering warmth simmered in my own veins, but I kept my features as cold as his were.

My gaze skipped past Leonidas and landed on the third and final person. Unlike his younger half siblings, this Morricone had wavy golden hair, along with tan skin and the ubiquitous amethyst eyes. He would have been quite handsome, if not for the sneer on his lips and the disdain that surged off him in bitter, caustic waves.

Crown Prince Milo Maximus Moreland Morricone glanced around with a bored expression, looking down his nose at everyone. Arrogant bastard. Rage sizzled through my body, burning hotter than a magier's lightning, and that familiar storm of emotion boiled up to new, dangerous heights in my heart, like a tornado spiraling up toward the sky. My hands clenched into fists, and it took every bit of self-control I had not to pluck the dagger off my belt, march across the floor, and bury the blade in the sadistic prince's chest.

Another man stepped out of the tunnel and slithered up behind Milo. Black hair, hazel eyes, bronze skin, heavily stubbled jaw. Captain Wexel was dressed in a short dark purple jacket, his hand curled around the hilt of the sword belted to his waist.

Maeven tipped her head to Ruri, as well as to Zariza, who both returned the gesture. Then she focused on my father. Maeven's lips puckered, as though she had bitten into something sour, but she headed toward him. Of course. She wasn't one to shy away from any unpleasantness. Why, the fact that she had let her oldest son torture me, allowed her younger son to be beaten, and threatened her own daughter was probably as inconsequential to her as worms were to a hungry strix—only good for pecking at and then gobbling down until something tastier and more substantial came along.

Maeven stopped in front of my father. An expectant hush fell over the crowd, and everyone's curiosity squeezed around my body, as though I was caught in a vise.

"Dominic." Maeven tipped her head to my father. Then her gaze flicked to me. "Gemma."

"Maeven," Father replied.

His cold, clipped voice was decidedly at odds with the anger surging off his body, the emotion hot enough to make my own cheeks burn in the cool arena air. Sometimes, I forgot Crown Prince Dominic Ripley hated Maeven just as much as I did, that his brother Frederich had been murdered and that he had almost lost me, Grandfather Heinrich, and his own life because of her schemes.

Maeven waited, but when it became apparent that was the sum total of my father's greeting, she gestured at her children. "This is my daughter, Delmira."

The princess dropped into a deep curtsy before rising. Her gaze locked with mine, then flicked down to my hands. Delmira's face remained blank, but sorrow radiated off her, and her thoughts whispered through my mind.

I'm so sorry, Gemma. So sorry . . . so sorry . . .

Her regret pinched my heart tight, and I found myself softening toward her. Delmira might not have been able to stop Milo from torturing me, but she had helped heal me afterward by slathering her homemade liladorn salve onto my whipped back and punctured hands. The Glitnir bone masters hadn't said so aloud, but I'd heard their silent thoughts about my gruesome injuries, and they had all agreed that Delmira's skill and kindness was the only reason I still had the use of my hands.

It's okay, I whispered the thought to her. *I'm grateful you helped heal me in Myrkvior.*

Delmira's head jerked back in surprise, but relief flickered across her face, and she gave me a small, tentative smile.

"This, of course, is Milo," Maeven continued with the unnecessary introductions.

The crown prince stepped up beside his mother. He didn't bother bowing to my father as protocol dictated. Instead, he focused on me. Another sneer twisted his face, and anger, hatred, and loathing blasted off him like steam from a screeching teakettle, burning just as hot as the rage still simmering in my own body.

"Princess Glitzma," Milo said, a mocking tone in his deep voice. "You're looking quite subdued. Not nearly as flashy as I had expected. Why, I thought you'd be dripping with diamonds at such a formal occasion."

I gave him a razor-thin smile. "I always save my diamonds for the final night of the Summit. Tell me, though, how are your hands? I heard you *severely* injured them a few weeks ago."

Milo stiffened, and his fingers clenched into fists. White gloves covered his hands, so I couldn't see if he was suffering any lasting effects of my punching his own lightning through his hands the same way he'd shoved his barbed arrows through mine. I wondered if his skin was as scarred as mine was. I fucking hoped so.

"Oh, I'm fully recovered from that little incident." Milo's voice was just as cold and cutting as mine was. "It was only a minor annoyance."

One I intend to eliminate, along with a great many other things. Just as soon as my experiments are finished.

His thoughts whispered through my mind, but the death threat wasn't nearly as alarming as his other musings. What experiments? Where were they taking place? Was he going to strike during the Summit?

"And finally, there is Leonidas," Maeven finished.

Leonidas stepped forward and dropped into a deep bow in front of me. He straightened up, his gaze locking with mine for a heartbeat, before bowing to my father.

Lightning crackled in Father's eyes, making them blaze like blue suns, and a fresh wave of anger blasted off him. Leonidas stared back at my father, his own features calm and smooth.

I discreetly touched my father's elbow in a silent warning. We could not afford to let our personal feelings get the better of us. Not here, with everyone watching. Such an outburst could potentially damage the pending trade agreements between the Andvarian nobles, merchants, and guilders and those in the other kingdoms, and if our people weren't happy, then their support for

King Heinrich and Crown Prince Dominic Ripley might diminish right along with their fortunes. Something my family couldn't afford with Andvari and Morta teetering on the brink of war.

Father released his magic, although he kept eyeing Leonidas like he wanted to rip the prince apart with his bare hands.

Leonidas stepped back, falling in line next to Delmira again.

In the distance, someone loudly, deliberately cleared their throat. Maeven's lips puckered again, but she jerked her hand, and a woman moved forward.

She was about my age, late twenties, and quite striking, with gray eyes, rosy skin, and long auburn hair that had more streaks of russet red than light brown. Her silver gown clung to her body, highlighting her toned arms and strong curves. Magic rippled off the woman, feeling cold, wet, and electric all at the same time, and my fingertips tingled again in warning. I'd forgotten what a powerful weather magier she was.

"And this is Corvina Dumond, Milo's fiancée," Maeven said in a flat, toneless voice.

Corvina curtsied to my father, then glared at me, hate clouding her gaze.

I bit back a groan. I should have realized Corvina would attend the Summit. No doubt she wanted to kill me because she mistakenly believed I had murdered her mother. Maeven and Milo were duplicitous enough, but I knew very little about Corvina, which made her dangerously unpredictable.

I glanced over at Maeven, whose lips curved up into a small, smug smile. Corvina's obvious ire with me greatly pleased her. Of course it did.

I thought about using my magic to silently tell Corvina that Maeven had murdered Emperia, but there was no guarantee Corvina would believe me, especially since I had no idea what lies Maeven had fed her.

Still, the perilous situation could also be an opportunity. The truth about Emperia's death was useless right now, but it might come in handy later, so I kept it to myself, like a trump card tucked up a cheater's sleeve during a game of kronekling.

Several seconds passed in silence, everyone tense and watchful. Maeven kept staring at me, as though she expected me to throw myself at Corvina's feet and vomit up the truth about Emperia's murder in some half-baked effort to turn the noble lady against her.

When it became apparent I wasn't going to do that, the Morricone queen's lips puckered again, and annoyance flickered off her. "Let us take our seats."

Maeven strode over to the Mortan dais on the opposite side of the arena, climbed the steps, and dropped into the large padded chair at the center of the long table. Delmira, Milo, Corvina, and Wexel followed her, but Leonidas bowed to both me and my father again before leaving.

Father watched him go, more anger blasting off his body. "I should electrocute the lot of them for hurting you. Starting with Leonidas."

Rhea stepped up beside us, her fingers curling around one of her daggers. "You kill Leonidas, and I'll gut Milo like a fish. Gemma can have the satisfaction of slitting Maeven's throat with her gargoyle dagger."

I might sometimes chafe at their overprotectiveness, but my father and stepmother would do anything to safeguard me. That comforting knowledge cooled some of my own anger. I threaded one arm through Father's, then my other arm through Rhea's, and drew them close.

"I love you both for your murderous sentiments, but we can't strike out at the Morricones," I murmured. "Not here, not tonight. That would damage our standing with the other kingdoms, even if our actions would be completely justified."

"That doesn't mean I have to like being civil to them." Rhea shot a dark glare at Milo.

Some of the tension eased out of Father's shoulders. "You're right, Gemma. I'm sorry you had to face them, though." He sighed. "I wish I could have shielded you from the Morricones, especially Maeven. But no matter what I do, she always seems to find a way to get the better of me and hurt our family. I don't know whether to admire or hate her for that."

My gaze drifted over to the Mortan queen, who was sipping wine from a goblet. "Me neither."

I escorted Father and Rhea over to the Andvarian dais, and we climbed the steps and took our seats. Zariza took her position at the Ungerian table, with Xenia sitting beside her, while Ruri and Tatsuo settled themselves at the Ryusaman table, with Kai standing guard behind them on the dais.

Only those invited to sit at the royal tables were on the arena floor, and the nobles, merchants, and guilders climbed the stairs and took their seats on the upper levels.

Reiko was at a table on the second floor, directly behind Ruri and Tatsuo. I had asked Reiko to sit with me at the Andvarian table, but she said she preferred to stay in the background. I wondered how much that had to do with the fact that Tatsuo didn't approve of his daughter's career as a spy—or her friendship with me.

Still, the longer I looked around, the more I realized I had been wrong before. The arena wasn't shaped like a queen's crown, with jewels and metal rising into the air. No, this was a bloody *theater*, where the royals were on display like brightly colored puppets, yanking on one another's strings while the crowd watched, smiled, and chortled at our foibles from on high.

I just wondered what drama would play out tonight.

A series of bells chimed, and servants carrying silver platters streamed out onto the arena floor, climbed up the steps of the various daises, and served dinner.

Dish after dish was deposited in front of me. First, there was a spiced tomato soup sprinkled with dill weed and topped with shredded sharp cheddar and sourdough croutons. Then came a warm salad of roasted brussels sprouts mixed with dried bloodcrisp apples, honey cranberries, toasted pumpkin seeds, and fat curls of parmesan cheese, all topped with a sweet, tangy apple-cider dressing. The breads were served next—thick, dark slices of pumpernickel, light-as-air yeast rolls, and hearty oat muffins, paired with sweet and savory butters that featured everything from sourwood honey to caramelized onions to lime zest.

The bread baskets were left on the tables, while the main course was rolled out—roasted chicken with apricot-glazed carrots and baby red potatoes seasoned with sea salt, black pepper, and mustard seeds. I washed everything down with a blueberry punch with a tasty zing of lemon.

Dinner was a quiet affair, with only a smattering of conversation. No one wanted to sour the delicious food with insults and threats, although that would probably change as the event wore on.

For dessert, there were vanilla and chocolate sweet cakes, still warm from the ovens and filled with orange, raspberry, fig, and other delicious jams.

I popped the last bite of a chocolate-raspberry cake into my mouth and sighed with happiness. The food at Caldwell Castle was always excellent, but the cook masters had truly outdone themselves tonight. Perhaps the sweet cakes would help drown out the anger, resentment, bitterness, and posturing that was sure to dominate the rest of the evening. Probably not, but it was the most pleasant thought I could muster on a full stomach.

Father rose to his feet and *tink-tink-tinked* a fork against his crystal water goblet. Everyone fell silent, and all eyes focused on Crown Prince Dominic Ripley.

Since the city of Caldwell stretched out into each of the three kingdoms, Andvari, Unger, and Morta all took turns hosting the Summit. This year, that duty fell to Unger, which meant the Ungerian contingent was responsible for arranging the dinners, entertainment, and other events, and more important, that Ungerian laws would be used to settle disputes. But no matter which kingdom hosted the Summit, Andvari always kicked off the festivities, since most of Castle Caldwell stood on Andvarian soil.

"Greetings to you all." Father's deep voice boomed through the arena. "Welcome to the Summit. We are all honored to meet here again, with friends both old and new."

He lifted his goblet in a toast, and everyone followed suit. I had to give Father credit for not stumbling over the traditional speech, especially since everyone knew the Ripleys and Morricones would never be friends. As for whose side Zariza and Ruri would come down on, well, that would depend on which goods they needed and which trade agreements would be the most lucrative and beneficial to their nobles, guilders, and merchants. The two queens had their own people and kingdoms to consider and protect, just as Father, Rhea, and I did ours.

"Tomorrow the plaza marketplace will open and formal negotiations for trade and other agreements will begin. But tonight we celebrate our hope for better days and more prosperity for all our kingdoms." Father raised his goblet in another toast.

Everyone took a drink, and Father sat down. At this point, another social hour would begin, and many folks would linger in here, talking, gossiping, and drinking late into the night—

A chair loudly *scraped* back from a table, shattering the relative quiet.

Maeven stood up.

Everyone froze, and all conversation abruptly ceased. Beside me, Father tensed. His right hand curled into a fist on his leg, and blue lightning crackled across his knuckles. Rhea discreetly plucked a dagger off her belt and made a small hand motion that had all the Andvarian guards snapping to attention. I also reached for my magic and dropped my hand to my own dagger.

But instead of unleashing her lightning or yelling for her guards to attack, Maeven glanced at Ruri, then Zariza, then Father. Finally, her gaze settled on me. Her lips twitched up into a small smile, and satisfaction gleamed in her eyes. Even worse, that same satisfaction rolled off her like a storm cloud growing darker and stronger as it gusted across a plain.

I'm going to enjoy this.

Her thought whispered through my mind, as low and smug as a cat's purr. I flinched. Suddenly, screams echoed in my ears, and the stench of blood flooded my nose. Maeven had thought those exact same words right before the Seven Spire massacre, and nothing good could come of her repeating that same sentiment now.

"I have some important business that must be attended to tonight," Maeven said. "As the old custom demands."

What custom? As far as I knew, there were no customs, old, new, or otherwise, that demanded any business be conducted the first night of the Summit.

Father glanced over at Zariza and Ruri, who both shrugged in return. Curiosity flickered off the queens, along with everyone else.

Father waved his hand. "Very well. State your business."

Maeven schooled her features into a more serious expression. "For far too long, our kingdoms have been at odds. Some of it is natural. Competition for food, resources, and the like. And of course every royal wants to lift their crown, kingdom, and people up to dizzying new heights."

Her words were benign, pleasant even, but with every sylla-ble she spewed, I felt like Maeven was hoisting an executioner's axe higher and higher into the air, and I found myself holding my breath, just waiting for her to swing the sharp blade at my head.

"But now we all face a dire new threat—a threat that we must unite against or risk all of us falling to it kingdom by kingdom."

Shocked whispers and worried chatter surged through the arena. What new threat? What did Maeven know that the rest of us didn't? Or was she just spinning another web of deception the way she had so many times before?

I studied the others at the Mortan table. Delmira's eyebrows were drawn together in confusion, and Corvina looked similarly befuddled. Leonidas's face was cold and blank as usual.

Milo didn't seem confused, though. His face was also cold and blank, but his lips puckered, just the faintest bit, as though he knew *exactly* what his mother was talking about and didn't like her revealing it to everyone else.

Was Milo the threat? Or his tearstone arrows and mysterious experiments? Or was Maeven talking about something—or someone—else?

"What is this new threat?" Father asked.

Maeven lifted one shoulder in a noncommittal shrug. "That is a private discussion for another time. Tonight I want to focus on the first step we can take to ensure that our kingdoms are better united—as the custom demands."

"What custom?" Ruri asked.

"Yes, what exactly are you proposing?" Zariza chimed in.

As soon as Zariza spoke, another small, infuriating smile

curved Maeven's lips. My heart sank. The Ungerian queen had just given Maeven the opening she had wanted all along.

"We all know the best way to unite two kingdoms is through a royal marriage," Maeven said.

More shocked whispers surged through the arena, and everyone stared at Milo, Leonidas, and Delmira. Speculation hung in the air like a wet, heavy blanket, dripping questions everywhere. Which one of them did Maeven want to marry off? And to which royal family?

At the far end of the Mortan table, Corvina visibly started. She cast a worried look at the queen, obviously wondering if Maeven was about to call off her engagement to Milo and offer him to someone else.

Behind her, Wexel stiffened, his jaw clenching tight and his gaze darting back and forth between Corvina and Maeven. While I was at Myrkvior, I'd discovered that Wexel and Corvina were fucking each other. I'd thought their dalliance was a mere convenience, but given the worry surging off Wexel, the captain had some genuine affection for the noble lady.

"And to whom are you offering the grand honor of marrying a Morricone?" Zariza drawled, derision rippling through her words.

"I am proposing a marriage between Morta . . ." Maeven's voice trailed off, and she glanced around, drawing out the moment and making sure everyone was literally on the edges of their seats. "And Andvari."

Shock jolted through me, as sharp as a spear punching into my chest. I'd never *dreamed* Maeven would make such a ridiculous proposal. Had the queen gone mad? Because she was out of her bloody mind if she thought I would *ever* marry Milo.

Maeven stared at me, another one of those smug, infuriating smiles spreading across her face. In that moment, I knew she was anything *but* mad. No, this was another clever trap she had sprung without warning, just like when she had exposed my real identity as Princess Gemma during her birthday ball. Only, I had a sinking feeling these consequences were going to be even more dire, dangerous, and hurtful.

Maeven paused, once again drawing out the moment and ramping up the tension and expectation. "I am proposing a marriage between my son Prince Leonidas and Crown Princess Gemma Ripley."

CHAPTER TEN

Spears of shock punched into my body. Suddenly, I felt like a gladiator's training dummy, with long, thick blades of surprise protruding from my arms, legs, and especially my chest. Only, instead of straw, my emotions were oozing everywhere, on full display for everyone to see.

Out of all the things Maeven could have said, out of all the things she could have proposed, I'd never expected her to utter those words. To suggest that Leonidas and I get *married*.

My gaze snapped over to the prince. Leonidas's face was still cold and calm, although heat burned in his eyes as he stared back at me. My stomach clenched, and an answering flush swept through my body, but all that mattered right now was stopping this mockery before it went any further.

Did you know she was going to do this? I silently demanded.

Leonidas shook his head the tiniest bit. *No, but that doesn't mean anything. Mother never shares her plans with anyone.*

His tone was as sour as mine was angry. Well, at least he hadn't had a hand in this ridiculousness.

By this point, a full-on smile creased Maeven's face, and her amethyst eyes actually fucking *sparkled*. The queen was exceptionally pleased with herself. Of course she was. Once again, she was manipulating me and her son like we were dolls set out on a table just for her amusement.

Beside me, Father sucked in a breath and shoved his chair back, as if to surge to his feet and yell at the Morricone queen, but I clamped my hand on his arm.

"No. She wants you to protest. I don't know why, but she does. Don't fall into her trap."

Father hesitated, although anger blasted off him, and his body remained as tense as a coiled spring. Several seconds ticked by. Then a long, shuddering breath escaped his lips. Anger kept surging off him, but his arm relaxed under my hand, and he remained seated.

"Well, Dominic?" Maeven called out. "What do you say?"

Father ignored her taunt. "You know her better than I do, Gemma. You know how she thinks and the games she likes to play. You speak to her."

I squeezed his arm in appreciation, then stood up, the *scrape* of my chair against the dais as loud and harsh as a saw tearing through a piece of wood.

The heavy weight of everyone's stares pressed down like a boulder slowly crushing my body. My gargoyle pendant heated up against my chest, but it couldn't stop everyone's silent thoughts from crowding into my mind.

Wonder what she'll say . . .

A Ripley would never willingly marry a Morricone . . .

This battle is already over. Glitzma is no match for Maeven . . .

That last snide thought made my own anger flare up again, but I drew in a deep breath, then slowly, quietly exhaled. Now was not the time to feel *any* emotion, either my own or someone else's.

No, right now, I needed to be as cold as Maeven always was, twice as clever, and three times as ruthless. Otherwise, I would end up doing exactly what she wanted, something I couldn't afford. Not now, when I was speaking for my father and all of Andvari. I needed to keep my freedom intact and my traitorous heart in check, especially when it came to Leonidas Morricone.

Maeven stepped around to the front of the Mortan table so that she was facing me. I did the same and moved in front of the Andvarian table. Now only empty air separated us, although the space crackled with tension and hostility.

"Well, Gemma?" Maeven purred. "What do *you* say to my proposal?"

Another smile tugged at her lips, and triumph blasted off her like a foghorn. The bitch thought she'd already won this game between us.

Still, the longer I stared at her, the more the air around her shimmered, as though it were full of heat waves. My magic roared to life, and suddenly, I was looking at another, younger version of Maeven—the one watching the Bellonans and Andvarians assemble on the royal lawn at Seven Spire, knowing they would all be dead in a matter of minutes.

Screams rang in my ears, and the stench of blood punched me in the nose. Sometimes, it seemed like the massacre had happened only yesterday, instead of some sixteen years ago. But as I focused on Maeven's smug, infuriating smirk, the memory of another woman from that awful day popped into my mind, and I latched onto it like a life ring tossed to a shipwrecked sailor.

The more I focused on that particular memory, the calmer my magic grew, and the clearer and sharper my mind became. The screams and stench of blood vanished, and the arena snapped back into focus, although rage continued to hammer in my heart.

"Well, Gemma?" Maeven purred again. "Do you have an answer? Or am I to take your silence as acceptance?"

"Forgive me, Your Majesty, but I was lost in my memories." I smiled at her, although my expression was all teeth. "Your proposal made me think of my uncle Frederich. I'm sure you remember him. After all, you arranged for him to be slaughtered at Seven Spire, along with Lord Hans and my other countrymen."

Shocked gasps rang out. It was one thing for everyone to know what the Mortan queen had done all those years ago, but it was quite another for me to so flatly, coldly state it. Sometimes, I thought that was one of the main problems with being a royal. I could never just speak the bloody *truth*, but always had to waltz around it in order to preserve the tenuous peace.

Maeven's smirk vanished. "The Seven Spire massacre is in the distant past. It has nothing to do with my current proposal," she retorted, a harsh bite in her voice.

For perhaps the first time ever, I'd managed to get under her skin. Excellent. Now to open a wound and really make the bitch bleed.

"Oh, I think it has *everything* to do with your current proposal."

Maeven opened her mouth to respond, but I cut her off. Let her dance to my words for a change.

"Your proposal also makes me think of Crown Princess Vasilia Blair. I'm sure you remember Vasilia too, since you helped her slaughter most of her Blair royal cousins, along with my uncle Frederich."

Maeven's fingers twitched as if she was fighting the urge to blast me with her lightning. "Vasilia Blair has even less to do with this than your dead uncle does."

"On the contrary, Vasilia has quite a lot to do with your proposal. After all, Uncle Frederich was to be engaged to Vasilia—at least before she killed him. Why, I still remember Vasilia standing over Uncle Frederich as he lay dead on the ground from the dagger she'd punched into his heart. Vasilia said something about him then. What was it, exactly?"

I tapped my finger on my lips, as though searching for the right words, but I had never forgotten them. I had never forgotten *anything* about that day, no matter how desperately I had tried to.

I snapped my fingers together, and several people flinched at the harsh sound, including Maeven. "Oh, yes. I remember now. Vasilia wasn't very impressed with the idea of being engaged to Uncle Frederich, since he was third in line for the Andvarian throne at the time. Just as I am not very impressed with the idea of being engaged to your son now, a bastard prince who will never wear the Mortan crown."

I deliberately trailed my gaze over Leonidas, from his onyx-black hair, down his angular face, and over his muscled chest, studying him as thoroughly as I would inspect a prize Floresian stallion that I was thinking about buying. He stared back at me, his features blank.

I hardened my heart, wrapping ice around my emotions, then lifted my chin and peered down my nose at him. "I'll tell you the same thing about your son that Vasilia said about my uncle Frederich: What a bloody *insult*. Really, Maeven. You could have done *so* much better."

Several people gasped, and even Maeven stiffened. Leonidas didn't move, but a muscle ticced in his jaw.

Part of me regretted wounding him, especially in this manner. At Myrkvior, Leonidas had confessed how difficult his life had been as a bastard prince, especially after his mother had killed King Maximus and taken the throne. I had never cared that Leonidas was a bastard, but I wasn't going to fall into

Maeven's trap, and if that meant being cruel to Leonidas, then so be it.

My gaze flicked over to Xenia at the Ungerian table. She nodded, and the ogre on her neck winked at me. Xenia had also been at the massacre, and she probably remembered Vasilia's words as clearly as I did. Even more important, she approved of how I was deflecting Maeven's attack now.

Maeven's cheeks flushed, her eyes darkened with fury, and her fingers twitched again. But after a few seconds, the emotion faded from her features, and she smoothed her hands down her skirt. "How ironic that you would use such harsh words to describe my son when your own uncle, Lucas Sullivan, is also a bastard prince."

Father rocked back in his chair, as if to rise up and defend his brother, but this time Rhea laid her hand on his arm, and he remained seated.

"Uncle Lucas is a bastard only because of the circumstances of his birth," I replied. "He's not a cruel, heartless bastard in deed, thought, and action like *both* of your sons are."

More shocked gasps rang out, although the arena quickly descended into silence again.

Hate blazed in Milo's eyes, and his cheeks turned a mottled red. I smirked at him, then focused on Maeven again.

Her fingers twitched for a third time, then curled into fists. *I'm giving you a gift, Gemma*, her voice snarled in my mind. *You should take it.*

I narrowed my eyes at her. *You never give gifts. Only traps that advance your own position.*

Leonidas glanced back and forth between the two of us, as if hearing our silent conversation with his own mind magier power.

Maeven glared at me a few seconds longer, but then a strange, abrupt calm settled over her, as though she were standing in the eye of a storm. My own worry ratcheted up to new heights, like a high tide swiftly sweeping up a shoreline.

"I thought you might be a bit reluctant about accepting my more-than-generous offer. But since we are at the Summit, I can call upon my right as queen to resolve the issue," Maeven said. "I invoke the Gauntlet."

Silence reigned, as if no one in the entire arena had any idea what she was talking about. I certainly didn't.

Xenia was the first to react. She blinked and blinked, as did the ogre on her neck. Understanding flared in Xenia's amber eyes, and worry surged off her, increasing my own concern.

Maeven looked around like a tutor educating a group of ignorant students. "For those of you who don't know, or don't remember, the Gauntlet is a series of challenges designed to show one's worth as a potential suitor."

A few audible whispers sounded, but far more thoughts exploded in my mind. The mental chatter was almost deafening, but the silent musings echoed my own turbulent thoughts.

The Gauntlet? Must be some ancient ritual nonsense . . .

What kind of challenges . . .

Sounds dangerous . . .

Maeven waited until the whispers died down before she spoke again. "If a suitor successfully completes all the challenges associated with the Gauntlet, then the two parties will be engaged and eventually wed—regardless of kingdoms, stations, or anything else."

Every single word she said sent another arrow of horror shooting through my body. My gaze snapped back over to Leonidas. For once, his icy mask had dropped away, and he was looking at his mother with a mixture of surprise and wariness.

I thought of something he'd said when we had spoken through our Cardea mirrors a few weeks ago, shortly after I had returned to Glitnir. *She's already scheming something else. She's been in her personal library all week, studying old books about courtly etiquette.*

Well, now I knew what Maeven had been plotting. She was trying to trap me into marrying her son—and she was bloody *winning.*

Shock spiraled through me, bringing with it an icy numbness, as though my fingers, arms, legs, and toes had all suddenly gone to sleep and stubbornly refused to wake up. I swayed backward and would have stumbled if I hadn't bumped into the table behind me. That motion cut through some of my shock, although it didn't douse any of my worry.

I had always known I would get married. After all, one of the main duties of any royal was to produce an heir, preferably more than one, and continue the familial line. But as a crown princess, I'd always expected I would be wed more or less on my own terms, in my own time—not be forced into it by a manipulative bitch of a queen.

And *why* did Maeven want me to marry Leonidas? She hated me as much as I despised her, and I doubted she was concerned with her son's happiness any more than she was with mine. No, Maeven wanted this alliance for some *other* reason.

The speculative murmurs died down, and silence dropped over the arena again.

Maeven smirked at me again, as though the battle were over, and I was a mouse clamped in a cat's jaws, well on my way to being torn apart and gobbled down.

White-hot rage roared through me, burning through that icy numbness, and I latched onto the emotion, letting its heat scorch through me. How *dare* that arrogant bitch think she could control me, that she could manipulate me, that *she* could dictate anything to *me*. Maeven had almost killed me during the Seven Spire massacre, and she had let Milo torture me in Myrkvior. She was *not* going to hurt me again.

Never again.

Protocol and niceties and courtly games be damned. I opened my mouth to tell Maeven exactly where she could shove her bloody Gauntlet when another chair scraped back from a table.

Xenia got to her feet. "I was here the last time a Gauntlet challenge was issued. It is an old Ungerian tradition, much like the Tanzen Freund dance. Strange that a Mortan would try to invoke it and impinge on *our* heritage."

Queen Zariza nodded, her eyes glittering with anger, and all around the arena, the other Ungers muttered their own displeasure.

Maeven lifted her chin. "That's the beauty of the Summit. Any royal in attendance can invoke the laws and traditions of the host kingdom. This year, the host kingdom just happens to be Unger. I'm not impinging on your heritage—I'm celebrating it."

Celebrating? More like twisting it around to suit her own purposes.

"If properly executed, then whatever laws and traditions that are invoked are binding on all parties concerned, even after the Summit is over and we all return to our respective kingdoms." Maeven gave Xenia a smile that was pure poison. "It's in the Summit charter. Read it for yourself, if you wish."

Oh, I was sure it was in the bloody charter, probably word for word. Maeven would have made absolutely certain she knew every possible outcome before springing her trap.

Xenia shrugged, as if she didn't care what the charter said. "In addition to stealing from another kingdom's culture, it seems you are forgetting something important about the Gauntlet."

"And what would that be?" Maeven asked.

Xenia shrugged again, although the ogre on her neck bared its teeth at the Mortan queen. "The mental and physical challenges of the Gauntlet are quite vigorous, which is the reason it is so rarely used."

"So what?"

"So your son will die if he fails *any* of the challenges," Xenia replied in an ice-cold voice. "The smallest mistake, the tiniest error, and Leonidas will forfeit his head to the executioner's axe. Are you really willing to take that risk? Is your son?"

For the first time, a bit of uncertainty flickered across Maeven's face.

"You're the one who is so eager to follow the letter of the law," Xenia continued. "And in Ungerian law, failure equals death."

Queen Zariza nodded, and the other Ungers let out harsh, agreeing mutters.

Thank you. I sent the thought to Xenia. She didn't look my way, but the ogre on her neck winked at me.

"Well, Your Majesty?" Xenia called out, her voice taking on a mocking note. "Do you still wish to proceed with the Gauntlet?"

More uncertainty flickered across Maeven's face. For as much as I despised the Morricone queen, even I had to admit she cared about her children. Oh, it certainly wasn't the traditional sort of love most mothers had for their sons and daughters, but what happened to her offspring did matter to her, at least in some small way. Was Maeven winning her game with me worth Leonidas potentially losing his life? Apparently, despite all her machinations, even she didn't know the answer to that question—

Another chair scraped back from a table, and Leonidas stood up.

The prince strode around to the front of the Mortan table, so that he was standing directly across from me. His gaze locked with mine, although his icy mask was fixed back into place, so I couldn't tell what he was thinking or feeling.

Still, the longer he stood there, the more worry filled my

heart. *No.* He wouldn't do it. He wouldn't give in to Maeven's madness, not at the potential cost of his own life—

"I accept," Leonidas called out in a loud, strong voice, his eyes still on mine. "I accept the challenge. I will participate in the Gauntlet."

CHAPTER ELEVEN

All around the arena, people surged to their feet, clapping, cheering, yelling, and whistling, but the noise sounded dim and distant compared to the roar of my heart in my ears. I stared at Leonidas, still stunned by his words, although my surprise quickly boiled up into anger.

Are you out of your mind? I hissed the thought at him. *You're doing* exactly *what Maeven wants you to.*

He shrugged, as if risking his life in such a ridiculous manner was of no consequence. *I do as my queen commands.*

Leonidas stared at me until the crowd's cheers died down, then turned and bowed, first to Zariza, then Xenia.

"Lady Xenia," he called out, "since the Gauntlet is an Ungerian custom, perhaps you will do me the honor of overseeing it. To ensure that it is properly executed and absolutely fair to all parties involved."

Maeven shot her son an annoyed look, but he ignored her.

Xenia glanced at Zariza, who nodded her approval. Next, she looked at Ruri, who also nodded. Then she eyed my father. He sighed, but he also tipped his head in agreement.

"Very well," Xenia replied, "I will oversee the Gauntlet. As such, my first order of business is to inform Princess Gemma and Prince Leonidas that they may both have a second to help them prepare for the challenges." She looked at me. "Princess Gemma, who do you choose?"

"Reiko Yamato."

"Lady Reiko," Xenia said, "please rise."

My friend was still sitting on the second-floor balcony, and she stood up so that everyone could see her—including her father.

Tatsuo twisted around in his chair and looked up at his daughter. His features were blank, but palpable waves of disapproval radiated off him, and the gold dragon on his neck belched out clouds of black smoke. Reiko stared down at him, color blazing across her cheekbones, but she lifted her chin in defiance.

"Prince Leonidas, who do you choose as your second?" Xenia asked.

"Delmira Morricone," he replied.

The princess also stood up. Her face was calm, but she kept twisting her liladorn ring around and around on her finger.

"Lady Reiko, Princess Delmira, do you accept your positions?" Xenia asked. "Do you both vow to support your charges to the best of your abilities?"

Reiko and Delmira both nodded.

"Then we are all agreed," Xenia replied. "As per custom, the first challenge will take place tomorrow at noon here in the arena. Prince Leonidas shall bring three items to please his intended. The items can be anything, large or small, expensive or not, but they must speak to Princess Gemma's body, mind, and heart."

"Who decides if the challenge is successful?" Maeven piped up, a snide note in her voice. "And whether my son loses his life?"

Xenia stared her down. "*I* do, along with the royals who are not directly involved. That would be Queen Zariza and Queen Ruri, if they are willing?"

They both nodded. Zariza smirked at Maeven, but Ruri maintained a neutral expression.

"Prince Leonidas, Princess Gemma, do you understand the first challenge?" Xenia asked.

Leonidas nodded. "I understand."

I jerked my head in acknowledgment. "As do I."

"Good," Xenia replied. "Then I will make the necessary arrangements."

She looked at the prince again, her amber gaze much sharper than before. "Know this, Prince Leonidas. You might not be an Unger, but you will be held to the same exacting standards, and you will suffer the same punishments as any Unger who would undertake the Gauntlet, up to and including death. For the last time—are you certain you wish to proceed?"

A tense, heavy silence dropped over the arena, but all I could hear was the roar of my heart in my ears, beating loud and fast.

Leonidas stared at me again. "I've never been more certain of anything in my life."

A shiver skittered down my spine, although I couldn't quite say if the sensation was one of dread or anticipation.

"Very well," Xenia replied. "The Gauntlet has begun. Good luck to you, Prince Leonidas. You're going to need it."

With that dire pronouncement, Xenia sat back down and started speaking to Zariza. Conversation exploded in the arena, the excited chatter rising all the way up to the glass roof and bouncing back down again.

I glanced up at the second floor, but Reiko had vanished, so I dropped my gaze to the Ryusaman table. Tatsuo was whispering to Ruri, who was nodding in response.

Over at the Mortan table, Milo, Corvina, and Wexel had

already left the dais, but Maeven had returned to her seat, and she mockingly saluted me with her wine goblet. I couldn't stand to look at her smug face any longer, so I spun away from her.

Father and Rhea were both on their feet, staring at me with expressions that were tight, furious, and sympathetic all at the same time. That icy numbness swept through my body again.

"What just happened?" I asked no one in particular.

Father came around the table and clasped my cold hands in his much warmer ones. "Don't worry, Gemma. No matter what happens, you are *not* marrying Leonidas Morricone. I don't give a damn about the Summit, the charter, or this arcane ritual Maeven has dredged up."

I nodded, still too stunned to say anything else.

"Come," Father said in a gentler voice. "I've had enough Morricone machinations for one night."

We trudged down the dais steps. Rhea followed us, along with several Andvarian guards, and we all headed toward the archway. Just before we stepped into the tunnel, I glanced back over my shoulder.

Xenia was still talking to Zariza, and Ruri had also joined them at the Ungerian table, although Tatsuo and Kai were nowhere to be seen. Maeven had also vanished, although Delmira and Leonidas were still at the Mortan table.

Delmira was chattering at her brother, who was looking at me again. The heat of Leonidas's gaze made equal parts worry and warmth spark in my heart, and his face was the last thing I saw before I stepped into the tunnel and the darkness swallowed me.

An hour later, I slammed a book shut and shoved it toward the large pile of volumes already littering the table in front of me.

"Nothing," I growled. "I can't find one single bloody *word* about this so-called Gauntlet. How did Maeven even learn about it?"

"I don't know," Father replied, poring over another book at his writing desk. "I'm not seeing anything about it either. But the Myrkvior library is rumored to be quite impressive. It certainly contains more books than what we have here at Caldwell."

After leaving the arena, we had retreated to my father's study. Floor-to-ceiling bookshelves covered two of the walls, but so far, none of the volumes had contained any information about the Gauntlet, much less a loophole that would let me wriggle out of Maeven's trap.

Rhea sighed and also pushed a book aside. She too was sitting at a table, searching for information. "Do you think Leonidas knew what Maeven was planning? After all, his life is the one she's risking."

I shook my head. "He claimed he didn't know about it."

"When did he tell you that?" Father's eyes narrowed. "Wait. You spoke to Leonidas? In the arena? With your magic?"

I shifted in my chair, suddenly uncomfortable. "Well . . . yes. We're both mind magiers. Tonight wasn't the first time I've spoken to him with my power."

I didn't mention all the *other* times I had communicated with Leonidas. And not just a few weeks ago, when I was in Myrkvior, or last week in the woods outside Haverton. When we were younger, after our encounters in the Spire Mountains, we used to talk all the time, although I had put a stop to that when I had started wearing my gargoyle pendant.

I rubbed the pendant between my fingers, and the sharp edges of the tearstone shards dug into my skin. For a long time, I'd told myself that I always wore the pendant to help block out my memories of the Seven Spire massacre, but I'd wanted to forget about Leonidas too, especially how alike we were and how I just couldn't quite seem to properly hate him. But to my great shame and total detriment, I had never been able to purge either the massacre or the prince from my mind or heart.

A knock sounded on the door, and Xenia stepped into the study, along with Zariza. Reiko also slid inside and shut the door behind them.

Zariza sashayed over and dropped down onto one of the settees by the fireplace. Xenia joined her, while Father and Rhea settled themselves in nearby chairs. I poured a round of apple brandy for everyone and handed out the glasses, then sat on another settee, along with Reiko.

Xenia nodded her thanks and downed her drink, as did Zariza. Apple brandy was a favorite among Ungers. Father, Rhea, and Reiko sipped their own brandies, but I set mine aside. I couldn't stomach it right now.

"So how bad is it?" I asked, forcing some false cheer into my voice. "Will I be married to Leonidas by midnight and murdered by Maeven by morning?"

Zariza snorted. "Things aren't quite *that* dire."

"But?" Father challenged.

Xenia sighed. "But they aren't good either. Maeven constructed her trap very well. Zariza and I have spoken to some of the Ungerian elders. As far as they know, there is no way for Gemma to escape the Gauntlet custom and refuse to marry Leonidas should he successfully complete the challenges." She paused. "Not without incurring serious consequences."

"What consequences?" Rhea asked.

"If Gemma were to refuse to honor the successful outcome of the Gauntlet, then Maeven could ask for recompense, most likely money or land commensurate to Gemma's standing as the crown princess of Andvari." Zariza paused. "Or she could call for retribution—and Gemma's execution."

Father, Rhea, and Reiko froze, all of them stunned into silence, but a bitter laugh spurted out of my lips.

"You have to admire Maeven's cleverness," I said. "No matter what happens, *she wins*. Either I marry Leonidas, or she squeezes a substantial amount of money out of the Andvarian royal treasury, or she finally finishes what she started at Seven Spire and has me killed."

"I'm sorry, Gemma," Zariza replied, sympathy filling her voice. "But as queen, I am honor- and duty-bound to enforce all Ungerian laws and traditions."

I nodded. It wasn't her fault I was in this mess. No, the blame for this situation landed squarely on Maeven's cursed head.

"The Morricones are determined to go through with this?" Father asked.

"Yes," Xenia replied. "I've already spoken to Maeven and Leonidas, and they both agreed to all the terms and consequences."

"Your best bet is to hope Leonidas fails one of the challenges," Zariza said. "If that happens, then I will happily swing the executioner's axe myself, and separate his handsome head from his equally handsome shoulders."

A wicked smile curved the Ungerian queen's lips, and the ogre on her neck winked at me. I forced myself to smile back at them, despite the sick sensation in my stomach.

"What are the challenges?" Rhea asked.

"The first challenge is the easiest, a mental exercise that involves Leonidas giving Gemma a series of gifts," Xenia answered. "For the second challenge, Leonidas will pit himself against other warriors in the arena. If he succeeds there, he will move on to the third and final challenge, which is an outdoor obstacle course, of sorts. All three challenges will be held on the castle grounds and open to Summit attendees."

Reiko snorted. "Gemma is a princess, and not just any princess, but the most pampered princess on the Buchovian continent. What could Leonidas possibly give Gemma that she doesn't already have?"

"And that's the challenge," Zariza replied. "Not to give gold or gems, but things that truly speak to the heart of your beloved."

"I am *not* his beloved," I muttered. "And I will *not* accept his gifts."

Xenia shook her head. "It's not that simple. The whole point of the Gauntlet is to overcome animosity and feuds. That's why those who are not directly involved in the Gauntlet serve as its judges. Just like Zariza, I too am honor- and duty-bound to uphold Ungerian tradition to its fullest extent, despite our long-standing friendship."

Xenia and her inner ogre stared at me, both of their faces completely serious. "We have to follow the rules, Gemma, and we cannot vote the way you want us to. Otherwise, Maeven will claim foul, the Gauntlet will be forfeited in her favor, and she can demand her prize, whether it's money, land, or your head."

Anger and frustration pounded through me that Maeven was fucking with my life yet again, and I had to unclench my teeth before I could answer. "I understand."

Xenia got to her feet, as did Zariza.

"I must go make the arrangements for the first challenge," Xenia said. "I will see you all tomorrow in the arena. Until then."

She left the study, with Zariza trailing along behind her.

The second they were gone, Father sighed, slumped back in his chair, and scrubbed his hands over his face. "What a bloody mess. Why would Maeven do this?"

"Because she is a cruel, petty, spiteful bitch who delights in making other people miserable," Rhea replied.

Father gave her a wan smile and clutched her hand. Rhea leaned over and kissed his cheek, and their mutual love filled the study, warmer than the heat blasting out of the fireplace. Even more impressive than the strength of their love was how simple, pure, and easy it was. It had always been one of my favorite emotions to feel, ever since I had first sensed it between the two of them after I had returned from the Seven Spire massacre. The depths of their feelings had helped to heal my own broken heart back then, and it renewed my determination now.

Maeven might think I was her puppet and doomed to dance to her tune, but I was going to cut my strings. The Mortan queen was *not* going to use me in her courtly games again—no matter what I had to do to thwart her scheme.

chapter twelve

Father and Rhea retired to their chambers for the night, and Reiko and I returned to my tower. Grimley was napping in front of the sitting room fireplace, although he cracked his eyes open as I hurried past him and strode into my bedroom.

Reiko crossed her arms over her chest and leaned up against the doorway. "What are you plotting, Gemma?"

I opened an armoire and started riffling through the clothes inside. "Why do you always assume I'm plotting something?"

"Because you *always are*. Topacia warned me that you never took a break from trouble, and she was absolutely right. You're like a hummingbird fluttering around, only instead of flowers, you zigzag from one disaster to the next."

"If one of us is a hummingbird, then it is most definitely *you*," I retorted. "Especially since you are far more addicted to sweet cakes than I am."

Reiko nodded, ceding my point. "True, but that doesn't change the fact that you're plotting something. Care to tell me what it is and how much more trouble you're going to get into?"

"Well, for starters, I'm going to fly Grimley over to the Mortan wing of the castle, land on one of the roofs, and slip inside."

Reiko blinked in surprise. "What? Why?"

"I want to see if Milo has set up some sort of tinkerer's workshop, like the one he had at Myrkvior. He has to conduct his mysterious experiments *somewhere* during the Summit."

"And you think he's stupid enough to conduct them at the castle? Right under Maeven's nose?"

"Probably not, but it doesn't hurt to check."

"Mmm." Reiko made a noncommittal sound. "And the *real* reason you're going to the Mortan wing?"

"So I can convince Leonidas to drop out of the Gauntlet," I muttered, wrestling with the buttons on the back of my gown. "I don't know why he agreed to Maeven's scheme, but I'm putting a stop to it—tonight."

"Why do you have to go to the Mortan wing to do that?" Reiko asked. "Why not just talk to Prince Leo with your mind magier magic?"

She was right. Leonidas was close enough that I could easily talk to him with my magic. Even now, despite all the walls separating us, I could still sense his presence, like an annoying feather tickling my skin.

"I want to hear what Leonidas has to say for himself. Plus, I will get a much better sense if he's hiding something if I see him face-to-face."

"Mmm." Reiko once again made a sound that was somehow disbelieving and full of judgment at the same time. "It still seems like a foolish risk."

"Perhaps, but I have to do *something*. I can't just sit around and wait to see what Milo and Maeven decide to throw at us next. Besides, I know every single inch of this castle, including the Mortan wing. I can sneak in and out with no one being the wiser."

I stripped off my gown and donned a dark gray tunic, along

with black leggings and boots, and a dark gray cloak. I also scrubbed the makeup off my face and pulled my hair back into a ponytail. For a final touch, I added my dagger to my belt like usual.

When I was ready, I stepped into the sitting room, along with Reiko.

Grimley yawned, stretched, and got to his feet. "What's this I hear about flying over to the Mortan wing?"

I told the gargoyle everything that had happened during the dinner.

He yawned again. "Oh, I already knew about all of that."

"How?" Reiko asked. "Haven't you been in here asleep this whole time?"

"Of course I've been asleep. It was finally nice and quiet," Grimley replied. "At least until Fern interrupted my evening nap. She showed up about fifteen minutes before you two did. Apparently, the glass panes on the arena roof are painfully thin, and she heard everything. Fern has already told all the other gargoyles. She's a terrible gossip."

Reiko frowned. "Gargoyles gossip?"

"We have to do *something* to amuse ourselves up on the rooftops all day long," Grimley replied. "And what's more entertaining than watching people frantically scurry about like ants below, making life far more complicated than it needs to be? Hunting, eating, and napping are what truly *matter*. Not convoluted rituals like this silly Gauntlet."

"It's not silly if Leonidas completes the challenges and I have to marry him," I muttered.

Grimley yawned yet again, unconcerned about the potential loss of my freedom. "If the worst happens and he succeeds, then I can always kill him. One swipe of my tail across the prince's throat should do the trick." His tail lashed from side to side, the arrow on the end whistling through the air.

I grinned. The gargoyle always knew exactly what to say to brighten my mood. "As much as I appreciate your murderous urges, Lyra would definitely disapprove of that."

"The bird could be a problem," Grimley agreed. "She is far more formidable than most of the strixes. Fern said Lyra was up on the arena roof too, listening to everything."

"And they didn't attack each other?" Reiko asked. "I thought gargoyles and strixes were natural enemies."

"They are in the wild," I replied. "But not here in Caldwell. The gargoyles and strixes share the sky, lake, and surrounding forests, just like the Andvarians share the castle with the Ungers and the Mortans."

"As much as I hate to admit it, Lyra is much easier to deal with than some of the gargoyles," Grimley grumbled. "Fern was complaining about some big brute who was also up on the arena roof. He kept telling her to be quiet so he could listen."

I thought of the creature I'd seen when we'd first arrived this morning. "Was the gargoyle's name Otto?"

Grimley frowned. "How did you know?"

"I tried to talk to him, but he brushed me off. He seemed like the type that would tell Fern to be quiet."

Grimley snorted. "Well, apparently, he didn't have any success."

I grinned again and looked over at Reiko. She nodded, but her eyes were distant, as though she were listening with only half an ear. She idly rubbed her index finger over the corner of the fireplace mantel, and the dragon on her hand looked troubled.

"What's wrong?" I asked. "Why aren't you changing clothes and demanding to go skulking about the Mortan wing with me?"

She sighed. "Unfortunately, I have my own mission. Kai approached me outside the arena after dinner. Tatsuo has requested an audience."

"Do you want me to go with you?"

Reiko gave me a small smile, although the expression quickly faded away. "I appreciate that, but I need to see my father alone. Sort of like how you need to see Prince Leo alone." She paused. "Actually, it's not like that at all. My conversation with Tatsuo will most likely be cold and stilted, whereas you and Prince Leo will be hard-pressed to keep your hands off each other."

I snorted. "I doubt that. Leonidas didn't seem any more pleased by Maeven's scheme than I did. Our conversation will probably be filled with half-truths and veiled threats, just as it was in the woods outside Haverton."

"Perhaps."

I rolled my eyes at her sly tone. "But?"

"But like Zariza said earlier, Prince Leo has a very handsome head attached to an equally handsome set of shoulders," Reiko replied, an appreciative purr in her voice. "I imagine the rest of him is equally as pleasing under all those clothes he always wears."

An image flashed through my mind of Leonidas's bare muscled chest, which I'd seen when I healed the stab wound Wexel had given him in Blauberg. He was far more than merely *pleasing*.

Reiko laughed at the telltale blush scalding my cheeks. "Perhaps instead of asking Leonidas to drop out of the Gauntlet, you should encourage him. Seduce him, secure his affections, and steal him away from Maeven and the rest of the Morricones."

I huffed. "I'm not usually in the business of *seduction*. Especially with a mortal enemy."

"I've seen you flirt at balls. You are quite skillful in that regard. As for the mortal enemy part . . ." Reiko's voice trailed off, and she shrugged. "As I've said before—sometimes, enemies make the best lovers. All that animosity can quickly turn to passion, if the circumstances are right."

"Like with you and Kai?"

She grimaced. "Yes."

"What happened?"

Her grimace deepened. "I joined the Crimson Dragons late in the season last year. Kai didn't appreciate Tatsuo pulling strings to get me a spot in the troupe, so Kai went out of his way to make sure everyone knew *he* was the best gladiator. I never could beat him, no matter how hard I tried. And I bloody *tried*—if only to have the satisfaction of knocking that arrogant smirk off his face. I never quite succeeded, though."

"So how did the two of you go from fighters to lovers?"

"After Kai knocked me out of the Tournament of Champions during the Regalia Games, he went on to win the title. That night, during the ball at the DiLucris' castle, all the Crimson Dragons were celebrating his victory—except for me. Kai followed me outside onto a balcony. Words were exchanged, and one thing just sort of . . . led to another." Reiko sighed. "It was a mistake. One that I have no intention of repeating."

Despite her muttered words, her eyes grew distant again, and a memory surged off her and filled my mind. Reiko and Kai locked in a heated embrace on a moonlit balcony, lips pressed together, hands roaming everywhere . . .

I cleared my throat, not wanting to intrude on her thoughts. Reiko blinked, and the memory faded away.

"But enough about Kai," she said. "We were talking about how you can use your wiles on Leonidas."

I thought of how Leonidas had held me when we'd danced at Maeven's birthday ball. There had been no animosity between us then, only his body against mine, and the music pulling us together time and time again. Not just the music, but my simmering attraction to him, one that I would be an absolute fool to indulge in, much less try to weaponize as some half-baked seduction scheme.

I shook my head. "Trust me. There will be no *seduction* tonight. But maybe I can find some answers about what Milo is plotting, or at least convince Leonidas to give up Maeven's madness."

"What if he refuses?" Reiko asked. "And decides to participate in the Gauntlet anyway?"

That worry had been brewing in the back of my mind ever since he had accepted the challenge during dinner. Leonidas Morricone was just as stubborn as I was, and he might very well participate in the Gauntlet just for spite, just to prove to me and everyone else he could conquer its challenges. But more likely, Maeven was manipulating him into it by holding Delmira's safety over his head, just as she had done in Myrkvior a few weeks ago. The queen wasn't above threatening her children and using Leonidas's and Delmira's love for each other to her own advantage.

"He won't refuse," I said, making my voice more confident than I really felt. "Leonidas doesn't want to be shackled to me for the rest of his life any more than I want to be bound to him."

Reiko and Grimley exchanged a look, as though they didn't believe my words. I didn't quite believe them either. Oh, I might be intensely attracted to the Morricone prince, but marriage was something else altogether. Perhaps even more important, I wouldn't risk my heart again where Leonidas was concerned. Doing so at Myrkvior had almost cost me my life, and I would not make the same mistake again.

Never again.

Reiko headed into her bedroom to change clothes for her meeting with Tatsuo. I stepped out onto the balcony, and Grimley followed me.

Caldwell Castle was far more beautiful at night than it was during the day. The darkness hid the castle's plain gray facade, even as the moon- and starlight gilded the walls, parapets, and towers in a soft silvery sheen. Pale blue fluorestones outlined many of the archways, while candles burned in many of the windows, looking like golden fireflies trapped in stained-glass frost.

"Are you sure you want to do this, Gemma?" Grimley asked. "Given everything that's happened, Maeven is certain to have extra guards patrolling the Mortan wing."

"Yes. I still haven't figured out what Milo is up to, and I have to stop the Gauntlet before it goes any farther. So let's go."

I climbed onto the gargoyle's back, and he flapped his wings and took off.

With his dark gray skin, Grimley melted into the night sky, and no guards looked up as he flew a loop around the castle. Most of the other gargoyles were roosting on the Andvarian rooftops, although a few were perched on the Ungerian towers, as well as the ones that housed the Ryusamans. Overall, though, I didn't see nearly as many gargoyles as usual. The creatures almost always returned to the castle around sunset to jostle for their favorite spots, but tonight, whole sections of the roofs were empty.

Grims, where are all the other gargoyles?

Apparently, Otto has been barking orders for the last few weeks, trying to tell the other gargoyles where to hunt and steering them away from some of the best islands around the lake so he can go hunt there himself. Fern told me that several gargoyles have flown south to other towns to get away from him.

Disputes among gargoyles were rare, but Otto seemed to dislike his fellow creatures as much as he did humans. How sad. Perhaps I could talk to him and try to get him to be less bossy and more cooperative.

Fewer gargoyles might be haunting the rooftops, but their

numbers were balanced out by the strixes—far more strixes than usual. Like Grimley, the birds blended into the night sky, except for their eyes, which glittered like purple torches. Some of the creatures were huddled together so closely I half expected the larger birds to jostle the smaller ones off the sides of the towers.

I frowned. Had Maeven brought extra guards to the Summit? That would certainly explain all the strixes, although I wondered why she had felt the need to bring so many men and creatures. Unless the Mortan queen was still worried about losing her crown to Milo—along with her life.

Grimley did another loop around the castle, but once again, none of the guards looked up. I pointed out a small tower that was free of strixes, and Grimley sailed down toward it, as silent as a cloud drifting through the sky, and landed with a soft *thump*. Careful of the steep slope, I slid off his back and picked my way down until I was close to the edge of the roof.

Below, three Mortan guards dressed in purple cloaks were patrolling a parapet.

". . . Black Swan troupe is going to win all the bloody championships again . . ."

". . . no hope for our gladiators . . ."

". . . might as well withdraw from the lead-up tournaments . . ."

Snatches of the guards' conversation drifted up to me. The royals, nobles, and merchants might be focused on the Summit, but these men were far more concerned with the upcoming season-ending sporting championships. Couldn't blame them for that. I'd much rather talk about gladiators than trade agreements any day.

The guards drew closer. Grimley might be almost invisible against the night sky, but I was not, so I dropped into a low crouch. One of my boots scraped against a worn tile, which cracked into a dozen pieces. Bits of stone *skitter-skittered* down the steep incline, then *plink-plink-plinked* onto the walkway below—right behind the guards.

"What was that?" The first guard spun around, his hand dropping to his sword.

I froze and held my breath, willing myself to be still and silent.

"Must be the wind," the second man replied.

"Yeah," the third guard chimed in. "It makes all sorts of weird noises when it gusts around the castle."

Those two guards walked on, but the first man held his position, his head swiveling back and forth, and his hand still on his sword. I gripped the dagger on my belt, ready to defend myself if the guard spotted me—

"Come on, Roddy!" the second guard called out. "Let's go inside and warm up."

Roddy looked around again, still suspicious, but he followed his two friends, and all three men headed into the castle.

I sighed with relief, then turned to Grimley. "Stay here and keep watch. Depending on how many guards are inside, I might not be able to get back up here. If we get separated, I'll meet you in my chambers."

He licked my hand. "Be careful."

Grimley settled down onto his stomach, looking like just another shadow on the roof. He was almost completely invisible, except for the bright burn of his sapphire-blue eyes.

I took hold of the edge of the roof, slid my body off the side, and dropped five feet onto the walkway below. Keeping low, I headed in the opposite direction of the guards until I reached a glass door, then opened it and slipped inside.

The Mortan wing was much the same as the Andvarian one, only here, purple banners featuring the Morricone crest covered the walls, and images of strixes were carved into the ceilings. Bits of polished onyx glimmered on the tips of the strixes' feathers, while amethysts glittered as their eyes, making it seem as though the creatures were going to swoop down and attack me at any moment. I shivered and hurried on.

Given the late hour, the corridors were deserted, except for a few guards and servants, but my magic let me sense their approach and thus avoid them. Alcoves full of books, weapons, and other treasures also filled this wing, so I ducked into one of the recessed spaces whenever I needed to hide. I peered into every room I passed, but they were all filled with ordinary furnishings, and I didn't see any signs of Milo having a workshop here. Reiko was right. The crown prince was conducting his experiments elsewhere, away from prying eyes like mine.

I made my way down to the third floor, where the Morricone royals traditionally stayed, and slipped into the appropriate corridor. Despite the fluorestone lamps blazing on the walls, dark shadows cloaked this hallway from top to bottom. I took a closer look at the nearest wall.

No, the corridor wasn't cloaked with shadows—it was covered with liladorn.

The black vines had punched through the stone and snaked along the walls here, just like they did at Myrkvior. I frowned. I had never noticed liladorn in the Mortan wing before—

Heels snapped on the floor behind me, and my fingertips tingled in warning. I hurried forward, darted past a set of closed double doors, and slipped into an alcove a little farther down the hallway. It too was covered in liladorn, and several thorns dug into my back like nails about to be driven into my spine.

Once again, I held my breath. My heart hammered so loudly I couldn't hear the footsteps anymore, although the tingling in my fingertips grew stronger and stronger, indicating that someone with powerful magic was headed this way—

"What do you possibly hope to accomplish by forcing Leonidas to participate in this sadistic ritual?" An irate feminine voice floated down the hallway.

My breath escaped in a soft hiss. I hadn't been spotted, so I eased up to the edge of the alcove and peered out into the corridor.

Delmira was standing in front of the double doors, her hands on her hips, glaring at Maeven. "I read that book you found in the Myrkvior library. I know *exactly* what the Gauntlet entails—and how very few people survive it."

Maeven waved her hand, dismissing her daughter's concerns. "And I've made certain arrangements that will help Leonidas complete the two more arduous challenges. Your job is to help him succeed in the mental one and come up with three things that will speak to Gemma Ripley's body, mind, and heart."

"Leo doesn't need my help with that, and you know it." Delmira's eyes narrowed. "Besides, if you'd had your way, Gemma would have died years ago at the Seven Spire massacre. But now you want her to marry Leo. Why?"

Maeven shrugged. "Plans change. And Gemma Ripley is crucial to mine, not just for the Summit, but far beyond."

Equal parts anger, worry, and dread shot through me. Once again, Maeven was playing with my life as though I were a bloody toy made solely for her amusement. What had I ever done to encourage such animosity? Why couldn't the bitch just leave me alone?

My anger boiled up, and my hands clenched into fists. I wasn't that scared little girl from the massacre anymore, or even the pampered princess I'd been a few weeks ago at Myrkvior. I was stronger now, especially when it came to my magic, and it was time I finally used it against Maeven.

I'd come here as a spy, but I was going to leave as an assassin.

I gathered up my power and raised my hand, ready to step out into the corridor, toss Maeven into the wall, and snap her spine—

A liladorn vine shot out and curled around my wrist, dragging my hand down. I struggled against the vine, but it tightened its grip, and a thorn slashed across the back of my right hand, drawing blood and adding a fresh new gash across my scar, next to the one that was still healing from where the liladorn in the Edelstein Gardens had gouged me a few days ago.

Stop it, that familiar presence said in my mind. *Don't make us hurt you.*

I glared down at the vine, but I ceased my struggles. The liladorn was incredibly tough and strong, and I wouldn't be able to break free without using a lot of magic and making a whole lot of noise, both of which would have every Mortan guard running here to cut me down.

"Fine. Don't tell me your plans," Delmira muttered. "But when are you going to stop treating Leo and me like your personal puppets?"

Maeven lifted her chin. "When your brother's future is secure, along with yours. And not a moment before."

Delmira threw up her hands in frustration. "What does that even *mean*?"

The queen's face remained impassive, but regret surged off her and doused me like a bucket of cold water. "Tomorrow will be a long day with the two Gauntlet challenges. I'm going to bed. You should do the same."

Delmira glared at her mother again, then spun around and stormed down the hallway. The liladorn vibrated in her wake, as though it were mirroring her anger.

Maeven eyed the vibrating vines, then let out a long, loud sigh. In that moment, she looked . . . *weary*, as if all her plots, schemes, and secrets were slowly crushing her the way the liladorn was still strangling my wrist.

"Someday, Delmira will understand," Maeven said, although I couldn't tell if she was talking to herself, the liladorn, or both.

She sighed again and waited for the vines to still. Then she opened one of the doors and stepped into her chambers.

But her regret lingered in the hallway like a cloud of cold fog and made me feel something I never thought I would for the Morricone queen.

Sympathy.

CHAPTER THIRTEEN

I waited until I was certain Maeven wasn't going to come back out into the corridor, then stepped forward. The liladorn finally released my wrist and retreated into the alcove.

Bloody vine, I hissed at it. *Stop scratching me.*

That presence sniffed. *Then stop being stupid, Not-Our-Princess.*

Once again, I wondered how I could possibly murder the sentient plant, but that was a puzzle for another time. I'd already pushed my luck by lurking in the Mortan wing this long, and I needed to leave before the liladorn snared me again, or worse, a guard spotted me.

I crept through the corridors, intending to climb back up to the tower where Grimley was waiting. But more footsteps rang out, forcing me to duck into yet another alcove, and a familiar figure appeared.

Wexel.

The captain strode through a pair of open doors. I hesitated, torn between escaping or sneaking around a little longer. But really, it was an easy choice. Reiko had been right earlier. I *was* a hummingbird, but instead of sugar water, I was attracted to danger.

So I followed Wexel.

I tiptoed down the hallway and glanced in through the doors, which led into a spacious library. From this angle, I couldn't see Wexel, but he couldn't see me either, so I eased forward. Free-standing bookcases ran down the middle of the library, dividing the room into two sections. I crept forward until I reached the end of the cases, then crouched down and peered around the side of one.

A fireplace dominated the back wall, which was shot through with liladorn vines. Milo was lounging on a settee, while Corvina sat ramrod-straight in a chair. A low table in between them featured platters of sweet cakes and other treats. Wexel was hovering in the space between Milo and Corvina.

"Well?" Milo asked, a clear command in his voice despite his lazy drawl.

"The men have returned from the island, and everything is ready for tomorrow," Wexel replied.

Milo took a sip of wine from a goblet. "Good. I just need to conduct a few final experiments, and then I can proceed with my plans."

"What *are* your plans?" Corvina asked. "Surely you're not going to attempt another coup against Maeven like the one that failed so miserably at Myrkvior."

Milo maintained his relaxed posture, although his fingers clenched around the goblet. He'd shed the white gloves he'd been wearing in the arena earlier, and red, mottled, puckered scars marred his hands, the marks eerily similar to the scars that adorned my own hands. Good. I was glad he had such vivid, lasting reminders of how much pain I had caused him.

"Of course not," he replied. "I never make the same mistake twice. My only error at Myrkvior was not thinking *big enough*, which is something I plan to correct just as soon as possible."

I frowned. What could be bigger or more important than trying to depose a queen?

Corvina arched an eyebrow at his vague answer. "Well, I would like to know what *my* money is paying for. My mother might have followed you blindly, but I will not."

And I'm never going to fuck you like she did. Corvina's thought snarled through my mind, and her disgust and loathing of Milo punched into my stomach.

Despite her less-than-charitable feelings toward her fiancé, Corvina had still aligned herself with Milo, just as Emperia Dumond had done before her. Why? What did she hope to gain?

Milo made a grand airy gesture with his goblet. "You know exactly what your money is paying for. Men, strixes, and tearstone, for starters. Everything I need to make my vision a reality and tear my mother down off her throne."

Corvina's eyebrow arched a little higher. "You should have killed Maeven on the way to the Summit like I advised. Now she's invoked that arcane Ungerian ritual, which means all eyes will be on her. And if Leonidas succeeds, then things will be even worse. Many of the Mortan nobles will laud him as a hero for finally managing to secure an alliance with the Andvarians, however forced it might be."

Milo laughed, and the low, ugly sound scraped against my skin like a razor blade. "Please. Leonidas won't succeed. Even if he does, Dominic Ripley will *never* allow his precious Glitzma to marry a Morricone. The Gauntlet isn't a problem—it's an *opportunity*. While everyone is watching Mother and Leonidas, we will implement our own plans."

"Which are?" Corvina asked, circling around to her previous question.

Milo huffed in annoyance. "If you must know, then I'll show you on the island tomorrow. But for right now, I have some details to discuss with Wexel. Leave us."

Corvina opened her mouth to protest the dismissal, but Wexel shook his head in warning. Corvina clamped her lips together, rose to her feet, and dipped into a curtsy.

"Of course," she murmured. "Until tomorrow."

Milo ignored her in favor of drinking more wine.

Magic crackled in Corvina's gray eyes, while anger stained her cheeks, although Milo didn't seem to notice either one.

Arrogant bastard. Once again, Corvina's thought snarled through my mind. *He's going to regret ignoring me.*

She stalked away from the fireplace and left the library. Her presence quickly vanished, like a storm cloud sweeping across the sky, but her words and animosity lingered in my mind and heart.

"You should take Corvina more seriously," Wexel said. "She's smarter than Emperia, and far stronger in her weather magic. She won't be content to wait for answers for much longer."

He was right. Corvina *was* smart and strong, and more important, she wouldn't make the same mistakes her mother had. Back at Myrkvior, Corvina had let Milo and Emperia's attempted coup play out, rather than involving herself in their plotting. That sly caution had allowed her to survive. Corvina might have aligned herself with Milo against Maeven, but I was willing to bet the noble lady was plotting against *both* the Morricones.

Milo shrugged. "And I won't need the Dumond fortune for much longer. Corvina thinks she's more important than she truly is, just like Emperia did. Once I have the rest of the necessary supplies, we can proceed with our plan to bring Andvari to its knees. After Andvari falls, I will finally have all the money, resources, and tearstone I need, and the Mortan nobles will be eager to follow me."

A shiver slid down my spine at him so casually discussing conquering my kingdom, even though he was talking in vague terms, just as he'd done when I'd eavesdropped in his workshop in Myrkvior. Milo had inherited Maeven's frustrating tendency to never reveal his true intentions until the last possible moment.

"What will you do with Corvina once you take the throne?" Wexel asked. "Will you honor the engagement and marry her?"

The captain's voice was level, but he couldn't quite hide his grimace, as if the thought of Corvina marrying Milo made him sick. Once again, the depth of Wexel's affection for the lady surprised me.

Milo scoffed. "Of course not. The Dumonds have been a thorn in my family's side for far too long. I'll kill Corvina, along with the rest of them, and add the Dumond fortune, land, and men to my own resources. Maeven once planned a massacre. Well, I can do the same. Only, I won't be so foolish as to let anyone escape like she did."

Wexel blinked in surprise. "But . . . you're talking about exterminating one of the oldest noble families in Morta."

Milo must have noticed the hesitation in the captain's voice because he finally deigned to glance over at his lackey. "Is that a problem for you, Wexel?"

The captain shook his head. "No, of course not."

"Good," Milo replied. "Because I would hate to have to find another captain, especially given all your years of loyal service."

Wexel's jaw clenched at the obvious threat.

Milo waved his hand again. "Get the servants to remove this mess. I have work to do."

He drained his wine and set the goblet on the table. I slid back behind the bookcase, stood up, and headed for the library doors. I needed to get out of here before the servants arrived—

My knee clipped a book jutting out on one of the shelves. The volume tumbled to the floor and landed with a loud *thump*.

"What was that?" Milo asked.

Stupid, stupid, Gemma! I cursed my clumsiness.

"Someone might be lurking out in the hallway," Wexel replied in a low voice. "I'll check."

A soft *rasp* sounded, indicating that Wexel had drawn his sword. I couldn't slip out of the library without his seeing me, so I crouched down and changed direction, heading deeper into the room.

I slipped from one bookcase to another, making sure to keep them in between myself and Milo, who was now standing in front of the fireplace, scanning what he could see of the library—

"Why are you just standing around out here?" Wexel snapped. "Come clear the table."

"Yes—yes, sir!" a high, nervous voice stammered.

More footsteps sounded, and a male servant entered the library, quickly followed by three more. I grimaced and kept moving, searching for another exit . . .

There.

I hurried over to a glass door in the far corner of the library and grabbed the knob. An electric shock zinged my fingers the second I touched the metal, which also felt strangely cold and damp, as though someone with lightning or other powerful magic had used the door recently. Had someone else been in here spying on Milo?

I grimaced, shook out my hand, and peered through the glass, but the room beyond was dark. More and more servants were invading the library, so I had no choice but to turn the knob, open the door, and step forward into the waiting blackness.

I plastered myself up against the closest wall and waited until my eyes adjusted to the dark. Lucky for me, I had stepped into an empty sitting room. With all the servants fluttering about, I couldn't risk moving through the hallways again, so I headed over to the back wall, which featured another glass door. I started to grab the knob and froze.

The door was cracked open.

I reached out with my magic, wondering if someone else was creeping through the Mortan wing, but I sensed only the servants in the library. Either way, I couldn't stay here, so I slipped through the open door and shut it behind me.

I wound up on a walkway that ringed this level of the castle. No guards were patrolling this section, so I rushed over to some steps and hurried down to the ground level. Then I sprinted forward, plunging into the gardens that lined the back half of the grounds.

In addition to the Summit, people also flocked to Caldwell Castle to stroll through its famed gardens, which were open to all. The Caldwell Gardens stretched out for more than a mile and were built on a series of wide, flat terraces that gradually stepped down to the lakeshore in the distance. During the summer, people would picnic in the open grassy spots on the terraces and gather in the stone amphitheater next to the shoreline to watch sailboat races. An enormous lighthouse also towered over the gardens, and the blue, white, and gray fluorestones spiraling up the structure made it look like an oversize yule tree gleaming in the night.

During the day, the gardens' flowers, shrubs, and trees would be awash in color, but tonight, they were dark, shadowy, and mysterious, which was perfect for my skulking.

Grimley. I sent the thought out. *I'm in the gardens on the Mortan side of the castle. I'm going to head up to the main plaza. I'll meet you back in my chambers.*

I heard him yawn in my mind. *So far, everything has been*

quiet, except for all these stupid birds. Did you know that strixes snore in their sleep?

As does a certain gargoyle, I reminded him.

At least I have a proper *snore. Loud, deep, and sonorous. Not a high, trilling, annoying wheeze. These bloody birds are giving me a headache.*

I grinned and plunged deeper into the gardens.

Blue, pink, and purple fluorestones clustered together like fallen petals along the stone paths that zigzagged across the terraces, while black wrought-iron lanterns filled with white fluorestones hung from tall poles, adding to the dreamy ethereal glow. Despite the late hour and the chilly wind gusting off the lake, several couples had ensconced themselves in the gazebos that dotted the terraces, and low murmurs curled through the air, along with louder, sharper cries of pleasure. My gargoyle pendant heated up against my chest, and passion gusted around me, the sensation as thick and heady as the perfumes wafting up from the flowers.

I ignored the burn in my cheeks and moved past the amorous couples. I was almost to the main steps that cut through the center of the gardens when a faint, feathery, electric presence tickled my skin.

Leonidas.

He was over . . . *there*. Deeper in the gardens and well on the Mortan side of the grounds. Of course he was. Because nothing about this could ever be *easy*.

I stopped, staring at the steps. All I had to do was walk up them, and I would be back on the main plaza. From there, I could slip through the marketplace and back into the Andvarian wing.

But part of the reason I'd risked sneaking into the Mortan wing was to convince Leonidas to drop out of the Gauntlet. Of course I wanted to undercut Maeven's mysterious plans for me, but I also wouldn't be able to sleep if I didn't at least *try* to persuade the prince not to participate in his mother's game.

And you want to see him again anyway, a treacherous little voice whispered in my mind.

I ignored the voice, changed direction, and headed back the way I'd come.

Some of the couples had spent their ardor and left the gazebos, so the gardens were much quieter than before. Still, the deeper I went into the lush landscaped vegetation, the more the back of my neck prickled, as though I were being watched. I looked around and reached out with my magic, but there were still too many couples and too many heady emotions for me to pick out any dark, malevolent intentions. I shivered and quickened my pace.

I trailed the threads of energy that surrounded Leonidas from one terrace to the next, like a child following breadcrumbs in an old fairy tale. And just like that foolish child, I was probably heading toward my own doom. Only, I would be gobbled up by a handsome prince instead of a warty old witch.

Finally, I reached a large gazebo at the end of this path. Gray and purple fluorestones curled up the gray stone railing, as well as the diamond-shaped columns that supported the low domed roof, but my gaze skipped past them and landed on the figure standing in the shadows.

Leonidas.

He was once again wearing a black cloak over a long black riding coat, along with a black tunic and leggings. He had one black boot propped up on the bottom section of the railing, and he was standing straight and tall, like a knight surveying the landscape he had just conquered. His hands were free of their usual gloves, and he was tapping his finger against the tearstone sword that was belted to his waist, along with a matching dagger. Both weapons glinted a dull gray against his dark clothes.

The fluorestones' moody gray-purple glows highlighted the sharp, angular planes of Leonidas's face, making him look even more handsome than usual, like a marble statue that had been placed inside the gazebo for everyone to admire, including me.

Especially me.

I flung that thought away, lest he overhear it with his magic. Then I stepped into the gazebo and stared out over the landscape, just as he was still doing.

The gazebo was situated on a high point that arced out over the rest of the gardens. Instead of another terrace, jagged boulders lay below, jutting up like teeth, as though they were a kraken that was trying to rise up and swallow the entire castle, gazebo, gardens, and all. A beautiful and dangerous view, just like the one of the man beside me.

"Did you know Mortans call this Fool's Bane Point?" Leonidas said. "Legend has it that long ago, a Morricone prince named Bane was desperately in love with a servant girl. But of course his father, the king, opposed the union and had the servant girl executed. Bane was so distraught that he threw himself off this point. Supposedly he impaled himself on one of the rocks, and flowers bloomed all around his body. The Mortans named the blossoms fool's bane after him. People claim you can see the prince's ghost wandering around the lighthouse and hear him wailing over his lost love whenever storms blow in off the lake."

I shivered. "Why do Mortan love stories always end in tragedy? I've never heard of one, not a single one, with a happy ending."

Leonidas shrugged. "Perhaps because we Mortans are a tragic people, always wanting things we can't have."

His words sent another shiver skittering down my spine. I knew all about wanting things I couldn't have, the chief of those standing right beside me.

"I've been waiting for you," Leonidas said.

"Why? Did your magic tell you that I was coming?"

"Of course. But I also knew you would come, given what happened in the arena."

I ground my teeth. I hated that he knew me so well, that I was so bloody *predictable*, but I wasn't about to let Maeven's scheme dictate the rest of my life. I'd already lost so much to her. I wasn't losing my freedom too.

"Did you learn anything interesting when you were creeping through the Mortan wing? You were in there for quite some time." Leonidas removed his boot from the railing and turned toward me. "I thought perhaps the liladorn had snagged you. Sometimes, the vines like to . . . play with visitors, just like the ones at Myrkvior do."

He gestured to the right, where several strands of liladorn twined through the railing.

I bristled at his teasing and eased away from the vines. "It scratched me. Apparently, it didn't like my eavesdropping on Delmira and Maeven. They were arguing about the Gauntlet."

Leonidas sighed. "Of course they were."

"Did you know what Maeven was up to?" I asked in a snide voice. "Did the two of you plan this little surprise for me like you planned the queen's birthday ball in Myrkvior?"

Leonidas sighed again, longer and deeper than before. "No. As I told you in the arena, Mother did not inform me of her plot. If she had, I would have put a stop to it."

Hope sprang up inside me. "You can still put a stop to it. You don't have to participate in the Gauntlet. Tell Xenia that you changed your mind. She'll understand."

He shook his head. "Mother and I met with Xenia earlier. She said that since I accepted the challenge in the arena, I am now bound by Ungerian customs and Summit laws to complete the tasks." He paused. "Or die trying. Her words, not mine."

My stomach clenched with worry. Despite everything that

had happened between us, I didn't want him to die. Perhaps that made me a grand fool, but Leonidas had suffered at Maeven's and Milo's hands just as much as I had at Myrkvior, maybe even more so, and King Maximus had done unspeakable things to him when he was a boy. Just thinking about the awful scars that lined his back made me want to reach out and comfort him, even now.

"Xenia did assure me that I will not be killed if I fail the first challenge," Leonidas continued. "Apparently, she and Queen Zariza have decided to be lenient and extend me the courtesy of failing two challenges before the Ungers lop off my head."

"Why did you even agree to participate in the Gauntlet? No one could have blamed you for refusing. Everyone knows how manipulative Maeven is. Despite its being an Ungerian tradition, Xenia and Zariza probably would have let you bow out gracefully."

Leonidas's face hardened, and his chin lifted. "I am a Mortan, a Morricone, and I was given a task by my queen. It is my duty to complete that task and bring honor and glory to my kingdom."

I threw up my hands in frustration. "You are *impossible*. You always have been, ever since we were children and ran into those bandits by the river."

The words popped out before I could stop them. Leonidas Morricone got under my skin in a way no one else ever had and made my tongue as uncontrollable as my magic so often was.

He arched an eyebrow. "*You* were the reason those bandits attacked us. If you had just come with me when I asked, then we could have slipped into the woods, and none of that would have ever happened."

I threw up my hands again. "I thought you were trying to kill me! Again! What was I supposed to do?"

"Trust me, Gemma. Just trust me."

His low, husky voice curled around me like a python, squeezing my heart tight. That was the real issue between us. It always had been. As attractive as I found Leonidas, as much history as we shared, as similar as we were, I simply couldn't trust him. The few times I had tried had ended in disaster, including most recently at Myrkvior, and I was too wary to risk it again, especially now when the stakes were so high.

"You know I can't do that."

Sadness flickered across his face. "I know."

An awkward silence sprang up between us, but something propelled me to try again.

"Forget about bringing honor to Morta," I said. "We both know that doing one's duty mostly involves courtly nonsense that doesn't change anything for the better. You know how dangerous Ungerian customs can be. If you insist on going through with the Gauntlet, then you are going to wind up dead."

"Would that bother you?" Leonidas asked in a soft voice. "My winding up dead?"

Part of me wanted to say no, of course not, that he was a Morricone and I was a Ripley, and I wouldn't care if he dropped dead right here and now. But I couldn't bring myself to utter the harsh words. No, try as I might, I could never truly hate Leonidas. Not even now, when he was being a stupid, stubborn fool.

"Think of Lyra." I sidestepped his question. "She would be devastated by your death. So would Delmira. Why, it might even give Maeven pause as well, if only for a few moments."

A bitter laugh erupted out of his lips. "Well, it's good to know that a few people care about me, even if you don't."

Leonidas kept staring at me. I drew in a breath, and his honeysuckle scent filled my nose, making my head spin. Sometime during our conversation, I had stepped closer to him, like a magnet being slowly, irresistibly drawn to another magnet. It had always been that way between us, even when we were children. I didn't know if it was a product of our similar mind magier magic or our families' bloody, tangled histories, but something *always* seemed to draw us together—even as people and politics conspired to tear us apart.

"I understand why you don't trust me, Gemma," Leonidas said in a low, regretful voice that made needles of sympathy prick my heart. "Truly I do. I wouldn't trust me either, given everything that's happened."

"But?"

"But the Gauntlet is a chance for me to finally change that."

I couldn't have been more surprised than if he had stabbed me in the heart with his sword. "What do you mean?"

"Perhaps if I complete the Gauntlet, then you will finally believe that I would never willingly let any harm come to you. Perhaps you will even learn to trust me, just a little bit."

Surprise filled me. "You're not . . . doing this for *me*?"

His icy mask cracked and fell away, replaced by a stubborn look. "I can't think of a better reason to do it than for *you*."

My surprise vanished, replaced by anger, and I poked my finger against his muscled chest. "You stupid, arrogant fool! You're going to get yourself *killed*. And for what, to prove a point to me? That's the most ridiculous thing I've ever heard!"

Leonidas kept staring at me. "As I said before, I can't think of a better reason than you, Gemma."

His voice was lower, softer, huskier than before, and it wrapped around me like a fine cloak, warming my entire body. The sound of my name on his lips made my toes curl and my fingertips tingle, but not from any lightning or other power. No, I was simply captivated by the magic of *him*.

I shook my head. "You don't have to prove anything to me."

Determination flared in his amethyst eyes, glowing even stronger and more brightly than the fluorestones around us. "Yes, I do. I was hoping to prove it by bringing you to Myrkvior, but that didn't work out the way I intended. Well, now I have a second chance, and I'm going to take it."

"A second chance that *Maeven* orchestrated," I shot right back at him. "The only reason she even invoked the Gauntlet is because it somehow furthers her own plans. She admitted as much to Delmira earlier."

Leonidas shrugged. "I know that."

"But?"

"But I don't care," he snapped back. "All I care about is proving you can trust me. Proving how much I—"

He stopped, biting back his words, although he kept staring at me, the determination in his gaze flaring up into something much hotter and far more intense. My heart hammered in my chest, and every part of me tensed, wanting him to finish his thought and yet dreading what he might say.

"How much you *what*?" I asked, my voice cracking on the last word.

Leonidas stared at me, his gaze sharp, hungry, and focused, like a strix spotting its prey from afar. That tense, expectant silence dropped over us again, although his emotions blasted over me.

Interest. Attraction. Need. Want. Desire.

They mirrored all the things I was feeling for him—all the things I *shouldn't* be feeling for him. Especially not here, now, with the two of us alone in the dreamy dark.

I shook my head again. "You—*this*—is madness."

I turned to leave, but Leonidas grabbed my hand. The heat of his skin against mine stopped me cold, and I whirled back around toward him.

"What are you doing? You don't like to be touched."

That stubborn look filled Leonidas's face again, and he threaded his fingers through mine as if to contradict my words, even though we both knew they were true, given the scars on his back.

"I don't like to be touched by people who wish me harm," he replied. "But you are not one of those people."

A harsh laugh spewed out of my lips. "In case you've forgotten, I tried to kill you multiple times when we were children."

"Oh, Gemma, I have never forgotten one single thing about you."

His voice wrapped around me again, and I found myself swaying toward him. Leonidas closed the distance between us, his other hand settling on my waist. My free hand instinctively went up and clutched his shoulder, although I wasn't sure if I was trying to push him away or pull him closer.

Memories of the last time he'd held me like this on the dance floor at Myrkvior flashed through my mind. Even though we were all alone and there was no music, in some ways we were dancing again, both of us pushing and pulling against this hum, this current, this energy that bound us together.

Leonidas's gaze locked with mine, his eyes dark with the same desire that was thrumming through my own body.

"Don't do this," I whispered, even as my fingers tightened around his and my heart hammered in my chest again.

"I can't *not* do it," he replied. "Not anymore."

Leonidas drew me closer and lowered his lips to mine.

CHAPTER FOURTEEN

The first touch of his lips against mine was as light as a feather tickling my skin, but the electric shock of it sizzled all the way down into my toes, making them curl inside my boots.

Leonidas drew back, his gaze locking with mine. Both of us stood rigid and tense, like springs about to snap from being coiled so tightly. Our breaths rasped against each other's cheeks, and his honeysuckle scent filled my nose again, making my head spin. Our bodies were flush together, and even though we were both fully clothed, the heat of him sank deep down into my bones like a wildfire that refused to be extinguished.

His gaze traced over my face, as if he was trying to memorize the line of my nose, the curve of my cheeks, even the point of my chin. I did the same thing to him, imprinting his sharp nose, high cheekbones, and strong jaw on my own mind.

I didn't know how long we stood there, holding on to each other, both of us frozen like dancers whose music had stopped. But I didn't want this to stop. Not now.

Not ever, that snide little voice whispered in my mind again.

I ignored the voice and did what I'd wanted to all along—I surged forward and pressed my lips to his.

I meant to kiss Leonidas as gently as he had me, but the firm feel of his lips against mine sent more of those hot, electric shock waves jolting through my body, and I surged forward again, hungry for more—more heat, more sparks, more of *him*.

Leonidas growled and pulled me even closer. His tongue darted out to stroke mine, and I melted into him.

We spun around and around the gazebo. Lips crashing together. Tongues dueling back and forth. Hands roaming everywhere. A far more physical and pleasurable dance than the one we'd engaged in at Myrkvior, but it still wasn't enough. Desire zipped through my veins like a caladrius streaking through the air, and a pounding ache settled between my thighs.

Leonidas tugged me over to a loveseat embedded in one side of the gazebo railing and sank down onto the cushions. I followed the motion, straddling him. Leonidas pulled me closer and rained kisses along my neck. I rocked forward, and his hard cock settled in between my thighs.

"Gemma," Leonidas rasped against my skin, the same aching need in his voice that was pounding through my body. "Gemma."

I rocked forward again and again, wishing there was nothing separating us, that nothing was keeping me from feeling every single inch of him—

Crack.

A twig snapped in the distance, and another presence filled my mind, the sensation as cold and wet as sleet soaking my body.

Leonidas and I both froze. Then I scrambled back onto my feet and grabbed the dagger from my belt. Leonidas also stood up and drew his sword.

That cold, wet presence vanished, but several more took its place, like candles lighting up a dark room one by one by one.

Shadows crept closer, morphing into men wearing black cloaks over black tunics, leggings, and boots. Most of the men were clutching swords, although a few were armed with crossbows.

"Milo's men?" I asked in a low voice.

"I don't know who they are," Leonidas replied.

One of the men lifted his crossbow and pulled the trigger. The arrow zipped through the air, heading straight for my chest. I reached for my magic to send it spinning away, but Leonidas stepped in front of me and whirled around, so that he was facing me.

Leonidas didn't even glance behind him. Keeping his gaze on mine, he stretched his left arm back and sent out a blast of magic that knocked the arrow aside. Another blast of his magic threw back the charging men and sent them all tumbling to the ground.

I rolled my eyes. "Showoff."

He grinned, then rushed out of the gazebo, waded into the group of men, and started swinging his sword left and right, cutting down first one enemy, then another.

Three men climbed to their feet and ran around to the opposite side of the gazebo. I hurried in that direction.

The man closest to me raised his crossbow, but I used my magic to wrench it out of his grasp and send it sailing through the air. Then I rushed forward and buried my dagger in his chest, making him scream. I ripped my dagger out and shoved him back into the other two men, and all three of them went down in a heap on the grass.

The two uninjured men climbed back onto their feet and charged at me again. Their thoughts washed over me, each one as vicious as a slap across the face.

This bitch needs to die . . .

Gotta do our job . . .

Can't retreat until they're both dead . . .

I'd thought Milo had dispatched these men to kill Leonidas,

but it sounded like they were here to murder me too. Who were they working for? And how had they even known I was in the gardens?

I swiped my dagger across one man's stomach, then turned and punched the blade into the other man's throat. They both dropped to the ground. The pain of their injuries crashed through my own body, but I gritted my teeth and blocked it out.

Another man erupted out of the shadows and plowed into me from the side. I hit the ground, and my dagger spurted out of my hand. I reached out with my magic, trying to yank the blade back toward me, but the man dug his fingers into my hair and slammed my head against the ground.

Pain exploded in my skull, and white stars erupted in my eyes. Stunned, I slumped to the grass. The man dug his fingers into my hair again and yanked my head back.

"Time to die, Gemma," Wexel sneered in my ear.

The low *hiss* of a blade sliding free of its scabbard sounded. Desperate, I flung my arm out and reached for my dagger again. Despite the ache in my head, my magic came to me easily—and so did the weapon, which flew through the air and settled into my hand.

Wexel yanked my head back a little more, and I stabbed out with my dagger, driving it into his right thigh. Wexel howled with pain, but he didn't release me, so I yanked the dagger out and stabbed it into his thigh again.

This time, Wexel did release me. I dropped back down onto the grass, the bloody dagger still clutched in my hand. I crawled forward, trying to get away from Wexel, even as I braced myself for another attack . . .

But it never came.

Instead, the gardens went eerily quiet, except for the *slap-slap-slap-slap* of footsteps, but those quickly grew fainter, then vanished altogether. Wexel, most likely. The captain was happy to fight when he had the advantage, but he scurried away like a frightened child the second the tables turned on him.

I reached out, grabbed hold of the gazebo railing, and pulled myself upright. My head spun around. I staggered forward and would have fallen, but a hand latched onto my arm. I snapped up my dagger to stab whoever had grabbed me, but Leonidas's face swam into view.

I blinked away the last of the white stars and glanced past him. Several dead men littered the grass around the gazebo like oversize flowers someone had picked and then tossed aside.

I lowered my dagger. "Wexel?"

"Gone. Again," Leonidas growled. "That bastard has more lives than a caladrius. But forget about Wexel right now. How are you?"

His eyes crinkled with concern, and he gingerly probed a goose egg on the side of my head. I hissed with pain, but no more stars flashed before my eyes.

"Here," Leonidas said. "Sit down."

He guided me over to the cushioned loveseat where I had been straddling him moments before. A blush scalded my cheeks, and I pulled away from him and stayed on my feet.

"I'm fine. Really." I gestured at the men. "Who are they? Mortan guards?"

Leonidas went from one body to the next, examining them all in turn. He shook his head. "I've never seen any of them before, so I don't think they are part of the royal guard. But if Wexel was here, then they work for him—and Milo."

Leonidas was still clutching his sword, but his longish black hair was mussed from where I'd tangled my fingers in it, and his cloak was askew from where I'd tossed it back so I could run my hands over his muscled chest. Despite the imperfections, he reminded me of a conquering knight, and I had been the kingdom he had been about to plunder. My lips and tongue still tingled from his kisses, and his honeysuckle scent was imprinted on my skin like a heady perfume.

I slid my dagger back into its scabbard to give myself a few seconds to cobble together some composure. To ignore the hot need still pulsing through my body and smother it with cold reason.

Leonidas also sheathed his sword, and we faced each other again. I drew in a breath, then let it out and strode forward, but he stepped into my path.

"Stay," Leonidas said in a low, strained voice. "Be with me."

Please. He didn't speak the word, didn't even think it in his mind, but it hung in the air between us, and desire crackled through my veins again. It would be so very easy to step back into his arms, press my lips to his again, and finish what we'd started.

Fuck him and forget him, Reiko's voice whispered through my mind.

I was tempted to do just that, only there would be no *forgetting* Leonidas Morricone. There never had been, ever since I'd first met him as a child in the Spire Mountains.

"This is madness." I repeated my earlier sentiment, although my voice lacked conviction.

"Then be mad with me," Leonidas replied.

Temptation rose inside me like a hungry gargoyle demanding to be fed, but I shoved it down, drowning it in the sea of emotion that was still boiling inside me.

"At Myrkvior, you said we all are who we are. Well, you were right. Maeven is never going to stop trying to manipulate us, and Milo is never going to stop trying to kill us. *Nothing* is ever going to change between our families—or us."

All the heat died in Leonidas's eyes, snuffed out by my harsh words, and his icy mask snapped back into place again. "Then I suppose this is good night. I will dispose of the bodies and see you tomorrow for the Gauntlet."

Anger spiked through me. "Forget about the bloody Gauntlet. Leave the Summit while you still can. Before Milo and Wexel try to kill you again."

A muscle ticced in Leonidas's jaw. "No."

"*No?*" I snapped. "Don't be a fool. Surely it has occurred to you that Milo will probably try to sabotage the Gauntlet. It would be the perfect opportunity for you to finally have that fatal *accident* your brother so desperately wants to bestow upon you."

He smirked at me. "Worried about my safety again?"

"Hardly," I lied. "I just don't want Maeven to blame me for your death, and we both know she will, even though she's the one who enacted the tradition."

Leonidas tipped his head, acknowledging my point. But then his face hardened again, and determination sparked in his eyes. "I'm not backing out of the Gauntlet. I must do my duty."

"Forget about your damned duty to Morta, Maeven, and the Morricone throne," I growled. "Save yourself. That's what your mother would do."

"I wasn't talking about my duty to Morta, my mother, or her throne," Leonidas replied in a soft voice. "I was talking about my duty to *you*, Gemma."

Shock jolted through me, and I shook my head, trying to ignore the feelings swirling in his eyes, the same ones that were shredding my heart like a strix's sharp talons. "You have no *duty* to me. We've been thrown together a few times over the years by chance or circumstance or whatever you want to call it. There's nothing more to us than that."

"Liar," he accused in that same soft voice. "You know we're more than that. We've *always* been more than that from the very first moment we met in the woods all those years ago."

Leonidas moved forward so that he was standing right in front of me. His gaze dropped to my lips, but instead of kissing me again, he went down on one knee, then reached out and gently took my hand in his. The warmth of his skin against mine again made me shudder, and I had to force myself not to curl my fingers into his.

Leonidas stared up at me, his amethyst gaze locking with mine. "I am going to earn your trust, Gemma Ripley," he said in a serious, earnest voice. "And your heart too, if I am lucky enough to manage it."

My eyes widened, and my breath caught in my throat, even as his words rooted me in place. Leonidas brought my hand to his lips and pressed a courtly kiss to my knuckles, one that burned through me far worse than Milo's torturous lightning had. That pain had been all sharp, electric stings, but this— whatever *this* truly was—seeped into my skin, muscles, veins, bones, and worst of all, my heart.

Leonidas kept staring at me, determination blazing in his eyes again. I ripped my hand out of his and backed away.

"Do the Gauntlet or not," I snapped, my voice as harsh as I could make it. "That's your choice. But don't say I didn't warn you when you get your fool self killed."

Leonidas climbed to his feet. He dipped into a bow, his eyes never leaving mine, then straightened. "Until tomorrow, Gemma."

I skirted around him and stalked away. Somehow I managed not to turn around, even though I could feel his gaze on my back. His feathery presence also tickled my skin again, reminding me of the heated kisses we'd shared and making me ache for how much more there could have been between us.

I hurried away from the gazebo, heading back toward the main steps in the center of the gardens. By this point, it was almost midnight, and the amorous couples had left the gazebos for the warmer confines of their beds inside the castle, but I still kept to the shadows. The last thing I needed was for someone to see Princess Gemma and wonder what I was up to—

"You need to come home, Reiko."

The sound of my friend's name cut through the air like a dagger. I glanced around, but I didn't see Reiko on this terrace, which wasn't terribly surprising. The wind gusting off the lake often blew people's words around, and voices could rise and fall from one terrace to another.

"Why?" Reiko's reply floated up to me. "So I can be a gladiator again? That didn't work out so well the last time I tried it."

I followed her voice over to the edge of the terrace and ducked behind a tree. On the level below, Reiko was facing Tatsuo, who was bathed in a pool of white light from a nearby lantern. Kai was there too, lurking in the shadows.

Tatsuo sighed, as if they'd had this same argument many times before. "That's because you never truly devoted yourself to the training. You could be an excellent gladiator if you only applied yourself."

A humorless smile curved Reiko's lips. "But my being *excellent* has never been good enough for you."

Tatsuo grimaced, just a bit. "I've never said that."

"You've never had to." Reiko shook her head. "I will *never* be as good a gladiator as you were. I will never be the best fighter in a troupe, or triumph in the Ryusaman fights, or win the Tournament of Champions at the Regalia Games. I don't love being a gladiator the way you did."

She lifted her chin. "But I *do* love being a spy, and I am most excellent at it."

"And what, exactly, is there to love about being a spy? Sneaking around and eavesdropping on people?" Tatsuo scoffed. "There's no *honor* in that. Being a spy is one step above being a common thief. Only, you're stealing information instead of pretty trinkets."

Reiko jerked back as though he'd stabbed her, and hurt rippled off her, as sharp as a sword twisting into my own heart.

Tatsuo kept staring at her, conviction blasting off him like heat from an oven. The longer Reiko looked at her father, the more she just . . . wilted, like a delicate orchid losing all its vitality beneath a scorching sun.

Anger boiled up inside me, and I stepped forward, ready to show myself and tell Tatsuo Yamato just how wrong he was—

"Well, this *common spy* has work to do." Despite Reiko's caustic words, there was no real venom in her voice. "What are Queen Ruri's orders?"

Despite my best intentions, I stopped, holding my position in the shadows. As much as I cared about Reiko, I was also a spy, and I would do whatever it took to protect my kingdom—even eavesdrop on a friend.

"You are to continue your mission to learn what Milo Morricone plans to do with the stolen Andvarian tearstone." Tatsuo paused. "And you have a new objective—undercut whatever relationship is brewing between Gemma Ripley and Leonidas Morricone."

I blinked in surprise, as did Reiko.

"Why?" she asked.

"Ruri believes Gemma and Leonidas are far friendlier than they appeared to be at dinner tonight."

My body thrummed at the thought of the kisses I'd shared with Leonidas, even as my inner spy winced. I thought I'd done a better job of hiding my attraction to him, but Ruri was no fool. The Ryusaman queen had a reputation for being particularly observant. Some folks claimed her inner dragon gave her an extra set of eyes and ears and that she could hear the smallest whisper of trouble in an arena filled with raucous cheers.

"The Gauntlet is another one of Maeven's manipulations," Reiko said. "Nothing more. Gemma, Prince Dominic, and Captain Rhea have already started researching the ritual. They'll find some way to stop it."

"Perhaps," Tatsuo replied. "And if they do, we shall support their efforts. At the very least, Ruri wants to maintain the status quo and current peace with Andvari and Morta. At best, she would like for Milo to proceed with his plots, especially when it comes to deposing Maeven and lashing out at the Ripleys."

Reiko's eyebrows shot up. "Ruri *wants* Milo to attack the Ripleys? But if that happens, then Morta and Andvari will go to war."

Tatsuo shrugged. "Then let them go to war. It doesn't have anything to do with us, with Ryusama."

Shock zinged through me. War was never good for anyone, but if the worst happened, and Andvari fell to Morta, then Milo would be able to get as much tearstone as his greedy tinkerer's heart desired. With that sort of arsenal, Milo could turn his murderous intentions toward Ryusama, which could be potentially catastrophic for the other kingdom. So why would Tatsuo—and by extension Queen Ruri—want Milo to succeed in his plots?

"But Andvari is our ally," Reiko protested. "We have a long-standing treaty to come to their aid, if war ever does break out between Andvari and Morta."

"A treaty that will be null and void if Leonidas Morricone makes it through the Gauntlet and becomes engaged to Gemma Ripley." Tatsuo's eyes glittered with a cold, harsh light, and icy animosity surged off him, making me shiver. "Ryusama will *never* ally itself with anyone—or any kingdom—who marries a Morricone."

Sick understanding pooled in my stomach. My family wasn't the only one who had been targeted by the Morricones over the years. Xenia had told me about several plots King Maximus had ordered Maeven and the rest of the Bastard Brigade to enact against the Yamatos, some of which had resulted in the deaths of Ruri's siblings and cousins—people that Tatsuo was also related to. So I could understand the Yamatos' ire toward the Morricones, especially Maeven, even if it could potentially doom my kingdom.

"Once the Summit ends, so does your mission," Tatsuo continued. "You will leave the Andvarians and Mortans to their incessant squabbling and return to Ryusama. With any luck, the Ripleys and the Morricones will destroy each other, and Ruri can swoop in and finally establish a foothold on the continent proper. Be a spy if you must, but you will do so at home."

"Are those the queen's orders or yours?" Reiko asked in a snide voice.

Tatsuo shrugged again. "Consider them one and the same."

Reiko's jaw clenched, and she gave her father a short, sharp bow before snapping upright. Tatsuo eyed her, as if he wasn't sure whether she was mocking him, but he stalked away and disappeared into the shadows.

Instead of following the lord, Kai stepped forward. The lantern light bathed him in a soft glow, bringing out his golden eyes, along with the pleasing angles of his face and the broad swath of his muscled shoulders.

"Your father is only trying to do what he thinks is best for Ryusama, and you too," Kai said.

Reiko snorted. "Tatsuo wants me to bow down to his will, like my sisters have always done. And for the record, I have no interest in your opinion on my relationship with my father."

She started to walk around him, but he slid forward, blocking her path. Reiko clenched her fists and held her ground as the gladiator-turned-guard loomed over her. Kai's expression was neutral, although the red dragon on his neck peered down at the green one on Reiko's hand with obvious longing.

"Your new life suits you," Kai said. "Your father is a fool if he can't see that."

Reiko huffed. "Well, your new life doesn't suit you at all. What are you doing here? I thought you would still be touring through Ryusama with the rest of the Crimson Dragons and celebrating your victory in the Tournament of Champions."

"I go where my queen commands, the same as you."

Kai's face remained calm, but heat sparked in his eyes as he stared down at Reiko, and her body inched toward his, as though she were irresistibly drawn to his warmth, despite her best intentions.

"Well, my queen has given me orders," Reiko muttered.

"And will you obey them?" Kai asked, a curious tone in his voice.

"What choice do I have?"

"There is always a choice."

Reiko rolled her eyes. "Yes, and I always make the wrong one, especially when it comes to *you*."

Kai stepped even closer to her. "Or maybe we were both just too stubborn to admit it was the *right* choice. It certainly felt right to me."

A blush stained Reiko's cheeks, but she shook her head. "That night at the Regalia ball was a mistake. One that I won't be repeating."

"What about if I want to repeat it?" he asked in a low, husky voice.

Reiko's eyes widened in surprise, although she quickly schooled her expression into a blank mask. "As I said before, I have orders from my queen. You should go follow yours, whatever they are."

She moved past him and stormed into the shadows. Kai watched her go, a hungry expression filling his face.

"Until we meet again, my spy," he whispered. Then he too vanished into the shadows.

I waited the better part of a minute before easing out of my hiding spot and continuing through the gardens. I wasn't really thinking about where I was going, but my steps led me to a silver bench in a large open space on the topmost terrace. This bench was identical to the one I'd visited in the Edelstein Gardens back in Glitnir, right down to the silver plaque that bore my mother's name.

I sat down on the bench and rubbed my fingers over the plaque, wishing I could summon my mother like a genie out of a bottle. Merilde Ripley had been a master of diplomacy, often able to solve problems with a few kind words and soft smiles. She would have known what to do, how to best navigate the tricky situations and opposing forces brewing around me.

But my mother was gone, and it was up to me. I might sometimes despise being a princess, but tonight, being a spy was even worse, especially knowing that Reiko had orders to betray me—

Something brushed up against my fingers, and I glanced down to find a liladorn vine snaking through the bench slats and stroking my hand, as if it was trying to comfort me.

I peered around the back of the bench, which was completely covered with liladorn, far more strands than I had seen in the Edelstein Gardens. Before I had gone to Myrkvior, I had never encountered the plant, but now it was everywhere I went. These vines were twisted and tangled together, just like my emotions and loyalties were hopelessly twisted and tangled up inside me.

Maeven wanted me to marry Leonidas, even if it meant risking her son's life. Tatsuo wanted Reiko to use our friendship to undercut my relationship with the prince. Ruri planned to ignore Ryusama's treaty with Andvari. Milo was using Corvina's money to further his plot against Andvari. My list of problems went on and on, much like the liladorn vines kept curling around and around one another.

Going to scratch me again? I asked the vine.

Only if you ask us to.

And now the plant had a personality, one that dished out dry, sardonic humor. Terrific. Just bloody terrific.

I pulled my hand away from the vine and got to my feet. A flicker of light caught my eye, and I glanced up.

Maeven was standing on a balcony in the Mortan wing, watching me. Her gaze dropped to the bench, and her lips puckered, as though something about it greatly displeased her.

Anger shot through me. She was the cause of so many of my current problems, along with so much of my past misery and heartache. Maybe Tatsuo was right about one thing. Maybe Milo's deposing his mother *would* be for the best. Eliminating Maeven would at least solve the problem of Leonidas risking his life in the Gauntlet. But then the prince would be in even more danger from Milo, as would Delmira.

My anger cooled, replaced by a crushing wave of weariness. There were no solutions here, only more problems.

Maeven kept watching me, but I ignored her as I stalked through the gardens, leaving the Morricone queen and her twisted, tangled machinations behind, at least for the rest of this night.

CHAPTER FIFTEEN

I made it back to my chambers without anyone seeing me. Grimley was stretched out in front of the fireplace, and he cracked his eyes open as I trudged past him.

"Want to talk about it?" he rumbled.

"No."

"Suit yourself." He rolled over to face the flames, then shut his eyes and went to sleep.

I took a hot bath, rubbed some healing cucumber-ginger ointment on my various bumps and bruises, and went to bed. Despite everything that had happened, my sleep was blank and black until a knock on the door woke me the next morning.

Yaleen, my thread master, bustled into my chambers, along with several servants. Grimley grumbled about their disturbing his nap, so I opened one of the balcony doors so he could go hunting with the other gargoyles while I was prepared for the luncheon.

Yaleen wanted me to wear a gown, but I opted for plain black leggings and boots, although I did don a gray tunic with the Ripley gargoyle crest stitched over my heart in black thread. Tiny black-thread gargoyles also adorned the sleeves and circled my neck, as though the creatures were flying all around me. I also threw a dark gray cloak around my shoulders and slid my dagger into the scabbard belted to my waist.

Given all the dangerous, competing agendas at the Summit, I wanted a weapon and clothes I could fight in if—or more likely when—I was attacked again. Besides, the luncheon couldn't last all afternoon, and I still needed to find the island where Milo was conducting his experiments.

Yaleen pronounced me fit for the luncheon, and she and the servants left. I was perched in a chair at the vanity table in the sitting room, dabbing some almond powder onto my nose, when Reiko opened the door that connected our chambers and strolled inside.

She was dressed in a green tunic, along with black leggings, boots, and a cloak, and a sword and dagger dangled from her black leather belt. Her inner dragon had migrated from her right hand up to the side of her neck, and little puffs of black smoke escaped its lips, as though it were angry or upset about something.

Should I try to read their thoughts? *No*, I decided. I wouldn't betray our friendship. Not like that. Guilt already gnawed at my heart about how I'd eavesdropped on her, Tatsuo, and Kai last night, even if the conversation had been most enlightening.

"Are you ready to be wooed by your beloved?" Reiko asked, sprawling in a nearby settee.

I huffed. "Please. There is no wooing in something called *the Gauntlet*. Probably only pain, suffering, misery, and death."

"Perhaps it's like the Pureheart tradition in Bellona, where someone climbs up the cliffs at Seven Spire palace in order to be with their true love. Like your uncle Lucas Sullivan did all those years ago with Everleigh Blair. Even now, people still talk about that. It's one of the great love stories of our time."

The wistfulness in her voice surprised me. "I wouldn't think a spy such as yourself would care much for love stories."

A blush tinged her cheeks, and her inner dragon dropped its eyes in embarrassment. "I might have a soft spot for a grand love story."

"Really? And is there a grand love story in *your* past?"

Kai certainly thought so, given how he'd looked at her in the gardens last night, although I couldn't mention that without revealing my eavesdropping.

Reiko clutched a hand to her heart and let out an overly loud and dramatic sigh, like a noble lady about to swoon. "Sadly, no. So far, I've had to make do with watching others' tales unfold. That's why I'm so interested to see what Prince Leo does in the first challenge."

She paused and wet her lips. "Speaking of the prince, how did your meeting go with him last night?"

Undercut whatever relationship is brewing between Gemma Ripley and Leonidas Morricone. Tatsuo's voice snaked through my mind.

Did Reiko want to know what had happened because she was my friend? Or because Tatsuo had ordered her to find out?

"Gemma? Is something wrong?" Reiko's question penetrated my worry.

I hesitated, but I told her the truth. "Yes, something is very wrong. Leonidas refused to drop out of the Gauntlet. He claims he has to go through with it for the honor and glory of his queen and kingdom and all the other usual nonsense."

Reiko's eyes narrowed. "Anything else?"

"He kissed me."

Her eyes widened, then narrowed again. "And?"

"And I kissed him back."

"How was it?"

I sighed. "Magnificent."

I told her everything that had happened last night, from my eavesdropping on Maeven and Delmira and then on Milo and Corvina, to meeting Leonidas in the gardens, and Wexel's attack. The only thing I didn't fully describe was just how passionate my encounter with the prince had been. Even now, the heat of his lips and tongue still lingered against mine, and my body ached to finish what we'd started.

"Perhaps I should take your advice after all," I mused.

"What advice?"

"To fuck him."

Reiko blinked, although she quickly wiped the surprise off her face. She hesitated before speaking again. "Perhaps that wasn't the best advice."

"What do you mean?" I slid the tin of almond powder into a drawer, even as I covertly watched her in the mirror.

Reiko wet her lips again, and her inner dragon winced. "I suggested that before Maeven enacted the Gauntlet. Having any kind of dalliance with Prince Leo now will only make things . . . more complicated."

My heart sank. There were so few people I could truly trust, and I'd thought Reiko was one of them, especially given all the times we'd saved each other's lives over the past few weeks. But she seemed to be following her father's orders after all, something that saddened me more than I'd thought possible.

Once again, I'd fallen into the royal trap of thinking feelings would trump duty, and I had no one to blame but myself. Reiko had always made it crystal clear that she was a spy first and foremost, that she reported to Queen Ruri and would do whatever it took to protect Ryusama from the Mortans. Our friendship had been a happy accident more than anything else.

Perhaps I should play my own long game with Reiko, feed her lies and misinformation to pass on to Tatsuo, Kai, and Ruri while I tried to figure out a way to get the Ryusamans to honor the treaty they'd made with Andvari.

No. I held firm to my previous decision. I wasn't willing to cross that line—not with my friend. And Reiko *was* still my friend, despite our divided, conflicting loyalties.

So I gave her an honest answer. "I might fuck Leonidas, and I might not. But you're right. No matter what I do, things will undoubtedly get more complicated."

Reiko's gaze met mine in the mirror. "Such is the life of a royal."

Her observation further soured my mood, and I slammed the vanity-table drawer shut with far more force than was necessary.

"Let's get on with things," I said, failing to keep the bitterness out of my voice. "We wouldn't want to keep the masses waiting to see how the epic love story of Gemma Ripley and Leonidas Morricone will play out."

Reiko and I left the tower and went to the main Andvarian courtyard, where Father and Rhea were waiting, along with several guards.

I drew Father and Rhea aside and told them everything I'd seen and overheard in the Mortan wing last night. I also mentioned Wexel's attack and my meeting with Leonidas, although I didn't say anything about the more amorous aspects of our encounter.

I also didn't say anything about eavesdropping on Reiko, Tatsuo, and Kai. I couldn't, not with Reiko standing here with us. But even more than that, part of me didn't *want* to reveal she was working against us. Father might insist that she leave immediately, or worse, have her tossed in the dungeon as a political prisoner to be traded back to Ryusama. I selfishly didn't want to lose my friend, even if she was using me to further Tatsuo's agenda.

Father grimaced. "You know I will never be happy about you putting yourself in danger, Gemma."

"But?"

"But good job," he replied. "Now that we know Milo is conducting his experiments on an island, we can start discreetly searching the lake for the one he's using."

Rhea nodded. "I'll also post more guards along the lakeshore, just in case Milo is thinking about bringing in extra men by boat to cause trouble."

"And I'll see if Tatsuo has learned anything useful about Milo," Reiko added.

My heart twisted at her words, but I remained silent about her betrayal.

We made a few other plans, then left the courtyard. The plaza marketplace was in full swing, with merchants loudly, aggressively hawking their wares, but instead of stopping and shopping, most folks were heading toward the arena.

No one wanted to miss the first Gauntlet challenge.

Our entourage was among the last to arrive. The four raised daises and tables representing Andvari, Unger, Ryusama, and Morta were still sitting in their semicircle positions from last night, but a fifth, much smaller table with a single chair had been added in the center of the arena floor.

At the sight of me, an expectant hush fell over the crowd, and the people on the upper levels pressed against the balconies and stood on their tiptoes, trying to get the best view possible. I kept my face blank, but my gargoyle pendant heated up at all the silent thoughts flying through the air.

Father climbed the dais to the Andvarian table. Rhea and I followed him, while the guards spread out on the floor behind us. Reiko vanished into the crowd milling around outside the arena wall.

When everyone was seated, Xenia rose to her feet at the Ungerian table.

"We are gathered here for the first of three Gauntlet challenges." Her voice boomed through the arena. "Princess Gemma, please take your seat at the center table."

So I was to be put on display like a prize milk cow at a country fair. Marvelous. But Xenia's stern, unwavering stare indicated that I had no choice, so I stood up, trudged down the dais steps, and took my seat at the empty table.

Father and Rhea gave me encouraging smiles and nods. I returned the gestures, then looked over at the Ungerian table. Xenia's expression was still stern, although Zariza winked at me, as did the ogre on her neck.

Over at the Ryusaman table, Ruri was relaxing back in her chair, a neutral expression on her face and a wine goblet in her hand. Tatsuo's face was also neutral, although wisps of smoke floated out of his inner dragon's mouth and skated across his skin, betraying his simmering ire. Kai was lurking behind Tatsuo on the dais.

I glanced up at the second-floor balcony. Reiko was sitting directly behind her father again. She smiled and nodded, as though everything was fine, but my heart twinged at the thought of her betraying me and then returning to Ryusama.

Finally, I focused on the Mortan table. Delmira also gave me an encouraging smile, while Milo sneered at me before taking another swig of his wine. Corvina studied me with a thoughtful expression, not nearly as hostile as she had been before dinner last night. Wexel was standing off to the side of the dais, talking to a guard.

And then there was Maeven, sitting in the center of the Mortan table like a spider perched in the middle of its web. I ignored her smug look, although I couldn't quite shove her sly satisfaction out of my heart. Maeven thought she had me exactly where she wanted me.

I was worried she was right.

"The first Gauntlet challenge is a mental task," Xenia said. "The challenger is required to present three gifts that speak to his intended's body, mind, and heart."

Xenia stabbed her cane against the dais three times, and I had to grit my teeth to keep from flinching at the ominous *thumps*.

Footsteps rasped against the flagstones, and Leonidas strode through one of the gates set into the arena wall and stopped in the open space between the Ryusaman and Mortan daises. He was once again wearing his black cloak, and the amethyst buttons marching down his black riding coat matched the gleam of his purple eyes. A ray of sunlight streaming in through the glass ceiling added a golden sheen to his black hair, and he once again looked like a shadow knight—a dark, handsome, unstoppable force.

Several appreciative murmurs rippled through the crowd, from women and men alike. My traitorous heart quickened, and memories flooded my mind. My lips seeking out his time and time again. My fingers gliding through his hair. My body rocking against his.

Leonidas stared at me, his face impassive, although heat shimmered in his eyes, as though he too was remembering our interlude last night.

He gestured, and three servants also stepped through the open gate. Two of the servants were holding covered silver platters, while the third was clutching a box covered with a purple cloth.

Leonidas strode forward, with the servants trailing along behind him. The prince stopped and bowed to Xenia and Zariza, along with Father, Ruri, and Maeven. Then he stepped in front of my table. His face remained blank, but his right eye twitched in a quick wink.

I had to press my lips together to hold back an answering smile. *Your arrogance is not appealing.*

It's confidence, not arrogance.

I arched an eyebrow. *You think you know me well enough to give me three gifts?*

Yes.

His simple, quiet declaration unnerved me far more than some smug retort would have.

"Prince Leonidas," Xenia called out. "Present your first gift."

He gestured, and the first servant placed a silver platter on the table in front of me. All around the arena, audible *creaks* rang out as people leaned forward in their seats, straining to see what the gift was. The servant placed her hand on the cover and looked over at Leonidas. He waited several seconds, drawing out the moment, before nodding. The servant removed the cover, revealing . . .

"A toasted cheese-and-jam sandwich," Leonidas called out. "Princess Gemma's favorite. A gift of food to delight her tongue and fill her belly on this chilly autumn day. I prepared it myself."

I blinked in surprise. Not what I was expecting. Not at all. But he was right—it *was* my favorite, something I'd told him in my cottage in Blauberg, after I'd healed the stab wound that Wexel had inflicted on him. Odd, that Leonidas would remember something so small and trivial.

Equal parts appreciation, amusement, and derision rippled through the crowd. A few chuckles sounded, but they were drowned out by several disappointed huffs, as loud and raspy as air leaking out of a child's balloon. Most people had probably expected Leonidas to shower me with jewels, even though And-vari was far richer than Morta, and I already had enough jewels to last three lifetimes.

The crowd quieted, and everyone stared at me. It took me several seconds to realize they all actually wanted me to *eat* the bloody sandwich. An exasperated sigh escaped my lips, and Leonidas grinned, knowing he'd won this round.

Determination settled over me. Two could play his confidence game. So I grabbed one of the triangles, held it up, and critically examined it from all sides, as though it were an expensive bracelet I was thinking about buying. A few more chuckles sounded, many of them coming from Zariza.

Leonidas's eyes narrowed. *Now you're just being contrary.*

When it comes to you? Absolutely.

I gave him a sweet smile, then sank my teeth into the sandwich. Golden toasted bread. Warm melted gruyère cheese. Sweet, tangy apricot jam. I wanted to moan at how good it was, but instead, I chewed slowly, as though I were thoroughly analyzing and critiquing every little thing about the sandwich.

"Well, Princess Gemma?" Xenia asked. "Is the gift to your satisfaction?"

I popped the last bite into my mouth and once again took my time chewing and swallowing. "It's perfect," I admitted in a grudging voice.

The crowd broke out into polite applause. The servant stepped forward to remove the tray, but I held out my hand, stopping her.

"Since Prince Leonidas has gone to such great lengths to prepare such a fine, elaborate meal, I should enjoy the fruits of his labor, don't you think?"

I reached out, grabbed another triangle, and sank my teeth into it. Laughter rippled through the arena. The Gauntlet might ostensibly be a challenge for Leonidas, but it was one for me too. Being sour and reluctant would not endear me to anyone, especially the other royals, but charming was another matter. I might have to adhere to the rules of the Gauntlet, but that didn't mean I couldn't put my own stamp on the challenges. Maeven might have manipulated me into this, but I needed to show her and everyone else that I wasn't just going to roll over and let my future be dictated by the Morricone queen.

Leonidas waited until the laughter subsided, and I had finished another piece of the sandwich, before he spoke again. "And now my second gift, one to delight Princess Gemma's mind and other senses and bring beauty to her day."

The second servant stepped forward and placed his silver platter on the table. Once again, silence and expectation dropped over the arena. At Leonidas's signal, the servant removed the cover to reveal . . .

"Ice violets," Leonidas called out.

The small purple wildflowers were tied together with a strand of liladorn, and the thorns on the black vine were all carefully curled inward, like the prongs on a jeweler's design, as though they were protecting the flowers. A simple yet beautiful display.

This time, more pleased murmurs than disappointed huffs rang out. A cheese-and-jam sandwich might be an acquired taste, but everyone could appreciate a pretty bouquet.

I picked up the violets and inhaled deeply. Their soft floral scent tickled my nose, and I also got the faintest whiff of lilac from the liladorn, even though it didn't have any blooms.

I looked up at Leonidas again. *Why ice violets? Most people would have given roses or orchids. Not a common wildflower.*

You told me once to keep giving flowers to Andvarian girls, so I decided to take your advice.

I *had* said that after he had given an ice violet to a little girl who'd run across him in Blauberg, a girl that he had decided to spare instead of kill. *I didn't think you remembered that.*

The corners of his lips curved into a rueful smile. *I remember everything about you, Gemma. I always have, and I always will.*

My hands curled even tighter around the bouquet. One of the liladorn thorns pricked my thumb, drawing a drop of blood, but it was a shallow slice compared to the much deeper wounds Leonidas was leaving on my heart. With a sandwich and some wildflowers, he was dangerously close to making me forget about all the obstacles between us.

"Princess Gemma?" Xenia asked. "Is the gift to your satisfaction?"

"Yes." I set the flowers on the platter. "And how very thoughtful of Prince Leonidas to gift me with violets that are the exact same color as his eyes. Why, it's almost like he doesn't want me to forget him whenever we're apart."

I made my voice light and teasing to hide my inner turmoil, and I was rewarded with a few more laughs.

Another round of applause rang out, a little louder and more enthusiastic than before. Leonidas waited until it died down, then gestured for the third servant to step forward.

Unlike the other two, who were much older, this servant was a girl of about thirteen, with gray eyes, rosy skin, and black hair that was piled on top of her head and secured with amethyst-studded pins. Anaka, the servant who'd helped me during my time at Myrkvior.

I gave the girl a genuine smile. She bobbed her head, then put the third and final gift on the table. Instead of another platter, a purple cloth was draped over a tallish box. Anaka removed her hands from the box and scuttled back in line with the other two servants, as though she didn't want to be near whatever was under the cloth any longer than necessary.

I glanced up at Leonidas. *What now? A necklace made of coral vipers to bite and poison me to death? Two gifts and a betrayal does seem to be the Morricone way.*

Yes, it was a snide, bitchy thing to say, but his other two gifts had pleased me far more than I'd expected, and I needed to put some distance between us—even if I had a sneaking suspicion that was already a lost cause.

Leonidas's eyes gleamed with mischief. *What a wonderful motto. Perhaps I can convince Mother to add it to our family crest. But for now, don't worry. I think this will be your favorite gift for many years to come.*

I wondered if he was mocking me, but he seemed more smug than sardonic. Still, his mysterious words intrigued me, and I found myself leaning forward, as eager to see what was under the cloth as everyone else was.

"And finally," Leonidas said, "a gift to warm Princess Gemma's heart."

This time, he stepped forward, took hold of the cloth, and drew it off the box with a grand, elaborate flourish that would have made any gladiator ringmaster proud. I'd been wrong. Instead of a box, the cloth had been hiding a small coldiron cage that contained . . .

A ball of purple fluff.

I frowned, wondering why Leonidas thought a cage full of feathers would warm my heart. Then the ball moved, hopping toward me, and a tiny head poked out between the bars. My eyes widened, and my breath caught in my throat.

It was a baby strix.

The creature was tiny, no larger than a kitten, and its feathers were a light lilac instead of the dark purple of full-grown strixes like Lyra. Its eyes were also a light bright lilac, while its beak, talons, and the tips of its wings were a dusky gray, although they would all blacken and harden as the strix grew older.

I was immediately enchanted with the creature, and I stretched my hand out toward the cage.

Hello. I gently sent the thought to the strix.

The baby's eyes brightened, and it leaned forward and rubbed its head against my fingers.

I desperately wanted to open the cage to see if the strix would come to me, but I was once again painfully aware of everyone's stares, so I dropped my hand and sat back.

Even more mischief danced in Leonidas's eyes. *You told me once that you always wanted to pet a strix.*

Yes, I *had* said that, back when I was severely injured and waiting to die in the Blauberg mine. I shifted in my chair, suddenly uncomfortable. Leonidas Morricone knew far too much about me, especially how to tug on my heartstrings.

"Could anyone resist the appeal of having their very own baby strix?" Leonidas asked, although it was clearly a rhetorical question, since my eagerness had just proven that I couldn't resist it.

More applause rang out, even louder and more enthusiastic than before.

I looked over at the Mortan table again. Delmira was beaming at both Leonidas and me. She had tried to play matchmaker between us at Myrkvior, so Leonidas's thoughtful gifts probably pleased her soft romantic heart to no end. Milo and Corvina were whispering to each other, far more interested in their conversation than in the challenge. Wexel had vanished, as had some of the Mortan guards.

And then there was Maeven. For once, she was smiling wide, as though her son's efforts and my subsequent reactions had greatly amused her. Even more unusual, she actually seemed . . . *happy*. Of course she was. Her scheme was working, and she was one step closer to shackling me to her son.

I pulled my gaze away from Maeven and looked over at my father on the opposite side of the arena. A deep frown creased his face, his arms were crossed over his chest, and he was glancing back and forth between Leonidas and me like he had never seen either one of us before. Rhea was also glancing back and forth between the prince and me, a thoughtful expression on her face.

The applause trailed off, and Xenia stood up again at the Ungerian table.

"Princess Gemma," she called out. "What do you say to this third and final gift?"

"Well, it does warm my heart," I drawled. "Even if the strix's feathers will undoubtedly make me sneeze."

More laughter rang out, but despite my mocking tone, it was clear Leonidas had given me three unusual but wonderful gifts.

Xenia glanced first at Zariza, who nodded. Then she looked over at Ruri. I couldn't tell what the Ryusaman queen was thinking, but beside her, Tatsuo's face was stone-cold, and the gold dragon on his neck was now belching out clouds of thick black smoke, indicating his displeasure. Kai's features appeared neither friendly nor hostile, although his eyes sparkled with amusement. After several long seconds, Ruri also nodded.

"Well done, Prince Leonidas," Xenia said. "You have successfully completed the first Gauntlet challenge."

Cheers erupted all around the arena, along with several encouraging shouts and whistles. Maeven gave me a smug look, while Delmira shot to her feet, leading the hearty applause. My father was also applauding, although it was more of a steady slap of his hands together, rather than any real approval.

Leonidas bowed to Xenia and Zariza, and then to Ruri, before repeating the gesture with Maeven. Then, he did the same thing to my father, who gave him a Crown Prince Dominic Ripley glower in return. And finally, Leonidas bowed to me. I ignored the gesture and got to my feet.

"As per Ungerian tradition, Prince Leonidas will advance to the second challenge, which will be held tonight in the arena,"

Xenia said. "In the meantime, Prince Leonidas receives a boon for successfully completing the first challenge—he will spend the rest of the afternoon with his intended."

Boon? Xenia hadn't said anything about a bloody boon last night, and Leonidas keeping his head should be reward enough. My surprise vanished, replaced by frustration. I'd been hoping to sneak away from the castle to find the island where Milo was conducting his experiments, not waste the rest of the afternoon preening like a peacock for an unwanted audience.

"Prince Leonidas," Xenia said, "do you have an activity in mind for the afternoon?"

For the first time, he hesitated, as though the boon had surprised him as much as it had me.

"A picnic in the gardens would be lovely," Delmira spoke up. "As Leonidas's second, I'll be happy to make the arrangements—if that is agreeable to everyone?"

Leonidas nodded, and I had no choice but to do the same.

Delmira clapped her hands together. "Excellent! I will come fetch Princess Gemma as soon as everything is ready."

"And so the first part of the Gauntlet is concluded." Xenia thumped her cane against the dais three more times.

Another smattering of applause rang out, and everyone got to their feet and started leaving. The show was over—for now—and the nobles, merchants, and others still had plenty of business to conduct in the plaza marketplace.

I eyed the table, wondering what I should do with my gifts. The two remaining triangles of the cheese-and-jam sandwich had gone cold, so I left them on the platter. I hesitated, then grabbed the bouquet of ice violets. I also took hold of the ring on the top of the coldiron cage and hoisted it up into the air. The baby strix peered at me, curiosity rippling off it.

Everything is okay, I gently whispered the thought. *My name is Gemma. I'm going to take good care of you, and we are going to be wonderful friends.*

Okay, the strix silently chirped back to me, although her voice was so high, tinny, and singsong I couldn't tell if she understood what I was saying or was just echoing my own word.

"Allow me," Leonidas murmured.

He held out his hand, and I passed the cage over to him. Then he offered me his other arm. Once again, I was aware of all the eyes on us. The first challenge might be finished, but he was still playing his part, and I had to do the same. I took his arm, and Leonidas escorted me over to the Andvarian dais.

Father and Rhea had stepped down off the dais, and they watched us approach. Reiko was there too.

Leonidas dropped my arm and bowed to my father again. "Your Highness."

"Leonidas," Father replied in an icy voice.

The prince met my father's glower with a cool expression of his own, then handed the cage to Reiko, who gave the baby strix a wary look.

Leonidas held out his hand to me. People were still watching us with avid interest, so I reluctantly placed my fingers in his.

"Until our picnic, Princess Gemma," Leonidas murmured.

He leaned down and pressed a courtly kiss to my knuckles. That one soft touch reminded me of how his lips and tongue had felt against mine in the gardens last night, and everything inside me clenched tight with renewed desire.

Leonidas straightened, his face still schooled in that impassive mask, but his thumb darted out and stroked across the back of my hand, as though he wanted to touch me just a moment more. I held back a shiver at the innocuous yet intimate touch.

He released my hand and bowed to my father again before

striding away. His black cloak rippled around his tall, muscled body, also reminding me of how delicious it had felt to be pressed up against him last night—and how I yearned to be that close to him again.

Leonidas might have conquered the first Gauntlet challenge, but I'd utterly failed this test. He might have given me three gifts, but he had received far more in return.

With a sandwich, a bouquet, and a baby strix, he had cracked the cold walls I'd erected around my heart, and I wasn't sure how much longer they would stand against his determined onslaught.

CHAPTER SIXTEEN

No one said anything as we returned to the Andvarian wing.

Father and Rhea had trade meetings to attend, so they left Reiko and me in the courtyard. More frustration filled me. Normally, I would have attended those meetings too, but instead, I had to go on a bloody picnic with Leonidas. At times like these, I didn't feel like a princess, a future leader of my people. No, right now, I was a doll set out for others to play with however they saw fit.

With that sour thought in mind, I returned to my chambers, along with Reiko. Grimley was napping in his usual spot in front of the sitting room fireplace, although he yawned and sat up.

A servant had already set out a crystal vase filled with water on one of the tables, and I slid the bouquet into the container. The violets didn't do anything, but to my surprise, the liladorn uncurled itself from around the other flowers and dipped down into the water, as though it were thirsty and wanted a drink. Apparently, being removed from the rest of a vine wasn't enough to kill the plant. Curious—and creepy.

I scooted the vase off to one side of the table, while Reiko placed the coldiron cage on the other side. The baby strix was staring at me with a hopeful expression, so I undid the bolt and opened the cage door.

The baby strix hopped out onto the table. Her eyes widened and darted around, as though she were trying to look at everything at once, from Reiko and me, to the furniture, to the sunlight streaming in through the balcony doors.

Grimley padded over, put his paws up on the table, and peered at the much smaller creature. "What is *that*?"

"One of my gifts from Leonidas."

He sniffed, completely unimpressed. "And you're actually going to keep it?"

The strix ignored his grumpy tone, leaned forward, and stared into the gargoyle's blue eyes. Her little head quirked from side to side in fascination.

Mine, I heard the strix whisper to herself.

The creature hopped forward and fluttered—well, more like fell—to the floor. Grimley stepped back, but the baby strix hurried over and rubbed her head all over his right front paw before wrapping one of her tiny wings around his leg. If she could have, I imagined that the strix would have snaked around the gargoyle like a coral viper curling around a tree branch.

"Gemma? Gemma!" Grimley called out, a note of panic in his voice. "What is it doing?"

"*She* likes you," I replied. "You're warm and hard, and you probably remind her of being safe and snug inside a rookery nest."

Grimley's forehead creased with confusion, but the strix gazed up at him with an adoring expression, as though he were the most wonderful thing she had ever seen. Grimley shuffled back and returned to his previous spot in front of the fireplace.

The strix let out a little squeak of alarm and scuttled over to him. A growl rumbled out of Grimley's throat, but the baby ignored the low warning sound. This time she hopped inside his two front paws, fluffed out her feathers, and settled down. An instant later, the strix's eyes were closed, and soft breathy sounds vibrated out of her chest, as though she was singing a song in her sleep.

"Your gift is presumptuous and annoying," Grimley grumbled, although he made no move to dislodge the creature from between his paws.

"Well, that makes her exactly like Leonidas." I fingered the petals on one of the ice violets, and a thought popped into my mind. "Violet."

"What?" Grimley asked. "What are you mumbling about?"

I gestured at the sleeping strix. "Violet. That will be her name, if she likes it."

Grimley sighed, but he laid his head down and closed his eyes. Soon, he was snoring right alongside Violet.

I kept stroking the petals, thinking about the three Gauntlet gifts. Leonidas was right. He *did* know me well—far too well for my peace of mind. Being attracted to him was one thing. But letting myself actually *care* about him was certain to end in disaster for me, and for my kingdom as well, especially if Queen Ruri decided to ignore Ryusama's treaty to aid Andvari during a Mortan attack.

"Leonidas's gifts were definitely . . . interesting," Reiko said. "Not what I expected from him—or you either."

"What do you mean?"

"Most people, especially a pampered princess like Gemma Ripley, would have been greatly disappointed by a sandwich, some wildflowers, and a strix, but you were quite pleased with his gifts."

"What's your point?"

She shrugged. "No point. Just an observation."

I wondered if Tatsuo had observed the same thing. Probably, given the displeasure that had radiated off him in the arena. I also wondered if Reiko was really going to follow her father's orders to manipulate me. She had a pleasant smile fixed on her face, but tension rolled off her, and her inner dragon was staring down at the floor.

A knock sounded, breaking the awkward silence.

"Enter," I said.

The door opened, and Delmira stepped into my chambers. An Andvarian guard was standing outside in the hallway, his hand on his sword, and a clear question on his face. I shook my head, telling him to stand down. The guard gave me a curt nod and retreated.

Earlier in the arena, Delmira had been wearing a purple gown, but she was now dressed identically to me in a dark gray tunic, along with black leggings and boots, with a dark gray cloak thrown over her shoulders. A small blade was belted to her waist, and she was clutching two boxes in her hands like they were daggers she was going to use to parry an attack.

"Gemma, Reiko." Delmira's face was smooth, her voice strong and confident, but unease rippled off her, and she rubbed her thumbs over the tops of the boxes in a nervous tell.

"Delmira," I replied.

Reiko crossed her arms over her chest and gave the Morricone princess a cold look. Delmira's jaw clenched, and stubbornness flared in her amethyst eyes. In that moment, she looked eerily similar to Maeven, and I realized Delmira Morricone was a force to be reckoned with in her own right.

Delmira turned to me and dropped into a deep curtsy. "First of all, I want to formally apologize for everything that happened at Myrkvior. It was never my intention for any harm to come to you, Gemma."

Sincerity filled her voice, and regret gusted off her in

waves—the same regret I had sensed when she had helped heal me after Milo's brutal torture. Once again, my heart softened. I might have to guard myself against Leonidas, but I didn't want to do the same to Delmira, especially when I'd seen how difficult and lonely her life was with Maeven as a mother and Milo as a brother.

"Thank you. I accept your apology."

Delmira nodded and faced Reiko. "I also never meant for any harm to come to you, Reiko."

The dragon morph snorted, but she didn't outright reject the apology.

"I brought you both a gift." Delmira held out the boxes.

Reiko and I each took a box and opened the lid. To my surprise, each box contained a black dagger resting in purple velvet. I plucked out my dagger and studied it. The blade was small, thin, and lightweight, but still razor-sharp. It also matched the weapon on Delmira's belt.

"Liladorn daggers," Delmira said. "I made them myself."

"Not bad, princess." Reiko admired her own blade before flipping it end over end in her hand. "Not bad at all."

"It's wonderful," I added. "But how did you shape the liladorn into a weapon? From everything I've read, it's extremely hard to cut, much less craft like this."

A pleased blush tinted Delmira's cheeks, and she gave a modest shrug. "Working with the liladorn has always come easily to me. Probably because we have so much of it at Myrkvior. I make all kinds of things with it. Daggers, ribbons, baskets."

I thought of how the vines in the Mortan wing had trembled with her wrath last night. Delmira seemed to have the same sort of connection to the vines as I did to Grimley, and Leonidas did to Lyra. Curious.

Delmira gave us a bright smile. "Now, if you'll come with me, I've arranged our picnic."

She turned to leave, but then she caught sight of Grimley stretched out in front of the fireplace. Delmira's eyes lit up much the same way the baby strix's had earlier. "A gargoyle!" she squealed.

Grimley's ears twitched, and he opened his eyes and raised his head. "A gargoyle whose naps keep getting interrupted."

Instead of being intimidated by his grumpy tone, Delmira crouched down beside Grimley. The baby strix remained asleep, still nestled in between his paws.

"You must be Grimley," Delmira replied. "Lyra has told me all about you."

She held out her hand, which Grimley eyed like it was a scorpion about to sting him.

Be nice, I told him. *She just wants to be friends.*

Grimley's answering sigh sounded in my mind, but he held out a paw to shake with Delmira, who also scratched his head, right in between his two horns, just how he liked.

Grimley's tail *thump-thump-thumped* against the rug in happiness, and he licked her hand. Delmira laughed and scratched his head again.

I rolled my eyes. *How easily your loyalty is bought.*

When it comes to head scratches? Absolutely.

Grimley grinned at me, licked Delmira's hand again, and returned to his nap.

Delmira gave the gargoyle a wistful look, then rose to her feet. "Come. Leonidas is waiting."

She strode through the open door. Reiko followed her, still flipping her liladorn dagger end over end in her hand.

I slid my own liladorn dagger into a slot on my weapons belt. Then I reached out and rubbed one of the ice-violet petals between my fingertips again, wishing I could just enjoy Leonidas's gifts without invoking any of the consequences that came along with them. But consequences were a way of life for Princess Gemma, so I sighed, dropped my hand from the flower, and trudged after Delmira and Reiko.

I asked a servant to bring Violet some water, along with toasted sunflower and pumpkin seeds to eat, then caught up with Reiko and Delmira. The three of us left the Andvarian wing, wound our way through the busy marketplace, and stopped at the top of the steps that led down to the gardens. Anaka, the servant girl from the arena, was waiting there with an enormous black picnic basket made of liladorn, just like the dagger Delmira had given me.

Anaka handed the basket to Delmira, then grinned at me. "It's good to see you again, Your Highness."

"You too, Anaka. I especially like the amethyst pins in your hair."

I winked, and she giggled and raised her hand to one of the pins, which I'd given her back at Myrkvior. Anaka bobbed her head at Delmira and ran off toward the Mortan wing.

Delmira hoisted the basket a little higher in her arms and headed down the steps. Reiko and I followed her.

Normally during the Summit, the gardens would be empty, except for a few folks taking a break from the bustling marketplace. But this afternoon, throngs of people were milling about, despite the chilly wind blowing off the lake. Of course they were. Everyone wanted to see this supposedly grand love story play out, if only so they could share the gossip with their friends.

My gargoyle pendant heated up against my chest, but it couldn't hold back all the thoughts zipping through the air like the bees buzzing over the flowerbeds.

Wonder what Princess Gemma really thinks of Leonidas . . .

Surely she won't actually marry him, no matter what happens during the Gauntlet . . .

I would never marry a bastard, even if he was a prince . . .

Anger filled me at that last thought, but I gritted my teeth and walked on.

Nobles and merchants weren't the only ones in the gardens. Zariza was sitting on an enormous blanket spread out on the ground, gesturing with a goblet at the people gathered around her. Xenia was perched in a nearby chair, clutching her own goblet. She nodded at me as we passed by the Ungers.

What are you plotting now? I sent the thought to her.

Xenia raised her goblet to her lips, but not before I saw her grin. *Pursuing a hunch.*

Well, that was decidedly cryptic. Then again, Xenia always had her own games in motion.

Delmira, Reiko, and I walked down the steps to the next terrace, where Ruri was ensconced in a cushioned chair behind a table, nibbling on grapes, cheeses, and other treats. Tatsuo was murmuring into her ear, with Kai standing guard nearby. Ruri seemed to be relaxing and taking in the sunshine, but her eyes narrowed when she caught sight of me.

I nodded to the Ryusaman queen, who tilted her head in return. Tatsuo did not acknowledge me, although he stared at Reiko. My friend's face remained blank, but worry rippled off her.

Engage the enemy, and you will dictate their actions, Xenia's voice whispered in my mind. *Wait for them to make the first move, and you will be snared in their trap.*

The ogre morph had told me that more than once over the years, and now was the perfect time to test her theory.

"Let's go say a proper hello to Queen Ruri," I told Reiko and Delmira. "I haven't seen nearly enough of her at the Summit so far."

"Do you really think that's a good idea?" Reiko asked, her voice a bit strained.

"Oh, I think it's an *excellent* idea."

"But the picnic—" Delmira began, but I cut her off.

"Will be just as delicious if we dig into it ten minutes later."

Delmira muttered something under her breath that sounded a lot like *stubborn Ripley princess ruining my plans*, but she followed Reiko and me over to the Ryusamans' table.

I curtsied. Delmira mimicked the motion, while Reiko bowed.

"Queen Ruri, so lovely to see you again," I said. "How are you enjoying the day?"

"The weather has been quite agreeable for this time of year," Ruri replied, her voice just as polite and smooth as mine was. "The events of the Summit less so."

"Mmm, yes. Some unexpected developments have occurred."

Ruri arched an eyebrow, but I stared right back at her, showing none of my worry and concern.

"Lord Tatsuo, so lovely to see you again as well," I said. "Reiko has told me quite a lot about you."

His gaze flicked over to his daughter, who was standing stiff and tall, as though her body had suddenly been turned to stone just by the force of her father's look.

"Has she?" Tatsuo replied. "My daughter doesn't usually sing my praises."

"Neither does my father sing mine," Reiko muttered, her voice brimming with bitterness.

Even though he was seated, Tatsuo still managed to peer down his nose at her. "Just because we both know you are wasting your time and especially your talents, trotting from kingdom to kingdom and chasing rumors."

An angry flush stained Reiko's cheeks, and hurt surged off her, as sharp as a sword stabbing into my own heart.

I opened my mouth to defend her, but Reiko discreetly waggled her fingers in a clear *no* gesture, and her inner dragon gave me a sad, resigned look.

Tatsuo swung his attention back to me. "As for you, Princess Gemma, I would think you would be most upset by the *unexpected developments* of the Summit. Especially Maeven Morricone's attempt to force you to marry her son." His eyes narrowed. "Unless you are not opposed to the idea. You and Prince Leonidas *did* seem rather friendly in the arena earlier."

And just like in the arena, everyone focused on me, although different emotions radiated off them all. Accusing Tatsuo. Watchful Ruri. Neutral Kai. Frustrated Reiko. Wary Delmira. As for my own emotions—well, I hadn't quite sorted those out, so I aimed for some common ground.

"Maeven Morricone delights in playing games," I replied. "So I will let her little game play out."

"But surely you won't actually marry Leonidas," Tatsuo continued. "Especially since Ryusama would deeply frown on such a union."

His words and tone were a bit softer and more polite than what he'd used with Reiko in the gardens last night, but his meaning of implied consequences was still razor-sharp. My gaze zoomed over to Ruri, but the queen's face was as blank and serene as the clouds drifting through the sky. I couldn't tell if she supported Tatsuo's harsh sentiments or just wanted to see how I would react to them.

"No matter what Ryusama frowns on, the rules of the Gauntlet are quite clear," Delmira chimed in, a bite in her voice. "If Leonidas successfully completes all three challenges, then he and Gemma *will* be engaged."

Tatsuo turned his cold gaze to the Morricone princess. Delmira's fingers tightened around her picnic basket, but she stared right back at him.

Tatsuo waved his hand, dismissing her words. "The Gauntlet is an old, outdated tradition. Even the Ungers rarely use it anymore. Prince Dominic *never* should have allowed it to proceed. Such things would *not* be tolerated in Ryusama."

Anger roared through me at the implication that my father was weak or somehow at fault for Maeven's machinations, and I finally let loose with some of the retorts I'd been holding back through all of Tatsuo's barbed insults.

"So you would have me break an Ungerian tradition, which in turn means ignoring the rules that we are all bound by under the Summit charter." I arched an eyebrow at him. "Tell me, Lord Tatsuo. Where is the *honor* in that?"

Tatsuo's nostrils flared with anger, and smoke boiled out of the mouth of his inner dragon. Delmira sucked in a breath, while Reiko stiffened again. Ruri regarded me with narrowed eyes, but Kai's mouth twitched, as though he were trying to hold back a smile, and the red dragon on his neck winked at me.

"Come," I told Delmira and Reiko. "We shouldn't keep Leonidas waiting. Suddenly, I'm very much looking forward to our picnic."

I curtsied to Ruri again and tilted my head to Kai. I stared down Tatsuo for a few seconds, then strode away from the table. Reiko and Delmira murmured their goodbyes to Queen Ruri and hurried to catch up to me.

"That was *amazing*," Delmira said, a reverent tone in her voice.

I grinned. "My tongue often gets me in trouble, but this time it was worth it."

Reiko shook her head. "You might be happy now, but Tatsuo

will find some way to make you regret your words. The only thing he hates more than being disobeyed is being embarrassed, especially in front of the queen."

Delmira placed a hand on the dragon morph's shoulder. "I'm sorry you and your father don't get along."

Reiko shook off her hand. "It's no concern of yours," she said in a cold, clipped voice.

"I do have some experience with a difficult parent. If you ever want to talk about it—"

"I *will not*," Reiko snapped.

Delmira's face remained blank, but hurt flickered off her like a thorn pricking my skin. She spun around and strode away.

I poked Reiko in the shoulder. "There was no need for that. She was just trying to be nice."

"*Nice?*" Reiko snorted. "First, she gives us both liladorn daggers, and now she's offering me a shoulder to cry on. Please. It's all an act, a way to ingratiate herself with us. Maeven knows you like Delmira, and she's using her daughter to play games with you, Gemma. The same way she is with Leonidas."

Just like your father is using you to play games with me. I didn't voice the thought, but Reiko must have seen the displeasure on my face because she snorted again.

"Let's get this farce over with," she muttered and stalked after Delmira.

A long, weary sigh escaped my lips. How had things gone so wrong so quickly? We hadn't been in the gardens fifteen minutes, and it already felt like a lifetime—

A gleam of glass caught my eye, and I looked up.

Maeven was watching me again.

She was on the same balcony as last night and peering down at me with a neutral expression, neither happy nor hostile. She *should* have been happy. Leonidas had made it through the first Gauntlet challenge, I was one step closer to being engaged to her son, and the Ryusamans were not quite openly threatening retribution against Andvari for my following the rules we were all supposed to abide by.

More anger boiled up inside me, and I snapped off a mocking salute to Maeven, as though I were a guard acknowledging a despised captain. The queen's lips puckered in displeasure.

Disgusted, I dropped my gaze and stormed deeper into the gardens. Reiko was right. It was time to get on with the next act in this laughable farce.

CHAPTER SEVENTEEN

I caught up to Reiko and Delmira, and we moved into the Mortan section of the gardens. We passed several more nobles and merchants, but none of them followed us, and we soon left the watchers behind.

"Don't worry," Delmira said. "No one will bother us, especially not the noble ladies who have been chasing after Leo lately."

I eyed the princess, wondering if she was trying to make me jealous by insinuating that her brother had other suitors. If so, she was succeeding.

"Mother ordered that this part of the gardens be closed," Delmira continued.

"How kind of her," I drawled.

Delmira grimaced and kept walking. A few minutes later, she rounded a large, tangled bed of liladorn, and a familiar structure came into view.

The gazebo where I'd met Leonidas last night. Where I'd kissed him like a fool. Where we would have done so much more if we hadn't been interrupted by Wexel and his assassins.

Heat flooded my body, making my cheeks burn, despite the cool air, but I followed Delmira and Reiko into the gazebo. Last night, the interior had been empty, except for the loveseat embedded in the railing, but a table was now positioned inside, along with four chairs. I glanced around. Leonidas had gotten rid of the assassins' bodies, just like he said he would, and no trace of last night's battle remained.

Leonidas was staring out over the rocks below, although he turned at our footsteps. His gaze flicked from Delmira to Reiko before settling on me. The heat in his eyes matched what was still simmering in my body, as though he too was remembering our kisses and caresses last night.

He bowed to Reiko. "Welcome, Lady Reiko. I spotted you in the arena last night and again earlier today, although I believe this is the first time we've formally met."

"Lucky me," Reiko muttered.

Leonidas ignored her less-than-enthusiastic greeting and bowed to me. "Gemma," he said in a husky voice that sent chills sliding down my spine.

"Leonidas."

The four of us stood there, an awkward silence dropping over the gazebo.

"Well," Delmira chirped in a cheery voice, "this food isn't going to eat itself. Let's sit."

Reiko and I took the two chairs on one side of the table, while Delmira and Leonidas slid into the opposite seats. The princess kept up a steady stream of chatter as she set out the food. I admired her determination to pretend like we weren't all at odds.

Fresh fruits, cheeses, spiced nuts, chocolates, sweet cakes. The basket contained an impressive amount of food, and my stomach rumbled. The only thing I'd eaten today had been part of the cheese-and-jam sandwich Leonidas had given me in the arena, so I enthusiastically dug into the spread. Everything was delicious, including the cranberry punch with its refreshing notes of orange.

Leonidas only nibbled on a few pieces of fruit, but Delmira ate just as much as I did, and she polished off one whole wedge of cheese all by herself.

Reiko crossed her arms over her chest. "I can't believe you're eating their food, Gemma. It could be poisoned. Why, this whole Gauntlet nonsense could be another elaborate plot by Maeven to try to assassinate you."

"You do realize that we're sitting right across the table?" Leonidas drawled. "I thought spies were supposed to be more subtle than that."

"Not when it comes to the Morricones," Reiko snapped back at him.

I took another sip of punch. "The food is not poisoned."

Reiko snorted. "You'll think that—right up until you keel over dead."

"Poison is just another form of magic, and I can sense it just like I can sense your magic whenever you morph." I brightened and popped another slice of bloodcrisp apple into my mouth. "Perhaps it would be better if the food *was* poisoned. Keeling over dead would solve a great many of my problems."

"Like having to marry me?" Leonidas chimed in.

I gave him a smile that was all teeth. "For starters."

"Now, now, children," Delmira chided. "Play nice."

Leonidas and I both shot her sour looks. Reiko huffed, but she finally deigned to eat some sweet cakes.

I waved another slice of apple around. "See? Not poisoned."

Reiko huffed again, but she kept right on gobbling down the delicious cakes.

All too soon, we finished eating, and another awkward silence descended over the gazebo. Delmira packed the leftover food into the basket, then walked over to the railing.

"Is our company truly that offensive?" Reiko asked in a sarcastic tone.

"Not when you're not accusing us of trying to poison you," Delmira said. "But right now, I'm far more interested in the view."

She stabbed her finger to the left, and Leonidas, Reiko, and I all got up to see what she was pointing at. In addition to the steep, rocky cliff, the gazebo also overlooked the garden terraces, along with the lakeshore.

Milo and Corvina were walking along a stone path by the water, with Wexel and several guards trailing them. Milo gestured with his hands, telling some story, while Corvina idly plucked petals off a bouquet of purple flowers and scattered them on the ground. The crown prince and his entourage followed the path over to one of the docks that stretched out into the lake like a compass needle pointing due north.

Milo marched over to a large sailboat, stepped onto the deck, and took the wheel. Corvina glared at her fiancé's back, but Wexel scurried forward and helped her on board. The guards, who were all carrying large picnic baskets, also hopped onto the vessel.

Corvina shoved the bouquet of flowers at Wexel and raised her hands. Gray magic crackled around her fingertips, and a gust of wind rose up to fill the boat's purple sail. Despite the distance between us, her power made my fingertips tingle in warning. This was the first time I had ever seen Corvina use her magic, and the weather magier was even stronger than I'd expected. She summoned up even more wind, and the boat started skimming across the water.

"Where are they going?" I asked.

"To Antheia, one of the Mortan islands farther out in the lake," Delmira replied. "Ostensibly, Milo and Corvina are having a picnic, the same as us. I overheard the servants gossiping about it when I ordered our own picnic basket."

"But?" I asked.

"But Milo despises picnics. He has ever since I dumped a jar full of ants on his head after he deliberately broke my favorite doll when we were children."

Delmira grinned, and a memory flickered off her—Milo screaming, dancing around, and desperately trying to claw dozens of tiny black ants out of his golden hair.

"Nicely done, princess," Reiko said, a bit of grudging respect in her voice.

Delmira tipped her head, acknowledging the compliment. "This gazebo has the best view of the Mortan dock. I thought Gemma might be interested in learning more about Milo's supposed picnic."

"Absolutely," I murmured.

Grimley. I sent the thought to the gargoyle. *Nap time is over. I need you in the gardens.*

A loud yawn sounded in my mind. *Fine. I'm not getting any sleep anyway, given the fluffball's snoring.*

Even though he couldn't see me, I still grinned. He didn't realize it yet, but Grimley was about a heartbeat away from being as enchanted with Violet as the baby strix was with him.

Now I just needed to find a ride for Reiko.

Fern? I sent the thought out as far and wide as I could, but I didn't sense the gargoyle anywhere nearby. *Fern?*

No response. She must be out hunting in the countryside. Perhaps that was for the best. I still didn't know how much I could trust Reiko, or how whatever we might find on the island would affect our kingdoms—and our friendship.

"Please don't tell me that you're thinking about following them over to that island," Reiko said. "It could be a trap."

"With Milo? It usually is. But this is my best chance to find out more about his experiments and how they relate to the stolen tearstone."

"What experiments?" Leonidas asked in a sharp voice.

"The ones I heard him crowing about to Corvina and Wexel when I was skulking around the Mortan wing last night. Milo mentioned an island, which I assume is Antheia."

"You can't go there by yourself," Delmira protested.

"Don't worry. I won't be going alone."

I stepped out of the gazebo and looked up. Grimley was circling overhead, and I waved my hand, getting his attention. He dove down and landed on the grass. Grimley let out another loud, jaw-cracking yawn that sounded like rocks exploding, then vibrated like a dog slinging water off its coat. When he finished, he looked marginally more awake.

A light, feathery presence tickled my mind, and Lyra dropped to the ground, landing a few feet away from Grimley. The two creatures warily eyed each other.

"What is Lyra doing here?" I asked.

Leonidas gave me one of his smug, infuriating smirks. "I can't let you have all the fun of spying on my brother."

Reiko stepped forward. "I should go with Gemma. Not you."

I couldn't tell if she was being a concerned friend or trying to keep me away from the prince, as per Tatsuo's orders. Or perhaps it was a bit of both.

Leonidas gave Reiko a cool look. "Lyra decides who she takes where and when."

The strix hopped forward. "Leo goes, you stay, dragon," she chirped in her singsong voice.

Reiko glared at the creature, but she didn't argue anymore.

"Excellent," Delmira replied. "Gemma and Leo can go check out the island, while Reiko and I stay here and keep up the illusion of the picnic."

She threw up the hood of her gray cloak, then threaded her arm through Reiko's the way I always did. From a distance, someone might mistake Delmira for me, although her simple disguise wouldn't fool anyone for long.

My eyes narrowed. "You knew I would chase after Milo. That's why you're wearing that cloak."

"Of course. Why else would I be dressed in Andvarian gray? It's a horrible color for me." Delmira grinned, then gestured at Leonidas and me. "If you hurry, you all can fly around to the back side of the island without Milo, Corvina, or Wexel spotting you."

I glanced at Reiko, who gave a reluctant nod.

"Go," she said. "I'll stay here with *Princess Gemma* until you return."

Leonidas was already climbing onto Lyra's back. Neither one of them was going to be left behind, so I had no choice but to mount Grimley and hold on tight as the gargoyle flapped his wings and took off.

As soon as we sailed up into the sky, all the tension drained out of my body, as though the wind was scrubbing my worries away the same way it was sloughing over my face. In an instant, I felt lighter and freer than I had since Leonidas had strode into the arena earlier today. I drew in a deep breath, filling my lungs with the crisp air.

Lyra was flying a few feet away, matching Grimley's steady rhythm. Leonidas was leaning down low on the strix's back, the wind tangling his hair and making his cloak billow out behind him. The prince glanced over at me, a smile on his lips, looking happier and far more relaxed than I had ever seen before.

I love this, don't you? He sent the thought to me.

More than just about anything else.

He shot Grimley an envious look. *You might have always wanted to pet a strix, but I've always wanted to fly on a gargoyle.*

I grinned back at him. *Race you to the island?*

Leonidas's smile widened. *You're on.*

Lyra let out a loud *caw!* She pumped her wings again, then tucked them into her sides and dove down toward the lake. Grimley growled, recognizing the challenge, and followed her.

The strix and the gargoyle skimmed over the surface of the water, so low that cold spray misted over my face. Sheer, exhilarating joy filled me, and I laughed, although the wind tore the sound from my lips and drowned it in the lake.

Lyra and Grimley eyed each other, then pumped their wings even harder and faster. I laughed again and again, and Leonidas's answering chuckles rang in my mind. His joy enveloped me like a warm cloak, mixing and mingling with my own.

After about twenty minutes of flying, with Lyra and Grimley still neck and neck, the Mortan island came into view. From a distance, Antheia looked like any other island in the lake—a gray sandy shore with a rocky incline that led up to dense woods. Milo's sailboat was already tied to a dock.

Follow us, Leonidas said.

Still skimming the surface of the water, Lyra veered to the right, giving the island a wide berth. Grimley followed her. I scanned the shore, but I didn't see any other docks, only more rocks and trees.

Lyra circled around to the opposite side of the island, coasted into a small cove, and landed on a large boulder. Grimley also coasted into the cove, although he plopped down into the water lapping up against the rocks.

"Muddy paws," he grumbled. "I *hate* having muddy paws."

"Then maybe you should have landed more carefully," Lyra chirped from her perch.

Grimley glowered at her. "I can still eat you, feather duster."

Lyra huffed. "You will not be eating me today or any other day, rocks-for-brains."

Grimley's tail lashed back and forth, while Lyra raked her talons across the boulder, making stone chips fly through the air.

"Enough." I slid off Grimley's back and stepped onto a rock rather than into the water. "We're here to spy on Milo, not threaten each other."

"For once, Gemma and I are in complete agreement." Leonidas climbed off Lyra. "We need to work together instead of engaging in insults."

Grimley dropped his tail, while Lyra stopped tearing into the boulder, although the two creatures kept glaring at each other.

"There's a cave in the back of the cove that comes out near the center of the island," Leonidas said. "Milo is most likely to be at the nearby manor house."

I nodded, then looked at Grimley and Lyra. "You two fly around the island and see if you can spot anything interesting."

The creatures flapped their wings and took off, leaving me alone with Leonidas. Now that the thrill of the race had worn off, I realized just how much danger I was in. Not just from Milo, Corvina, Wexel, and however many guards might be on the island, but also from Leonidas. Flying beside him had been far more wonderful than I'd expected, and the emotion hummed in my heart like a happy song.

He held out his hand to me. "The rocks are slippery."

I stared at his fingers, but there was no real reason to protest, so I slid my hand into his. The warmth of his skin against mine made me shiver.

Leonidas stepped from boulder to boulder, leading me deeper into the cove. The rocks gave way to the sandy shore, and he led me over to a black chasm in the cove wall.

"The cave is only wide enough for one person to walk through at a time," Leonidas said, dropping my hand. "Follow me."

I waited until he had turned away, then shook out my hand, trying—and failing—to fling off the sensation of his skin against my own. I let out a frustrated breath and stepped into the cave behind him.

The passageway was quite narrow and climbed steadily upward. I couldn't see anything in the dark, and the only sounds were our raspy breaths and soft footsteps scraping against the stone. I didn't know how long we walked, ten minutes, maybe twenty, but eventually, we stepped out into a small clearing.

Leonidas drew his sword, while I grabbed my dagger. We crossed the clearing and plunged into the trees beyond. Once again, I followed Leonidas, being careful to step exactly where he did, just in case Wexel or someone else had laid trip wires in the woods.

I didn't spot any, but I did see something unusual—nets.

Rope nets dangled from the tree branches like thick spiderwebs. Most of the nets were old and rotten, as though they'd been hanging for years, but I spotted a few newer ones strung up here and there. What was Milo doing—trapping—on this island?

About half a mile later, the woods gave way to a grassy lawn that rolled up the hill to an enormous manor house. Like Caldwell Castle, the house's gray stone facade was quite plain. Only a few carvings of flowers and vines adorned the walls, although silver weathervanes shaped like strixes *creak-creak-creaked* back and forth on the rooftops. The manor house and grounds looked well-maintained, but an emptiness filled the air, as though no one ever stayed here for long.

"Mother used to bring us here every summer when we were young," Leonidas said. "Delmira would pit her dolls and stuffed animals against one another in gladiator tournaments in the garden, while Lyra and I would fly around and explore the island."

"And what would Milo do?" I asked.

"Milo spent a lot of time in the woods."

"Exploring?"

Leonidas's jaw clenched. "Hunting. He would build and set snares for rabbits, squirrels, and the like. Then he would bring the poor creatures back to the house and torture them with sticks, daggers, and more. He called them his *experiments*. Even back then, Milo wanted to be just like Uncle Maximus."

I thought back to the strange nets hanging in the trees. At some point, Milo had moved on to bigger prey. I shuddered.

"This side of the house is too exposed to approach," Leonidas said. "Follow me."

Still keeping to the woods, he led me around to the opposite side of the manor, where a large garden butted up against the trees. Thick strands of liladorn choked most of the vegetation, but several flowerbeds were curiously bare, as though someone had recently removed all the plants and left only the dirt behind.

Leonidas crept over to the house and used his magic to unlock a door. We stepped inside and moved through a long corridor with several rooms branching off it. Gray sheets covered the furniture, giving the tables and chairs odd lifelike shapes in the gloom, as though a family of ghosts had taken up residence and were just waiting to haunt whoever walked by. Cobwebs clustered in the ceiling corners, and a thick layer of dust coated everything.

Despite the grime, I spotted a few signs of life. Dirt and smudged footprints marred the floors, along with blades of grass, as though several people had tromped through the garden and into the manor. I reached out with my magic, but I didn't sense anyone else inside the house. Where were Milo and the others?

"Let's see where the trail leads," Leonidas murmured.

Together, we followed the dirt, footprints, and grass into a large dining room. Several picture windows were set into the wall, allowing the afternoon sunlight to stream inside. Unlike the rest of the house, no sheets covered any of the furniture, and everything gleamed as though it had been recently cleaned.

Several tables were clustered together in the center of the room, while books covered a writing desk in the back corner. I didn't see any of Milo's barbed tearstone arrows, but deep nicks and long scratches gouged all the tabletops, which were also spattered with dull brown stains.

No, not stains—dried blood.

Sick understanding pulsed through me. "This is another one of Milo's workshops."

"Apparently so," Leonidas muttered. "I'm not surprised. He used this room the same way when we were children."

"How so?"

"One day, Milo caught a baby gargoyle in one of his nets and brought it in here. Mother had taken Delmira and me into Caldwell to shop, so we didn't return home until late."

"What happened?"

Leonidas's nostrils flared with disgust. "Milo had the gargoyle tied down to the dining room table, and an assortment of swords, daggers, and tools laid out on another table. He'd spent the whole day trying to figure out how to kill the poor creature. When we found him, Milo was beating the gargoyle with a hammer. He stopped, looked at Mother, and said he wanted to know if the gargoyle's blood was as red as that of all the other animals he'd killed."

Images flickered off Leonidas and filled my mind. Young Milo clutching a gleaming light gray hammer and looming over a baby gargoyle lashed down to a table. Milo grinning and raising the hammer high. The gargoyle growling and desperately trying to break free of the thick ropes. The crown prince smashing the tool down onto one of the gargoyle's horns over and over again until it snapped off with a loud, sickening *crack*—

That long-ago *crack* jolted me out of Leonidas's memories and back into the present. Revulsion roiled in my stomach, and I fought the urge to vomit.

"I rushed forward and shoved Milo away from the gargoyle," Leonidas continued. "Milo was so angry at me for stopping his fun that he hit me with the hammer. He would have killed me with it if Mother hadn't intervened. That was the first time I realized just how much Milo hated me."

"What did Maeven say about Milo's experiment?"

Leonidas shrugged. "Nothing, really. She sent Milo to his room while I helped the servants carry the gargoyle outside and release it. I don't know if the creature lived or not, but Milo was incensed that she'd ruined his experiment. We left Antheia the next day, and Mother never brought us back."

But Milo had come back, and now he was conducting more experiments in his childhood haunt. Determination rose up inside me, overcoming my revulsion, and my hand tightened around my dagger. I'd come here to spy on Milo, but if I got the chance, I would happily kill him. Not just for the threat he posed to my kingdom now, but for all the innocent creatures he'd tortured, just as he had tortured me a few weeks ago.

But for right now, I still needed to figure out what Milo was plotting, so I forced myself to examine everything again. Besides the bloodstains, there was nothing else noteworthy about the tables, so I headed over to the desk covered with books, while Leonidas prowled through the rest of the room.

I flipped through several books, but they were all dry, boring tomes discussing theories about how magic was created, used, absorbed, transferred, and more. Milo had had these same sorts of books in his Myrkvior workshop, and I didn't see any obvious clues in the volumes.

"Find anything?" Leonidas called out.

"Not yet. You?"

"Nothing."

We continued with our respective searches. I had just set another book aside when I felt something odd emanating from the desk.

Magic.

I closed my eyes, reaching out with my own power and trying to find that one invisible thread of energy among the dozens of books on the desk. The magic was faint and felt strangely cold and wet, but I managed to grab that thread with my mind, careful not to grasp it too tightly, lest it crumble away like a damp piece of paper. Then, with my eyes still closed, I leaned down and started sorting through the books.

I wasn't sure how many books I picked up and set aside, or how many minutes passed. All that mattered was tracking that tiny thread of magic back to its source. Milo had come here for a reason, something far more important than muddying up the floors, trapping creatures, and carving them to pieces, and I wanted to know what it was.

"You might have better luck if you opened your eyes and actually looked at those books," Leonidas said in a teasing tone.

"Shhh. I'm concentrating."

"If you say so," he replied. "I'm going to check the other rooms."

I tuned out the sound of his retreating footsteps and concentrated on the cold, wet thread of magic again. The more books I sorted through, the thicker and stronger it became, like I was coming to the anchor on the end of a ship's chain. Still keeping my eyes closed, I reached out and grabbed . . .

Another book.

My eyes popped open, and I studied the slender volume in my hands. The cover was purple, with the title on the spine standing out in silver foil—*A Treatise on Mortan Plants: Their Properties and Uses*.

Well, that sounded vague and boring. Why would Milo be interested in a book about plants? Especially when the rest of the volumes on the table were either about magic or creatures?

Curious, I opened the book, careful not to crack the spine, and leafed through it.

The book was exactly what its title suggested—a treatise filled with long, detailed passages about all sorts of plants, from ice violets to pear trees to amethyst-eye cactuses. I flipped through the pages, although the magic was so faint I couldn't get a sense of what Milo had been looking at. Still, I did find something odd—a jagged shard of stone tucked in between two pages like a ribbon marking where someone had stopped reading.

I plucked out the stone and held it up to the light. It was a simple gray rock, although its edges were jagged and blackened, and it had the same burned-glass look as the stone I'd picked up in the Haverton mine. Strange. I slid the rock into my pocket to study later.

I kept looking through the book, and I found something else odd—a couple of pages near the center had been ripped out.

Anger exploded inside me. Books were precious treasures, and Milo's treating one so cruelly made me want to tear his heart out of his chest, just like he had ripped the pages out of this book.

Leonidas strode back into the dining room. "Find anything?"

I showed him the damage. "Milo was too lazy to take the entire book. He just ripped out the pages he wanted and left it here with all the others."

Leonidas frowned. "Can you tell what was on the missing pages?"

I flipped to the table of contents and ran my finger down the list of entries. "Milo tore out a section about how to grow some rare flowers, although it doesn't mention the exact plants." A thought occurred to me. "Do you think he could be researching poisons?"

Leonidas shrugged. "It wouldn't surprise me. Milo is probably looking for a less obvious way to murder Mother, since his coup at Myrkvior failed a few weeks ago. Poison could potentially help him with that."

An old, familiar worry gnawed at my heart. "Like amethyst-eye poison?"

"Perhaps, but not likely. Mother built up an immunity to that poison years ago, so it wouldn't have any effect on her."

"Why did she do that?"

He shrugged again. "Because Emperia Dumond and several other people tried to kill her with it."

"Just like Maeven and Dahlia Sullivan tried to kill Grandfather Heinrich with it at Glitnir all those years ago."

Leonidas grimaced at my accusing tone, but he didn't shy away from the ugly truth simmering in the air between us. "Yes. Just like that."

And just like that, I was reminded why we could never be anything more than two people who occasionally worked together against our common enemies. There was simply too much bad blood between our families, too many plots and assassination attempts and fucking long games, including the one Maeven was playing right now with the Gauntlet.

Anger boiled up in my chest again, and I snapped the book shut with far more force than was necessary. "There's nothing here. We should go."

Leonidas stared at me, clearly wanting to argue, but he strode out of the dining room.

More anger roiled in my chest, along with a fair amount of disgust. I started to toss the purple book back down onto the desk with all the others, but at the last moment, I changed my mind. Perhaps I could find a copy of it in the Caldwell Castle library and at least figure out what plant—and potential poison—Milo was interested in.

It wasn't much of a clue, but it was the only one I had, so I tucked the book under my arm and left the dining room, once again feeling like Milo was three steps ahead of me.

CHAPTER EIGHTEEN

eonidas and I went back out into the garden.

Grimley? I asked. *Where are you?*

The feather duster and I are hiding in the trees. Milo and the other Mortans are already back on the sailboat. They're leaving the island.

I looked at Leonidas. "Did Lyra tell you about Milo?"

"Yes. Milo has already done whatever he needed to do here. You're right. We should go."

Leonidas headed toward the woods, but a presence tickled my mind, and I glanced back over my shoulder. Otto, the gargoyle with the gray moonstone eyes, was perched on the manor house roof. What was he doing here?

Otto glared down at me, his nostrils flaring wide in anger. His tail lashed from side to side, while his long black talons dug into the tiles like he wanted to rip the roof to pieces, along with the rest of the house. My gaze locked onto his broken left horn, and sick realization shot through me.

He was the baby gargoyle Milo had tortured.

Memories surged off the gargoyle and slammed into my mind. A young Otto flying over the island. Swooping down to chase a rabbit and getting caught in one of those horrid nets. A young Milo grinning wide, snapping his fingers, and ordering some servants to drag a struggling Otto to the manor house, net and all . . .

Screech. Screech-screech. Screech.

Otto's talons dug into the tiles again, and even more anger roared off him than before, scattering the rest of his memories. No wonder he had been so rude to me before at the castle. He probably didn't like humans at all, given his suffering at Milo's hands.

Otto has been barking orders for the last few weeks, trying to tell the other gargoyles where to hunt and steering them away from some of the best islands around the lake, Grimley's voice whispered in my mind.

Otto hadn't been hogging the best hunting grounds. He'd simply been trying to keep the other gargoyles out of Milo's nets so they wouldn't suffer as he had suffered. Sympathy filled me. I stepped in Otto's direction, but before I could send a thought to him, the gargoyle flapped his wings and took off.

"Gemma?" Leonidas called out. "Is something wrong?"

I shook my head. "Let's go. I don't want to stay here any longer than necessary."

Leonidas and I quickly returned to the cove, where Lyra and Grimley were waiting, and the creatures flew us back to Caldwell Castle. The second we landed, Reiko and Delmira rushed out of the gazebo.

"Well?" Reiko demanded. "Did you find anything?"

"Just another one of Milo's horrid workshops," I muttered.

Leonidas looked at Delmira. "He had tables set up in the dining room. There was blood all over them, although he didn't leave any bodies behind, so we couldn't tell if the blood was from animals, creatures, or people."

Delmira's lips curled with disgust. "Knowing Milo? Probably all three."

"We think he might be experimenting with plants," I said. "Maybe even concocting some rare poison to try to assassinate Maeven."

Delmira nodded. "Milo is still pissed that his attempted coup failed so miserably a few weeks ago. He won't stop until either he or Mother is dead."

She shuddered, as if suddenly cold. The princess ducked back into the gazebo to grab her picnic basket, then returned. "I should go check on Mother. Reiko, please escort me."

Delmira clamped her free hand on Reiko's arm and tugged the dragon morph along behind her. Reiko looked over her shoulder at me, but I nodded, telling her to go ahead.

"If my services are no longer needed, I'm going to return to my midafternoon nap," Grimley said.

"Thanks, Grims."

The gargoyle flapped his wings and sailed up into the air.

"Me too," Lyra chirped, then followed him.

That left me standing alone with Leonidas. Rather than look at him, I focused on the gazebo, but it just reminded me of how good it had felt to be in his arms last night.

I cleared the dryness out of my throat. "I should go too."

"Wait." Leonidas threaded his arm through mine, as if to escort me through the gardens.

The whole side of my body tingled where it was pressed up against his, but I rolled my eyes and tugged my arm free. "You don't have to pretend. No one is watching right now."

"Who says I'm pretending?" he drawled.

I drew a little circle in midair with my finger. "Your own smug expression."

Leonidas smirked at me again, although a more thoughtful look quickly filled his face. "This afternoon was . . . nice."

I frowned in confusion. "The picnic?"

"The picnic, flying over to the island, even skulking around

Milo's workshop. It was nice just . . . being with you." He paused. "Without someone trying to kill us."

A genuine laugh bubbled out of my lips. "If no one trying to kill you is your idea of a good time, then yes, this afternoon was *quite* the grand affair."

Leonidas grinned, the warm expression sweeping away the ice that so often coated his features. In this moment, he looked like the boy who had whispered thoughts to me and walked through my dreams for months as though we were true friends. Before I had donned my gargoyle pendant and shut him out. Before I had used the pendant to try to shut out my memories of, and especially my cowardice during, the Seven Spire massacre. Both battles that I was still losing, to this very moment.

"Yes." The word slipped out before I could stop it, and my tongue just kept tripping along. "It was fun. Much more so than I expected."

He arched an eyebrow. "You almost sound disappointed."

"Just waiting for the other sword to fall—and for someone to stab me in the back."

Leonidas shook his head. "I told you weeks ago—I will never lie to you again, Gemma."

"And I told you weeks ago—I don't believe you, and I will never trust you." I shrugged. "So I would say that we are at an impasse."

An insurmountable one. Despite being a royal and knowing there would most likely be a political component to my marriage, I had been holding out some small hope that I would love—or at least respect—the man I wound up marrying. But respect was built on mutual trust, and without that trust, there could be nothing at all. Not respect, and most definitely not love, no matter how strongly I was attracted to Leonidas.

"Were the Gauntlet gifts your idea or someone else's?" Once again, my tongue got me into trouble, and the question popped out before I could stop it.

Hurt flickered across Leonidas's face, as though I should have already known the answer. "The gifts were my idea, although Delmira arranged the flowers and helped me pick out the baby strix. She's good at finding the right creature for the right person. I did make the sandwich myself, though," he said in a lighter tone. "I know how important a proper toasted cheese-and-jam sandwich is to Gemma Ripley."

I smiled a little at his teasing, although my mood turned serious again. "Why those particular gifts?"

"I explained them to you in the arena."

"No, we both put on a show for the crowd. Royal gladiators dueling with words instead of weapons. I want to know why *you* specifically chose *those* gifts for *me*."

Leonidas considered my words. "Because I knew you would like them. And they all . . . reminded me of you, of the time we spent together in Blauberg, when we talked in your cottage and then later down in the mine. Before everything went so dreadfully wrong at Myrkvior. I hoped the gifts might please you, or at least might remind you of happier, simpler times between us."

They had certainly done that, although I would never admit it. That confession was too personal, too heartfelt, and it would make me even more vulnerable to him. Oh, who was I fooling? *Everything* about Leonidas Morricone made me confused and raw and vulnerable, especially the way he was looking at me right now, with heat sparking in his eyes.

"Well, thank you," I said in a stiff tone, trying to put some emotional distance between us. "The gifts were lovely and thoughtful."

I paused, but once again my tongue got the better of me. "Although I doubt Grimley would agree."

Leonidas's eyebrows drew together. "What does your gargoyle have to do with the gifts?"

"Violet, the baby strix, is quite enamored with Grimley. It's like she took one look at him and immediately fell in love."

"That's a feeling I know very well," he murmured.

Suddenly, we weren't talking about the gifts anymore. A hot blush scalded my cheeks, and Leonidas's gaze dropped to my lips, as though he was thinking about kissing me. Everything inside me tensed, aching for him to do just that.

But he didn't reach for me, and I didn't sway toward him either. Slowly, the moment passed, although I still felt as fragile as a piece of glass, one that could shatter at any second.

"Until tonight, Gemma," Leonidas said in a husky voice that did all sorts of unwanted things to my insides.

He bowed to me, then left the gardens, taking another precious piece of my heart along with him.

I should have headed back to the Andvarian wing, but I didn't want to see Father, Rhea, or anyone else. Not when my emotions were still sloshing back and forth and making a thorough mess of me. So I strode past the gazebo, stopped at the edge of the cliff, and stared out over the lake.

The sailboat that Milo, Corvina, and Wexel had taken to the island was tied to the dock again. Corvina must have been an even stronger weather magier than I'd realized to take them to and from the island so swiftly.

The thought further soured my mood, and I dropped my gaze to the jagged boulders below the gazebo. Tiny purple flowers were growing in between the rocks, looking like little splotches of colorful paint on dull gray canvas. Fool's bane, Leonidas had said, named after the Morricone prince who'd jumped to his death rather than be without his love.

Bitterness filled me. How appropriate that I was standing

in this spot. After all, I was a fool too, just as Prince Bane had been.

Still, the longer I stared at the purple flowers, the more familiar they seemed, even though I'd never heard of fool's bane until last night. A thought popped into my mind, overpowering my bitterness. I glanced around, but this section of the gardens was still deserted, so no one saw me drop to the ground, wiggle forward, and carefully step off the side of the cliff onto the closest rock.

The large boulders had plenty of hand- and footholds, so it was easy enough for me to climb down to where the flowers were poking up between the crevasses.

By this point, I was just above the lake, and the waves slapped up against the rocks, throwing spray into the air. Careful of the slippery stones, I sat on one of the boulders, leaned over, and plucked some of the fool's bane.

Each flower had a fuzzy green stem, along with three small purple petals that reminded me of clover. The blossoms looked exactly the same as the dried flower the Mortan boy had had in his pouch in Haverton. That flower was tucked away in my jewelry box in my chambers, along with the burned glasslike rock I'd picked up in the old tearstone mine.

If anyone could make a pretty little purple flower deadly, then it's the Morricones, Alvis's voice whispered through my mind.

No obvious magic emanated from the fool's bane, but it had an odd scent, more rotten fish than sweet pollen. My nose crinkled with disgust, but I tucked the flowers into one of my cloak pockets, right next to the book I'd taken from Milo's island workshop.

Once again, I thought about returning to the castle, but it was peaceful here, so I stared out over the lake instead. Perhaps it was the sparkling gleam of the water or the cool spray tickling my face, but my magic boiled up inside me, much the same way the water was relentlessly *slap-slap-slapping* up against the rocks.

The air around me shimmered, transforming into another place and time. I tried to throttle my magic into submission, but that just made it boil up even quicker and faster. I ground my teeth, but I couldn't move, not without potentially falling on the slippery rocks, and I had no choice but to let my power sweep me away . . .

I blinked. I was still sitting on a rock, but instead of staring out over Caldwell Lake, I was back by that nameless river in the Spire Mountains, watching Farena and her two bandit brothers approach young Gems and Leo.

Gems shot Leo an angry glare. This is all *your fault.*

Even though she was sending the thought to him, I still heard it in my own mind, thanks to my magic.

He narrowed his eyes at her. My fault? This is *your* fault. If you had just listened to me, we could have run into the woods before they ever even saw us. Now they're going to rob and kill us.

Gems's hand tightened around the stick she was still clutching. Give up if you want to, but I am *not* going to be murdered by bandits.

Anger flared in Leo's eyes, making them burn a dark, dangerous purple. Neither am I.

Farena grinned and made an airy gesture with her hand. "Now, if the two of you will be so kind as to empty your pockets, we'll take everything you have and be on our way."

Gems snorted. "Sorry to disappoint, but I don't have anything."

"Me neither," Leo added.

Farena stabbed her sword at him. "That pretty pin says otherwise."

Leo's hand shot up to his neck. A silver pin shaped like a flying strix with amethyst eyes secured his cloak around his shoulders. "My father gave me this," he growled. "You can't have it."

"I wasn't asking, boy." Farena stabbed her sword at him again. "You can either give it to me, or I'll take it off your cold, lifeless body."

Instead of being intimidated, Leo's spine straightened, and his hands clenched into fists.

"Not afraid of me, huh? Perhaps you'll feel differently when I kill your little friend." Farena swung her sword in Gems's direction.

Gems also straightened her spine and lifted her chin in defiance. Farena's eyes narrowed, and she snapped her fingers. Her two brothers brandished their swords and stepped up on either side of her.

"Kill the girl first," Farena ordered. "And make it hurt."

The two male bandits grinned and headed toward Gems—

"Wait!" Leo held his hands up in surrender. "Just wait."

Gems looked at him. *What are you doing?*

Distracting them, he replied, still looking at Farena. *Get ready.*

Leo let out a loud, dramatic sigh. "Fine. You win. Here. Take it."

He unhooked the silver pin, and his purple cloak dropped from his shoulders and landed in a puddle of water. Leo held the pin up where the bandits could see it.

"You want this? Then go get it!"

He reared his arm back and pretended to toss the pin over their heads. All three bandits looked in the direction of Leo's throw, not realizing that he was shoving the pin into a pocket on his leggings.

"Now!" Leo shouted.

He curled his hand into a tight fist and used his magic to yank Farena's sword out of her hand. The bandit's eyes widened in surprise, but she charged at him.

"Kill the girl!" Farena screamed. "I'll take care of the boy!"

My gaze snapped over to Gems, who was still clutching her stick. Even though this had happened years ago, my heart pounded in time with hers, and a strange, exhilarating mix of anger, fear, and magic surged up inside me.

Gems ducked the first bandit's swing, then cracked her stick across the head of the second man. He staggered back and lost his grip on his sword, which clang-clang-clanged off first one rock, then another.

Gems dropped her stick and lunged for the sword, but the first bandit dug his fingers into her hair and yanked her back. Gems yelped, and pain spiked through my own scalp, as though the man was tearing my hair out too.

"Farena might want you dead, but she never said I had to make it quick," the bandit hissed. "I like making little girls scream."

Gems shuddered and tried to break free, but the bandit tightened his grip, yanking even harder on her hair. She yelped again, and tears of pain streamed down her face.

The second bandit shook off his daze and staggered over to his sword, which was lying in a puddle of water.

I will not be killed by bandits. I will not be killed by bandits. I will not be killed by bandits . . . Gems chanted the words over and over again in her mind, and they echoed through mine as well.

She stretched her hand out, reaching for the strings of energy wrapped around the bandit's sword, and I found myself mimicking her motion. On the ground, the sword rattled back and forth, once again clang-clang-clanging against the rocks. The second bandit stopped, clearly confused about why his sword was moving on its own.

"Come on," Gems growled. "Come on! COME ON!"

She screamed the last few words, and a wave of magic zipped off her, picked up the sword, and flung it at the second bandit. The blade punched into his stomach, and he yelped and dropped to the ground.

Gems screamed again, and the sword ripped out of the man's stomach and flew over into her hand. She drove her elbow into the gut of the bandit behind her, who grunted and lost his grip on her hair. Gems raised the sword high, then spun around and whipped it down, slashing the blade across his chest.

That bandit also dropped to the ground, yelling and blubbering, just like his brother was still doing, although their cries were rapidly growing faint and weak as they bled out.

Still clutching the sword, Gems whirled around again.

Farena and Leo had waded out into the river, and the female bandit had her hands locked around the boy's throat. Leo was trying to pry her fingers off his neck, but he wasn't having any luck, and I could hear him gasping for air, even above the gurgling river.

His gaze darted over to Gems. Please, he whispered. Please . . . help . . . me . . .

Gems hesitated, then rushed over to the edge of the water and held the sword out. Leo lifted his hand and grabbed the weapon with his magic. The blade flew out of Gems's grasp and punched into Farena's back, making her scream and release her grip on Leo's throat.

This time, Gems grabbed the sword with her magic and yanked it out of the bandit's body, making the weapon fly *back into her outstretched hand. Farena screamed again and stumbled forward—straight into Leo.*

He tried to dodge her, but Farena crashed into him and bounced off. The bandit slipped underneath the water, and Leo staggered around, trying to find his balance. He lurched to the side, and his feet flew out from under him.

"Leo!" Gems screamed. "Watch out!"

But it was too late, and he couldn't quite catch himself. Even now, all these years later, the crack of his head hitting one of the rocks sounded as loud as a thunderclap in my mind. I flinched, as did Gems.

Leo's eyes rolled up in the back of his head, and he toppled over into the water. Like Farena, he too slipped below the surface.

"Leo! Leo!" Gems screamed again, and I found myself mouthing the words right along with her.

He finally bobbed up, but he was facedown in the river, and the current quickly pulled him along.

"Stupid Morricone," Gems snarled. "I should let you drown."

But an instant later, a sigh escaped from her lips, and she dropped the sword, tore off her cloak, and waded into the river. Gems sucked in a breath, then dove into the water, chasing after Leo . . .

Another spray of water splattered up against my face, breaking the stranglehold of my magic, and I sucked in a breath, just as I had done that day so long ago. Perhaps it was the remnants of my magic or the vividness of the memory, but I could still feel that first cold crash of water enveloping my body as I dove into the river after Leonidas.

I shuddered out a breath and wiped the spray off my face with a trembling hand.

Leonidas was right. We had *always* been connected. First by chance and the Seven Spire massacre and who our families were. Then at the river, by necessity, trying to survive the bandits. And now . . . Well, I didn't know what our connection was now—or what I even *wanted* it to be.

My mind said we were on opposite sides, even as my body desperately burned for his and my heart whispered softer, more treacherous things. Enemy, attraction, emotion. I simply didn't see a way to reconcile any one of those things with the other two.

I couldn't forget about Leonidas, but I couldn't draw him closer either. The stakes were far too high to indulge in my fascination with him, no matter how much I might want to. Not when Maeven was manipulating us both for her own mysterious ends, Milo was still a threat to us all, Reiko was spying on me for Tatsuo, and Ruri was considering ignoring the treaty between Ryusama and Andvari, which would leave my kingdom even more vulnerable to Morta.

I felt like a wire walker in a gladiator troupe trying to cross a tightrope strung high above a crowded arena. One wrong move, one small misstep, and I would slip, fall, and plunge to my death—and doom my kingdom along with me.

CHAPTER NINETEEN

I carefully climbed down the rest of the slippery rocks, then circled around the lake to the main steps. By this point, it was midafternoon, and most people had crowded into the plaza marketplace to conduct their business.

I skirted around the boisterous merchants and bargain-hunting shoppers and returned to the Andvarian wing. Father and Rhea were each sitting at a desk in the study, poring over documents.

"How go the trade negotiations?" I asked, closing the door behind me.

Father sighed, tossed a paper down onto the pile in front of him, and leaned back in his chair. "Even slower and more tedious than last year."

"How was your picnic with Leonidas?" Rhea asked.

"Fine. Although it turned into more of a mission than a picnic."

I took a seat and told them everything that had happened, from picnicking with Reiko, Delmira, and Leonidas to flying to the island to finding Milo's latest workshop of horrors. I also showed them the fool's bane, although neither one of them knew anything about the flowers.

"Milo didn't leave any guards behind on the island?" Rhea asked. "That doesn't make any sense. Why not leave at least a few men behind to make sure no one came snooping around?"

"I don't know why Milo went to the island, but he didn't stay long, and he didn't leave much behind. Nothing that tells us where he's storing all the tearstone arrows he's made, or how and when he plans to use the weapons."

Father eyed the fool's bane I had laid on his desk. "But you think he's somehow using these flowers in his scheme."

"Perhaps. I'm going to see if I can find a copy of Milo's book in the castle library. Maybe I can find the missing pages and learn more about the fool's bane or whatever plant and poison Milo might be tinkering with."

I drew in a breath, then let it out. As much as I would like to keep this next bit of information to myself, I had a duty to share it—even if it ended up costing me a friend. "There's something else."

"What has Maeven done now?" Father muttered.

"Not Maeven—Reiko."

I told Father and Rhea everything I'd overheard Reiko and Tatsuo say in the gardens last night, as well as my own conversation with Tatsuo and Ruri earlier today. When I finished, Father's face was as dark as a storm cloud, and lightning crackled in his blue eyes.

"Andvari and Ryusama have a bloody *treaty*," he snapped. "One that does not have anything to do with you and Leonidas Morricone."

Rhea's topaz eyes glittered with similar anger. "I've sent men to Ryusama several times over the past few years to help them clean up storm damage and the like. And *this* is how they repay us?"

I sighed. "I'm sorry. This is all my fault."

And it *was* my fault. Perhaps if my attraction to Leonidas hadn't been so bloody *obvious* at Myrkvior, then Maeven would have never dreamed up this scheme, and Andvari's relationship with Ryusama wouldn't be hanging in the balance. And I still didn't understand *why* Maeven wanted me to become engaged to Leonidas. She certainly had no love for me, just as I had none for her. Perhaps she wanted Andvari's relationship with Ryusama to crumble, although I still got the sense Maeven had something even more sinister in mind. She always did.

So I started looking at the Gauntlet from Maeven's perspective, especially what she—and Morta—could gain from it. I still couldn't puzzle it out, but the exercise did help me consider what *Andvari* might gain from the Gauntlet.

My mind whirred, and I thought about something Milo had said when I was eavesdropping on him in the library last night. "Perhaps we should look at the Gauntlet not as a problem, but as an opportunity."

Father frowned. "What do you mean? Surely you don't want Leonidas to succeed."

I ignored the traitorous twinge in my heart and waved my hand. "Forget about whether Leonidas completes the challenges. All we have to do is convince Ruri and Tatsuo that we *do* want him to succeed."

"How does that help Andvari?" Rhea asked.

"Right now, Queen Ruri thinks we don't want Leonidas to succeed any more than she does. Ruri thinks that we are so reluctant that she feels comfortable breaking our treaty without fear of any consequences for Ryusama."

"So?" Rhea asked.

I leaned forward, determination surging through me. "So let's give her some bloody *consequences*. We have resources that Ryusama needs—coal, gold, gemstones, tearstone. Things that would be a lot cheaper to send across our land border to Morta than they are to ship across the sea to Ryusama."

Understanding filled Father's face. "Ah. You want us to pretend we are seriously considering new trade agreements with Morta—ones that will completely cut out Ryusama."

I nodded. "Exactly. Let's make Ruri worry for a change. No matter how much she hates Maeven and the Morricones, she still has a kingdom to run, and she still needs our resources. Ruri might be more amenable to honoring our current treaty if she thinks she has more to lose than gain."

"And what about Leonidas and the Gauntlet?" Rhea asked.

Her gaze settled on me like a lead weight, as did Father's, but I didn't have an answer for them. Until I knew exactly what Maeven hoped to gain from the Gauntlet, I couldn't do much to counter her scheme.

I blew out a breath. "One problem at a time. Let's see if Leonidas actually makes it through the next two challenges before worrying about how I can wiggle out of my impending engagement without losing my head."

By the time I finished plotting strategy with Father and Rhea, the sun was setting and I had to get ready for dinner—and the second Gauntlet challenge.

I returned to my chambers to find Grimley galloping around the sitting room like he was a Floresian stallion. Even more curious, he had his tail wrapped around Violet's tiny body. The baby strix was hoisted up behind him, and the gargoyle was racing around the chamber like Violet was a purple kite he was flying through the air.

Grimley was grinning, and Violet's eyes gleamed with happiness, even as her wings fluttered, as though she were flying herself, instead of Grimley doing the work for her.

"What are you doing?" I asked.

Grimley froze in mid-gallop, his tail still wrapped around Violet. A guilty look flickered across the gargoyle's face, and he lowered the strix to the floor and released her.

Violet squeaked in protest and waggled her wings, clearly wanting to continue their game. Grimley gently patted her head with the flat side of the arrow on the end of his tail.

"Were you actually *playing* with Violet?" I drawled. "I thought you vehemently disliked tiny balls of fluff."

Another guilty look flickered across Grimley's face, but he perched primly on his front paws. "Of course I wasn't *playing* with the strix. She woke me up from my nap and was chasing me around. I was doing my best to escape her."

I arched an eyebrow. "Escape her? When she's not even the size of one of your paws? She must be a fearsome ball of fluff indeed."

Violet squeaked and fluttered her wings again, as if agreeing that yes, she was extremely fearsome, despite her small size.

"Fine," Grimley grumbled. "We were playing. And she's not so bad . . . for a strix."

He muttered the last few words, but affection rippled through his voice. I wasn't the only one who'd fallen in love with the baby strix.

I laughed and sat down on the floor. Violet hopped over to me, rubbed her head against my fingers, and then climbed into my outstretched palm. I lifted her up and stroked my fingers along her fluffy feathers. Her chest vibrated with happiness, and a squeaky little song trilled out of her beak.

Leonidas truly had given me a wonderful gift, and I had to

remind myself it came with a steep price—one that I didn't want to pay.

Grimley and Violet settled down for another nap, so I took a hot bath, then summoned Yaleen, my thread master, along with the usual servants, to help me get dressed.

The Gauntlet challenge aside, tonight's dinner was a formal occasion, so Yaleen dressed me in a beautiful light gray gown shot through with silver thread that made it—and me—sparkle like a star. The low necklace highlighted my cleavage, along with my gargoyle pendant, while the pockets in the billowing skirt were large enough to hold my gargoyle dagger, along with the li-ladorn blade that Delmira had given me earlier.

I dismissed the servants and went into the sitting room. Reiko's door had been shut all afternoon, and I hadn't seen my friend since she'd left me with Leonidas in the gardens. Guilt churned in my stomach that I'd shared her conversation with Tatsuo with Father and Rhea, and I hesitated, wondering if I should knock on her door—

As if in answer to my silent question, the door opened, and Reiko stepped into the sitting room wearing a beautiful gown made of crimson silk. The gauzy, sequined panels were draped together to look like overlapping dragon scales, and they shimmered with every step she took. Smoky shadow and liner brought out her green eyes, while her lips were stained a deep vibrant red.

"You look stunning," I said.

She tipped her head, acknowledging the compliment. "As do you. Once again, you are certain to turn Prince Leo's head."

Her voice was neutral, and I couldn't tell if she was sincere, so I changed the subject.

"What did you do after Delmira dragged you out of the gardens?"

Reiko shrugged. "Skulked around the plaza marketplace, picking up news and gossip."

I wondered if she'd had another meeting with Tatsuo and Ruri, or a more personal one with Kai, but I didn't ask. I knew how awkward it was to be caught between royals—especially since I was currently caught between Maeven and my father—and I wasn't going to put my friend in that same position. So I opted for a safer question.

"Did you find out anything more about Milo's trip to the island?"

Reiko shook her head. "I eavesdropped on some Mortan guards, but none of them knew anything specific about Milo's trip. They all thought he and Corvina had just gone for a pleasure ride."

I snorted. "Milo takes pleasure in slaughter, not pretty scenery."

"What about you? Did you learn anything new after you left the gardens?"

Once again, Reiko's voice was strangely neutral, and once again, I changed the subject. "I might have found part of the answer."

I showed her the fool's bane flowers I had picked earlier, then fished the dried purple blossom that the Mortan boy had been carrying out of my jewelry box. They all looked identical.

Reiko poked one of the fresh flowers with her finger, but it just lay there like a dead fish. "But Alvis tested the dried fool's bane on that tearstone shard in your grandfather's study before we left Glitnir, and nothing happened."

Frustration coursed through me. "No, it didn't. But I still feel like the flower is important."

I thought about telling her my plan to search the castle library for the same book I'd found in Milo's workshop, but I kept quiet. I *hated* this. I hated not knowing whose side Reiko was on, and if she was genuinely interested in helping me figure out Milo's plot or just spying on me for Tatsuo, for Queen Ruri and Ryusama.

In some ways, Reiko was just as much my enemy now as Maeven, Milo, Wexel, and Corvina were, although her potential betrayal could wound my heart far worse than the Mortans ever could.

"Well, I'm sure you'll figure it out," Reiko replied. "But it's time to go see what new Gauntlet challenge Prince Leo must overcome."

Her voice remained neutral, and I once again couldn't tell what she really meant. But then her lips twitched and she snickered, as did the dragon on her hand. I rolled my eyes at their teasing, but a knot of tension loosened in my chest. No matter what happened between us and our respective kingdoms, at this moment, Reiko was my friend.

So I threaded my arm through hers and swept my hand out wide. "Reiko the Resplendent, please do me the great honor of escorting me to my beloved Leonidas so that the next chapter in our epic love story can begin."

Reiko snickered again at my light tone and grandiose words. I grinned back at her, but worry still crackled through my body.

Leonidas Morricone wasn't my beloved or some other courtly admirer. No, he was something far more dangerous—an enemy who had wormed his way into my heart, despite my best efforts to prevent such a dangerous, treacherous thing.

Reiko and I left my chambers and went down to the courtyard where Father, Rhea, and several guards were waiting.

"Gemma, Reiko, you both look lovely." Father murmured the benign sentiment as though nothing was wrong.

Reiko bobbed her head, not seeming to notice that my father's smile didn't quite reach his eyes when he looked at her.

Together, we left the Andvarian wing, crossed the plaza, and entered the arena. Once again, we were among the last to arrive, and most people had already taken their seats on the upper levels. Excited chatter filled the air, and my gargoyle pendant heated up as it strained to block out everyone's thoughts.

We strode out onto the arena floor. Zariza was ensconced in a cluster of nobles, gesturing with her goblet and telling some story while Xenia looked on. Ruri and Tatsuo were standing apart from everyone else, as though they didn't want anyone to overhear their conversation, although Kai was lurking nearby as usual.

Murmurs rippled through the crowd at my arrival, catching the other royals' attention. Father, Zariza, Xenia, and I all exchanged nods. Father tipped his head to Ruri, who returned the gesture before focusing on me. After a few seconds of silent contemplation, Ruri resumed her conversation with Tatsuo, who was staring at Reiko. Smoke once again boiled out of the mouth of his inner dragon, and he crossed his arms, wrinkling the front of his gleaming gold jacket.

Reiko stiffened and dropped my arm. "I should go find a seat."

Before I could ask her to sit at the Andvarian table, she melted into the crowd. I glanced back over at Tatsuo, whose face was filled with satisfaction. He eyed me a moment, then turned back to Ruri.

I looked out over the arena. The main floor had been rearranged since the first challenge. The four royal daises had been pushed much farther back so that they hugged the arena wall, leaving the center of the floor completely empty. The tables had changed as well. Instead of the long rectangular ones, much shorter, squarer tables perched on the daises. Curious. Xenia had said Leonidas would have to pit himself against other warriors, but neither the open space nor the new furnishings gave me any clue as to exactly what was planned.

More murmurs rippled through the crowd, and heavy footsteps thumped against the floor. Father, Rhea, and I turned to find Maeven striding toward us, along with Delmira. Milo and Corvina were trailing along behind them, as was Wexel, but there was a clear divide between the three of them and the Mortan guards flanking the queen.

Smart of Maeven not to trust the crown prince, although part of me cursed her wariness. One of them murdering the other would solve at least some of my problems, but I wasn't sure which would be better—or worse—for me, and especially for Andvari.

I glanced toward the tunnel archway, but Leonidas did not appear. He must be getting ready for the challenge.

The queen stopped in front of us. "Dominic, Rhea."

"Maeven," Father replied, his voice dripping with cold disdain.

She ignored him and focused on me. "I am here to collect Gemma, so that we might sit together, as Ungerian custom dictates for the second Gauntlet challenge."

Sit with Maeven? I'd rather chew broken glass than dine with the Morricone queen again. I'd barely survived the meals I'd shared with her at Myrkvior, and I had no desire to repeat those hostile experiences.

Maeven gestured at Delmira, who curtsied to Father and Rhea. "Delmira will dine at the Andvarian table, to uphold the proper protocols."

I looked over at Xenia, who nodded, indicating that Maeven had every right to hold me hostage at the Mortan table. Wonderful.

"It will be a good way for us to get to know each other better,"

Maeven purred, a sly light gleaming in her eyes. "After all, we will be family soon."

"We will *never* be family," Father snarled.

His harsh tone boomed out like thunder. Everyone went quiet, and all eyes fell on us, including those of Ruri, Tatsuo, and Kai.

I placed my hand on his arm and gave the Morricone queen my sweetest smile. "I would be *delighted* to dine with Maeven. It will give us a chance to discuss those new trade agreements between Andvari and Morta. The ones we've all been working so diligently on during the Summit. Right, Father?"

"Yes," he replied in a smooth voice, following my lead. "You're absolutely right, Gemma."

Maeven blinked rapidly in surprise, Ruri stiffened, and Tatsuo crossed his arms over his chest again, further wrinkling his gold jacket. Zariza looked back and forth between everyone. The Ungerian queen's face remained blank, but her inner ogre opened its mouth in a silent laugh. Well, at least my predicament amused someone.

"Of course we can discuss the new trade agreements," Maeven said. "Why, I'm sure this is just the start of *many* mutually beneficial relationships between Morta and Andvari."

Her voice boomed out just like Father's had, breaking the tense silence. Since their talk didn't seem as though it was going to devolve into outright confrontation, everyone slowly returned to their previous conversations.

I gave Maeven another sweet smile. "Perhaps we *should* start thinking of you as family."

Her eyes narrowed with suspicion. "Why is that?"

"Well, if you were family, then we could bury you in the Glitnir cemetery, right next to Dahlia Sullivan. Wouldn't that be lovely? To be reunited with your cousin? Especially since your scheme is the reason she's dead?"

Maeven's fingers flexed, as though she wanted to reach out and strangle me. Delmira sucked in a breath, and Milo, Corvina, and Wexel stared at me like I was a strange, dangerous creature they had never encountered before. Even Father and Rhea seemed startled by my venomous words.

"And of course if you were buried at Glitnir, then Father and I could visit your grave any time we wanted to." My smile widened. "Oh, yes. Thinking of you as family is a *marvelous* idea."

No one spoke, and another tense silence dropped over our group.

"Please allow me the honor of escorting you, Your Majesty." Before Maeven could protest, I stepped over and wound my arm through hers. "I wouldn't want you to fall trying to navigate up the steps, especially given your advanced age."

Delmira coughed, although it sounded suspiciously like a laugh. Maeven swung her angry gaze around to her daughter, but Delmira grinned back at her, then went over to my father.

"Your Highness," Delmira said, "please allow me that same honor."

Father looked at me.

Don't worry. I sent the thought to him. *I'll be fine.*

Father held his arm out to Delmira and led her toward the Andvarian dais, with Rhea and the guards following them.

That left me in the middle of the Mortans, with my arm still entangled with Maeven's. She wasn't doing anything even vaguely threatening, but my fingertips still tingled from the magic coursing through her body, as well as her plethora of amethyst jewelry. The sensation reminded me that I was quite literally playing with lightning. The queen eyed me much the same way I was eyeing her—with anger, disgust, and hatred.

"Your tongue has sharpened since we last dined together at Myrkvior," she murmured. "Good. I would hate to think I promised my son to some witless princess in a pretty gown."

My tongue might have sharpened, but it was still a dull, rusty spoon compared to hers.

Maeven smiled, knowing she'd bested me. "Come, Gemma, darling," she cooed. "We have *so* much to talk about during dinner."

And just like that, the Morricone queen took complete control of the situation and dragged me along in her dangerous wake.

CHAPTER TWENTY

Maeven and I strode over to the Mortan dais. The queen yanked her arm free of mine, climbed the steps, and took her seat at the head of the table, so that she was facing out toward the arena floor.

She tilted her head, indicating the chair to her right, and I climbed the dais and dropped down into it. Milo took the seat on Maeven's left, directly across from me, while Corvina seated herself next to him. Wexel also stepped up onto the dais.

The seating arrangement was eerily similar to how we had dined together at Myrkvior, only this time, I didn't have Delmira and Leonidas flanking me as buffers, and everyone knew my real identity. My gargoyle pendant heated up again, this time from the collective hate blasting off Milo, Corvina, and Wexel, and I had to resist the urge to yank the hot disc away from my bare skin. I'd be lucky if it didn't burn me before the dinner was finished.

Milo sneered at me. "I still can't believe Mother wants to marry Leo off to *you*. Then again, I suppose it makes sense, since you both have the same kind of cursed magic."

"Oh, Milo," I purred, "your jealousy is showing. And so are the scars on your hands."

He glanced down, but white gloves covered his hands, just as they had last night in the arena. Milo's head snapped up, and he glared at me. "One day, Gemma, you're going to pay for insulting me."

"But not today," I purred again.

A muscle ticced in Milo's jaw, and even more hate blasted off him, hot enough to make sweat prickle the back of my neck.

"Let's talk about something more pleasant," Corvina said in a deceptively light voice. "Gemma, have you thought about what kind of gown you'll wear when you and Leo get married? Mortan purple would look *wonderful* on you."

Her words seemed innocent enough, but the sly curve of her lips indicated she knew exactly what she was doing—reminding me of how Maeven was manipulating me yet again. Well, two could play that game.

I didn't kill Emperia. I sent the thought to her. *I didn't kill your mother. That was Maeven's doing, not mine. If you want to be pissed at someone, then be pissed at her.*

Corvina blinked, as if startled to hear my voice in her mind, but no shock surged off her at my revelation. No wonder, no worry, no fear. At the very least, she should have been mildly surprised, unless . . .

She already *knew* Maeven had murdered her mother.

When had Corvina figured it out? And how was she planning to retaliate against the queen? I reached out with my magic, hoping to probe a little deeper and get some answers, but power rippled off her, like the electric charge in the air before a violent storm, and my fingertips tingled in warning.

Corvina's gray eyes narrowed. *Get out of my head, you Andvarian bitch. Or I'll fry you with my weather magic the same way you fried Milo with his own lightning.*

"Enough," Maeven said, sensing the animosity between us. "We're stuck here together for the evening, so let's keep the insults and posturing to a minimum."

Corvina swung her angry gaze around to the queen. More power surged off her, although the sensation quickly wilted away under Maeven's icy, steady glare.

On the back of the dais, Wexel grimaced, and sympathy gusted off him. Once again, the depth of his feelings for Corvina surprised me, but I supposed that every pot had a lid, as the old saying went. Even those as cunning, cruel, and conniving as the two of them.

A series of bells rang out, and servants entered the arena, climbed the daises, and started serving dinner.

Hot, spicy soups. Fresh, crispy salads. Warm breads. Succulent meats. Seasoned vegetables. The food was just as scrumptious as it had been last night, but everything tasted like wet ash in my mouth, and every *scrape* of a knife on a plate made me tense in anticipation of Wexel's shoving his sword into my back.

Eventually, dessert was served—a peach cake topped with fresh peaches in a warm syrup, toasted slivered almonds, and a generous dollop of cold whipped vanilla-bean sweet cream. That finally woke up my taste buds and overpowered my unease, and I enjoyed every single bite of the dessert, despite the hostile company.

"Tell me, Gemma. How was your picnic with Leonidas?" Maeven eyed me over the rim of her crystal goblet. She had forgone dessert in favor of sangria, and thick slices of peaches floated in her drink, along with blueberries and other bits of fruit.

Giving some benign answer would have been the safest, smartest course of action. But so far at the Summit, safe and smart had gotten me absolutely nowhere, so I decided to engage my enemies, rather than retreat from them.

"Oh, the picnic was fine, but I had a much better time exploring the island."

Milo and Corvina froze, as did Wexel, who was now standing behind the queen.

"What island?" Maeven asked.

"The one that Milo, Corvina, and Wexel visited earlier," I replied. "Antheia Island, where you used to holiday when your children were younger."

Everyone fell silent, although tension hung over the table like a wet blanket about to drop down and smother us all.

"Leonidas told me about all the things your family used to do on the island. I was especially interested in how Milo trapped a baby gargoyle in the woods, brought it back to the house, and tried to butcher it on the dining room table."

I carefully gathered up my magic, as though I was plucking needles off the floor. This time, instead of dipping my fingers into the sea of thoughts that constantly churned around me, I reached out toward Milo, subtly trying to worm my way past his lightning power so I could hear his inner musings.

She knows nothing. Milo's thought rasped through my mind like sandpaper scraping across my skin. *The Ripley bitch is just fishing for information. My plans remain on track.*

Frustration filled me. His thoughts were too vague. I needed more details about what he was plotting and what it had to do with his barbed tearstone arrows. I tried to probe deeper, but anger blasted off the crown prince, burning through the threads of his thoughts and knocking my own power aside.

"Gargoyles. Horrible creatures." Milo shuddered, as though he was talking about something truly vile. "I was trying to do us all a favor and rid the island of the pests."

Otto's broken horn and angry face filled my mind. Somehow I kept my voice even, despite the rage sizzling inside my heart. "Getting rid of pests? Why, the way I heard it, you pitched a royal fit when your mother ordered the gargoyle be released."

A furious flush stained Milo's cheeks, and his hand strangled his napkin. Corvina snickered, although her laughter cut off under Milo's hot glare. Maeven drained her sangria and held the empty goblet out, as if she needed another libation to endure our bickering. Wexel grabbed a pitcher off a table along the back of the dais and shoved it at a servant, who scurried forward and poured more sangria into the queen's glass.

I once again reached out with my magic, straining to hear Milo's thoughts, but his pounding anger drowned out everything else. So I turned to Corvina.

"Did you have a pleasant time on the island? I saw you and Milo boarding the sailboat with Wexel this afternoon. How odd, that you would take a captain on a pleasure ride with your fiancé."

Corvina's eyes narrowed again. I tried to read her thoughts, but just like with Milo, all I could sense was her anger at me.

Still, Corvina recovered much more quickly than Milo did, and she placed her hand on top of his, even though he was still strangling his napkin.

"Why, yes," Corvina cooed, "Milo gave me a tour of the island and the manor house. We're thinking about taking our own holiday there after our wedding. Isn't that right, darling?"

It took Milo several seconds to unclench his jaw. "Of course."

Maeven eyed the two of them, obviously not believing a word they said. Yeah, me neither.

I opened my mouth to keep prodding, to try to provoke a response and get some clue as to what Milo, Corvina, and Wexel had been doing on the island, but at the last second, I clamped my lips shut. My fingertips were tingling again, even more violently than when I had taken Maeven's arm earlier.

Someone here was using magic—a *lot* of magic.

My gaze flicked from Corvina to Milo to Maeven, but the noble lady and the crown prince were merely glaring at me, while the queen was leaning back in her chair, watching the drama play out between us. Next, I glanced over at Wexel, who was also glaring at me, but the captain was holding his position, and none of the servants on the dais seemed to have any power.

So where was the magic coming from?

Too many people were on the dais for me to immediately suss out the source, so I dropped my head and closed my eyes, as if I was gathering my thoughts. Then I reached out, sorting through all the threads of energy pulsing, bobbing, and weaving around me.

Maeven's lightning, Milo's similar, slightly weaker power, Corvina's weather magic, Wexel's strength. None of them was the source of the power, so I stretched my mind out, searching for that one particular thread of magic . . .

There.

I carefully grabbed hold of the thread in my mind, reeling it in the same way I would a fish on a line. Then, when I was firmly focused on that thread of power, I opened my eyes.

The source of the magic? The goblet in Maeven's hand.

Confusion filled me, but the longer I stared at the crystal container, the more the tingling in my fingertips intensified. The magic wasn't coming from the queen or the amethyst rings on her fingers, but rather from the goblet itself, which could mean only one thing.

Someone was trying to poison Maeven.

"What's wrong, Gemma?" Corvina asked in a snide tone. "Have you run out of insults and innuendos already?"

I ignored her, schemes and scenarios spinning through my mind. I didn't particularly care that someone was trying to kill the queen. In fact, part of me applauded their ruthlessness in doing it in such a public fashion. If I had been sitting over at the

Andvarian table, I would have let this long game play out and watched and waited to see if Maeven succumbed to whatever foul thing had been slipped into her drink.

But I was sitting at the Mortan table, within arm's reach of the queen, and if Maeven died, then I would most likely be blamed for her death. I might not even make it off the dais before Milo blasted me with his lightning or Wexel rammed his sword into my back—

As if picking up on my dark thoughts, Maeven lifted the goblet to her lips.

Instinct took over. I immediately slammed my dessert fork down onto my empty plate. A quick blast of my magic flipped the plate up off the table and smashed it into Maeven's hand, making her lose her grip on the goblet. Sangria and fruit bits splattered all over the queen and the table, while the crystal goblet hit the stone dais and shattered into a dozen pieces.

All around the arena, everyone stopped eating and talking to stare at the Mortan dais.

Maeven shot to her feet and held her right arm out to her side, sangria dripping off her fingers like peach-colored blood. "You clumsy fool!" she hissed.

I also stood up, grabbed my napkin, and started dabbing at the mess on the table. "It was an accident!"

A servant rushed forward and handed Maeven a towel, so she could wipe the sangria off her fingers. Another servant fell to his knees, picking up the pieces of the broken goblet.

"I'm sorry! So sorry!" I dropped to my knees beside the servant, subtly elbowing him out of the way.

I glanced over the mess on the dais. Peaches, blueberries, a few chunks of bloodcrisp apple. Nothing unusual, so I picked up the largest piece of crystal. My fingertips tingled again the second they closed around the sharp shard. Yes, Maeven's sangria had definitely been poisoned.

I helped the servant pile the remaining pieces on a napkin. Then he hurried away with the shattered goblet, while I slowly stood up.

By this point, everyone was staring at me, including Milo, Corvina, and Wexel. I reached out again, trying to read their thoughts, wondering if one of them might have tried to poison the queen, but this time, Maeven's ire drowned out everyone else's inner musings.

I dipped into a deep curtsy and strove for a contrite tone. "I apologize, Your Majesty. It was an accident."

Several long seconds ticked by, but I kept my head down and my body locked into the curtsy.

A loud, annoyed huff sounded. "Rise," Maeven commanded in a curt tone.

I popped back upright and clasped my hands together, trying to strike a remorseful pose. Maeven eyed me, but I stared right back at her, my own face carefully blank.

A servant stepped forward to hand the queen another towel, but she waved him off.

Maeven snapped her fingers. "Remove this mess."

The servants swiped the dishes off the table, disposed of the soiled cloths, and fetched some fresh linens. In less than two minutes, the table had been reset, and you wouldn't have known that anything untoward had happened, except for the sangria stains on Maeven's gown and the sweet scent of peaches filling the air.

Maeven sat back down. I waited until she was settled, then dropped into my own chair.

Several more seconds passed in tense silence, but when it became apparent that Maeven wasn't going to fry me with lightning for soaking her gown, everyone returned to their previous conversations.

Maeven didn't ask for any more sangria, and she eventually

growled at the servants to leave. I watched them go, but none of them was acting suspiciously. I also glanced at Milo, Corvina, and Wexel. They too weren't doing anything suspicious, although so much anger was blasting off them that I couldn't tell if it was just their general hatred of me or because Maeven wasn't dead yet.

But someone had tried to kill the Morricone queen, and instead of letting them get away with it, I had saved the bitch's life.

What had I done?

An expectant hush dropped over the crowd, and everyone turned their chairs around so they had the best view possible of the arena floor. I did the same, trying to ignore my rising dread.

Xenia rose to her feet at the Ungerian table. She thumped her ogre-head cane against the dais three times, drawing everyone's attention.

"We are gathered here for the second challenge of the Gauntlet," she said. "Earlier today, Prince Leonidas proved how well he knows Princess Gemma by giving her three gifts. Tonight, he will battle for the honor of her applause."

Xenia stabbed her cane at one of the gates in the wall. The black iron creaked open, and Leonidas strode into the arena.

He was dressed in traditional gladiator garb—a tightly fitted sleeveless shirt, along with a knee-length kilt and flat sandals with straps that wound up past his ankles. Instead of Mortan purple, Leonidas was clothed in a more neutral pale gray, which was eerily similar to the colors of the Black Swan troupe.

His black hair gleamed like polished onyx under the white light cast out by the fluorestones. The sleeveless shirt showed off the muscles in his arms and chest, while the kilt did the same thing for his toned legs. Leonidas was always darkly handsome in his black cloak and riding coat, but tonight, he was stripped down to what he truly was—a fierce, dangerous warrior.

Appreciative murmurs rippled through the crowd, and I had to press my lips together to keep from joining in the admiring chorus.

I forced my gaze away from him and studied the enemies gathered around me. Maeven's expression was neutral, but Milo, Corvina, and Wexel were all openly sneering at Leonidas. No surprise there.

Over at the Andvarian table, Father and Rhea also wore neutral expressions, but Delmira was leaning forward, her hands clasped against her chest. Over at the Ungerian table, Xenia was still standing, while Zariza was relaxing back in her chair, a goblet in her hand.

And finally, I glanced over at the Ryusamans. Ruri was also relaxing back in her chair and enjoying some wine, although Tatsuo and Kai were not on the dais. I looked up at the balcony above Tatsuo's empty chair, but I didn't spot Reiko amid the crowd. Perhaps the three of them were having another clandestine meeting. Bitterness swirled through me at the thought.

Leonidas bowed first to Xenia, then to Zariza, Father, and Ruri. He also bowed to Maeven, then focused on me.

A smile creased his face, brightening his eyes. *I always wanted to be a gladiator.*

Don't be a fool, I replied. *Gladiators can die just as easily as everyone else can.*

Perhaps. But not me. Not when I have love, fate, and destiny on my side.

I rolled my eyes. *Is that speech part of your Gauntlet theatrics tonight?*

No. It's just for you, Gemma.

Leonidas dropped into a low formal bow, his smile widening, and his hot, intense gaze never leaving mine.

Answering sparks of desire exploded like fireworks in my chest, and I struggled to keep my face blank. I would *not* be swayed by pretty words, not when I knew how empty the promises behind them truly were. Leonidas Morricone was like a poisoned sweet cake—pleasing to the tongue, but deadly to the body. One small bite, one tiny taste, one brief surrender to temptation would be more than enough to doom me forever.

Leonidas straightened and strode to the far end of the arena, close to the main entrance tunnel. He shook out his arms and legs and cracked his neck from side to side, getting ready for whatever was coming next.

At the opposite end of the arena, Anaka walked through the open gate carrying a sword and a dagger, along with a gladiator shield. Instead of taking the weapons to Leonidas, the servant girl placed them on the floor in between the Andvarian and Mortan tables.

Next, several guards dressed in their respective kingdom's colors entered and took up positions around the appropriate daises, as though they were needed to protect the royals. Some wooden beams were also brought out and placed in front of the daises, forming a crude ring and clearly dividing the arena floor from the royals. Unease trickled through me. Why were guards and beams required for this challenge?

The servants retreated, and a dozen men and women strode out onto the arena floor. They were all dressed in gladiator garb—sleeveless black shirts, kilts, and sandals—but they had two things that Leonidas did not. These gladiators were all wearing silver helms that protected their heads and obscured their faces, and every single one of them was carrying a weapon. Swords, daggers, shields, maces. One man even clutched a crossbow.

The men and women spread out, putting themselves in between Leonidas and the sword, dagger, and shield still lying on the floor.

"Tonight's challenge is simple," Xenia said. "Prince Leonidas must battle his opponents, retrieve his weapons, and be the last person standing." She paused, letting the interest and tension build, before she spoke again. "This Gauntlet challenge is the equivalent of a black-ring gladiator match."

My gaze dropped to the low beams cordoning off the daises from the rest of the arena floor. Sure enough, the wood was painted a dull, flat black. Worry and dread filled my stomach. A black-ring gladiator match was usually a bout between two people to the death, but Leonidas was battling twelve other gladiators, not just one other warrior.

This was a true *gauntlet* in every sense of the word—one he might not survive.

CHAPTER TWENTY-ONE

I spun around in my chair toward Maeven. "Are you out of your mind?" I hissed. "You have to put a stop to this!"

"Why, Gemma, you almost sound like you're concerned about Leonidas," Maeven purred. "How sweet."

Smug satisfaction rolled off her, adding to my own anger. Despite the fact Milo, Corvina, and Wexel were staring at me, I leaned in closer to the queen.

"I don't know why you invoked this custom, but are you really going to risk your son's life to get whatever it is you want?"

Maeven gave an airy wave of her hand, brushing my words aside. "Leonidas is a fine warrior. He has battled far more dangerous people than this."

"Where did you get the gladiators for the challenge?" Corvina asked.

"I called for volunteers from among the royal guards," Maeven replied. "I told the guards they would get to participate in a gladiator match in front of everyone. They were all quite eager to have that honor."

"And did you mention they would have to die for that so-called honor?" I asked in a snide voice.

Maeven waved her hand again, brushing my words aside. "The guards are loyal to me, and they wished to bring honor and glory to Morta."

She sidestepped my question as neatly as if we were performing a complicated waltz. More anger shot through me, and my hands clenched into fists on top of the table. Wexel stepped forward, his hand curling around his sword and anticipation rippling off him. The captain might not be loyal to his queen, but he would take great pleasure in cutting me down if I physically attacked her.

"Besides, Gemma," Maeven continued, "you should know by now I never play a game I can't win."

One corner of her mouth quirked up into a sly smile, and even more smug satisfaction rolled off her.

The bitch had cheated.

Her words implied as much, as did her emotions. Somehow, some way, Maeven had arranged for Leonidas to win the challenge, even if it meant sacrificing her own guards. Equal parts admiration and frustration coursed through me. I didn't want Leonidas to die, but I didn't want him to win the challenge either. Not with my life, freedom, and kingdom hanging in the balance.

"Something wrong, Gemma?" This time Milo spoke, a mocking tone in his voice. "Your scars are showing."

My hands had clenched into even tighter fists, making the red starburst scars stand out in stark relief next to my white knuckles. More anger spiked through me that the bastard had thrown my own words back in my face, but I forced myself to relax my hands.

"Nothing is wrong," I replied. "Watching Mortans bleed is always an amusing spectacle. I quite enjoyed it in Blauberg, and I'm sure now will be no different."

Rage crackled in Milo's eyes, along with his magic, and he planted his elbow on the table, leaned forward, and stabbed his finger at me. He opened his mouth, most likely to insult me again—

"Enough," Maeven snapped. "We are here to watch the challenge. Nothing more, nothing less."

Milo turned his irate gaze to her. Once again, he opened his mouth, but Maeven's cold stare made him reconsider, and he pinched his lips together, leaned back, and sulked in silence.

Corvina's expression remained blank as she looked back and forth between the crown prince and the queen, but a thought whispered off her. *Milo is such a fucking* coward. *He'll never do what needs to be done to destroy Maeven.*

For once, I heartily agreed with her.

Xenia thumped her cane on the Ungerian dais again, and everyone fell silent. Leonidas stood alone on one side of the arena, with those dozen gladiators standing in between him and the three weapons.

"As per the rules of the Gauntlet, there is to be no interference from anyone in the arena. Neither to help Prince Leonidas." Xenia looked at Maeven. "Or to hinder him." She glanced over at my father. "If anyone does interfere, then they will lose their heads, as will Prince Leonidas. Agreed?"

One by one, Maeven, Father, Zariza, and Ruri all nodded.

Xenia lifted her cane high in the air. Anticipation, excitement, and bloodlust swelled up like tidal waves. The combined force of everyone's emotions made my gargoyle pendant burn against my chest again, even as it pressed me down into my seat and kept me from rising, from yelling, from doing something to help Leonidas. Despite all my tangled, conflicting emotions about the Morricone prince, he didn't deserve to die because of Maeven's manipulations. But I couldn't help Leonidas any more than I could help myself right now.

Xenia's cane slammed down against the dais, and her voice boomed through the arena as loud as a crack of thunder. "Begin!"

The last echoes of Xenia's voice hadn't even faded away before the gladiators screamed and rushed forward. Leonidas watched them come, his fingers flexing, his face eerily calm.

A mutt with speed magic reached the prince first and whipped his sword back and forth in a series of rapid moves. The man wasn't pulling his blows, not a single one, and each move was designed to kill Leonidas outright. I frowned. If Maeven had cheated, if she had rigged the challenge, then why was that man trying so hard to murder her son?

Leonidas ducked left, then right, zigzagging back and forth to avoid the strikes. Then he spun past the man and charged at the next closest warrior, moving deeper into the gauntlet of gladiators. Leonidas slammed his fist into the second man's face, then yanked the man's dagger out of his hand and shoved him away. The second man staggered back, but he charged forward again and locked his hands around the prince's throat.

Beside me, Maeven leaned forward. Her brow creased in confusion, and worry pulsed off her, strong enough to make my own stomach churn.

No. Her thought rasped through my mind. *This is wrong. My orders were to hurt, not kill. Those . . . those aren't my men.*

My gaze snapped back over to the prince. *Leo! I don't know what's going on, but those gladiators aren't Mortan guards. They want to kill you!*

A muffled grunt sounded in my mind, although I couldn't

tell if it was an acknowledgment of my warning or just him trying to breathe.

Leonidas brought up the dagger in his hand and punched it into the left eye of the gladiator throttling him. The prince ripped the dagger out, and the other man fell to the floor screaming.

A woman clutching a large mace rushed up on Leonidas's blind side, but he must have sensed her weapon slicing through the air because he ducked at the last possible second. The woman's mace punched into the chest of another gladiator creeping up on the prince, killing that man and sending him toppling to the ground.

Two enemies down, ten more to go.

Leonidas ducked and spun and lashed out with his dagger over and over again. He managed to kill two more gladiators, the mutt who'd first attacked him and the woman with the mace, before another woman stepped up and sliced her sword across his left forearm.

Pain pulsed off Leonidas, and the sting of the wound blazed through my own skin, making me hiss.

Maeven gave me a sharp look, having heard the sound over the crowd's raucous cheers, and I had to grind my teeth to keep from hissing again. The last thing I needed was for the queen to realize how strangely attuned I was to her son.

That first wound was like a floodgate opening. The remaining gladiators gathered around Leonidas, forcing him into the center of their deadly circle. Then they lashed out with their weapons, slicing their swords and daggers across every single part of the prince they could reach.

His right shoulder. His left thigh. His right calf.

Leonidas managed to bury his dagger in another gladiator's throat, but the seven remaining warriors tightened their circle and attacked him again with renewed vigor.

By this point, everyone was on their feet. Screams roared through the arena, but the spectators didn't care who won. They only wanted to see *more*—more blood, more pain, and especially more death.

The crowd's continued bloodlust bubbled up like hot lava in my veins, while its collective hunger squeezed around my chest, as though a kraken was gnawing on my ribs. My magic rose up in response, freezing me in place, and I was unable to do anything but suffer through the crowd's raucous frenzy, as well as Leonidas's pain.

A female gladiator slammed her fist into the prince's face, sending him spinning down to the ground. The other gladiators lunged forward and started kicking him, driving their sandaled feet into his arms, chest, legs, and back. I flinched at each and every blow, and Leonidas's pain flooded my body as if I were the one being pummeled, instead of him.

That's it. Beat the bastard down. Make him suffer as I have suffered.

The thought rose above all the others in the arena and slithered through my mind like a coral viper dripping venom and malice in its wake. The crowd was so loud that I couldn't tell exactly whose thought it was, but it seemed to belong to Milo, who was punching his fist into the air over and over again and screaming at the gladiators to kill his brother. Beside him, Corvina was watching the fight with narrowed eyes, a cruel smile on her red lips. Wexel was also smiling. Maeven's face was calm, but worry rippled off her again.

The gladiators kept kicking Leonidas, who was down on his hands and knees. Despite the beating, he was trying to crawl toward the sword, dagger, and shield, which were still more than a dozen feet away.

"Forget about the weapons," I muttered. "Get up before they beat you to death."

There was no way Leonidas could have heard me above the crowd's roar, but he lifted his head, and his pain-filled gaze locked with mine, despite the people and distance separating us.

Get up, Leo! I yelled. *You can't earn my trust if you're dead!*

To my surprise, he grinned, the motion making him look even more handsome, despite the blood and bruises covering his face. *As my lady commands.*

Leonidas stopped crawling and closed his eyes, as if gathering his strength. The gladiators increased their attacks, while the crowd cheered even louder.

Suddenly, Leonidas's eyes snapped open, burning a bright electric violet, and an invisible wave of magic blasted off him, tossing all seven of the remaining gladiators away from him. My fingertips tingled, and my ears popped from the sudden release of power and pressure.

The gladiators flew through the air and landed hard, their weapons tumbling from their hands. Leonidas staggered back up onto his feet and limped forward, hurrying toward the sword, dagger, and shield.

One of the female gladiators scrambled to her feet, grabbed her sword, and charged at him.

Behind you! I yelled.

I didn't know if he heard me or not, but Leonidas took hold of the shield, then spun around and snapped it up, shoving it straight into the gladiator's face and breaking her nose. Next he slammed the shield into the side of the woman's head, cracking her skull and sending her tumbling down to the ground.

Another gladiator charged at Leonidas. This time he used his magic to toss the shield straight into the man's throat, crushing his windpipe. The gladiator dropped like a stone, struggling to breathe, although he soon stilled.

Leonidas flicked his fingers, and the sword flew up off the

arena floor and settled into his hand. The crowd gasped, then roared again.

The prince's eyes blazed with rage, pain, and magic, and he dove into the remaining gladiators. Bones crunched. Bodies flew through the air. And blood coated the arena floor like dull rust-colored paint.

Back in the Haverton woods, Leonidas had claimed I was getting stronger in my magic. Well, he was far more skillful with his power than I was with mine, and he manipulated all those strings of energy around the gladiators like a music master playing an instrument to its fullest, loudest, most violent potential.

By this point, Corvina and Wexel were both frowning, while a sly smile was creeping across Maeven's face. Milo's expression was flat and blank, but two surprising emotions surged off him—jealousy mixed with a healthy dose of fear.

And just like that, I realized why Milo wanted Leonidas dead so badly. The crown prince was envious of his brother's mind magier magic—and worried that it was greater than his own lightning power.

The last gladiator standing was the one with the crossbow, who had largely kept to the fringes of the fight. He aimed the weapon at Leonidas, and everyone in the arena fell silent again.

"Drop the crossbow, and I won't kill you," Leonidas growled, magic still blazing in his eyes.

The gladiator shifted on his feet, his gaze flicking over the bloody broken bodies lying between him and Leonidas. The man wet his lips, and his gaze darted in this direction, as though he was looking at someone on the Mortan dais. He grimaced and lowered the crossbow as if to surrender. Leonidas relaxed his watchful stance a fraction of an inch—

The man's eyes narrowed, and he lifted the crossbow and pulled the trigger.

A collective gasp rang out. Leonidas snapped up his hand and caught the bolt with his magic, stopping it in midair.

Leonidas shook his head. "I gave you a chance."

He flicked his fingers and sent the bolt shooting back at the other man. The projectile plunged into the man's throat, and he joined the other dead gladiators on the floor.

For a heartbeat, silence filled the arena. Then, everyone sucked in a breath and started cheering, yelling, screaming, clapping, and whistling.

I cheered and screamed and clapped as well, completely caught up in the heady moment. My gaze locked with Leonidas's, and he grinned and slowly, awkwardly bowed to me again. My heart soared. He was so arrogant, but still so very attractive, even with the blood and bruises covering his face, and cuts, scrapes, and other injuries dotting his hands, arms, and legs—

Enjoy your victory, Morricone. It's the last one you'll ever have.

The thought sliced through my mind like a dagger, and malevolence washed over me like a bucket of cold water dousing my body from head to toe. My hands froze in midclap, even as my gaze darted from one person to the next.

Milo's arms were crossed over his chest, and his face was tight with fury. Corvina and Wexel looked equally pissed that Leonidas had survived. Xenia, Zariza, Father, Rhea, and Ruri were all politely clapping on their respective daises, so I looked up at first one level, then another, still searching for the source of the icy malevolence—

A bright silver gleam caught my eye. A figure wearing a black cloak, along with a hood that obscured their features, was lurking in the shadows on the third-floor balcony. They adjusted the position of the crossbow in their hands, making the silver bolt wink at me again.

The assassin pulled the trigger, and the bolt shot out—heading straight for Leonidas.

CHAPTER TWENTY-TWO

Everything slowed down.

The assassin pulling the trigger. The bolt flying out of the crossbow. The projectile zipping toward Leonidas's back.

Then, in the next instant, everything returned to normal speed, and I sprang into action.

I lunged forward, my fingers flexing wide and my magic zipping outward faster than a gargoyle streaking through the sky. Every ounce of my concentration was focused on reaching, reaching, reaching for the invisible string of energy attached to that bolt. I had to stop the projectile before it punched into Leonidas's back, before it *killed* him—

The bolt froze in midair, inches away from his body. Leonidas must have sensed my magic because he whirled around, his eyes widening as he realized just how very close he had come to dying.

The cheers snuffed out, and the guards snapped to attention and rushed forward, surrounding their respective royals. Still more guards hustled through the gates in the arena wall, climbed the stairs, and spread out, controlling the crowd, as well as searching for the would-be assassin.

But as the seconds passed, and no more bolts rained down on the arena floor, the guards slowly relaxed. Soon, everyone was glancing back and forth between me and the bolt still hovering in front of Leonidas. These people had heard rumors I was a mind magier, just like the folks in Haverton had, and now they had all seen my power in action.

"Thank you, Gemma," Milo called out in a loud, snide voice. "You interfered in the challenge, which means my brother's life is forfeit, along with yours. Isn't that right, Xenia?"

I silently cursed. The assassin might have failed, but of course Milo would try to twist the situation to his own advantage. One way or another, he was determined to see Leonidas dead, and me too.

Xenia tilted her head to the side, looking first at Leonidas, then me. No one else moved or spoke, and that tense silence dropped over the arena yet again.

"Well, Xenia?" Milo challenged. "Aren't you going to follow your own rules of engagement?"

Xenia arched an eyebrow and gave him a look that would have cut glass. "Princess Gemma interfered with an assassin, not the challenge itself, as anyone with half a brain would realize. Then again, brains have never been in abundance among the Morricones."

Anger stained Milo's cheeks a mottled red, and he opened his mouth to snipe back at her—

"Why don't we let Princess Gemma decide whether I live or die?" Leonidas said, his voice booming out even louder than Milo's had. "She is the one who intervened, so let her determine my fate."

Agreeing murmurs rang out, along with several yells of encouragement. A muscle ticced in Milo's jaw, but he had clearly been outvoted by the crowd.

Leonidas eased forward. The bolt was still hovering in midair, but now it was pressed right up against his chest. He raised his gaze to mine and held his arms out wide.

All I had to do was flick my fingers, and I could shove the bolt straight into his heart—and he wouldn't do a thing to stop me.

The crowd quieted, and all eyes landed on me. Half the spectators wanted to see me kill the prince, while the other half were just as eager for me to spare him. Xenia, Zariza, and Ruri were eyeing me with avid interest. Father and Rhea were both frowning, while Delmira kept twisting her liladorn ring around and around on her finger. I still didn't see Reiko, Tatsuo, or Kai anywhere in the arena.

On the Mortan dais, Milo, Corvina, and Wexel watched me with narrowed eyes and murderous eagerness. They all wanted me to kill Leonidas and save them the trouble of doing it themselves. Maeven's face was as smooth as ever, although she was holding her breath, uncertainty blasting off her body, not quite knowing what I would choose.

I didn't know either.

I *should* kill Leonidas. I should kill Maeven's son in retribution for her orchestrating Uncle Frederich's murder at Seven Spire, as well as poisoning Grandfather Heinrich and trying to assassinate Father at Glitnir.

My hand clenched into an even tighter fist, and the bolt twisted in midair, as though it were a screw about to sink into Leonidas's heart. Not a flicker of fear crossed his face, and he remained steady and confident. In that moment, I realized something I had never even considered before.

Leonidas Morricone trusted me—completely, utterly, absolutely.

A Morricone trusting a Ripley was momentous enough, but

the fact that Leonidas Morricone trusted Gemma Ripley *not* to kill him was quite extraordinary, especially given how I had tried to hurt him when we were children.

Even more remarkable was that this trust wasn't born out of circumstance, necessity, or survival. Not like our childhood encounters had been. This trust hadn't come about because I'd saved Leonidas from being murdered a few weeks ago by Wexel in Blauberg, and then again more recently in the woods outside Haverton. And this trust wasn't because he knew vital secrets and information that I didn't, like he had during our time at Myrkvior.

No, this trust went so much deeper than anything as simple as circumstance, necessity, or survival. This trust burrowed into my chest like a tearstone mine diving straight down into the heart of the mountains, and the rock-solid strength of it shook me to the core. I had often dreamed of having this power over Leonidas, of taking my revenge on him, but now that the moment was here, I couldn't cut him down. Not because I was soft or squeamish or didn't want an arena full of people to see me murder someone.

I simply couldn't kill *him*.

Never. Not tonight or any other night.

Even though Leonidas Morricone was my mortal enemy, my greatest bloody weakness, I simply didn't have the rage or hate or malice in my heart to strike him down. I had never felt that rage. Not really, not truly, not for him.

No, I felt far too many *other* things where Leonidas was concerned. Sympathy. Respect. Kinship. And other stronger, hotter, more intense things I didn't want to think about. Maybe I would always feel these things for Leonidas. Maybe that made me weak or gullible or stupid, but I would *not* be petty or cruel or vindictive.

That would make me far too much like Maeven.

Oh, I had taken the lessons the Morricone queen had inflicted on me to heart, especially her masterful manipulation at Myrkvior. But part of learning from Maeven also meant moving *past* her, and given her conversation with Delmira last night, I got the sense Maeven had *never* been able to move past all the petty, cruel, vindictive things she had done—and all the ones that had been done to her.

I wouldn't add to that cruelty by killing her son in front of her.

Not this son, anyway.

But that didn't mean I couldn't take my anger out on someone else. The guards hadn't reached the third-floor balcony yet, and the cloaked, hooded figure was still lurking there, watching the show, just like the rest of the crowd. So I tightened my grip on the bolt, then flicked my fingers, sending the projectile shooting back up at the would-be assassin.

Thwack!

Pain spiked through my mind, along with a surprising image. The figure jerked back, then fled from the balcony and disappeared.

My gaze dropped back down to Leonidas. For once, his icy armor had fully cracked away, and emotions flashed like lightning strikes in his eyes—heat, desire, want, and an aching need so deep and intense that it stole my breath.

Those same intense emotions raged inside me, making me sway from side to side and adding to the perpetual storm in my body, my mind, and especially in my heart. Even worse, I felt like everyone watching could *see* my feelings too, as though I were a rag doll that was slowly losing her stuffing. An embarrassed blush scalded my cheeks, but I lifted my chin and kept right on staring at Leonidas. I would not back down from the silent challenge in his eyes.

A second passed, maybe five or ten or twenty. Or maybe it

was no time at all. But all around us, the crowd roared again, cheering, yelling, clapping, screaming, and whistling even louder than before. They were ecstatic that the prince would live to see another day and compete in another challenge for their amusement.

Despite the raucous applause, I had never felt like more of a failure. By sparing Leonidas's life, I had doomed my own.

PART THREE

THE
GAUNTLET

CHAPTER TWENTY-THREE

I stood on the Mortan dais, doing my best to keep my face calm and blank, as though my deciding *not* to kill a prince was an ordinary everyday occurrence. The applause slowly died down, although people remained in the arena, waiting to see what would happen next.

A Mortan guard rushed across the arena floor and climbed up onto the dais. Maeven waved him over, and he whispered something in her ear. The queen's nostrils flared, and anger surged off her. What was going on?

Maeven murmured something to the guard, who nodded and hurried away, disappearing through an open gate in the arena wall.

She snapped her fingers at Wexel. "Take Leonidas to be healed, and make sure no one else tries to murder my son."

The captain started to leave the dais, but the queen speared him with a hard look.

"Do *not* fail me in this, Wexel," Maeven said, her tone full of icy fury. "Or I will have your head stuffed and mounted like a trophy."

Wexel's face paled, but he leaped off the dais and scurried away. Within seconds, the captain was standing by Leonidas's side, along with half a dozen Mortan guards. Together, the men formed a protective ring around the prince and ushered him through an open gate in the wall, taking him deeper into the arena.

"As amusing as it was to watch Leonidas get thrashed, I have more important things to do." Milo snapped his fingers much the same way Maeven had done. "Come, Corvina."

He left the dais without even waiting to see if she would follow. Corvina's jaw clenched and she shot daggers at Milo's back with her eyes, but she trailed after him.

That left Maeven and me standing alone on the Mortan dais.

"You should be happy," I said in a flat, toneless voice. "You got what you wanted. Leonidas made it through another challenge."

Maeven gave me a look that was almost pitying. Even worse, the same emotion surged off her, and I had to grind my teeth to keep the soothing sensation at bay.

"Leonidas might have survived the second challenge, but I haven't gotten what I wanted." She shook her head. "Not yet."

Not yet? What did that even mean? I didn't know what to say to her mysterious words, so I skirted around the Mortan queen, trudged down the steps, and headed for the Andvarian dais.

Delmira was going in the opposite direction toward the Mortan dais. "Thank you for sparing Leo's life," she murmured.

More weariness filled me, so I just nodded and kept walking. Father and Rhea were standing at the base of the Andvarian dais, surrounded by guards.

"I've sent men to the upper levels to see if they can find any trace of the assassin." Rhea was clutching a dagger, and her eyes were snapping back and forth, as she scanned for potential threats.

Father pulled me into a tight hug, then held me out at arm's length and gave me a critical once-over. "Gemma? Are you okay?"

"Fine," I lied.

"What happened? What did Maeven say about the assassin?"

"Assassins," I corrected him.

I drew Father and Rhea off to the side and told them everything that had happened at the Mortan table, including the thoughts and silent threats I'd overheard and how surprised Maeven had been when the gladiators had tried to kill Leonidas, instead of just wounding him, like she had planned.

Father frowned. "Who do you think ordered those gladiators to kill Leonidas? Was it Milo?"

"I don't know for certain, but he is the most obvious suspect. He definitely wants Leonidas dead."

I didn't say anything about the assassin with the crossbow. Thanks to the image that had popped into my mind when I'd wounded that person, I knew exactly who had been behind the attack, although I was still wrestling with how to handle the ramifications.

Maeven and Delmira had disappeared deeper into the arena, along with the Mortan guards, but Xenia, Zariza, Ruri, and Tatsuo were still here, all of them also surrounded by guards. Even though Leonidas had been the assassin's target, none of the royals were taking any chances.

Xenia gestured at us, and Father, Rhea, and I went over to the ogre morph and the other royals.

A flutter of movement caught my eye. Reiko was standing on the second-floor balcony, and she fluttered her fingers at me again.

Are you all right? Her thought whispered through my mind.

For now. We'll talk later. Okay?

Reiko nodded and vanished into the crowd.

I dropped my gaze back down to the other royals. Zariza's face was creased in thought, as was the one of her inner ogre. Ruri and her dragon wore a similar expression, while Tatsuo was fiddling with a loose thread on the sleeve of his rumpled red jacket. He noticed my stare and dropped his hand to his side. Kai glanced back and forth between Tatsuo and me, his own face carefully neutral.

Xenia cleared her throat. "One of Zariza's guards has informed me of a disturbing incident. A dozen people have been found dead in one of the arena dressing rooms. They appear to be Mortan guards, and Maeven has gone to identify them."

So someone had murdered Maeven's guards and substituted their own people in hopes of killing Leonidas during the challenge. The bold, risky gamble might have worked if Leonidas had been less of a warrior or just a little bit weaker in his magic.

"How did the guards die?" I asked.

"Poisoned wine," Xenia replied. "Several empty bottles were found in the dressing room."

"What kind of poison?" Ruri asked.

Xenia shrugged. "I don't know, and I doubt Maeven will share anything that she or her men find with me."

"So you're just going to let the Mortans remove the bodies and be done with things?" Father asked.

Xenia shrugged again. "As per the rules of the Summit, the arena is neutral territory, and each kingdom handles any incidents involving their own people, including murders. So this is Maeven's mess to clean up."

Poison suggested someone had put serious thought and planning into killing the original Mortan gladiators, just as someone had put serious thought and planning into spiking Maeven's sangria during dinner. But there was no way the attack on Leonidas and me in the gardens last night could have been planned, since even I hadn't known when and where I was going to meet him. Still, all the attacks had had the same goal—killing Maeven and Leonidas.

My mind kept churning, thinking about who would benefit the most from Maeven's and Leonidas's deaths. Of course the obvious answer was Milo. With his mother and brother out of the way, he would be the king of Morta and finally free to implement whatever horrible thing he was planning against Andvari. Corvina would benefit too and become the queen of Morta, but only if Milo chose to honor their engagement and actually marry her. But even then, she would just be a figurehead, and Milo would be the one wielding the true power.

But Milo wasn't the only suspect. Ruri and Tatsuo had made it crystal clear they were not pleased about a potential Morricone-Ripley engagement. Assassinating Leonidas would be one way to ensure he didn't survive the Gauntlet and thus maintain the status quo among Ryusama, Morta, and Andvari.

As for Zariza . . . Well, the Ungerian queen had her own reasons to hate Maeven. Although knowing what I did about Zariza, I was sure she would prefer to kill the queen herself, with her ogre teeth and talons, rather than use poison, but she was still quite capable of planning an assassination.

As was my father.

I eyed Father, who was whispering to Rhea. Perhaps it was wrong to consider the possibility that your own father had been behind an assassination attempt, but I couldn't discount him. Crown Prince Dominic Ripley would do just about anything to keep his heir Princess Gemma out of Maeven's clutches, especially since he'd been unable to protect me from her during the Seven Spire massacre.

"Well, I am more than happy to let Maeven deal with this incident," Ruri said. "Dominic, Zariza, I'll see you in the morning to continue our negotiations."

The royals nodded at one another, and Ruri strode away, followed by Tatsuo, Kai, and the Ryusaman guards.

"What a bloody mess," Father muttered. "This was supposed to be a peaceful Summit, not one rife with assassination attempts."

Zariza tossed her long red hair over her shoulder. "Well, as long as no one is trying to assassinate me, you, or Ruri, then what does it matter? Maybe we'll get lucky, and someone will finally succeed in killing Maeven."

Father returned her smile with a faint one of his own, although the expression quickly faded away. "As much as I would dearly love to see Maeven lying dead at my feet, Milo won't be any easier to deal with."

Zariza shrugged. "Morricones are never easy to deal with."

Xenia cleared her throat again. "I'm afraid the second challenge isn't quite over yet." She gave me an apologetic look.

I sighed. "What new torture is this?"

"According to the Gauntlet rules, for every challenge that Leonidas wins, he receives a boon," Xenia replied. "He would like to speak with you—alone."

Father shook his head. "No. Absolutely not."

Xenia also gave him an apologetic look. "I'm afraid that if you or Gemma refuse, then I will have no choice but to declare the rest of the Gauntlet as forfeit and Leonidas as the winner."

Father opened his mouth to keep arguing, but I laid a hand on his arm. "It's all right. I'll go talk to Leonidas. I have some things to discuss with him anyway."

Like who he thought had slaughtered the Mortan guards and tried to murder him.

Father tilted his head to the side, as if he was seeing something in my features he hadn't noticed before. "Very well," he murmured. "Go speak to Leonidas. But I expect a full report at breakfast."

"Of course."

Father studied me a moment longer, then strode away. Rhea followed him, along with the Andvarian guards. Zariza also departed with her own men. A few of the Ungerian guards lingered, but Xenia waved her hand, and they withdrew. That left the ogre morph and me standing alone.

The arena had been filled with so many people and so much noise over the past few hours that it was a bit disconcerting to see the structure empty of life, as though its heart had been plucked out of its chest, leaving only a hollow cage of ribs behind.

My gaze dropped to the flagstones. No one had removed the bodies or mopped up the blood yet, and death and scarlet stains stretched out as far as I could see.

I shuddered and looked at Xenia. "I suppose this is the part where you say I should have killed Leonidas when I had the chance."

Xenia shrugged. "He gave you that choice, and you chose something else."

"Aren't you going to tell me what a grand fool I am?" I asked, bitterness seeping into my voice. "For choosing to spare Maeven's son? Especially given everything she's done to my family?"

Xenia shrugged again. "Choosing mercy is not a weakness, Gemma. Sometimes it is much, much harder to be kind than it is to be cruel. We both know that."

Yes, we did. Sometimes, I forgot Xenia had had her own adventures and faced her own challenges and enemies over the years.

"What about the third challenge? Will it involve more fighting on Leonidas's part?"

"Yes, although it's more about Leonidas conquering physical obstacles rather than wading through gladiators. But don't worry. Now that I know someone is targeting Leonidas, I will take precautions so no one interferes or tries to assassinate him again." Xenia's face hardened, and the ogre on her neck drew its lips back in a silent snarl. "*No one* makes a mockery of Ungerian traditions. Leonidas will win or lose the Gauntlet on his own merits."

"They're not just targeting Leonidas. Someone wants Maeven dead too." I told her about the poisoned sangria.

Xenia *tap-tap-tapped* her index finger on the silver ogre head on top of her cane. "I knew you were making a fuss for some reason. I just didn't realize it was to save Maeven."

"Stupid, I know."

"Sometimes, someone dying is far worse than their living. As much as I despise Maeven, she has been a good ruler for her people." Xenia paused. "As much as a Morricone could ever truly be a good ruler."

I snorted out a laugh, although the sound quickly faded away in the empty arena. "What happens if Leonidas completes the third challenge tomorrow? Will I be forced to marry him right then and there?"

"The Gauntlet started out as a way for two lovers to be together, despite the objections of their warring families," Xenia replied. "Later on, it was invoked to settle disputes and avoid unnecessary bloodshed. It was never meant to be used as a weapon, but trust Maeven to deploy it in that way."

I opened my mouth to demand a real answer to my question, but the ogre on Xenia's neck shook its head. No matter how close we were, my friend wasn't going to reveal anything else. Once again, Xenia was playing her own long game, just like Maeven was, and Leonidas and I were caught in the middle of them both.

"I wonder what Maeven thinks she's really going to gain," Xenia murmured.

"What do you mean?"

"Forcing you and Leonidas together this way is a big risk for her to take. Sometimes, the Gauntlet ends well."

"But?"

"But most of the time it doesn't. Either someone is killed during one of the challenges or assassinated during the Summit or murdered soon afterward. So why would Maeven take such a huge gamble with her son's life?" Xenia arched an eyebrow at me. "Unless she knows something about you and Leonidas that I don't?"

I sidestepped her question the same way she had mine. "You know Leonidas and I met as children in the Spire Mountains. How he handed me over to a turncoat guard in the woods. And I told you about everything that happened between us at Myrkvior. How he let me prance around like a fool when he knew who I really was."

"You and Leonidas do have a far more complicated history than most Gauntlet participants."

"Leonidas told me that he wouldn't lose the challenge tonight because he had fate and destiny on his side." A bitter laugh escaped my lips. "Sometimes, I think he's an even bigger fool than I am."

"Not fate or destiny," Xenia countered. "Just you, Gemma."

And that was the thing that annoyed and rankled me most of all—that Leonidas Morricone *always* seemed to get the better of me one way or another.

"Well, I suppose I should go see my *beloved*. I wouldn't want Maeven to force me into marriage by forfeit."

Xenia chuckled at my caustic humor. "The bone masters should be done healing him by now. Do you want me to escort you?"

"I can find him." I'd already revealed too much to Xenia, and I needed a few minutes alone.

"Very well," she replied. "I'll have the guards sweep the arena to make sure no one is lurking around, and I'll leave a few men posted outside to make sure no one disturbs you."

I squeezed her hand. "Thank you, Xenia."

She squeezed my hand back, then whipped up her cane and poked me in the shoulder with it.

"Ouch!" I rubbed the throbbing spot. "What was that for?"

"A reminder not to be a fool where Leonidas is concerned."

I huffed. "I think it's far too late for that."

"Only if you waste what you've been given."

With those mysterious words, Xenia strode away, the steady *tap-tap-tap* of her cane on the flagstones echoing in my ears like nails being driven into a coffin.

My coffin, since I had already lost all my previous battles against Leonidas Morricone.

I waited until the echoes of Xenia's cane and footsteps had faded away. Then I reached out with my magic, searching for Leonidas's hot, electric, feathery presence. He was over . . . *there*.

I left the arena floor, walked through an open gate, and headed into one of the tunnels. A couple of hallways branched off the long corridor, circling around the arena, while several rooms were set into the walls. I didn't pass anyone, although I sensed a few of Xenia's guards in the distance.

Finally, I reached a closed door near the end of the corridor. I reached out with my magic again, but Leonidas was the only person on the other side. Good. I had no desire to battle more assassins tonight. I drew in a breath and slowly let it out, trying to settle my roiling emotions. Then I opened the door, stepped through to the other side, and closed and locked it behind me.

This dressing room was eerily similar to the ones I had seen at the Black Swan and other arenas throughout Bellona and Andvari. Racks of brightly colored, sequined costumes lined the walls, along with vanity tables covered with pots of face paint. Large wooden balls, hoops, and other props were piled haphazardly in one corner, while racks of weapons were clustered together in another corner.

My gaze reluctantly landed on Leonidas, who was sitting on a large gray velvet settee. He got to his feet, and I walked over to him.

Leonidas's muscled chest was bare, as were his feet, although a pair of black leggings was slung low on his hips. The bone masters had healed his injuries, so no cuts, scrapes, or bruises marred his skin, although he radiated weariness. His ruined gladiator outfit was draped over the side of a porcelain tub, the water inside pink with blood. I grimaced at the sight.

My gaze skipped back over to Leonidas, then moved past him to one of the vanity-table mirrors. The bone masters might have healed the injuries he'd gotten tonight, but old white scars crisscrossed his back from the tops of his shoulders all the way down to his leggings. Most of the marks were long and thin from where King Maximus had whipped him as a boy, but burn marks and other larger, more gruesome scars also dotted and puckered his skin, caused by things I didn't even want to imagine.

"Come to finish the job?" Leonidas gestured at his sword, dagger, and shield, which were lying on a nearby table.

His tone was light, but his face was guarded and serious, and memories of the gladiators' vicious attacks flickered through his mind, and mine too. Despite playing his words off as a joke, Leonidas was still a bit shaken up from the arena fight. The echoes of all the brutal blows he'd received pummeled my ears, along with my heart. I grimaced again.

"Xenia sent me. She said you wanted to talk, as per your boon for surviving the second challenge."

"Ah, so this meeting is by necessity, rather than by choice." More weariness colored his voice.

For all intents and purposes, this meeting *was* by necessity. I was bound by the rules of the Gauntlet just as much as he was, and I wasn't going to do anything to forfeit and give Leonidas—and by extension Maeven—an easy victory. But part of me had wanted to make sure he was okay. The need to do that surprised and unsettled me in ways I didn't want to admit to anyone, least of all him.

Leonidas kept staring at me. I shifted on my feet, uncomfortable under his silent scrutiny, and said the first thing that popped into my mind.

"Someone tried to poison Maeven during dinner."

His face hardened. "Tell me."

Leonidas listened to my story, more and more anger blasting off him. "Fucking Milo," he spat out. "He won't be happy until Mother and I are both dead. Delmira too. Then no one will stand in the way of him being king of Morta."

"Someone else could have poisoned Maeven's sangria," I pointed out. "And used the same poison on the Mortan guards who were supposed to participate in the gladiator challenge."

I didn't say anything about the assassin who'd fired the bolt at him. I knew exactly who'd done that, although not how to deal with them.

"True," Leonidas admitted. "Plenty of people hate Maeven Morricone, but we both know Milo is the most likely suspect. He and Mother are playing a deadly game with each other, and Delmira and I just happen to be caught in the cross fire." He paused. "Along with you. For that, I am truly sorry, Gemma. Sometimes, I feel like I'm always apologizing to you for how horrible my family is."

Leonidas ran his fingers through his black hair in a rare show of frustration, and the motion caused a few drops of water to slide out of his longish locks and drip down his bare chest. My stomach clenched, and my fingertips itched to follow those trails of water down his glorious body. I dug my nails into my palms, trying to get rid of the sensation, but it didn't work.

Nothing *ever* bloody worked when it came to Leonidas Morricone.

He hesitated, then dropped his hand to his side. "I would like to know one thing, though."

"What?"

"Why did you stop the assassin from killing me?"

Even though I had been expecting the question, I still tensed. I didn't want to answer. I didn't want to say the words out loud to anyone, but especially not to *him*. That would be an even bigger defeat than all the unwanted emotion I'd shown in the arena for everyone to see.

I gave a casual shrug. "I could hardly let you be murdered after such a grand display of courage, strength, and fighting prowess. Why, the crowd would have rioted if you had been killed."

Leonidas's face remained blank, but hurt rippled off him and pinched my own heart. "And here I thought you might actually be concerned about me."

I snorted. "As you so aptly proved in the arena, you are more than capable of taking care of yourself."

"Yes, but it's . . . pleasing to know someone cares enough to protect me." His low, husky words sent a chill zipping down my spine, even as more heat flared in his eyes.

"Don't mistake necessity for choice," I snapped, echoing his earlier words. "I was sitting at the Mortan table, remember? If you had been killed, Maeven probably would have blasted me with her lightning in retribution."

"Perhaps," he agreed. "But I appreciate you saving my life all the same. Once again, I am in your debt, Gemma. It seems as though I am forever falling deeper into your debt, falling deeper and deeper into *you*."

My heart squeezed tight. "Don't say things like that."

"Like what?"

"Things like *that*," I snarled. "Soft things, sweet things, lovely things that you don't really mean."

He eased closer until only a few inches separated us, and the heat from his body arced out like lightning dancing across my skin. I balled my hands into fists and held my ground. I'd made a vow to myself weeks ago that I would not run from him, never again, despite all the unwanted feelings he stirred.

Leonidas's eyes glittered with amethyst fire. "I *never* say things I don't mean when it comes to you, Gemma. I never have, and I never will."

"I don't believe you," I snapped back, although my voice had lost much of its previous conviction.

"Sooner or later you're going to have to believe me or else kill me."

"Well, then perhaps I should have let the assassin finish the job earlier."

Frustration filled his face. "Perhaps you should have. At least then I would have been put out of my misery."

"What misery?"

"The misery of wanting you so bloody *badly* and having you push me away at every single turn." He ground out the words as if each one was a dagger ripping into his heart.

My eyes widened, and shock and disbelief filled me. Despite everything that had happened, everything we had been through together, both as children and in recent weeks, this was the first time he had ever so openly, boldly admitted his feelings for me . . . whatever they truly were.

I shook my head, desperate to ignore my quickening heart. "You don't want me. Not really. I'm just difficult, and you enjoy a challenge. You're a royal, and royals always want the few things we can't have."

"That's not true, and you know it. We've had this connection ever since we were children. I felt it then, and I feel it even more strongly now."

I shook my head again. "You're confusing our magic and history together with something else, something *more*."

"I have *never* for one single *second* been confused about how I feel about you, Gemma."

Leonidas's low, husky voice wrapped around me from head to toe, warming me like the softest cloak, even as his words vibrated through my bones. Still, I tried my best to push those feelings down, the way I always did.

"Whatever you feel for me isn't *real*. It can't possibly be. There can *never* be anything other than death between a Morricone and a Ripley."

Leonidas reached out and took my hand, the way he had so many times before. Then he lifted my hand and settled it on his bare shoulder. That itching in my fingertips intensified, as did the urge to stroke his skin. Leonidas placed one of his hands on my waist, then captured my other hand in his free one.

"What—what are you doing?" I asked, my words coming out in a ragged whisper.

"Do you remember when we danced together in the throne room at Myrkvior?" he asked, his voice curling around me again. "Because I do. Every single detail. How the color of your gown mirrored your eyes. The way you smelled like fresh lilacs mixed with magic. The way you held yourself. The way you moved against me, *with* me."

Heat glittered in his eyes, making them blaze like stars, and I found myself unable to tear my gaze away from his.

"I think you felt the same things I did that night," Leonidas said.

He started moving, swaying from side to side. Despite my best intentions, I found myself falling in step with him, the two of us dancing around the dressing room to music that was only in our minds.

"Perhaps I did feel those things," I admitted. "Perhaps I even thought about acting on them, especially in the gardens last night."

We came to a beat in that phantom music. Leonidas spun me away, then pulled me right back into his arms again.

"But?" he asked as we fell back into the pattern of the dance.

"But there can never be anything between us."

"Why not?"

I let out an exasperated sigh. "Because your mother has tried to kill me multiple times, and no doubt she'll try again. I don't know what long game Maeven is playing, but she can't possibly want us to get engaged, much less be married."

"I have long since given up trying to figure out what my mother truly wants." His face hardened with determination. "But I know what I want, and that is *you*, Gemma."

Leonidas stepped even closer to me, and my hand tightened on his shoulder, even as my fingers threaded through his. The feel of his skin against mine was intoxicating—*he* was intoxicating, especially his honeysuckle scent, which made desire bloom in my body with every breath I took.

"And what if I don't want you?" I asked, my voice a ragged whisper.

Leonidas immediately released me. "Then I will take my leave of you and try to convince my mother to forgo her plot. The choice is yours, Gemma. It always has been."

But the choice wasn't mine. Not really. My treacherous heart had made it long ago, and even now, it was hammering in my chest, trying to overpower my common sense.

As a mind magier, I always felt *too much*, but never more so than when it came to Leonidas Morricone. When he'd been down on the arena floor tonight, surrounded by gladiators, I'd felt as though part of myself would die right along with him if he were killed. And I'd felt the same way when the assassin had targeted him. And no doubt I would feel the same way tomorrow during the third challenge.

But for tonight, he was whole and here with me and I was so bloody tired of denying what was so obvious to everyone, including myself. So for once, I ignored my mind and drowned in the emotions flooding my heart.

I stepped forward and lifted my lips to his.

Chapter Twenty-Four

Despite the desire pulsing through my veins, I made my kiss sweet, soft, and gentle, just as Leonidas had made his first kiss to me in the gardens last night. I brushed my lips against his once, twice, three times, then drew back.

Leonidas stared at me, hunger filling his face. Slowly, very, very slowly, I placed one hand on his bare shoulder and lifted my other hand to his face. Leonidas stood absolutely still, as though I were a hummingbird he didn't want to scare away from a beautiful flower. Well, he was the flower, and I wanted to drink deeply of him.

I skimmed my fingertips across his cheek and down his jaw. His breath hitched and his body inched closer to mine, the delicious heat of his skin warming me from head to toe. He didn't touch me, but he didn't have to. The amethyst fire in his eyes hypnotized me as quickly and easily as a coral viper charming its prey, and the pure, raw hunger blasting off him wrapped around me like the silken strands of a spider's web, drawing me even deeper into this tangled snare of desire that constantly pulsed, thrummed, and shimmered between us. I was thoroughly enchanted and completely ensnared by him, and for once, I didn't want to escape. I wanted only to revel in my feelings for him and his for me.

"Is this okay?" I whispered, still tracing my fingertips across his jaw.

"It's not enough," he growled. "That's the problem, Gemma. I always want *more*—more of *you*."

So I gave him more, easing in closer and lifting my lips to his again. I still went slowly, gently, treating him as though he was a delicate treasure I didn't want to damage in any way. The faintest flicker of my fingertips on his skin, the lightest brush of my lips against his. Even though he had asked for more, Leonidas didn't like to be touched, and I didn't want to cross any boundaries I shouldn't. He had been hurt so very badly, and I didn't want to be another person who had wounded him. Not when it came to this.

I don't know how long we stayed like that, with me just brushing my lips against his, as though I was taking tiny sips of a delicious drink and wanted to make it last as long as possible. He tasted sweet, like his honeysuckle soap, yet completely masculine. The same scent filled my nose, adding to the dizzying sensations cascading through my body.

The kiss began to change, to deepen, and his lips pressed back against mine, as though he was finally ready to drink me in just as I was still doing to him. Leonidas's tongue teased my lips, then dipped inside my mouth. My hand slid up, tangling in his silky hair, even as my simmering desire boiled up into sharp, aching need.

Leonidas growled again and yanked me toward him. Our kisses grew longer, harder, deeper, our tongues striking against each other like matches and further fueling our desire. He tore his lips away from mine and trailed hot kisses down my neck.

"I want to touch more of you," he rasped. "All of you."

"Yes," I rasped back. "I want to touch you too. More of you. All of you."

He kept kissing my throat, and I snaked my hands around his body, stroking my fingertips up and down his back. Leonidas shuddered and raised his gaze to mine. My hands froze, and I was suddenly, painfully aware of the scars on his skin, the ones I had been tracing with my fingertips.

"Don't stop," he whispered. "Never stop touching me."

I resumed my exploration of his muscled back. Leonidas's hands crept up in between us, and he hooked his thumbs in the sides of my neckline and gave me a questioning look. I nodded my consent. I took all the proper herbs and precautions, and I wanted to feel all of his skin against mine.

He moved his fingers back and forth, slowly pushing the gown aside until it slipped over my shoulders. I drew back and tugged my arms free of the fabric, then pushed the rest of it down so that it fell to the floor. I stepped out of the gown, along with my heels, my chest and stomach bare and only my silken undergarments covering the rest of me.

Leonidas's gaze tracked up and down my body. "Beautiful," he said in a low, reverent voice. "So beautiful."

"Are you just going to stand there and look at me?" I teased. "Because I had something a little more hands-on in mind."

A wicked grin curved Leonidas's lips. He stepped forward, but I backed away, crooking my finger at him. Another growl erupted out of Leonidas's throat, and he followed me over to the settee.

He reached for me, but I gently pushed his hands away and stroked his hard erection through his leggings, making him hiss with pleasure. Then I hooked my fingers into the waistband and eased the fabric down. Leonidas lifted one foot, then the other, letting me strip the leggings off him. I rose to my feet, then reached out and stroked his cock again.

Leonidas's hands balled into fists by his sides, but every slide of my fingers against his hard, thick erection made his entire body jerk and twitch. Desire surged off him, mixing with the sharp, aching need still throbbing in my own veins.

Leonidas lowered his head and kissed my right breast. That first touch of his tongue against my nipple made a whirlpool of heat spiral inside me. Suddenly, my body was the one that was jerking and twitching. Leonidas scraped his teeth against my nipple, then sucked on it hard.

I groaned and tangled my fingers in his hair. He lavished that same attention on my left breast, then put his hands around my waist, picked me up, and laid me down on the settee. He hooked his fingers into my undergarments, slid them down my legs, and tossed them aside.

Leonidas braced his hands on either side of me. "I've dreamed about you, about this moment, so many times."

"Me too," I confessed. "But it doesn't have to be a dream any longer."

I pulled his head down to mine. Leonidas kissed me back, hard and deep, his tongue crashing against mine. His hands drifted lower, and he rolled my stiff nipples in between his fingers before sucking first one, then the other. I arced up against him, a relentless ache building between my thighs.

Leonidas's hand glided down my stomach, and his fingers trailed down through my curls before caressing that most intimate part of me.

"Ah," I rasped and dug my fingers into his back as pleasure spiked through me. "More."

Leonidas gave me another wicked grin. "As my lady commands."

He lowered his head and put his tongue where his fingers had been. The first hot, electric lick made me buck up off the settee, but he kept going, dipping his tongue in and out of my folds, along with his fingers.

It was too much, and yet not enough. He had been right before. I needed *more* of him, *all* of him.

Leonidas lifted his head, and I pushed his shoulders back, swung my legs around, and rose up onto my knees. He swung around too, his back resting against the settee. I straddled him, stroking his cock again. Leonidas leaned forward, teasing my nipples with his tongue and teeth.

Our kisses and caresses grew harder, faster, until we were both in a frenzy, trying to bring as much pleasure to the other as possible. Somehow I ended up on my back, with Leonidas bracing his hands on either side of me again.

His beautiful amethyst eyes locked with mine, so dark with passion that they looked more black than purple, and his feelings crashed over me. Need. Want. Desire. And other warmer, softer things that made my heart soar. In that moment, I couldn't tell where his feelings left off and mine began. Or maybe they were one and the same. Maybe they had *always* been one and the same.

Gemma.

Yes, Leo. Now.

Leonidas slid forward, plunging inside me. We both shuddered and stared into each other's eyes. Then I locked my legs around his waist, and he pumped his hips forward, going deeper inside me. I dug my fingers into his back and buried my face in his neck, nipping at his throat as we rocked together.

We drove each other higher and higher, getting closer to the release we both craved. Leonidas thrust into me again, and the need, want, and desire coalesced into liquid fire scorching through my veins. The orgasm exploded deep inside me, and I fell back against the settee, crying out with pleasure.

Leonidas thrust into me again and shuddered, his head dropping to my shoulder as he found his own release.

We lay there on the settee, our bodies still entwined, the storm of emotion we had created together sweeping us both away and drowning us in a sea of pleasure.

Sometime later, that storm of emotion went still and silent, and the fire inside me simmered down to a warm, languid afterglow. Leonidas slowly withdrew from my body. He kissed me again, gently this time, then collapsed on the settee beside me.

For several minutes, we lay there, arms and legs tangled, drinking in each other's presence. But as the heady highs from the sex wore off, more and more doubts crept into my mind, eventually jelling into one single troubling thought.

What had I done?

I abruptly sat up, swung my legs over the side of the settee, and got to my feet. I shimmied into my undergarments and gown and shoved my feet back into my heels. Leonidas also got up and pulled on his leggings.

I smoothed my hands through my hair, trying to tame it, along with my runaway heart. "I should go."

A resigned look settled over Leonidas's face. "Back to wanting to have nothing to do with me again?"

My spine stiffened at his sharp words. "I didn't say that."

"You didn't have to," he accused. "I can *feel* how eager you are to escape."

"We both know I can't stay here, and neither can you. More assassins could be lurking around. Plus, sooner or later, people will start to wonder where we are."

He arched an eyebrow. "And you're worried what they'll say if they realize we've been together?"

"*This*," I said as I waggled my hand back and forth between us, "doesn't change anything."

"It changes *everything*," Leonidas snapped. "Especially since all I want to do right now is press you up against that door and fuck you senseless again. Until all you can do is scream out my name, and all I can do is scream out yours."

Heat exploded in my body like fireworks, and I had to curl my hands into fists to keep from reaching for him, to keep from begging him to do just that and more—so much *more*. But no matter how heady they were, a few moments of pleasure couldn't just erase all the past pain and betrayals.

"And I want to sit you back down on that settee and ride you like a Floresian stallion," I snapped right back at him. "But we can't always have what we want."

Leonidas threw up his hands in frustration. "Why not? If what we both so desperately want is each other?"

"Because you're a Morricone, and I'm a Ripley. That's *never* going to change, no matter how much we might want it to."

Determination flared in his eyes. "It will change if I win the Gauntlet tomorrow."

A bitter laugh tumbled out of my lips. "No, it won't. Because the Gauntlet wasn't your idea or even mine. It was *Maeven's*. And I will be damned if I let her dictate anything else about my life."

He threw his hands up again. "So you're going to throw away everything we could have, everything we could be, just because it didn't start out the way you wanted it to?"

His words wrenched my heart, and I had to swallow the hard knot of emotion in my throat before I could speak again. "It's not just about you and me. We each have our own kingdoms to think about, along with our duty to our families."

Leonidas shook his head. "Not me. Not anymore."

"What do you mean?"

He prowled over and stopped right in front of me, his body inches away from mine. My fingertips tingled with awareness, and I had to resist the urge to wrap my arms around his neck, lean in, and kiss him again.

"I've helped my mother hold on to her crown for the last sixteen years," Leonidas replied in a flat voice. "I've done my damned duty to her *and* to Morta. Well, no more. I want something of *my own*. I want *you*, Gemma. I always have."

His confession squeezed my chest like a vise, making it hard to breathe, but once again I shook my head. "You want to fuck me again, nothing more. And we both know you would never truly be *mine*. Part of you would always belong to Morta and your family, the same way I will always belong to Andvari and my family."

"We could belong to each other, but even after this, you still don't trust me," Leonidas said, his voice brimming with bitterness.

"No, I don't."

Even as I said the words, I wondered if they were a lie. Because I *did* trust Leonidas—to an extent. I'd trusted him with my life in the past and with my body tonight. But I couldn't quite take that final step and trust him with my heart.

It was ironic, really. Just when I thought Coward Gemma was finally gone for good, something happened that brought all my fears bubbling right back up to the surface. If Leonidas betrayed me again, especially after what we had shared here tonight, then I might never recover from the blow. And I just couldn't risk that.

Not even for him. No matter how desperately I wanted to.

I shoved those thoughts down, lest he overhear them with his magic. Because if he touched me again, if he kissed me again, then I would fall back into his arms, consequences be damned.

"I'm sorry. That things aren't different. That *I'm* not different. I wish . . ."

"What?" he growled.

That I was braver. That I was stronger. That I didn't want you so much. That I didn't care about you so much.

I shoved those thoughts down too. Because if I ever said the words out loud, if I ever admitted them, then I would be irrevocably lost.

"It doesn't matter. Not even Princess Gemma can make this wish come true."

Leonidas kept staring at me, anger, want, desire, and anguish flickering across his face. I couldn't stand to look at him a second longer, so I turned around, unlocked the door, and threw it open. I held my head high as I stepped back out into the corridor and marched away from the dressing room.

With every step I took, my pace quickened. Soon I had picked up my skirt and was sprinting through one corridor after another, trying to find a way to escape from the arena.

No matter how hard I tried, though, I couldn't outrun my own traitorous heart, which longed to return to Leonidas.

CHAPTER TWENTY-FIVE

I finally reached one of the arena exits and slipped outside. The night had grown quite cold while I was with Leonidas, and a few flakes of snow were fluttering down from the sky. I shivered, hugged my arms around myself, and headed toward the Andvarian wing.

It was almost midnight, so no one was skulking about, except for a few guards, whom I easily avoided, and I made it back to my chambers without running into anyone.

Low snores rumbled out of my bedroom, along with high singsong notes. I peeked inside. Grimley was sleeping in front of the fireplace, with Violet cuddled in between his paws. I eased the door shut so I wouldn't disturb them—

I spotted movement out of the corner of my eye and spun in that direction. Reiko was standing by the sitting room fireplace, still dressed in the same gown she'd worn to dinner.

I gasped and pressed my hand to my chest, trying to slow my racing heart. "You scared me."

Her gaze lingered on my messy hair and rumpled gown. "You and Leonidas?"

"Yes."

"How was it?"

I flopped down onto one of the settees. "Glorious."

An amused smile curved her lips. "It must have been truly glorious for you to swoon like a noble lady having a fainting spell."

Reiko ignored my scowl and dropped into a nearby chair. "Well, while you were experiencing a night of sublime passion with Prince Leo, I was skulking about, seeing what gossip I could pick up about the attack."

"Which one?" I muttered.

"What do you mean?"

I sat up and told her about Maeven's sangria being poisoned, along with the Mortan guards' wine.

"What kind of poison do you think Milo used?" Reiko asked.

"I have no idea." I paused. "If Milo was actually behind the attacks."

She frowned in confusion. "You *don't* think he poisoned Maeven's goblet, along with her men?"

"I'm not saying he *didn't* do it, but plenty of people would love to see Maeven dead, or murder her son right in front of her, or both."

Restlessness surged through me, and I got to my feet and started pacing back and forth, thinking about all the attacks over the past two days. First, someone tried to kill Leonidas and me in the gardens. Then, Maeven's sangria was spiked and her men poisoned. And finally, the assassin had shot that bolt at Leonidas in the arena. Different attacks, all with different methods of execution—guards, poison, and a crossbow.

"Something's wrong," I muttered. "At least more so than usual. The attacks just don't make sense. If Maeven is the target, then why not focus on killing her and her alone? Why try to kill me in the gardens? Or Leonidas in the arena? It's almost like . . ."

"What?" Reiko asked.

"Like there's more than one person behind the attacks. Different people with different motives and different agendas. I know that's the case with the arena assassin." The last few words slipped out before I could stop them, and I once again cursed my runaway tongue.

Reiko's eyes narrowed. "Do you *know* who fired the crossbow at Leonidas?"

"Yes." My stomach clenched with dread, but I forced out the words anyway. "It was Tatsuo."

Reiko blinked, while her inner dragon's eyes went wide. Shock blasted off both of them, the emotion strong enough to punch the air from my lungs. She shook her head, as if flinging off my words. "No—no. You're wrong."

"When I sent that bolt flying back at the assassin, I managed to hit him—in the shoulder, I think. As soon as the bolt slammed into his body, I felt his pain—and Tatsuo's gold dragon face roared in my mind."

Reiko kept shaking her head, but I kept talking, trying to convince her.

"Tatsuo wasn't on the Ryusaman dais with Queen Ruri during the gladiator challenge. And when I saw him afterward, he had changed his jacket from gold to red. He would only do that if he didn't want someone to see his *original* jacket—like if it was torn and bloodied."

A tense, awkward silence fell over us. Reiko jumped to her feet and started pacing back and forth, much the same way I had done.

"I knew it," she muttered. "I *knew* Kai had some ulterior motive. He must have been the one who planned the attack on Leonidas."

I frowned. "Why would you say that?"

"Because Kai sidled up to me right before the gladiator

challenge started and claimed he had important information. I followed him into one of the arena hallways, so I didn't even see the attack on Leonidas. Kai must have lured me away so that one of his guards could fire that bolt. Some morph with a gold dragon face, just like my father has."

Kai being with Reiko made him even less likely to have been part of Tatsuo's scheme, although I didn't point that out or repeat my certainty that Tatsuo had shot the bolt. "Did Kai have information?"

Reiko huffed. "Of course not. He just hemmed and hawed about nothing."

I thought of the way Kai had looked at her last night in the gardens. That certainly hadn't been *nothing*.

"I don't believe Tatsuo was part of Kai's scheme, though," she muttered. "I *can't* believe it. My father would never . . ."

"Kill a Morricone to maintain the status quo with Ryusama, Andvari, and Morta?" I finished her thought. "We both know he would do that—and worse."

She stopped pacing. "What do you mean *worse*?"

I drew in a breath and let it out. "I heard you and Tatsuo talking in the gardens last night. Your father told you to undercut my relationship with Leonidas—and that Queen Ruri plans to ignore Ryusama's treaty with Andvari if I get engaged to him."

Reiko's lips pressed together into a tight, unhappy line, and the dragon on her hand grimaced. "So that's why you've been acting so strangely."

"Not just me."

This time she grimaced, right along with her inner dragon.

I gathered up my courage and asked the question that had been nagging me all night long. "Did you help Tatsuo try to kill Leonidas?"

Reiko jerked back, and more shock blasted off her. "Of course not! Why would you even ask me that?"

"Because I didn't see you in the arena right after the challenge ended."

Anger sparked in her eyes, and she slapped her hands on her hips. "So you think what, exactly? That I'm *lying*? That I just made up the story about Kai luring me away? That I snuck off and played lookout for Tatsuo while he tried to murder Prince Leo?"

"First rule of being a spy—anyone can betray you at any time," I said, repeating her words to me in Haverton. "Even someone you think is a staunch ally."

More anger filled her face, and Reiko stared at me like she had never seen me before. Hurt blasted off her and stabbed into my own chest, prompting me to speak again.

"Tatsuo is your father, and Ryusama is your kingdom. You've always said you were a spy first and foremost. I also know how strained your relationship is with your father and how much it would mean to you to finally win his approval."

"And you think I would betray you, my friend, in order to get that approval?" Reiko's lips curled with disgust. "You really have been spending too much time with Prince Leo. *He's* the one who betrayed you at Myrkvior, not me. *I* came to your rescue in Blauberg, like a fool."

This time I was the one who jerked back. My own hurt flooded my heart, but I couldn't stop my tongue from getting me into even more trouble. "You told me this morning I shouldn't have anything to do with Leonidas. Which was in direct contrast to your earlier advice in Haverton to fuck him and forget him."

Reiko's lips pressed into a tight, unhappy line again. "You're right. I did say that. But not for the reasons you think."

"Then why?"

She threw her hands up in the air. "Because I can see how much you care about Leo, and I didn't want him to hurt you again."

"But would you have said anything if Tatsuo hadn't ordered you to?"

Reiko opened her mouth, but no words came out, and she didn't deny my accusation. That tense, ugly silence dropped over us again.

Weary resignation washed through me. "You should do what your father wants. You should tell Tatsuo that I took your advice to distance myself from Leonidas."

Her eyes narrowed again. "Why? What happened between the two of you?"

A caustic laugh spewed out of my lips. "I fucked him, and then I fucked things up between us. I ran away, just like I did at the Seven Spire massacre, just like I *always* do. Because I'm still a bloody *coward* at heart."

Sympathy flickered across her face, but I ignored it, steeling myself for what I had to do now. "After the Summit, you should go home—to Ryusama."

A muscle ticced in Reiko's jaw. "Why would I do that?"

"Because Tatsuo is your father, your family, and you love him. But mostly because you're a spy, and your queen and kingdom need you."

Reiko didn't say anything, and no obvious strong emotions flickered off her. For once, even her inner dragon's face was blank.

"War is coming between Andvari and Morta," I continued. "Tatsuo is right about one thing. My feud with Milo doesn't have anything to do with Ryusama. So you should leave while you still can."

Reiko kept staring at me, that same cold, flat look on her face. My heart squeezed tight again. So many words dangled on the tip of my tongue. I wanted to tell Reiko that she was magnificent in every way, and so much more than what Tatsuo saw her as. And I especially wanted to say that our friendship had been one of the best things that had ever happened to me. But for once, I controlled my tongue and held the words back.

Reiko had already done so much for me, and I was determined to do this for her, even if it broke my own heart. I would *never* ask her to choose between our friendship and her duty to her queen, father, and kingdom. Leonidas and I might be hopelessly snared in the royal trap with our families, but Reiko could still escape it.

"Well then, since the great Gemma Ripley has decided my fate, I will start packing my things." Reiko's voice was even colder than her expression was. "Goodbye, princess."

She gave me a low, formal Ryusaman bow and shot right back up again. I opened my mouth to say . . . something, but I was too late.

Reiko stepped back into her own chambers and shut the door. The soft *click* of the lock sliding home boomed as loud as a thunderclap in my mind, like a death knell tolling out the end of our friendship.

I didn't get much sleep, and I woke up the next morning feeling groggy, grumpy, and heartbroken. Somehow, in the space of a few short hours last night, I'd made a mess of everything.

Grimley and Violet were still sleeping when I snuck out of my bedroom into the sitting area. Reiko's door was still shut, and I didn't hear her moving around in her chambers. I thought about knocking on the door, but there was no point. She had her queen and kingdom to serve, and I wasn't going to stand in her way.

I went downstairs to my father's study. He and Rhea were eating breakfast, so I piled a plate high with food, even though the eggs, bacon, and breakfast potatoes tasted like bland mush in my mouth. Even the blackberry pancakes were unappealing. Even worse, they reminded me of how Leonidas had claimed they were one of his favorite treats during the breakfast we'd eaten together a few weeks ago in Myrkvior.

Father and Rhea filled me in on how the trade negotiations were going. I smiled, nodded, and made the appropriate responses, but my happy face must not have been terribly convincing because Father and Rhea exchanged a look, and she got to her feet.

"I need to check in with the guards," she said. "I'll leave you two to talk."

Rhea kissed Father, then left the study. He stared at me, and I did my best to hold on to the benign smile on my lips. But this expression must not have been terribly convincing either, because he placed his napkin on the table.

"Let's take a walk," Father said.

We left the study and stepped outside. The October morning was clear and bright, with only a few clouds drifting through the sky. The air was chilly, although it would warm up nicely by noon. The merchants in the plaza marketplace were already setting out their goods, but Father led me past the people and carts and toward the gardens. His strides were quick and purposeful, and he didn't stop until we reached my mother's memorial bench on the top main terrace.

Given the early hour, we were alone in this section of the gardens, although I spied Xenia down by the lakeshore. She was stabbing her cane at several workers who were constructing a large wooden platform, presumably for the third challenge.

My stomach clenched with nausea, wondering if Leonidas would even participate in the final Gauntlet challenge, given how badly things had ended between us last night. And what would happen if he won? How could we ever be anything more than enemies given who our families were and all the horrible things we'd done to each other?

Father eyed the workers before gesturing at me. "Let's sit."

He settled himself on one side of my mother's bench, while I took the other. He smiled and rubbed his fingers over the silver plaque that bore her name.

"I don't know if I ever told you this before, but I met your mother right here in this exact spot." He paused. "Sort of."

"What do you mean *sort of*?"

"I was sitting here, on this bench, surrounded by a gaggle of noble ladies, all of whom dearly wanted to be the next queen of Andvari. Back then, I was more popular than a rosebush to a horde of bees." Father laughed and pointed to a spot a few feet away. "Then this shadow fell over me. I looked up, and your mother was standing right there, her arms crossed over her chest, her foot tapping with annoyance, and a thoroughly disgusted look on her face."

Memories flickered off him and filled my mind. My father handsome and dashing in his gray jacket, and my mother glaring down at him, fierce and beautiful, with a crown of blue frost pansies circling her head.

"You make it sound like you and Mother didn't get along."

His lips curved up into a wry smile. "Oh, Merilde absolutely *hated* me. She thought I was arrogant, rude, and puffed up with self-importance—and she was right. All princes are a bit puffed up, at least when they are first venturing out into the world and trying to make a name for themselves, trying to step out of the shadows of all the kings and queens who have come before them."

"So what happened?"

Father's eyes softened with memories. "We fought *constantly* during the Summit. Heinrich and Jeeves, Merilde's father, didn't much care for each other, and they disagreed about a great many things. Naturally, that bled over into my relationship with Merilde. We used to have the most long-winded arguments about trade agreements and what was best for Andvari."

His smile widened, and bittersweet longing surged off him and washed through my own heart. "Those were some of the most thrilling conversations of my life."

"How did you move past your differences? Obviously you did, or I wouldn't be here."

A thoughtful look filled Father's face. "I'm not quite sure when or how it happened. But the more I talked to Merilde, the more I realized I loved the way she challenged me, the way she pushed me to be a better man, to be a better leader. I had all these grand ideas, but Merilde showed me what true love really is."

"And what is that?"

My father's eyes locked with mine. "Trust. Respect. Caring enough about someone else's feelings to put them above your own, no matter what the stakes are or how badly the outcome might damage you. That's what true love is, Gemma, and it is far more precious than any gold or gems we have at Glitnir."

He fell silent, as if choosing his next words carefully. "You care for Leonidas."

I opened my mouth to deny it, but he waved his hand, cutting me off.

"Just because I'm your father doesn't mean I'm blind. The gifts he gave you for the first challenge were perfect for you, and I saw how you looked at him in the arena last night."

"How was that?" I whispered.

"Like your heart was being beaten the same way those gladiators were beating him."

I grimaced. His words were so very unfortunately, regrettably true, but I still tried to deny them, struggling like a rabbit caught in a hunter's snare.

"How I feel about Leonidas doesn't matter. Especially since I can barely be in the same room with him without wondering when he's going to betray me next. How he is going to choose Morta and his family over me, just as he did in Myrkvior." Bitterness poisoned my voice and strangled my heart.

"From what you've told me, Leonidas was in an impossible situation. Maeven is the one who forced him to choose between saving you and protecting Delmira."

I sighed. "I know, and I would have made the same choice if you or Rhea were being threatened. But it still hurts all the same."

"Why do you think that is?"

His question made me uncomfortable, but I answered it anyway. "I have to do so many things as Princess Gemma. I always have to appear brave and strong and noble and kind and good. I have to be *perfect* every single second of every single day. Some of that is of my own doing, by letting people think I was Glitzma and nothing more over the past few years."

"And now?" Father asked.

I sighed again, longer, louder, and deeper than before. "And now . . . I want someone to see all the *other* parts of me, the broken, jagged pieces that are decidedly *imperfect*, and help me hold them all together." Emotion clogged my throat, but I forced out the truth I had never spoken aloud before. "Leonidas . . . sees all those pieces of me. He always has, ever since we were children."

"But?"

A third sigh escaped my lips. "But I don't know if I can ever fully trust him with all those pieces, all those sharp edges that could so easily shred my heart."

"Because he's a Morricone? Maeven's son?"

"Yes . . . and no. Leonidas being a Morricone, especially Maeven's son, makes me even more wary. But the truth is I don't know if I can ever trust *anyone* that way."

I surged to my feet and started pacing back and forth. "I've just seen too many betrayals in my life. First, Uncle Frederich was murdered at Seven Spire by Crown Princess Vasilia, the woman he was supposed to marry. Then Dahlia Sullivan poisoned Grandfather Heinrich, even though he loved her and she had some affection for him. And finally, Leonidas turned me over to Maeven at Myrkvior, even though he claimed to care about me. Care, concern, love. They all pave a path to certain destruction."

Father rose to his feet. "Betrayal is a way of life for royals, Gemma. Nothing will ever change that. Even now there are some Andvarian nobles who would dearly love to see themselves on the throne, instead of our family."

"But?"

Father put his hands on my arms and gave them a gentle squeeze. "But with the right person, love *is* worth the risk— *any* risk. Merilde taught me that, Rhea too, and I think you and Leonidas could teach each other that as well."

"What about him being a Morricone? And Queen Ruri threatening to break our treaty?"

Father harrumphed. "Well, I won't pretend I'm *happy* Maeven's son is the one who has caught your eye, but I will try to judge Leonidas on his own merits." His face hardened. "As for the Ryusamans, if Ruri thinks she can break our treaty without consequences, then she is gravely mistaken."

Determination glinted in his eyes, and in that moment, Dominic Ripley looked every inch the future king that he was.

"But first things first," Father said. "We will see if Leonidas actually manages to complete the last challenge."

"And if he does?"

More determination filled my father's face. "Then we will negotiate terms with Xenia and Maeven. But know this, Gemma. I will do whatever it takes to protect you."

Hot tears pricked my eyes, and I hugged him. "Thank you, Father."

He hugged me back. "Of course, my darling."

We kept hugging, drawing what comfort we could from each other. My gaze dropped to my mother's plaque, which was once again surrounded by curls of liladorn, and a tiny tendril of hope bloomed in my heart. My parents had overcome all the obstacles between them. Perhaps Leonidas and I could do the same—if we survived the rest of the Summit.

CHAPTER TWENTY-SIX

Father offered to stay with me, but I knew he had work to do, so I told him that I was fine. And I truly was. My mind and heart were clearer than they had been in weeks.

Father returned to his study, but I headed toward a building located off the plaza marketplace, in between the Andvarian and Mortan wings. The front door was open, so I slipped inside, walked down a short hallway, and stepped into a large library.

Tables and chairs were clustered together in the center of this first main room, flanked by several rows of bookcases. Colorful tapestries of historic battles adorned the walls, along with faded maps. The air smelled slightly musty, and dust motes swirled in the sunlight streaming in through the stained-glass windows.

No guards were stationed in here, and the library was a common area that anyone could use during the Summit. A few people held meetings in the library's rooms, but most gatherings took place at the tables on the plaza, where everyone could see and gossip about everyone else.

The thousands of library books got little use during the

Summit, unless someone needed to look up an obscure bit of lore that had some impact on their trade negotiations. I wondered if that's what Maeven had done. If she had wandered into the library sometime in the past, seen a book about the Gauntlet, and tucked the information away in the back of her mind, to be used when the time was right. If so, that would have been a particularly impressive Bellonan long game, even for someone as smart and cunning as Maeven.

I went to the section that dealt with plants, flowers, gardening, and the like. I moved from one shelf to the next, scanning all the volumes, but I didn't see any books with purple covers or titles that matched the one I had taken from Milo's island workshop.

Frustrated, I headed to a different section that focused on magiers and their powers and abilities. I scanned all the volumes about plant magiers, but once again I came up empty.

More frustration surged through me, and I started pacing back and forth. Instead of focusing on my mission, I thought back to what Father had told me about how he and my mother had met. Their love story had been difficult enough with only their own prejudices against each other to overcome. They hadn't had the added strain of being from two different kingdoms, or two families that had such a long bloody history, like Leonidas and I did—

A thought popped into my mind, and I stopped pacing. There was one more place in the library where I might find a copy of Milo's book.

I left the room with the magier books and went to a reading nook in the very back of the library. The space wasn't very large, only about twelve feet wide, and hidden behind a row of bookcases. A cushioned settee stood in between a cold fireplace and a small bookcase. A low table was positioned in front of the settee, with a single chair sitting on the opposite side. A layer of dust coated everything, as if the servants who cleaned the library had forgotten this reading nook even existed.

Still, dust and all, the sight brought a smile to my face. When I was younger, my mother used to bring me here, to *our secret spot*, as she called it, and we would curl up together on the settee and drink hot chocolate while we read one book after another. Wistful longing filled my heart. If only I could go back to those simpler times when my greatest worry had been wondering if a story was going to have a happy ending. But there was no going back, only forward, so I walked over to the bookshelf and scanned the titles.

Most of the volumes were the same storybooks I remembered, the covers worn and faded, but my mother had often read other books while I had been doing my studies. Plus, Merilde had loved to garden, even though she had been a time magier, instead of a plant magier.

I glanced through those books, but none of them had a purple cover. With each shelf, my heart sank a little lower with disappointment. By the time I reached the bottom shelf and the last of the books, my heart was level with my toes. I should have known better than to get my hopes up. It had been a long shot that Merilde might have read the same book as Milo, once upon a time.

I started to turn away from the bookcase when a title done in silver foil caught my eye—*A Treatise on Mortan Plants: Their Properties and Uses*. My heart lifted, and I grabbed the book. The cover was black instead of purple, but the titles were the same.

A gray ribbon was nestled in the book, as if to mark someone's place. I rubbed the ribbon between my fingers, and a memory filled my mind of my mother smiling and tying it in my hair the last summer we had come to Caldwell before she had gotten sick. Why would this ribbon still be here all these years later? And in this specific book?

I frowned. Had my mother *seen* this moment with her time magier magic? Had she known I would someday come looking for this book? But how could she have possibly known that? From what I remembered, Merilde's power had been modest at best, and she usually got only glimpses of the immediate past or future.

Even more curious now, I tucked the ribbon into my pocket, then flipped through the book. It was *exactly* the same as Milo's book, and the gray ribbon marked the start of the missing pages. I read through the information.

> Fool's bane poison is derived from the flower of the same name. Despite its small, seemingly innocuous appearance, fool's bane is a most interesting plant, able to grow in harsh environments that would destroy other vegetation. It can be used to make everything from perfume to poison, although the poison is of particular interest. It can be given in small doses, to cause a seemingly natural decline in a person, or in a concentrated form that is lethal within minutes . . .

So Milo *was* brewing up a rare poison. Not surprising, given how Maeven's guards had been killed and the magic I'd sensed in her goblet at dinner last night.

A few recipes were included, although I couldn't tell if they were for making the poison, the perfume, or both. The passage was also accompanied by an illustration—three small purple petals on a fuzzy green stem—that looked exactly like the fool's bane I'd picked yesterday afternoon and the dried flower the Mortan boy had in his pouch in the Haverton woods. I kept reading.

> The full extent of the uses of fool's bane are known only to a few extremely skilled plant magiers and tin-

kerers. Some magiers theorize that, in addition to its
lethality, various concentrations of the poison can also
be used to affect magic, either increasing or removing
it from people, creatures, and even objects . . .

I skimmed the rest of the passage, but there was nothing
else of interest, so I shut the book and placed it on the top shelf.
Learning which flower and poison Milo was using was helpful,
but it still didn't give me any real clue as to what his ultimate
goal was—

My fingertips tingled in warning, and footsteps whispered
behind me, along with a steady *swish-swish-swish* of fabric.

"You should be in your chambers getting ready, Gemma,"
a soft familiar voice cut through the air. "It's not every day a
crown princess gets engaged."

I froze, my hand still on the book. I had been so caught up in
my reading that I hadn't sensed her approach. I cursed my lack
of attentiveness, even as I dropped my hand from the book and
turned around.

Queen Maeven stood in front of me.

My gaze darted past Maeven, but no guards were lurking behind
her in the hidden nook, and I didn't sense anyone else's presence farther out in the library. She had come here alone, which
made me even more curious—and wary.

"What are you doing in here?" I asked in a snide voice.
"Come to research more arcane rituals to further torture me?"

"Oh, I think the one arcane ritual is torture enough." She
arched an eyebrow. "And that was a sad attempt at mockery. I
thought you had more imagination, Gemma."

"Well, give me a moment to hone my wits and sharpen my

tongue, and I'm sure I can come up with several insults that are appropriately clever and cutting enough for you."

An amused laugh tumbled out of her lips and splattered all over me. "There is literally *nothing* you can say that I haven't heard before, either being shouted directly to my face or slyly whispered behind my back."

Maeven stepped forward and I skirted to the side, keeping the low table between us. I also reached for my power, ready to block any attack she might make with her lightning.

Maeven arched her eyebrow again. "If you're thinking about killing me, I would advise against it. I have several guards posted outside the library. You would not escape. Surely murdering me isn't worth your own life."

I bared my teeth at her. "I'm tempted to try it and find out. I escaped from Myrkvior. A library shouldn't be too much of a challenge."

Another laugh tumbled out of her lips. "You do have spirit. I can see why Leonidas likes you so much."

She said the words calmly, casually, but a sly look filled her face, and I knew she was testing me, waiting to see how I would respond. I might not be able to draw my dagger and attack her, but we were still dueling, so I kept my own face blank, even though it was a losing battle. Father had noticed my feelings for Leonidas in the arena last night, and I had no doubt that Maeven had as well.

She continued her slow circuit around the reading nook. I matched her step-for-step, moving in the opposite direction and keeping the same amount of distance between us. We'd done this same stalemate dance in Milo's workshop in Myrkvior, with me trying to lunge around a table to kill her and her just as easily skirting around it, skirting around *me*, just like she was now.

Just like she *always* did.

Maeven reached the bookcase and trailed her fingers over

the volumes. Worry filled me. Had she noticed the book I had been reading? Would the title mean anything to her?

Maeven had seen King Maximus's tinkerings and experiments firsthand, and she probably knew more about fool's bane poison than the writer of the book did. But she merely trailed her fingers over a few more volumes, then stopped and faced me again.

"I'd forgotten how cozy this little space was. I can see why Merilde liked it so much."

Once again, I froze. "What do you know about my mother?"

"I used to see the two of you roaming through the gardens when I would come to Caldwell for the Summit. And at other times, when Maximus would summer on Antheia Island for a few weeks. Merilde was always quite friendly to me, much more so than I expected."

I eyed her, wondering if she was lying, if this was some new ploy to throw me off balance and fuck with my emotions, something she always took great delight in doing. But the queen's features were more thoughtful than cunning, and her voice rang with truth.

"Merilde even invited me to have tea with her a time or two, right here in this very room," Maeven continued, moving over to the settee. "Why, I remember her sitting right here, with you curled up beside her, your nose stuck in one of those inane storybooks you loved so much."

Her hands curled around the back of the settee, her short dark purple nails digging into the gray cushions like strix talons about to rip through the fabric. Maeven glanced downward, and a memory surged off her—my mother and me sitting on the settee, just as she had described. She *was* telling the truth. She had been here before. Why?

"I always envied your mother," Maeven said. "Merilde had both a husband who loved her and a child whom she adored. She had such an easy, happy, carefree life, even for a future queen consort. That was one of the reasons why I hated her so much."

Anger exploded in my heart, but I forced myself to shove it down. Snapping at her wouldn't do me any good, and it certainly wouldn't get me any answers about her relationship with my mother—or why she was telling me about it now.

"As a Mortan, I didn't think you needed a reason to hate an Andvarian, future queen consort or otherwise."

Maeven shrugged. "Sometimes I do, sometimes I don't. But Merilde was kind, unlike the other Andvarian nobles, who always peered down their noses at me, as if they all didn't have a bastard relative or two haunting the halls of their estates. So I hated Merilde a little more than all the others. I even thought about killing her, once, in this very room. I was going to dose her tea with amethyst-eye poison."

My heart squeezed tight. I'd always known Maeven was cruel, but to murder someone just because they had shown you a tiny bit of kindness, respect, and mercy . . . Well, she was even more of a heartless bitch than I'd thought, and she gave me yet another reason to despise her.

Maeven's nails dug a little deeper into the settee cushions, and purple lightning crackled around her fingers, singeing the fabric. I reached for my own magic again, ready to block her power if she threw it at me. But just as quickly as it appeared, the lightning vanished, and Maeven drew in a deep breath, as though steadying herself.

"But I had forgotten one small thing about Merilde, and it ruined my entire plan."

"Which was?"

"That she was a time magier," Maeven replied, a rueful smile curving her face. "Merilde had already had a vision of me trying to poison her. She knew what I was going to do before I even did it."

"So what happened?"

Because I knew Maeven hadn't poisoned my mother. No, Merilde's sickness had been a by-product of her magic, as was so often the case with time magiers. They saw too much, experienced too many glimpses of the past and future that pulled them in too many different directions, and their visions simply wore out their bodies, especially their minds and hearts. At least that was the theory.

"We sat down to have tea, and Merilde picked up her cup." Maeven stared at the low table as if she was replaying the scene in her mind. "She told me that it was my choice. If I wanted, then she would drink the poison and I could kill her."

"And what was your other choice?"

Maeven's gaze locked with mine. "That I could be queen of Morta."

Shock sizzled through me just like her lightning had scorched the settee cushions. "*My mother* told *you* that you could be *queen of Morta?*"

My voice screeched out a little louder and higher with every single word. I couldn't even *imagine* such a thing. Why would Merilde do that? Why would she say that? Perhaps it had been a ploy to keep Maeven from poisoning her. But if that had been the case, then why hadn't my mother just summoned some guards to deal with the other woman? Why tell Maeven that she could be queen?

"Of course I didn't believe her," Maeven continued. "I thought Merilde was just trying to save herself. But she claimed she'd had a vision of my future and that I could have everything I ever wanted if only I did one small thing."

I couldn't stop myself from asking the inevitable question. "And what was that?"

"When Leonidas turned thirteen, I had to send him to stay with one of my cousins who lived in the Spire Mountains near the Bellona-Andvari border. Merilde was *quite* insistent about it. She said if I did that, then I would one day be queen of Morta."

"And you believed her?"

"Not at first."

"What convinced you?"

Maeven's lips puckered in thought. "It was the look on Merilde's face. She was so bloody *certain* of herself, her magic, her vision—but she wasn't happy about it. In fact, she was rather disgusted about my becoming queen. Plus, I was already plotting how to get Leonidas and Delmira away from Myrkvior and Maximus."

"So you didn't believe my mother," I replied. "Not really. Her suggestion just fit in with your own plans."

"I suppose that's one way to look at it. Although now, thinking back on our conversation, and remembering what she asked me to do . . ." Her voice trailed off suggestively.

"What?" I growled.

"I can see now that Merilde was far more interested in securing *your* future than she ever was *mine*."

Every word she said only confused me more. "What do you mean?"

"Haven't you ever wondered how Leonidas ended up in the Spire Mountains at the *exact same time* you were fleeing from Bellona?"

I frowned at her implication. "But my mother's magic was modest at best. She couldn't have possibly foreseen that the two of us would meet."

Or everything that would happen between us back then. Or again in Blauberg and Myrkvior a few weeks ago. And especially in the arena dressing room last night. Merilde couldn't have possibly known about everything I would feel for Leonidas. All the ways I so desperately wanted him, and how very afraid I was to fully trust him, especially with my heart.

Unless . . . my mother had lied about her power the same way I had lied about mine for so long.

The stronger a time magier was in their magic, the shorter they tended to live. Most time magiers with moderate powers made it to at least fifty, but my mother had still been in her thirties when she'd died.

"Merilde saw *something*," Maeven hissed. "And like a fool, I fell for her long game. Sometimes, I wish I had never taken her advice. Sometimes, I wish I had forced that poison down her throat and then done the same thing to *you*, Gemma. Perhaps if I had, then Leonidas wouldn't have almost died in the arena last night."

Rage exploded in my heart, and I stabbed my finger at her. "Don't you *dare* speak about my mother that way, you arrogant, duplicitous, manipulative bitch. And don't you dare blame her for *any* of this. *You're* the one who thrust Leonidas into the Gauntlet, so *you're* the reason he almost died. You and all the enemies you've made."

I kept glaring at her. "And to think I actually saved your life last night."

"How did you . . ." Maeven's eyes narrowed. "My sangria. It was poisoned, just like the bottles of wine my guards drank in the arena dressing room."

"Yes, and I should have let you drink it. Maybe then Leonidas would finally be safe—from *you*."

Maeven winced, as if my words had finally managed to wound her, although her features quickly smoothed back into that icy, haughty expression I knew so well, the one that so often encased Leonidas's features in a similar armor.

"I don't blame your mother," she replied. "I wanted to believe her vision so very badly that I didn't see how it would benefit her. But Merilde tied our two families together that day, as snugly and neatly as a ribbon on a yuletide present, and I haven't been able to break that connection, no matter how hard I've tried over the years—and I have certainly tried."

No one will bother us, especially not the noble ladies who have been chasing after Leo lately, Delmira's voice whispered through my mind.

I'd thought she had been trying to make me jealous, but now I wondered if the sudden influx of female suitors had been another manipulation on Maeven's part. A way to tempt her son away from me, even though I still wasn't sure I wanted to be bound to him in any way.

"Merilde's vision still doesn't have anything to do with you thrusting Leonidas into the Gauntlet. Did you think Xenia would go easy on him? She has far too much pride in Ungerian tradition to do that. So does Zariza."

Maeven huffed with annoyance. "I'll admit that was a . . . miscalculation on my part. I thought the Ungers would merely hurt Leonidas if he failed one of the challenges, not threaten to kill him. But I should have known they would adhere to their tradition. Ogres always do. Barbaric, bloodthirsty idiots."

She shook her head, as though the Ungers doing exactly what she had manipulated them into doing was a great disappointment. Then she looked at me again, her face even colder than before. "No, Gemma. I don't blame Merilde for Leonidas being in danger. I blame *you*."

The venom in her voice slapped me across the face. "How can *you* possibly blame *me* for something that *you* put into motion?"

"Because Leonidas will not admit defeat. He will not quit the Gauntlet, no matter how much I've begged him to."

My eyes bulged. "Wait. You've tried to talk him *out* of participating in the Gauntlet? When?"

"Last night, after the second challenge. I even commanded it as his queen, but he refused." Maeven speared me with another icy glower. "He refused because of *you*, Gemma. Leonidas fool-ishly thinks that if he makes it through the Gauntlet that it will *prove* something to you. That you will finally consider him *worthy* of your affection or some such nonsense. Romantic fool."

Her tone was harsh, but grudging respect rippled through her words, as if she both hated and admired her son for sticking to his principles.

I am going to earn your trust, Gemma Ripley, Leonidas's voice whispered through my mind. *And your heart too, if I am lucky enough to manage it.*

I'd thought his confession had been just another pretty ploy, another way he could seduce me, sway me to his side, and then betray me later on. But anger and frustration poured off Maeven like rain from a cloud. She wasn't lying about her son's actions—just like Leonidas hadn't been lying to me.

In an instant, all the rage in my heart evaporated, replaced by something much, much stronger—hope.

Hope for so many things. For Leonidas, for myself, but mostly, for the two of us—together.

Maeven's lips curled with disgust. "Look at you. I can *see* the desire on your face. You want Leonidas to succeed in the Gauntlet, despite yourself."

"I don't want Leonidas to die," I said, sidestepping her ac-cusation. "But even if he succeeds in the final challenge, we are not getting engaged, much less married. I will *not* let you dic-tate the course of my life."

"Fool," Maeven hissed right back at me. "I told you before that I was giving you a gift—my son. You should take him and be grateful for my generosity."

"Maeven would never let her son marry anyone less than a princess," I murmured.

She blinked. "What? What is that nonsense you're spout-ing?"

"I overheard someone say that at Myrkvior." Well, over-heard it with my mind, but she didn't need to know that. "And they were right. You might sit on the Mortan throne, but you have three children and only one crown to give them. So you de-cided to try to marry Leonidas off to a princess of some other kingdom and get your hands on another throne that way. Just like Dahlia Sullivan wanted to kill my father and grandfather so that she could convince Uncle Lucas to take the Andvarian crown and marry some Mortan noble lady."

Disgust rolled through me. "You might claim that Merilde tricked you into all of this and that Leonidas is thwarting you now by refusing to drop out of the Gauntlet, but you are play-ing your own long game in order to further your own agenda. I might be a fool when it comes to your son, but I'm not stupid when it comes to *you*."

Maeven glared at me, but once again, a faint bit of grudging respect rippled off her.

"Well, I'm not falling for any more of your tricks. You might have started this game with Leonidas and me, but *I* will be the one to finish it."

Maeven took a menacing step forward. "And I know *you*, Gemma Ripley. I've been watching you from afar for years. I know how you think, and I especially know what your heart de-sires."

"You know *nothing* of my heart," I hissed.

"I know it's so soft and weak that it wouldn't let you kill Leonidas in the arena last night, even though you had the per-fect opportunity," she hissed right back at me. "I would *never* make such a mistake, and neither would any of the queens you hold in such high regard."

Her words punched into my stomach, but this time, instead of shock, they made a fresh wave of rage rise up in my chest. Now I was the one who took a menacing step forward.

"I *do* hold the other queens in high regard. Do you know why? Because I have learned things from every single one of them. Everleigh, Zariza, Ruri. And Xenia too. How to be cold and ruthless and calculating. Even how to be a spy. Oh, yes. I have learned from *all* the queens, including you. Sometimes, I think I've learned more from you than all the others combined."

Maeven blinked, as if she had never expected me to confess such a thing. I wasn't sure what to make of it either, but I'd said the words, and I wasn't going to take them back.

"Oh, yes. I have learned quite a lot from you, Your Majesty," I snarled out her title. "First at the Seven Spire massacre all those years ago. Then several months after that, when you came to Glitnir to try to kill Everleigh Blair. And then again at Myrkvior just a few weeks ago. So I know you have some other plot in mind when it comes to the Gauntlet, and I will *never* believe a word you say to try to convince me otherwise."

Anger painted red splotches on her cheeks, and more purple lightning crackled around her clenched fists. "I am trying to ensure my son's happiness," she snapped. "And I am especially trying to save his life!"

Maeven grimaced, as though she'd never meant to confess such a thing to anyone, least of all me. But once again, truth rang through her words. Even more telling, pure, raw fear surged off her, along with an image of Milo plunging a sword into Leonidas's back.

"So that's why you want Leonidas to marry me. Not so he will be happy, but so that he will be far away from Morta where Milo can't get to him."

A bitter laugh tumbled out of Maeven's lips, and her fear burned through me like acid. "There is no place where Milo can't get to Leonidas, but at least with you, he has a chance of surviving."

She paused, and when she spoke again, her voice was

pitched much lower and softer than before. "He might even have a chance at happiness too."

Maeven dropped her gaze from mine as if she couldn't bear to look at me right now. "You're right. You have learned from me, Gemma. I just hope you were paying attention—and that you use those lessons to save my son."

With that dire pronouncement, Queen Maeven spun around and stalked out of the reading nook, once again leaving me with far more questions than answers.

chapter twenty-seven

I waited until I was certain Maeven was gone, then left the library. I hurried across the plaza and returned to my chambers.

Reiko's door was still shut, and I didn't sense her anywhere nearby. I wondered if she'd already gone to Queen Ruri, if she'd already told Tatsuo that she would be returning to Ryusama with them. Hurt rippled through my heart at the thought, but I was the one who'd pushed my friend away, and I had no one to blame for her loss but myself.

Grimley and Violet were stretched out by the sitting-room fireplace. The strix was fast asleep, but the gargoyle lifted his head at the sound of my footsteps. I plopped down on the floor and hugged his neck.

Grimley leaned into me, one of his wings coming around to pat my back. I sighed and hugged him again.

I drew back, and Grimley regarded me with a serious expression. "What was that for?"

I didn't feel like explaining my conversation with Father,

my latest run-in with Maeven, or my conflicting feelings about Leonidas, Reiko, and everything else. "I just needed a hug."

Grimley opened his mouth to question me further, but a knock sounded on the door. Xenia entered my chambers, followed by Yaleen, my thread master, and the usual servants.

"Come to prepare the lamb for the slaughter?" I asked.

Xenia arched an eyebrow at my sarcastic tone. "The day has barely started. Don't jinx it, Gemma. Besides, we're going to do our best to avoid slaughter today."

Grimley got to his feet, stretched, and announced he was going hunting. Violet squeaked in protest, but the gargoyle lifted her up onto the settee in front of the fireplace, and she hunkered down on a cushion. I scratched Grimley's head. Then he went out to the balcony, flapped his wings, and sailed up into the sky.

I watched him go, wishing I could fly away from all my problems, but I had no choice but to trudge back inside and hand myself over to Yaleen and the servants.

First, they dressed me in traditional gladiator fighting leathers—a tightly fitted light gray sleeveless shirt, a knee-length kilt, and flat sandals with straps that wound up past my ankles. I added my tearstone dagger to the weapons belt around my waist, and my gargoyle pendant hung from my neck as usual.

Next, Yaleen and the servants worked on my hair and makeup. Brushing, tugging, pulling. Powdering, perfuming, painting. I had never felt more like a doll being dressed up and primped for someone else's amusement.

Eventually they retreated, and I studied my reflection in the vanity-table mirror. My dark brown hair had been pulled back into three knots, each one of which was bristling with strix feathers that looked like purple arrows sticking out of my head. Light gray paint covered my face, while black shadow and liner rimmed my blue eyes. My lips had also been stained a deep flat black. But the most unusual part of the makeup was the three black snarling gargoyle faces that adorned my face—one on each cheek and a third in the center of my forehead.

"Come. Let me look at you," Xenia called out from her chair by the sitting-room fireplace.

I got to my feet and walked over to her.

Xenia leaned forward, her hands resting on her silver cane, and inspected me from head to toe. "Well done. Very well done."

Yaleen grinned. Then she and the servants exited the chambers, leaving me alone with Xenia.

"Why a gladiator outfit?" I asked. "Mixed with strix feathers and gargoyle faces?"

Xenia stabbed her cane at my hair, then my face. "The strix feathers symbolize Leonidas, while the gargoyles represent you, along with the three Gauntlet challenges." She waved her cane at my chest. "As for the fighting leathers, well, the Ungers of old might have . . . borrowed those from the Bellonans."

My eyebrows shot up. "You're actually admitting that this grand Ungerian tradition has some of its roots in the Bellonan gladiator fights?"

Xenia shrugged. "Even the barbaric Bellonans have good ideas on occasion."

I laughed, although the sound quickly faded away. "Tell me what Leonidas is facing in the final challenge. *Please.*" The last word came out much harsher than I intended.

"Nothing too strenuous," Xenia replied. "As I've said before, it's an obstacle course of sorts. He'll start by swimming out into the lake, retrieving a flag from a wooden platform, and swimming back to shore. Then he will work his way up the various terraces, stopping to engage in three gladiator fights."

"Nothing too strenuous? The swim alone could kill him,

given how cold the lake is. Not to mention how badly last night's fight went in the arena."

"Don't worry," Xenia continued. "I handpicked the gladiators, and these fights are only to first blood. If Leonidas makes it past the fighters, he will climb up the rocks and then the side of the lighthouse, where you will be waiting on the observation deck at the top."

I frowned. "That last part sounds an awful lot like the Pureheart challenge, where the Bellonans scale the side of Seven Spire palace to be with their love."

Xenia harrumphed, but a grudging smile creased her face. "As I said before, the Bellonans have some good ideas on occasion."

"What happens if Leonidas makes it to the top of the lighthouse?"

"Well, in ideal circumstances, the two of you would loudly proclaim your love for all to hear, swoon into each other's arms, and share a passionate kiss. Or two. Or three."

I snorted. "We both know these are far less than ideal circumstances."

Xenia tipped her head, acknowledging my point. "What happens at the top of the lighthouse is entirely up to you, Gemma. You could always shove Leonidas off the side. He'd probably fall to his death."

"Or?"

She speared me with a hard look. "Or you could finally admit how you feel about him."

I snorted again. "I did that in the arena last night when I didn't kill him."

"Regardless, what happens between you and Leonidas is your business. Mine is just to make sure the Gauntlet proceeds without any more assassination attempts." Xenia got to her feet, and her face softened. "Whatever you decide about Leonidas, I'll support you, Gemma."

I nodded, too much emotion clogging my throat to speak right now. Xenia squeezed my arm, then left, closing the door behind her.

Over on the settee, Violet fluttered her wings. The strix had remained largely quiet while Yaleen and the servants had been working on me, although she'd watched their ministrations with wide eyes. I went over, crouched down in front of her, and smoothed my hand over her light purple feathers.

"What do you think?" I murmured. "Should I throw Leonidas off the lighthouse? Or perhaps myself? Really, I'd like to toss Maeven off the side, but sadly, that is not an option."

Violet let out a sympathetic cheep. I petted her again, then straightened up.

My gaze landed on the crystal vase that held the bouquet of ice violets Leonidas had given me during the first Gauntlet challenge. I rubbed one of the purple petals between my fingertips. Leonidas had given me a truly lovely bouquet, even if the violets' color reminded me of the fool's bane I had picked by the lakeshore yesterday—

My fingers froze, crushing the silky petal. Suddenly, I remembered *another* person who'd had a bouquet of purple flowers by the lakeshore yesterday.

Corvina.

At the time, I'd thought her bouquet had merely been a prop to sell the illusion that she and Milo were out for a pleasant stroll. But what if Corvina had purposefully picked some fool's bane just as I had?

My mind skipped from that memory over to the missing pages in the book in Milo's workshop on Antheia Island. Milo wouldn't have needed to tear the pages out of that book—it was *his* book, and he could have simply taken it with him. But what if Corvina had wanted the fool's bane recipes? What if *she* had ripped out those pages so she could brew her own batch of poison?

My mind kept whirring. Corvina might have aligned herself with Milo, might be supplying him with men and money, but that didn't mean she didn't have her *own* agenda. A few weeks ago at Myrkvior, Corvina had stood by and watched while Milo and Emperia had tried to depose Maeven. What if she was doing the same thing again? What if she was letting Milo battle Maeven and then making her own plans to kill whichever Morricone was left standing?

The more I thought about it, the more sense it made. Then I remembered the gladiators who had tried to kill Leonidas in the arena last night. What if Corvina had bigger plans than just murdering Milo or Maeven? What if she wanted to kill *all* the Morricones?

More worry spiked through me. If so, then Leonidas was still in danger—and Corvina probably had something horrible planned for him during the third Gauntlet challenge.

Behind me, the chamber door creaked open. Violet squeaked, fluttered her wings, and drew back, jamming her tiny body into the space between the settee cushions.

I turned around. "Xenia! I'm so glad you came back. I need to warn you about—"

My words died on my lips. A woman stood before me dressed in gray fighting leathers and a weapons belt, just like I was. Her auburn hair was also pulled back into three knots and bristled with purple strix feathers, just like mine was. Gray paint covered her face, although black lightning bolts zigzagged down her cheeks and forehead instead of gargoyles. Recognition shot through me, along with more than a little shock.

"Corvina," I whispered.

"Hello, Gemma," she purred, then snapped up the crossbow in her hand and fired it at me.

I jerked to the side and reached for the string of energy attached to the arrow zipping toward me—

Too late. The arrow sank into my upper left arm. Pain exploded in my body, and I screamed and staggered back. I bounced off a table, my feet flew out from under me, and I hit the floor hard.

Anger spiked through me, along with more pain, but I scrambled to my feet, whirled around, and reached for my magic to kill her—

Wexel was now standing in front of me. He gave me an evil grin, then plowed his fist into my face. Pain rippled through my jaw, and I once again staggered back and fell to the floor.

More anger spiked through me, and I started to get up to kill them both, but Wexel planted his right boot on my chest, pinning me in place with his strength magic.

"Stop fighting, or I'll crush your fucking ribs," he growled.

I had no choice but to lay on the floor and glare up at him.

Corvina strolled over, propped the crossbow up on her shoulder, and stared down at me with a dispassionate expression. "Given your heroics in Blauberg, I thought you'd put up much more of a fight, Gemma. How disappointing."

She reached down, took hold of the shaft, and yanked the arrow out of my arm. I screamed again, tears rolling down my face, and blood oozed out of the deep, jagged wound.

Corvina held the arrow up where I could see it. Horror filled me. Not just any arrow—one of Milo's barbed monstrosities.

She twirled it back and forth between her fingers. "Milo was right. Blood really does make the tearstone change color."

More blood—*my* blood—dripped down the shaft like paint rolling across a blank canvas, turning the light gray tearstone the same dark blue as the barbed arrowhead. Vomit rose in my throat, but I choked it down.

All this time, I'd thought Milo had been coating his arrows with something. I was right about that—and wrong too. Because I had never considered that *blood* could be part of his foul formula.

Corvina tossed the arrow down, and it landed with an ominous clatter on the floor beside me.

"Not going to use the arrow to torture me with your weather magic like Milo did?" Once again, my tongue kept tripping along, despite the dire situation. "How disappointing."

A merry laugh erupted out of her lips. "Please. I'm not wasting my power on you like that. Besides, the poison on the arrow will kill you soon enough."

Icy fingers of dread curled around my heart. "Fool's bane," I croaked. "You coated the arrow with fool's bane poison."

"Of course," Corvina replied. "I got the idea from Milo. He claims that coating his arrows with dried fool's bane helps the tearstone amplify and better conduct his lightning magic, along with a person's blood."

So that's why the dead Mortan boy in Haverton had had the dried flower in his pouch. He'd been using it on the arrows as part of Milo's experiments.

"The dried fool's bane by itself isn't poisonous—unless you grind it up and mix it with salt and water." A sly light filled Corvina's eyes. "Milo gave me *quite* the lesson about the flower when we were on Antheia. He had my men cultivate an entire garden of fool's bane on the island, just so he could harvest the blossoms for his arrows. But of course I found a better, more efficient use for them."

I thought of the empty flowerbeds outside the island manor

house. Wexel and the rest of Corvina's men must have pulled up all the plants right before Leonidas and I had arrived.

"The poison is surprisingly easy to make for something so lethal," Corvina continued. "You should already be feeling the effects."

I concentrated, pushing away the pain of the wound, Wexel's punch, and his boot still pressing against my chest. She was right. I *could* feel the poison slowly creeping through my veins, cold and wet, like the soil that the fool's bane grew in by the lake. A rotten, watery stench also filled my nose, and a tired lethargy was quickly rising inside me.

More icy fingers of dread curled around my heart, but I forced myself to stay calm. Corvina thought she had killed me, and she was here to crow about how clever she was. Well, I was going to let her talk all she wanted. Maybe she had killed me, but I was going to get to the bottom of her scheme before I died—and find some way to stop her from hurting Leonidas.

"I'm surprised Milo didn't come here and kill me himself," I said.

"Oh, he wanted to. But I convinced him that it would be better if he was seen in the crowd with Maeven and Delmira while Wexel and I killed you."

"Why is that?" I prompted, trying to get her to keep talking.

Corvina laughed again. "Milo thinks I'm following his orders to eliminate Leonidas and Maeven so he can take the throne, but I've been implementing my own plans during the Summit."

So I was right. Corvina *was* playing her own long game with the Morricones—and I just happened to be in her way.

"*You* poisoned Maeven's sangria at dinner last night with fool's bane. Well, Wexel did it for you, since he handed the sangria pitcher to the servant, and he probably gave Maeven's guards those bottles of poisoned wine too. Once they were dead, you replaced them with your own men for the gladiator challenge to try to kill Leonidas. Did Milo tell you to do that too?"

"Oh, please. Milo could *never* be that clever. I subtly suggested the ideas, and he ordered me to execute them. My plans would have worked, and Maeven and Leonidas would both already be dead, if you hadn't interfered." Anger sparked in Corvina's eyes, turning them a dark, stormy gray, and her magic gusted over me, cold, hard, and wet, just like the poison still creeping through my veins.

I remembered the whispered thoughts I'd heard during the dinner and gladiator challenge. The crowd had been so loud that I'd assumed they belonged to Milo, but they had really been Corvina's musings.

My mind kept churning. "But poisoning the gladiators wasn't your first strike during the Summit. You were also behind the attack on Leonidas and me in the gardens two nights ago."

"An opportunity presented itself to eliminate you both, so I took it." Corvina shot a sour look at Wexel. "Although I apparently didn't give Wexel enough men to get the job done. Another unfortunate setback."

"But how did you even know Leonidas and I were in the gardens?"

"After I left Milo and Wexel in the library that night, I snuck back in through a side door. I wanted to hear *exactly* what my dear fiancé said about me. But surprise, surprise, I spotted you in the library instead."

I thought of the cold, wet, electric magic on the door I'd used to escape the library and the similar presence I'd sensed sneaking along behind me in the gardens. Corvina had been spying on me, just like I'd been spying on the Morricones. Only, I'd been too distracted by my thoughts about Leonidas to realize it.

Bitterness surged through me. What a fool I was. Reiko would have never made such a mistake.

Corvina snapped her fingers. "And just like that, I saw a way to get everything I had ever wanted."

One way or another, I will be queen of Morta, Corvina's voice whispered through my mind. She'd said those words to Wexel at Myrkvior, and now she was doing everything in her power to make them a reality.

"But you just kept interfering, so I decided to come here and kill you myself to make sure you wouldn't ruin any more of my plans."

"Why kill me? I never did anything to you. I told you last night in the arena—Maeven murdered Emperia, not me. Something you already knew, given your lack of surprise."

Corvina scoffed. "I knew Maeven was up to something as soon as she offered to take Emperia to Milo's workshop to see you being tortured. I just didn't think the bitch was going to murder my mother and then blame it on you." She sneered down at me. "As if Princess Glitzma could have *ever* bested my mother or any other Dumond. You might be a mind magier, but you're no match for me."

Corvina raised her hand. Gray magic crackled on her fingertips, a tiny whirlwind of lightning and cold, hard pellets of ice. She waggled her fingers, and the lightning and pellets merged together, morphing into a thin flat disc lined with sharp serrated edges—a deadly hailstone.

The weather magier admired her creation, then flicked her wrist and tossed it into the fireplace. The hailstone hissed as it hit the flames, although the fire quickly consumed it.

"Even though I knew the truth, I still pretended to believe Maeven when she claimed that you had murdered my mother. I snarled and cursed and stomped around and made all sorts of nasty threats against you." Corvina's chin lifted with pride. "I gave *quite* the grand performance."

"You were brilliant," Wexel chimed in.

She smiled and blew him a kiss. Ugh.

I looked at her gray fighting leathers, and more sick understanding filled me. "You're going to take my place in the Gauntlet and kill Leonidas."

Her black lips split into a wide smile. "Exactly. The lighthouse is high enough that no one will realize I'm not you. Except for Leonidas, of course. Assuming he manages to get to the top, I might give him a few seconds to think he's won before I shove him off the side."

My heart clenched with dread.

"Once Leonidas is dead, I'll leave the lighthouse, strip off this ridiculous costume and face paint, and slip back into the crowd of spectators. Sometime later, Xenia and the rest of your friends will find your body in here, along with Milo's arrow." Corvina clucked her tongue in mock sympathy. "It will be *quite* the tragic end to yours and Leo's twisted little love story. Why, some of the music masters might even write a ballad or two about it."

I ignored her taunts. "So everyone will think I killed Leonidas, and then that Milo killed me in retribution. Clever, but you still have to get rid of Maeven."

"That's the easiest part." Corvina waggled her fingers again, and gray lightning shot out and hit the tearstone arrow on the floor, making it skitter a little farther away from me. "While everyone is running around screaming about Leonidas being dead, I'll creep through the crowd and shoot the bitch in the back. If the arrow doesn't kill her outright, then the fool's bane poison will."

Another piece of her plan snapped into place in my mind.

"And then you'll turn on Milo because you won't need him anymore. That's why you shot me with one of his arrows. You're going to frame him for my murder, and Maeven's too."

Even though she'd poisoned me, I respected her cleverness—and I still needed to know more about her plot.

"Milo won't go down without a fight, but you've already made plans to deal with him too."

Corvina grinned, but it was a sharp, cruel expression. "Over the past few days, I've quietly been sneaking my men from Antheia Island over here, into Caldwell Castle. Milo thinks those men will follow him after I kill Maeven, but they are loyal to *me*. With Wexel's help, we'll capture Milo and kill anyone loyal to him. Then I'll turn Milo over to your father as a sign of good faith and to help cement my rule. I'm sure Dominic Ripley will be eager to execute the person responsible for his daughter's murder."

"But that still leaves Delmira," I pointed out.

Corvina laughed again. "Please. Delmira isn't even worth the effort of killing. If she's lucky, I'll let her stay on at court in Myrkvior. I've always wanted a Morricone servant."

Every word she said chilled me to the bone. I'd thought Milo and Maeven were the most dangerous enemies I'd ever encountered, but Corvina easily rivaled them. The noble lady pretending to serve Milo even as she'd been usurping his plans was particularly brilliant—and ruthless. She had definitely learned from Emperia's mistakes, and she was going to eliminate everyone who stood between her and the Mortan throne.

"We need to go," Corvina said. "The challenge will be starting soon."

"You should just let me go ahead and squish her like a bug." Wexel increased the pressure on my chest, and my bones *pop-pop-popped* in protest.

Corvina shook her head. "No. Milo doesn't have your

strength magic, and I don't want to give anyone a reason to doubt that he killed Gemma. We stick to the plan. The poison will finish her off."

Wexel increased the pressure a little more, then removed his foot from my chest. I sucked in a breath, tears streaming out of my eyes.

Corvina stepped over me and wound her arms around the captain's neck. "Although I always love it when you offer to murder people for me."

Wexel grinned, leaned down, and kissed her. Corvina moaned into his mouth and hooked her leg up around his waist. Wexel growled in response and squeezed her ass, and lust blasted off both of them. Ugh. If I had to lay here and watch them fuck . . . Well, that would be yet another humiliation.

Corvina pulled back. "Not now," she purred. "We still have work to do."

She pressed another kiss to the captain's lips, then looked down at me again, her gray gaze as cold as the hailstone she'd created earlier. "Goodbye, Gemma. I'm sorry I can't stay to witness your suffering. From what I've read, fool's bane poison is supposedly a particularly painful way to die."

Corvina smirked at me, then strode out of the sitting room. Wexel followed her and shut the door behind them, leaving me to die.

CHAPTER TWENTY-EIGHT

As soon as Corvina and Wexel left, I reached out with my magic.

Leo! The Gauntlet is a trap! Corvina is going to kill you!

I sent the thought out again and again, but there was no response. I couldn't even sense Leonidas, even though I knew he had to be somewhere around the lake. The fool's bane must be killing my magic, right along with my body.

Since I couldn't reach Leonidas, I tried calling out to Grimley, but he didn't answer me either. He was probably still out hunting, which meant he was even farther away than Leonidas was.

I also tried calling out to Father, Rhea, and Xenia. No response from any of them.

There was only one other person I might have a chance of reaching—if she would even bother to listen to me. Despite how painfully aware I was of every second ticking by, I closed my eyes and pictured Reiko, along with her inner dragon. Then I reached out, searching for the smoky presence that was uniquely theirs.

I finally—*finally*—got a flicker of emotion, and I seized onto that thin thread. *Reiko! The Gauntlet is a trap! Corvina is going to assassinate Leonidas—*

The flicker vanished, and emptiness filled my mind. I desperately searched for the thread again, but no matter how hard I tried, I couldn't find it.

Well, if I couldn't reach anyone with my magic, then I would have to make it to the gardens before the poison killed me.

And it *was* killing me.

Cold sweat was streaming down my face, my heart was racing, and my breath was puffing out in ragged gasps. Strangely enough, I felt like I was drowning on dry land, as if every bit of air I drew in was pumping water into my lungs.

Still, I had to try.

So I forced myself to roll over onto my side. The one good thing about the poison was that it had numbed my arm so I didn't feel the pain of the arrow wound anymore. Of course that also meant the poison was that much closer to my heart.

It took me much, much longer than it should have to push myself up onto my hands and knees. Those small efforts left me sweating even more profusely and gasping for each and every watery breath. I would never be able to get to my feet, but maybe I could at least crawl over to the main chamber door, although I didn't know how I would open it—

Sunlight sliced in through the balcony doors, and a glint of crystal caught my eye. I glanced up, and my gaze locked onto the vase that held the ice violets Leonidas had picked for me, along with the strand of liladorn Delmira had wrapped around the flowers—

Liladorn also has powerful healing properties . . . Legend has it the sap from a single vine is enough to counteract the effects of coral-viper venom, along with amethyst-eye and other deadly poisons . . .

The passage I'd read in Lord Eichen's book back in Haverton floated through my mind. I had no idea if liladorn could heal fool's bane poison, but it was my only chance. So I changed direction, crawling over to the table. It was only about five feet away, but it seemed like five miles, as slowly as I was moving and as hard as it was to breathe—

Gemma? A small high singsong voice sounded in my mind.

It took most of the strength I had left to lift my head. Violet had emerged from her hiding place between the settee cushions and was regarding me with a puzzled expression.

"Violet," I rasped. "Hop up . . . onto the table . . . Push the vase . . . off the side . . . Please . . . *Please* . . ."

My voice deserted me, choked by my own waterlogged breathing. I reached out with my magic, but it too was completely gone, so I swiped my hand out, trying to get the strix to understand what I wanted her to do. Violet quirked her head from side to side in confusion.

I motioned again and again, but she just kept staring at me. Finally, I dropped my hand. Maybe I could still crawl over to the table, although I had no idea how I was going to get the vase off the top—

Thunk. Thunk-thunk. Thunk.

Wearily, I raised my head again. Violet had hopped from the settee up onto the table, and the baby strix was headbutting the heavy crystal vase. Fresh hope bloomed in my heart, but I didn't have the breath left to encourage her.

Thunk. Thunk-thunk. Thunk.

Violet kept headbutting the vase. Each blow scooted it a little closer to the edge of the table until—

Thunk!

One final headbutt from the strix sent the vase crashing to the floor. The crystal shattered into a hundred pieces, some of which flew through the air and stung my skin with their sharp edges, but I didn't care. All that mattered was making it over to the liladorn and seeing if it could counteract the poison.

I gathered up the remaining scraps of my strength and inched in its direction like a worm trying to wiggle through dry, hard-packed dirt that had absolutely no give to it. I reached the shattered vase, but going that short distance ate up the remaining scraps of my strength, and my hand dropped into the puddle of water just short of the liladorn.

By this point, the entire left side of my body was cold and numb, and I couldn't feel anything, not even the fresh cuts from the crystal shards. Desperation filled me, and my gaze locked onto the black vine, which was so close and yet so far away.

Please, I rasped in my mind. *Please, please help me.*

My head dropped to the floor, my gaze still locked on the liladorn, but the vine just sat there in the mess of water, violets, and broken crystal. I didn't know if it was as dead as the violets were or just ignoring me, but despair filled me all the same. Of course it wouldn't help me. It was connected to the Morricones, to Delmira, not to me—

The liladorn twitched.

I blinked, wondering if I was just imagining the vine's movement, but it twitched again before arching back, like a person yawning, stretching their arms wide, and getting out of bed.

Helpless, I watched as the vine lowered itself to the floor and snaked toward me. Violet hopped down off the table, almost landing on the vine, then scooted off to the side, watching it with wide eyes, her little beak snapping open and shut, as if it was a worm she wanted to gobble up.

The vine stopped in front of me and arced up again, like it was putting its thorns on its hips in place of hands. If a vine could even have hips. Did fool's bane poison drive people mad before it killed them? Because I certainly felt like I was going mad right now.

We told *you that you would ask us to scratch you again, Not-Our-Princess.* A smug voice filled my mind. *We see everything, just like your mother did. We liked Merilde. She planted us everywhere she went.*

Questions crowded into my mind, but before I could ask any of them, the liladorn snaked around my left wrist and punched its long thorns deep into my skin. My arm was so cold and numb that it didn't hurt, not even when the liladorn tightened its grip and blood gushed up and spattered onto the floor.

Violet squeaked in alarm and stabbed her beak at the vine, trying to break its grip on me, but one of the thorns shot out toward her, making the strix scuttle back.

Still helpless, all I could do was lay there while the liladorn sank its thorns deeper and deeper into my body . . .

I must have passed out. One second, I was staring at the liladorn tightening its grip on my wrist, more and more blood dripping down my skin. Then, in the next instant, I was standing in the middle of the sandy lakeshore.

On either side of me, people were crammed into the two halves of the amphitheater that overlooked the lake, with even more folks on the terraces in the gardens behind and above me. Everyone was on their feet, cheering, screaming, yelling, and whistling, and dozens of folks were waving flags bearing the crests of the various kingdoms, as though this were a gladiator match.

I was ghosting again. It sometimes happened when I was severely injured—or dying, like I was right now in my chambers. Still, if this was my last gasp of magic, then I was going to use it to help Leonidas.

I shielded my eyes against the noon sun. Father and Rhea. Zariza and Xenia. Ruri, Tatsuo, and Kai. All the royals were in attendance, each group standing a little apart from the others on the top terrace. Maeven was there too, along with Delmira, and Milo was loitering nearby, watching the proceedings with a sneer on his face.

I glanced up. Corvina was standing on the lighthouse's observation deck, her hands resting on the railing like a queen lording over her subjects. The bitch was right. From this distance, she *did* look enough like me to fool the crowd. I didn't see Wexel anywhere, but he had to be lurking nearby, probably with Corvina's men, ready to spring her trap to kill Maeven and capture Milo.

A loud roar rose up from the crowd, and I whirled around toward the lake.

Leonidas had made it back to shore.

He splashed through the mud, a sodden gray flag clutched in his left hand. His movements were slow and stiff, his lips blue with cold, and water sluiced off his light gray fighting leathers and sandals. But he kept putting one foot in front of the other until he was out of the water.

A couple of Ungers wiped the prince down with towels while another shoved a mug of something hot into his hand. Leonidas tossed back the steaming drink, then held the wet flag up high. The crowd went wild, cheering and yelling even louder.

My heart clenched with equal parts hope and dread. He'd made it through the first part of the challenge. He was one step closer to winning—and being murdered by Corvina.

One of the Ungers took the flag from Leonidas, while another buckled a weapons belt with a sword and a dagger around his waist. A third Unger handed him a gladiator shield. Leonidas staggered forward, his eyes focused on the main steps that led up to the gardens.

I darted in front of him, the sand sucking at my feet and slowing me down, even though I wasn't really there. "Leo!" I yelled. "Leo, stop! It's a trap!"

For a split second, he hesitated and glanced in my direction, his eyes flicking back and forth as if he'd heard me but couldn't figure out where I was.

"Leo! It's a trap!" I yelled again.

His mouth settled into a hard, determined line, and he moved forward, putting his foot on the first step that would take him up into the gardens and the second part of the challenge—

I sucked in a breath. My eyes snapped open, and I found myself staring up at a carving of Queen Armina on the ceiling, riding her gargoyle Arton into battle against the Mortans.

I sucked in another breath. Instead of feeling weak and waterlogged, the air smoothly, easily filled my lungs. I dug my elbows into the floor and pushed myself up to sitting. My head spun around, and pins and needles stabbed through my body, as though my arms and legs were waking up from a long, awkward sleep.

I glanced down. Ugly red scratches ringed my left wrist, and my upper arm was still a torn mess from where Corvina had yanked out the tearstone arrow, but I could actually feel the limb again. The liladorn was curled up in the puddle of water on the floor, like a person soaking itself in a soothing bath. I shuddered and looked away from it.

Gemma? A soft singsong voice sounded in my mind, and Violet hopped over and peered up at me. *Better now?*

Love flowed through me, and I scooped her up, kissed the top of her head, and placed her on the settee. "Yes, I am better now. You are also the best strix ever, but you need to stay here, where it's safe."

I grabbed the edge of the settee and hoisted myself upright. The motions made my head spin, and more pins and needles stabbed through my body, but they were small discomforts compared to the worry and dread pounding in my heart.

I had to get to Leonidas—before it was too late.

There was no way I could get out of my chambers, across the plaza, and through the gardens before Leonidas made it past the gladiators and started climbing up the side of the lighthouse, where Corvina was waiting to kill him.

Not without help.

I staggered out onto the balcony, more pins and needles shooting through my body, and clutched the railing. I scanned the surrounding rooftops, but I didn't see any gargoyles. Of course not. It was the middle of the day, which meant they were all out hunting—

A pair of gray eyes glowed in the shadows on the tower next to mine. I stumbled forward a few steps, and the eyes crept closer, morphing into a familiar gargoyle—Otto.

I stretched out my hand, beckoning him to come closer, but he stopped and remained hunched in place.

Help me. Please.

Otto's eyes narrowed to slits. *Why should I? You've never helped me, princess.*

I'm so sorry for what Milo did to you. I know what it's like to be tortured by him. But if you help me now, maybe I can put an end to him.

Otto's lips drew back in a silent snarl. *You lie. You can't stop him. No one can.*

You might be right. I might not be able to stop him, but I can bloody well try. Starting by saving Leo's life right now.

The gargoyle kept staring at me, unmoving, unblinking. Frustration pounded through me, but I didn't have time to convince him to help me. I also didn't have time to go down the stairs, so I peered over the railing, wondering if I had enough magic to float myself down to the ground—

A shadow blotted out the sun, air rushed over my face, and Otto dropped to the balcony beside me.

"Were you actually going to try to climb down the side of the tower?" he asked in a low, gravelly voice.

"To save Leonidas? Absolutely."

His eyes narrowed in thought. Then he sighed. "Very well. I'll help you save your prince. I owe him that much for how he tried to help me all those years ago. But don't blame me if we both wind up getting killed."

I lurched forward, threw my arms around his neck, and hugged him. Otto stiffened, but he didn't shove me away.

"Thank you," I rasped. "You don't know what this means to me."

I released his neck and scrambled up onto his back. I'd barely gotten settled when Otto flapped his wings and took off.

I'd flown on many gargoyles over the years. Most of the creatures, including Grimley and Fern, glided gracefully through the air, but Otto tore through the sky like it was an enemy he was determined to slay. I gripped the bases of his wings, tightened my legs, and held on.

Otto was the only gargoyle soaring through the sky, and I didn't spot any strixes on the Mortan towers either. They must be out hunting too. Still, I reached out with my magic again.

Lyra! I sent the thought out as far and wide as I could. *Leo is in trouble!*

Nothing. No flickers, no awareness, no sense that she had heard me.

Next, I tried Grimley, repeating the same message. I got a faint flicker off him, but nothing more, indicating that he was still out in the surrounding countryside. I tried Fern too, with the same faint response.

Up to me then.

Otto zoomed across the plaza and out into the gardens. He flapped his wings, hovering several hundred feet above the topmost terrace. *Where do you want to go?*

I scanned the gardens below. Three gladiators were clustered together, each one leaning heavily on their swords while a couple of bone masters tended to them. Leonidas had already defeated the Ungerian warriors and was trudging toward the rocks below the lighthouse to begin his climb. The crowd was on its feet, and everyone was once again yelling, screaming, and cheering him on.

Leo! Leo, it's a trap! I sent the thought out, but he didn't answer me, and he didn't waver from his resolute trek. Frustration boiled up in my veins.

I can't hover here all day, Otto said. *Where do you want to go?*

My gaze zipped over to the lighthouse. Corvina was still standing on the observation deck, waving to the crowd and urging them to cheer even louder for Leonidas. Of course she was. She didn't want anyone to hear him call her name when he finally recognized her. Fury filled my heart. I might not be able to stop Leonidas, but I could definitely stop her.

The lighthouse. Drop me right on top of that bitch.

You got it, princess.

Otto flapped his wings and headed in that direction. Murmurs rose up from the crowd, along with a wave of confusion so strong that it threatened to unseat me. People were shielding their eyes and peering up at Otto and me.

"Look! Up there! On the gargoyle! It's Princess Gemma!" Someone bellowed in a loud voice.

I frowned. That sounded like . . . Reiko. I glanced down, but I didn't spot my friend anywhere in the crowded halves of the amphitheater or on the lakeshore—

Magic crackled in the air, and my gaze snapped up.

Corvina had also spotted Otto and me. Her mouth gaped, and I felt every ounce of her surprise, despite the distance between us. Then her mouth snapped shut, and even more gray lightning flared on her fingertips. She drew her arm back, but Otto pumped his wings, flying even harder and faster.

The gargoyle sailed over the top of the lighthouse. I slid off his back, landed in a low crouch, and rolled across the flagstones, absorbing the impact of the fall. Pain bloomed in my left arm, making me hiss, but I scrambled to my feet.

Corvina tossed her gray lightning at Otto. The gargoyle veered sharply to his left, but the blast clipped one of his wings. He bellowed with pain and dropped like a stone.

"No!" I screamed and lurched over to the railing.

Otto was still pumping his wings, trying to stay aloft, but he was fighting a losing battle. I snapped up my hand and reached out with my magic, trying to slow his fall. For a split second, I grabbed the strings of energy around the gargoyle, and he jerked in midair. But he was large and heavy, and I was still weak from the poison, and my magic slipped through my fingers.

And so did Otto.

He plummeted toward the ground, landing on top of a gazebo. The wooden roof caved in, and I lost sight of him—

More magic crackled, and a chill filled the air. On instinct, I spun away from the railing.

Thwack-thwack-thwack.

Hailstones slammed into the spot where I'd been standing. The cold, hard projectiles made several stones explode out of the railing and fall to the ground far, far below.

I rushed back over to an intact section of the railing, watching in horror as the debris streaked toward Leonidas.

"Leo!" I screamed. "Watch out!"

His head lifted, as did his hand. My breath caught in my throat, wondering if he had enough magic to stop the debris from crushing him—

The stones jerked to a halt a couple of feet above his head. Leonidas flicked his wrist, and the stones sailed off into the gardens below. His gaze locked with mine, his amethyst eyes burning fierce and bright.

Leo.

Gemma.

His thought mixed with mine. Both of our names echoed in my mind, while his worry beat in my heart, right next to my concern for him—

For the third time, magic crackled through the air. I glanced back over my shoulder. Corvina stalked toward me, more of those damned gray hailstones swirling around her fingertips.

"It's over," I called out. "You've lost."

Corvina stopped and glanced over the broken railing. The crowd had gone completely silent, and everyone was staring up at us, from the people in the amphitheater to those gathered on the lakeshore to the royals on the topmost terrace. The only person who was ignoring us was Leonidas, who had reached the top of the rocks and was now running toward the lighthouse.

Corvina stepped forward, and I tracked her gaze down to Milo. The crown prince's hands were curled into fists, and fury darkened his cheeks. He was clearly pissed she had failed to kill me. Wexel was down there too, a tense, worried expression on his face.

Several dozen guards flanked the captain. They were all wearing purple cloaks, but metal helms covered their faces, and several of them were clutching crossbows. Those weren't Maeven's guards—they were Corvina's men, already in position to strike.

"Don't do it," I warned. "Escape with your life while you still can."

Corvina looked at me, fury flaring in her gray eyes. "Escape with my life? After everything Maeven has done to me? After all the Dumonds she's killed over the years? After she murdered my mother just a few weeks ago? It's not much of a life if everyone you've ever loved is *dead*."

I flinched at her words, but I couldn't deny the harsh truth in them.

"*You* might be able to turn a blind eye to that bitch's actions, but *I* will not," Corvina snarled. "I'd rather be dead than bow down to Maeven Morricone for one more fucking *second*."

"Your plan is ruined." I kept trying to reason with her. "You can't frame Milo for my murder anymore."

A loud, bitter laugh erupted out of Corvina's mouth. "You're right. My plan *is* ruined, thanks to you." Her face hardened, and even more magic flared in her eyes. "But who needs a plan when you have power and numbers on your side?"

I sucked in another breath to try again, but she cut me off.

"Dumonds! Attack!" Corvina screamed. "Kill the royals! Kill Maeven! Kill the queen!"

Down below, the guards ripped off their purple cloaks, exposing their black tunics underneath, then yelled, raised their weapons, and charged forward, heading straight toward Maeven and the rest of the royals.

Including my father.

He lifted his hand and summoned up his lightning magic, even as Rhea drew her sword and stepped in front of him.

"Protect the prince!" she screamed. "Protect Prince Dominic!"

The Ripley guards answered her summons, as did the Ungers, who flocked around Zariza and Xenia, and the Ryusamans, who did the same thing to Ruri, Tatsuo, and Kai.

The Dumond fighters cut down the first line of Mortan guards and headed toward the royals. My heart wrenched, but there was nothing I could do to help Father, Rhea, or anyone else on the terrace.

"As much fun as it would be to watch you mourn your father and the rest of your friends, I have a battle to win and a crown to claim," Corvina said. "And you're in my way, Gemma."

She reared back her hand and threw her hailstones. I did the only thing I could—I ran away.

I careened around the corner of the lighthouse just as her hailstones slammed into the railing, tossing more chunks of stone out into the open air.

A door was set into this side of the lighthouse, and I skidded to a stop and tried it. Locked. Corvina's shadow slithered along the flagstones, heading in this direction. I swallowed a curse, sprinted down the length of the walkway, and careened around the next corner. Another door was set into this side of the light-house, but it too was locked, and I didn't have the time to force it open.

Less than a minute later, I ended up right back where I had started on the side of the observation deck facing out toward the gardens and the crowd still watching below. I had run out of room, and I had no choice but to stand and fight, so I flattened myself up against the wall, watching Corvina's shadow creep closer and closer.

"You can't run around the lighthouse forever, Gemma." Corvina's smug voice drifted over to me. "Do us both a favor and let me kill you quickly—"

She stepped around the corner, and I put my shoulder down and rammed into her. My weak, clumsy blow didn't do any real damage to the weather magier, but it was hard enough to make her hand slam into the railing and send her hailstones dropping to the ground.

I surged forward to shove her over the side of the railing,

but Corvina spun away. More hailstones hovered around her fingertips, and gray lightning started dancing from one icy serrated projectile to the next.

"Stand still and let me kill you!" she hissed.

She stalked toward me, even more hailstones and lightning swirling and crackling around her fingertips. An evil smile split Corvina's lips. She had me trapped like a rabbit in a hunter's snare—

Gemma! Gemma!

I glanced down through the gap in the railing. Leonidas had reached the bottom of the lighthouse. He stared up at me, worry and magic flickering through his eyes.

You have to get away from Corvina before she kills you! Jump, Gemma! Jump! I'll catch you!

I looked around, hoping there was some other way, but I was trapped on the observation deck, and Corvina was coming to murder me. I looked down at Leonidas again, my eyes locking with his.

Please, his voice whispered in my mind.

My heart wrenched. Not because Leonidas was commanding me to jump, but because he was *asking* me to. He was asking me to trust him.

And I did.

Part of me had *always* trusted him, ever since we were children. Even after everything that had happened at Myrkvior, part of me had trusted him still, and I trusted him to save me now. I had simply been too stubborn, too much of a coward, and especially too caught up on past hurts and betrayals to admit it to myself until right now. I couldn't kill Leonidas, and he would never willingly hurt me.

Corvina was still approaching, crowing about how much she was going to enjoy murdering me, but I ignored her and scrambled up onto the nearest section of the railing that wasn't broken.

"No! Gemma! Don't!"

Down below, Father's voice rang out above the shouts and screams of the fight, but I ignored his cries, along with Corvina's continued threats. I had eyes only for Leonidas, and he for me.

Even more magic surged through the air as Corvina gathered up her power to deliver a killing strike. I was out of time.

I drew in a breath. Then, still staring at Leonidas, I leaped forward and hurled myself off the side of the lighthouse.

CHAPTER TWENTY-NINE

I plunged through the air faster than a strix streaking toward its prey. I didn't scream, but I couldn't keep my arms and legs from flailing as I instinctively tried to find some thread of energy to grab onto. But there was nothing, only empty air, and the hard, unyielding flagstones rushing up to meet me in three, two, one—

I jerked to a stop less than ten feet above the ground.

The motion jarred me from head to toe, like I was an unwanted puppet that had been forcibly wrenched off a stage. More pain exploded in my body, especially in my injured left arm, and a strangled cry escaped my lips.

When my mind and eyes finally stopped spinning, I looked to my right. Leonidas was standing about five feet away, his hands up and out, his face creased in intense concentration. Sweat poured down his forehead, and his entire body was trembling from the effort, but he had caught me, just like he'd promised.

So many emotions crowded into my heart, but the strongest one was love—so much love for him. Not because he had saved my life, although I was certainly grateful for that. No, I loved him because despite everything, he saw those jagged little pieces of me, the ones I kept hidden from everyone else, and I knew he would never, ever let them shatter.

Leonidas shuddered out a breath, then slowly dropped his hands. Those strings around my body tightened again, twisting me around and gently lowering me to the ground. I landed on my feet and staggered forward, but Leonidas was there to catch me. Or maybe we caught each other, since he seemed to be just as unsteady on his feet as I was on mine.

"Gemma!" he rasped. "Are you okay?"

I curled my fingers around his bare biceps. I needed to feel the solid strength of him right now, needed to feel his body, his magic, his mind brushing up against my own—

Over his shoulder, a bright, wicked flare of magic erupted.

"Leo!" I screamed.

I tried to shove him out of the way, but purple lightning punched into his back. Leonidas yelped like a wounded animal and stumbled forward.

I tried to catch him with my arms the same way he had caught me with his magic, but he slipped through my fingers and collapsed to the ground. A shadow fell over me, and my head snapped up.

Milo Morricone was looming in front of me.

The crown prince was wearing a gold breastplate over a purple tunic, leggings, and boots. A purple cloak fluttered around his shoulders, and a gold sword was belted to his waist. He was clutching a crossbow, and the weapon was loaded with one of his tearstone arrows, although I couldn't tell if this projectile was coated with fool's bane poison, like the one Corvina had shot me with earlier.

Behind Milo, the battle between the Dumond fighters, the

royals, and their guards raged on. So many bodies and weapons were crashing into one another that I couldn't tell who was winning—and who might already be dead.

Worry and dread punched me in the chest. This had morphed from an assassination scheme into a full-fledged battle—and quite possibly a war.

On the ground, Leonidas groaned. My heart lifted that he was still alive, and I stepped over him, putting myself in between him and his brother. Leonidas had saved me from Corvina, and I was going to do everything in my power to protect him from Milo now.

The crown prince looked me over from head to toe, his gaze lingering on the deep, ugly gash in my left arm. "Corvina can't do anything right. I knew I should have murdered you myself."

Milo lifted his hand and threw his lightning at me. I tried to lurch out of the way, but the bolt clipped my left shoulder. I screamed as the electric sizzle of his power washed over me, reigniting the pain of all my injuries. Even worse, the force of the bolt picked me up off my feet and tossed me back.

Once again, I scrambled for something, anything, to hold on to in order to stop me from falling, but there was nothing. Milo's lightning threw me clear of the rocks and sent me plummeting down into the lake far, far below.

The *crack* of my back hitting the water was even harder and sharper than the sting of Milo's lightning. The sound, force, and impact reverberated through my entire body, punching the air from my lungs and stunning my mind.

But even as the cold water closed over me, my magic rose up just as quickly. I opened my lips to yell, to scream, to try to shove the power away, but water rushed into my mouth, silencing my cries. I slipped below the surface of the lake, drowning in another place, another time . . .

I was back on the riverbank in the Spire Mountains, standing next to the dead Farena and her two equally dead bandit brothers, and watching the younger version of myself dive into the water and swim after Leo.

I grabbed my gargoyle pendant, which had gone ice-cold against my skin. "Let me go! I don't have time for this!" I screamed at my magic, but it ignored me like usual, and nothing changed.

Desperate, I ran along the riverbank, keeping pace with Gems in the water. Maybe if I could hurry the vision along, I could save myself before I drowned in the real world. Not bloody likely, but it was the only thing I could do.

Gems popped back up to the surface of the water and sucked in a breath. Her doing that seemed to ease the burn in my own lungs ever so slightly, although my entire body remained cold. I wasn't sure if the chill had to do with her being in the river or my current body sinking deeper into Caldwell Lake. Either way, I watched while Gems stroked her arms through the water, turning around and around.

"Leo!" she yelled. "Leo!"

"Over there," I muttered, even though she couldn't hear me. "He's over there."

Young Leo had gotten caught in a tangle of driftwood lodged up against a boulder in the middle of the river. Gems caught sight of him and swam in his direction. The swift current tried to pull her past him, but she fought against it and latched onto a driftwood branch.

Gems used the driftwood like a sideways ladder to pull herself over to Leo. Then she sank her hand into his wet hair and yanked his face up and out of the water. My heart wrenched. I'd forgotten how pale his face had been back then.

"Wake up!" Gems screamed. "Wake up, Leo!"

He didn't respond, so she hooked one arm around his chest, still keeping his face turned up toward the sky. She tried to swim back to shore, but the current was too swift, and the water kept pushing Gems up against the driftwood. Her fear and frustration punched into my heart, adding to the pressure in my chest.

He's dragging me down. I should just let him go. I can make it back to shore without him.

Her thoughts whispered through my mind. The burn in my lungs increased, but it was nothing compared to the shame flooding my heart for thinking about letting Leo go, letting him drown.

Gems loosened her grip on Leo. The current tugged him away, and his face rolled to the side, more in the water than out.

Gems gasped, reached out, and snagged Leo again, yanking him back toward her side. No. *Her thought filled my mind again.* I won't let him die. I won't be like the Morricones. I won't be like Maeven.

Anger and frustration rose up in her chest, making my lungs burn a little more.

Gems slapped at the water with her free hand. "No!" *she screamed.* "I am not going to die here! You are not going to kill me!"

She slapped at the water again, then raised her hand and focused on a thick tree branch hanging over the river. Determination blazed through Gems, and I felt her, my, our magic close around the strings of energy connected to that branch. My own hand closed into a fist, and I yanked on those strings right along with her.

Slowly Gems moved herself and Leo away from the driftwood tangle. The water slammed into her face over and over again, and the current threatened to suck her under, but she kept a firm grip on her magic and used it to guide herself and Leo over to the tree branch like it was a fishing pole reeling them both in.

Gems reached out, wrapped her hand around the actual branch, and pulled herself into the shallows. Then she turned around, grabbed Leo under the shoulders, and dragged him through the mud and back over to the shore.

I hurried over and stood beside Gems, even though she couldn't see or hear me and this had all happened long ago. She banged on Leo's chest a few times, then leaned down and put her mouth on his, forcing air into his lungs.

Gems repeated the process a few more times, but Leo didn't stir.

"Come on," she muttered. "Wake up. Wake up!"

She banged her fist on his chest again, and again, and again. Gems was in a frenzy, so she didn't feel the magic surging off her own body.

But I did.

I frowned. I didn't remember using my power on Leo, but magic poured off Gems, strong enough to make my fingertips tingle. Her magic, her emotions, flowed through Leo's body, mixing with his own mind magier power and wrapping around the strings of energy that surrounded his heart—

Leo jerked and started coughing.

Gems rolled him over onto his side so he wouldn't choke. After several seconds, Leo stopped coughing, and Gems eased him over onto his back again. He sucked down several gulps of air, as if he couldn't get enough of it into his lungs. His face was still pale, and an ugly gash on his forehead oozed blood, but he was alive.

"You . . . saved *me*," Leo said, a wondrous note in his voice, as though he couldn't believe she had done such a thing.

Gems held out her hand, which he took, and helped him sit up.

"You saved *me*," Leo repeated, as if it was the strangest, most nonsensical idea he had ever encountered.

Gems flopped down on the riverbank beside him, the water lapping at their soggy boots. She shuddered and yanked her feet clear of it. "Yes, I saved you. Wouldn't you have done the same for me?"

He shrugged, seemingly as uncomfortable about this turn of events as she was. "You saved *me*."

Gems frowned. "Why do you keep saying that?"

Leo's eyes were dark and haunted in his pale battered face. "No one's ever done that before."

"Saved you from drowning? Well, I hope you don't make a habit of falling into rivers. Surely no one is that clumsy, not even a Morricone."

Her tone was light, and she nudged him with her elbow. Leo nudged her back, joining in her teasing. Then he smiled, his entire face lighting up with warm, soft emotion.

Gems's lips parted, and she sucked in a breath. Her heart hammered in her chest, and mine also quickened its beat.

Leo's smile dimmed, and his gaze turned dark and serious again. "No one has ever saved me from anything before. Not drowning, and certainly not my uncle's cruelty."

His last few words escaped as a low, strained whisper, as though he were confessing a horrible secret he had never dared to tell anyone before. Gems kept staring at him, her heart hammering and softening and soaring all at the same time, just as mine was doing right now.

Leo looked right back at her, his eyes bright, as if she

was the most beautiful thing he'd ever seen, despite the fact that she was soaked to the bone, covered in mud, and smelled slightly fishy. His gaze dropped to her lips, which were blue with cold. Gems's eyes widened, and she jerked back. Even now, I couldn't tell if I'd been afraid of him kissing me or anxious for him to just go ahead and do it.

Leo cleared his throat, then pulled something out of his pocket with shaking fingers. "Here," he said, pressing the object into her hand. "Take this. As thanks."

The silver strix pin the bandits had wanted to steal glittered in Gems's palm. Her fingers slowly curled around the pin—along with Leo's hand. They sat there, staring into each other's eyes, both of them slowly leaning in toward each other—

"Gemma? Gemma! Where are you?" Xenia's voice sounded, and tree branches rustled farther back on the shoreline.

Gems and Leo broke apart and scrambled to their feet, as if they'd been caught doing something they shouldn't.

She held the strix pin out to him. "I can't take this. You said your father gave it to you."

Leo covered her hand with his. The hot shock of his skin rasped against mine just as it had back then, and I clenched my hand into a fist, trying to hold on to that warmth.

"Keep it," he said. "As something to remember me by."

A shudder swept through Gems's body. "What if I don't want to remember you?"

Sympathy filled his face. "I imagine this will be as hard for you to forget as it will be for me."

His gaze dropped to her lips again, as though he was once again thinking about kissing her. Gems swayed toward him, so many emotions blasting off her. Attraction.

Eagerness. Worry. But the strongest one was the softness in her heart, this strange, unexpected kinship she felt for him. The same mix of emotions also surged off Leo, and the two of them leaned toward each other again—

"Gemma!" *Xenia called out again.*

Leo tightened his grip on Gems's hand, then leaned down and brushed a kiss across her knuckles, as though the two of them were standing in the middle of a royal ball instead of on a rocky riverbank.

This was it, I realized.

This was the moment when I'd first fallen in love with Leonidas Morricone.

"Thank you, Gemma Ripley," he murmured. "Until we meet again."

Leo held on to her hand a moment longer, then dropped it and limped into the woods. Gems watched him go, me too, both of us with a smile on our lips—

"Gemma." A familiar voice sounded, but it wasn't Xenia yelling for me. No, this voice was calmer, softer, and one that I hadn't heard in a long, long time.

Gems kept staring at the woods where Leo had vanished, but I whirled around. A woman stood on the riverbank a few feet away. Dark blond hair flowing past her shoulders. Warm blue eyes. Rosy skin. And most of all, a kind smile that made her glow from within.

"Mother?" I whispered.

Merilde Ripley nodded, and her smile widened. I hurried over and stopped in front of her, drinking in every little detail of her face, from the arch of her brows to her straight nose to the freckles that dotted her cheeks. Of course I had portraits of her at Glitnir, but seeing her like this was different, more intense, and somehow more real than all those cold, still, flat portraits could ever be.

"How are you here? You were never *here in real life. You had already died by the time this had happened."* As soon as the words spewed out of my lips, the answer came to me. *"You saw this. With your time magier power. When you were still alive. You really did see everything you told Maeven about, including how she would become queen of Morta."*

Merilde shrugged. *"I saw a lot of things. More than I ever told anyone about, except for Maeven."* She stepped forward, her eyes locking with mine. *"But most of all, I saw the brave, strong, smart woman you would become. That you are today, Gemma."*

A bitter laugh tumbled out of my lips. *"Perhaps if I was truly brave and strong and smart, I wouldn't have been poisoned by Corvina and currently drowning in the lake."*

"Ah, yes, the lake. That is a problem," Mother said. *"You need to go back now."*

"But I want to stay here with you."

Mother shook her head. *"We both know you can't do that. You'll see me again, though. Sooner than you might think."*

She winked, just as she used to when she was reading a storybook to me and had come to an especially good part. Then, from one heartbeat to the next, she vanished.

I spun around and around, but my mother was gone, and I was all alone on the riverbank, except for Gems, who was still staring at the spot where Leo had gone into the woods . . .

Leo—Leo was in trouble.

With that thought, my magic finally released me, my eyes snapped open, and I sucked in a breath. But instead of sunlight and fresh air, I was greeted with murky darkness and another mouthful of cold water. I choked, the burn in my lungs increasing to a painful level.

I clawed up with my arms and kicked out with my legs, but my entire body was cold, heavy, and numb, and it was such a bloody effort to *move*, to do anything but slowly sink deeper into the water . . .

No! I roused myself out of my lethargy. I hadn't given up in the river that day, and I wasn't going to give up now. Not when Leo was wounded. Not when Father, Rhea, and everyone else were under attack from Corvina and her men. I was *not* going to let them be slaughtered like I had Uncle Frederich, Lord Hans, and everyone else at the Seven Spire massacre.

I kicked and clawed again, trying to reach the surface, but the water in my fighting leathers weighed me down, and my sandals felt as heavy as anchors strapped to my feet. I tried again and again, but I simply didn't have the physical strength to make it to the surface. That left me with the only other bit of strength I did have.

My magic.

Despite the steadily increasing burn and pressure in my lungs, I forced myself to close my eyes and reach for my magic. I was too deep in the water to reach out and latch onto something on the lakeshore, like I'd done that day with the branch hanging over the river. So this time, instead of grabbing onto the force produced by something else, I concentrated on my *own* power, on the storm of emotion that constantly churned deep inside me.

Trying to wrestle the storm into submission had always been a losing battle, so I didn't even attempt it. Instead, I dove into that crackling mass of energy and emotion and focused on everything I had been feeling over the past few days. Anger. Frustration. Worry. Dread.

Love.

All the love I had for Leonidas, all the feelings I had tried to push down and bury for so long. For the first time ever, I embraced them. The storm of energy and emotion flared up inside me, and I pulled it up, up, up, imagining it as a geyser under my feet that was going to shoot me out of the depths of the lake and straight back up to the surface of the water.

I wasn't sure it would work—but it did.

I clawed my arms, kicked my legs, and pushed with my magic, and I finally managed to break through to the surface. I sucked down a giant breath and almost choked on the air filling my lungs. I sucked in another breath, smaller this time, and the burning in my chest slowly eased.

I treaded water, getting my bearings. Even though he'd been trying to kill me, Milo had saved me instead. His lightning blast had thrown me clear of the rocks on this side of the lake. I probably would have broken every bone in my body if I'd tumbled down the boulders instead of hitting the water.

I listened, but the only sound was the steady *slap-slap-slap* of the water against the rocks, and I couldn't tell what was happening in the gardens. If people were still fighting. If the battle had ended. If everyone I cared about was captured—or dead.

My heart squeezed tight at the thought, but I swam back toward shore and whatever dangers might still be waiting for me there.

CHAPTER THIRTY

Milo's blast hadn't tossed me as far out into the water as I'd thought, and it didn't take me long to make it to the shore. I slogged onto the sand and listened again, but I still only heard the water crashing up against the rocks.

Leo? Father? Grimley? Lyra? Reiko?

I sent out the thoughts, but no one responded, and only an eerie, buzzing silence filled my mind. Dread surged into my chest, even colder than the water still lapping at my feet. I needed to get back up to the gardens. But how?

Milo might have inadvertently tossed me clear of the boulders, but he hadn't given me an easy way to escape the lake. These rocks formed a small cove, curving around a tiny crescent-moon patch of gray sand. I could either climb up the rocks or plod back out into the water and swim around them. I was already shivering, and my teeth kept chattering, no matter how tightly I clenched them. I wouldn't survive any more time in the water, which left the rocks.

Determination flared in my heart. Leo had been willing to swim in the frigid lake, fight gladiators, and climb up the side of a lighthouse for me, and I'd be damned if I wouldn't do the same for him. So I stepped forward and took hold of the closest rock.

The stones were slick from the water that constantly sprayed up into the air, but many of them still had sharp, jagged edges from where they had moved, shifted, and cracked against one another. By the time I scrambled up and over three boulders, sweat dripped down my face, and nicks, cuts, and scrapes covered my hands, arms, and legs. But I kept climbing, swiftly moving higher and higher.

I was about halfway up when I got stuck.

I reached the top of a boulder only to find that I was on a sort of plateau. The next rock up was too high for me to reach, and the surrounding stones were too far away to leap onto. Even if I bridged the gap, I risked slipping and falling to my death.

More frustration surged through me, but I kept looking around, trying to figure out how to get off the plateau. A shelf of rock jutted out from the side of the cliff about fifteen feet above my head. From there, I could easily climb the rest of the way back up to the gardens, but the problem was actually getting up there. Oh, I could pull the shelf down to me, but that would set off a chain reaction of rocks that would bury me alive.

My eyes narrowed. Maybe I didn't have to pull the rocks down to me. Maybe I could hoist *myself* up to the rocks, just as I'd pulled myself and Leonidas over to that branch in the river, and just as I'd propelled myself out of the lake a few minutes ago. It was the only chance I had, so I held out my hand and focused on the strings of energy around the rock shelf.

Most of the time, when I used my mind magier power, I moved an object in whatever position it was currently in, like turning a key that was already embedded in a lock. But this was different. I wasn't trying to move an object so much as I was trying to move *myself*.

Oh, sure, I could occasionally float myself up a wall at Glitnir, but there were no handholds here and nothing to catch me should my magic give out and I start to fall. Using my power like this was a potentially fatal risk, but it was one I had to take. Leonidas had asked me to trust him, and now it was time to trust in my magic, to trust in *myself*.

So I reached for even more of my power, gathering up all those strings of energy attached to that rock shelf. Only this time, instead of yanking on the strings, I wrapped them around my own body, as though I were a puppet and the rock shelf was the stage I was attached to. Then, when I had a firm grip on my magic, I started hoisting myself up those strings.

It was hard—so fucking *hard*—like trying to climb a series of invisible ropes I couldn't see, touch, or feel, except with my mind. But slowly my body rose an inch off the ground. Then two, then three, then an entire foot.

All the while, I kept pulling and pulling on those invisible strings, my arms pantomiming the motions, even though my fingers were only clutching empty air. Sweat poured down my face, and my entire body trembled, but I kept my gaze locked onto the rock shelf.

I didn't know how much time passed. A minute, two, five, ten. My sole focus was on hoisting myself up those invisible strings. Nothing else mattered. Not the wind whipping around my body, or the slap of water below, or the rocks subtly shifting all around me.

I stretched my hand up again and . . . and my fingers finally curled around hard, solid stone. I quickly threw my other hand up, gripping the shelf, then hoisted my right leg up there as well. My left leg followed, and I rolled over onto my back, with my body fully resting on the rock shelf.

More sweat poured down my face, and my chest heaved from the exertion. Right now, all I wanted to do was lie here, close my eyes, and sleep for days, but I couldn't do that. Not while Leonidas and the others were still in danger. So I got to my feet and kept moving.

It didn't take me long to scale the rest of the rocks and make it back to the main, top level of the gardens.

I hurried forward, moving from one tree to the next, and scanning the grounds. No one was in sight, and the gardens were utterly, eerily quiet. Even the birds and bugs had stilled, as if frightened away by the earlier shouts, screams, and violence. I headed toward the main open space on the topmost terrace, where the royals had been gathered. The closer I got, the more people I sensed, along with their silent chatter.

What is Milo doing . . .

He truly hates his family . . .

Milo is mad. He's going to murder us all . . .

More worry spiked through my heart, but I crept forward until I could peer around one of the trees and see what was happening.

It was even worse than I'd feared.

Down at the lakeshore, the nobles, merchants, and other spectators had been herded into the open space between the two halves of the amphitheater. Dumond fighters stood in front of the crowd, keeping them in place. Most of the fighters were holding swords, but a few were clutching crossbows, which were loaded with arrows that gleamed a light telltale gray. Along with undermining Milo's plans, Corvina had also stolen some of his tearstone arrows and given them to her men. Smart.

The royals were still on this topmost terrace, each one surrounded by what was left of their guards. Father stood with Rhea and a few Andvarians, while Ungers clustered around Zariza and Xenia. Ruri and Tatsuo were all alone, with only Kai to protect them.

But the Morricones were front and center.

Maeven's hands were clenched into fists, and her features

had hardened into a mask of icy fury. Delmira was beside her, supporting Leonidas. His fighting leathers were scorched from Milo's lightning and burns covered his back, but he was still on his feet, still alive. A knot of tension unwound from around my heart.

Milo was standing in front of his mother, his usual sneer on his face, and still holding the crossbow I'd seen him with earlier. He snapped his fingers and held out his arm, and Corvina sidled forward and took the weapon from him.

She hefted the crossbow, a sly smile stretching across her face. She was waiting for the right moment to strike, not just against Maeven, but Milo too. Wexel was hovering off to one side of the terrace, along with the Dumond fighters, who were facing off against the remaining Mortan guards.

"Well, Mother?" Milo asked, his voice breaking the tense silence. "What do you think of my plot now?"

He held his hands out wide, encompassing the terrace, along with everyone else in the gardens.

"It's not too late to stop this," Maeven said in a clipped, angry voice.

Milo laughed, the sound colder than the water still lapping at the shore. "Oh, please. You're just jealous *you* didn't think of this. How many times have you attended the Summit over the years? And yet, you never considered using this as an opportunity to attack. In one spot, you could have killed many of Morta's enemies, but instead, you remained frozen, weak, and useless."

My only error at Myrkvior was not thinking big enough. Milo had said that in the library a few nights ago, and now I knew exactly what he meant.

My heart seized in my chest. Milo's plan was far more ambitious than I'd realized. He didn't just want to kill Maeven and Leonidas. No, the crown prince wanted to murder every single royal here.

"You stupid fool!" Maeven hissed. "Of course I thought about it. I could have done it too, and with far more cunning and finesse than you've shown."

A muscle ticced in Milo's jaw, and his eyes glittered with a dark, dangerous light.

"But unlike you, I'm not reckless enough to let my ambition rule me and cloud my judgment," Maeven continued. "You might very well murder everyone here, but there are still many more royals back in Andvari, Unger, and Ryusama to take their places, rise up, and attack Morta, attack *you*."

Milo sneered at her again. "You've always been weak that way, too afraid of consequences that will never come to pass."

She shook her head. "Your ambition is going to be the death of you, but I'll be damned if it is the death of Morta too."

"The death of Morta?" He let out another laugh, although his face quickly turned hard and cruel again. "*You* have been the death of Morta, with your new trade agreements and ludicrous attempts to make peace with the other kingdoms. I still can't believe you actually tried to marry Leonidas off to Glitzma Ripley. Why bother with a royal marriage when we can just *take* what we want? What should have been *ours* all along?"

He spun to the side and spread his arms out wide, addressing the wary royals, as well as the frightened crowd down on the shore. "The Morricones have *always* been the strongest royal family. *We're* the ones with the most power, the most magic, the most ambition. For far too long, we've let the other kingdoms do as they wish, but no longer. I'm finally going to finish what Uncle Maximus started—and create a *new* Morta that stretches from one side of the Buchovian continent all the way to the other."

Greed, lust, and malevolence blasted off him, the poisonous emotions twisting, burning, and writhing around like a nest of coral vipers trapped in my chest. Ever since I'd gone to Myrkvior, I'd known Milo was a dangerous enemy, and he'd shown me exactly how sadistic he could be when he'd tortured me. But for the first time I realized the true rotten depths of his depravity. Milo didn't care about anything other than amassing power and then using that power to inflict his cruelty on as many people as possible, including his own flesh and blood.

"This new Morta, *my* new Morta, starts here today," Milo continued. "I have so many wonderful plans . . ."

He spread his arms out wide again, droning on and on about all the horrible things he was going to do once Maeven and the other royals were dead. I ignored his rant and eyed the Dumond fighters clustered around the royals. I needed help if I had any chance of saving Leo, Father, Rhea, and everyone else.

Grimley? I sent the thought out. *Where are you?*

Gemma! His voice finally filled my mind, although it was faint, and he still felt far away. *I'm with Fern and Lyra! We heard you before! We're on our way back to the castle!*

Good. I need your help.

I told the gargoyle what I planned to do and what I wanted him, Fern, and Lyra to do in return. Grimley didn't like it, but he grumbled his agreement.

Next, I looked over at the gazebo with the caved-in roof. *Otto? Are you okay?*

Of course I'm okay, he snapped, and a few of the broken wooden boards shifted in confirmation. *It takes more than a little fall to keep me down for long.*

Another knot of tension loosened in my chest. *Do you feel like fighting with us?*

His snort sounded in my mind. *I've been fighting my whole life, princess. Why stop now?*

I grinned and told Otto what I wanted him to do as well. He agreed, and I looked out over the crowd of Dumond fighters again. My gaze flicked from one person to another. No, no, no . . .

There.

I focused on a fighter lurking close to Ruri, Tatsuo, and Kai. Like the rest of the Dumonds, this fighter was also wearing a silver helm and clutching a sword, but they were shorter and leaner than the others, and a bit of green shimmered on their right hand, just below their black tunic sleeve.

I see you. I sent the thought out. *Hiding in plain sight again, just like you always do.*

The guard maintained a tense, watchful pose, although their head slowly turned in my direction.

Gemma? Reiko's voice filled my mind. *Is that you?*

Who else would it be?

Despite the helm that covered her face, I could still see her roll her eyes. *Oh, I don't know. Some other annoying mind magier who likes to whisper thoughts to me out of the blue and scare me half to death.* She paused. *I saw Milo blast you off the cliff. I thought you were dead.*

Not yet. Although the day is still young. This time, I paused. *I'm sorry about last night, and everything I said.*

I know. Me too.

Reiko's regret mingled with my own, but I set our emotions aside. *Grimley, Fern, and Lyra are on their way. Otto is with us too.*

What's your plan? Reiko asked.

Save as many people as possible.

I told her what I had in mind. Like Grimley, Reiko grumbled her displeasure, but she agreed.

". . . if you won't kneel to your new king, then I will take my crown the old-fashioned way, the Morricone way," Milo said, finishing up his speech.

He jerked his head. Corvina moved forward, raised the crossbow in her hands, and pointed it at Maeven.

"Last chance," Milo said, his voice eager, as though he was just waiting for her to refuse.

Maeven stared at her son, her face still set in that icy mask. In addition to her fury, another emotion washed off her—complete, utter, unrelenting sadness.

As if now that this moment, the betrayal she'd known was coming for so long, had finally arrived, she was helpless to do anything but *feel* every single agonizing second of it. Her sadness, along with the strong undercurrents of hurt and bitterness, filled up my heart like water being poured into a bucket until the liquid overflowed and drowned everything in its vicinity in that cold, aching sadness.

Maeven lifted her chin, still defiant. "No matter what you do to me, no matter how you plot and scheme and murder, one thing will always remain the same."

"What?" Milo asked.

"You will *never* be king of Morta." Her words came out as a simple pronouncement, as if Milo's fate had already been decided long ago, and there was nothing he could do to change it.

I saw a lot of things. More than I ever told anyone about, except for Maeven. My mother's voice echoed through my mind. Was this one of the things she had told the Morricone queen?

Milo threw his head back and laughed. "Still trying to scare me with fairy tales? Please. You should know better."

"So should you," Maeven replied in that same eerily calm voice. "Especially since I'm not the only one here being betrayed."

She tilted her head to the side, and Milo followed the motion over to Corvina, who was now pointing her crossbow at his chest.

He frowned. "Corvina? What are you doing?"

She smiled. "Following your mother's advice."

Still keeping the crossbow trained on him, Corvina backed away until she was standing in the open space between Milo and Maeven, right in front of the Mortan guards, who were still surrounded by Wexel and the Dumond fighters.

Corvina glanced over at the other royals. "As Milo has stated, he wants nothing more than to see you all dead."

"And what do you want?" Zariza snarled, blood still dripping from the black talons on her fingertips.

"To tear down the throne. For the Morricone reign to finally fucking *end*." Corvina's gray eyes glittered with hate as she looked back and forth between Milo and Maeven. "Milo is wrong. The Morricones aren't the Mortan family with the most power, magic, and ambition. The Dumonds are, and *I* am the Dumonds."

"What's your price for our lives?" Ruri asked.

"Support me as the new queen of Morta, and my men will stand down."

Another tense silence dropped over the terrace, and the royals all looked at one another. Zariza shook her head no, while Ruri nodded yes.

Father stared at both of them. Then his gaze flicked over Maeven, Milo, and Delmira before lingering on Leonidas. "And the Morricones?" he asked.

Even more hate glittered in Corvina's eyes. "They all die here and now."

Father shook his head. "No."

"*No?*" Corvina asked in an incredulous voice. "You should want the Morricones dead more than anyone else, Prince Dominic."

Father's face hardened. "I have never been a fan of royal assassinations, Morricone or otherwise."

Corvina blinked, as if it had never occurred to her that my father might *not* go along with her plan to murder people, even if they were his enemies.

"Fuck you and your assassination plot," Milo hissed. "No one is taking the throne away from me. Least of all *you*."

He snapped his hand up, purple lightning sparking on his

fingertips, but Corvina gave him an amused look and took a little better aim with her crossbow.

"When we were on Antheia Island, you told me that your tearstone arrows can punch through *anything*, even a gargoyle's stone skin," she purred. "I'd be happy to test your theory for myself."

Milo's nostrils flared with anger, but he lowered his hand. Corvina had been right last night in the arena. He really was a fucking coward at heart.

I stared at Corvina. Her words echoed in my mind, like a key unlocking a door, and giving me a glimpse of what Milo truly wanted, of what he had been trying to do for years now—

Gemma, Grimley's voice sounded. *Fern, Lyra, and I are in position.*

Good. Wait for my signal.

My plan had been to move as soon as Grimley arrived. But now that the moment was here, I hesitated, torn between letting Corvina kill Milo and saving everyone on the terrace. I wanted the crown prince to suffer for everything he'd done to me, and I needed him to die in order for Andvari to be truly safe—

Corvina's finger curled around the crossbow trigger. "Consider yourself lucky, Milo. At least for a few more minutes."

"Why is that?" He ground out the words.

She grinned. "Because there is one person here that I want to murder slightly more than you."

Corvina whirled around and fired the crossbow—at Maeven.

chapter thirty-one

Even as the arrow exploded out of the crossbow, I lifted my hand and reached out with my magic, trying to stop the projectile before it sank into Maeven's chest.

For a moment, I thought I had it. But I was tired from my forced swim and climb up the cliffs, and I wavered, just for an instant, and the arrow squirted out of my grasp and punched into Maeven's shoulder. She screamed and toppled to the ground.

"Mother!" Delmira yelled and dropped to her mother's side.

Milo growled and started toward Corvina, but she plucked another tearstone arrow from a slot on her weapons belt, slapped it into the crossbow, and leveled the weapon at him again.

"Ah, ah, ah," she purred. "I'm not ready to kill you yet. But soon, my darling fiancé. Soon."

Milo stopped, anger staining his cheeks. Corvina blew him a mocking kiss. Off to the side, Wexel appeared amused by his lover's antics, and his lips twitched up into a small grin.

"Now," Corvina said, looking at Father, Zariza, and Ruri again. "You can either accept me as the new queen of Morta, or you can die right alongside the Morricones. Your choice."

Hate blasted off her and burned through me like a wildfire. Corvina meant what she said. She would slaughter the Morricones first, then the rest of the royals, then the people on the shore, until everyone bowed down to her as the new queen of Morta.

Unless I stopped her.

My hesitation vanished, and I stepped out from behind the tree and strode forward. "I don't think you're going to be killing anyone else today," I called out.

Corvina turned around, her eyes widening. "You! I thought Milo blasted you off the cliff!"

"He did, although he fucked that up, just like he fucked up this latest coup." I glanced over at the crown prince. "You're not very good at playing capture-the-crown, are you, Milo?"

He glowered at me, even more rage and hate sparking in his eyes than when he'd realized Corvina had betrayed him. But my gaze skipped past him and everyone else to land on Leonidas.

Leo—

Gemma—

We both sent thoughts to each other, but the words didn't matter. No, the only thing that mattered right now was the love twining through my heart—my love for him mixed with his for me.

In an instant, that love blotted out everything else. The hate, rage, and bitterness blasting off Corvina and Milo. The pain rippling off Maeven. The worry, stress, and dread emanating from Delmira, Father, Zariza, and Ruri. The anxious fear surging through the spectators. Our love throttled it all, like liladorn run amok in a garden, and leaving only the most beautiful blossoms behind. That love gave me the strength to keep going, to keep moving forward.

I stopped in front of Corvina. In some ways, it was like staring into a mirror, especially since we were both still dressed in gray fighting leathers. But Corvina's hair and face paint were still perfect, while mine were a sodden, ruined mess.

"You have an annoying habit of escaping all the traps I set for you," she said.

"Then perhaps you should set better traps." My hand dropped to my gargoyle dagger on my belt. Despite everything that had happened, I'd managed to hang on to the weapon. "You want to be queen of Morta? Then come and fucking *earn* it."

"Are you actually trying to invoke a royal challenge?" A merry laugh erupted out of Corvina's lips. "I don't have to fight you." She gestured at the Dumond fighters on the terrace. "You can't win, Gemma. Not alone. Not against all of us."

In the distance, three shadows appeared in the sky, dropping lower and lower, like arrows streaking toward their targets. Off to the left, another shadow crept through the bushes, slinking toward the shore. And finally, off to the right, a fighter sidled forward a few steps.

I grinned at Corvina. "Who said I was alone?"

With loud, ominous grumbles and a sharp, answering shriek, Grimley, Fern, and Lyra dropped onto the Dumond fighters on the terrace. Down by the lake, Otto loped out of the bushes and plowed into the men there. And Reiko darted forward, putting herself in between the Dumond fighters and Ruri and Tatsuo, and protecting her queen and father. Kai stepped up beside her.

Corvina's head snapped back and forth. Horror flickered across her face, but it was quickly replaced by rage. "No!" she screamed. "You're not ruining my revenge! Kill them! Kill them all!"

Chaos erupted in the gardens.

Grimley and Fern raked their talons across the chests of a couple of fighters, while Lyra stabbed her beak into another man's throat. Down by the water, Otto ran back and forth, using his broad, strong body to knock the fighters down and then trample them like they were pins in a child's game he was trying to smash to smithereens.

A couple of Dumond fighters charged at Reiko, but she slashed her sword across one man's stomach, then spun around and killed the other man the same way. She ripped off her helm and tossed it aside, shifting into her larger, stronger form. Kai, Ruri, and Tatsuo all did the same thing, and the four dragon morphs dove into the pack of guards, using their talons and weapons to cut down their enemies.

Zariza and Xenia also fully shifted into their ogre forms, while Father unleashed his blue lightning, and Rhea chopped guards down with her sword and strength magic.

Leonidas lifted his hand and tossed a guard away from him, even as the man's sword zipped forward and settled into his palm. He cut down another guard, while Delmira punched her liladorn dagger into the chest of another enemy.

Wexel was caught in the middle of the Mortan guards and Dumond fighters, furiously swinging his sword back and forth, although I couldn't tell exactly who the captain was battling. I didn't spot Milo among the mass of clashing bodies, but that didn't surprise me. Now that his latest assassination plot had failed, the crown prince was probably trying to escape the fighting like the coward he truly was.

Corvina snarled and aimed her crossbow at Leonidas, but I clenched my hand into a fist and wrenched the weapon away. It jerked out of her hand and skittered across the flagstones.

"I don't think you'll be going back to Morta in triumph now," I called out.

Corvina bared her teeth at me. "There's always another move to make and another game to play, Gemma. I've killed Maeven, and I can kill you too. That will be *more* than enough to convince the Mortan nobles that I'm strong enough to be their new queen."

Gray lightning exploded around her fingertips, and she hurled her magic at me. I grabbed hold of all the strings of energy pulsing, crackling, and hissing around the lightning. Corvina *was* strong—much, much stronger than I'd realized—and her lightning fought against me like a gargoyle caught in a net, twisting, writhing, and desperately trying to wrench free.

Inch by inch, the magic crept closer, and I was shaking and sweating from the strain of trying to hold it back. I couldn't stop her magic, so I shoved it aside with my own power and sent it spinning into a nearby tree. The gray lightning slammed into the trunk, cleaving the wood in two and making the tree topple to the ground with a thunderous roar. The branches crashed down onto several of the Dumond fighters, crushing them.

Corvina snarled, and more gray lightning sparked on her fingertips, quickly congealing into hailstones. She flicked her fingers, and the hailstones streaked through the air, growing larger and sharper as they headed toward me like a cloud of icy knives. Once again, I used my own magic to send them spinning away. The hailstones *punch-punch-punched* into a stone bench, shattering it. My stomach clenched. That could have been me, that could still *be* me, if Corvina managed to blast past my defenses.

"You want to see the true power of the Dumond family?" Corvina crowed. "Well, here it is, Gemma."

She raised her hands out high and wide, as though she were a tree stretching its branches toward the sky. Only Corvina wasn't interested in soaking up sunlight.

The weather magier started calling down lightning instead.

Ominous gray clouds cloaked the sky, and thunder boomed in a low, rolling drumbeat that made my teeth ache. Corvina laughed and stretched her hands up a little higher and wider.

The wind howled around her, and lightning streaked down from the sky and danced all around her body, as though she were a living, breathing lightning rod. Even worse, hailstones spewed out of the magical storm, turning into huge chunks of sharp, serrated ice.

I glanced over my shoulder. Father, Rhea, Zariza, Xenia, Ruri, and Tatsuo were still battling the Dumond fighters. Reiko and Kai were there too, lashing out with their swords, while Grimley, Fern, and Lyra darted back and forth, swiping out with their talons, wings, and tails. Leonidas and Delmira were still guarding Maeven, cutting down anyone who came near them.

"Run!" I screamed. "Get off the terrace!"

The continued roar of thunder drowned out my voice. My fingertips tingled in warning, and my head snapped back around. Corvina grinned, her gray eyes burning like stars, even as the lightning kept dancing around her body, as nimbly as a partner spinning around her in a ballroom waltz.

"Well, Gemma?" she yelled. "What do you think of the Dumond power now?"

Instead of responding, I dove into the storm of emotion inside me and pulled my own magic up, up, up. Corvina's power danced around her, but I wrapped mine around me like a cloak covering me from head to toe.

Corvina flicked her fingers, tossing a bolt of lightning at me. Once again I sent it spinning away with my own power. Next, she shot hailstones in my direction, but I sent those flying away too.

Over and over, Corvina attacked me with her weather magic, hurling lightning, hailstones, and even needle-like sheets of sleet in my direction. But I held on to my magic and used the storm of emotion churning inside me to redirect all her attacks.

Sometimes, I managed to send her lightning into a group of Dumond fighters, but most of the time it was all I could do just to keep her from killing me. Sweat ran down my face, arms, and legs, mixing with her sleet, and my entire body trembled from using so much of my magic to deflect so little of hers. But I gritted my teeth and held on, not letting any of her power move through my invisible cloak, the shield I had created around myself and everyone behind me.

After a furious exchange where Corvina tried to pummel me with more sheets of needle-like sleet, she lowered her hands to her sides, a smile creasing her face.

"You're getting slower, Gemma," Corvina crowed. "Weaker too. Admit it. Your mind magier power is no match for my weather magic."

She was right. The poison, my forced swim, and the climb up the rocks had drained me, and tossing her power aside was sapping what little strength I had left. It wouldn't be long before my magic gave out completely. Then Corvina could take her time electrocuting and cutting me to shreds. I had to end the fight—end *her*—before that happened, or Corvina would turn her wrath on the royals next. On Leonidas and Father and everyone else I cared about.

Corvina sneered at me again. "No one can stop the weather, especially not you, Glitzma."

Her calling me that damned insulting nickname made a fresh wave of rage surge up inside me. Even now, after all the skill and power I'd displayed, the bitch *still* thought I was nothing but a spoiled, pampered princess she could crush and then brush aside on her way to the Mortan throne.

Still, the nickname made me reconsider our battle. I couldn't kill Corvina with my magic, not now, when I was teetering on the brink of exhaustion. But she was still underestimating me. All I had to do was find a way to twist her arrogance to my advantage, the same way she had twisted Milo's scheme around to suit her own plot—

An idea popped into my mind, and I scanned the wet, scorched, hailstone-covered ground. Where was it? Where was it?

My gaze landed on the crossbow I'd torn out of Corvina's hands earlier. Despite all the violent blasts of magic, the crossbow was still in one piece, although it was half buried under a mound of hailstones. All I had to do was get to it—or rather, get *her* to it.

Corvina lazily tossed another bolt of lightning at me. Instead of shoving it aside with my magic, I dodged it and took off running, heading in the opposite direction of the crossbow, as though I were finally admitting defeat and retreating.

My fingertips tingled in warning again, and a bolt of lightning slammed into the ground five feet in front of me, causing me to stagger to the side and spin around—right into a cloud of hailstones.

I pushed back with my own power and managed to send most of the hailstones spinning away. Most, but not all.

Thunk-thunk-thunk.

Three stones slipped past my defenses. One clipped my upper right arm, slicing through my skin, while two punched into my right thigh, severely cutting and bruising my leg and making it buckle. My ass hit the ground, and pain spiked through me like cold nails being hammered into my limbs.

"Gemma!" Leonidas screamed. "Gemma!"

He cut down another Dumond fighter and stepped in this direction, as if to put himself in between me and Corvina. My gaze locked with his, and I sent a thought to him.

Trust me.

He hesitated, and then it was too late, as another fighter engaged him.

Corvina's sandals crunched through the hailstones littering the ground, and the ice shattered like she was stalking through a field of bones. The weather magier loomed over me. The wind was still whipping around her body, making strands of her auburn hair ripple like fiery ribbons, while gray lightning continued crackling around her head, as though she were wearing a molten silver crown that hadn't quite solidified into a sure, hard shell yet.

"Not so fancy now, are you, Glitzma? I can't believe Milo had such trouble killing you in Blauberg. Then again, he's not *nearly* as strong as he thinks he is. He has no imagination, no creativity with his power. None of the Morricones do. All Maeven and Milo know how to do is blast things with their lightning. Completely unoriginal."

Corvina sniffed, as though *unoriginal* was the worst thing to be. Maybe she was right about that. Because if I didn't do something very, very creative, then she was going to kill me.

My gaze flicked past her to the crossbow still lying on the ground. Slowly, very, very slowly, I grabbed hold of the strings of energy wrapped around the weapon and tilted it upward, so that it was free of the hailstones littering the ground. My body trembled again, and even more sweat poured down my face, stinging my eyes, but I ignored my many aches and pains and focused on those few thin strings of energy.

Corvina raised her hand, and a single hailstone filled her palm, a wicked-looking thing that was all hard, heavy ice and sharp edges that would easily tear through my body. "Well?" she asked. "Any last words from Glitzma Ripley?"

"You were . . . right about . . . one thing," I rasped through the pain still spiking through my body.

Her eyes narrowed with suspicion. "What?"

I grinned in the face of my impending death. "There's always one more game to play."

I lifted my hand and pointed my index finger at her. Corvina's eyebrows creased together in confusion, and she looked down at her chest. The second her gaze dropped, I curled my finger back, pulling the trigger on the crossbow.

Thwack!

The tearstone arrow shot out of the crossbow and punched into Corvina's back.

She screamed and staggered forward, her eyes bulging and the deadly hailstone falling from her grasp. I lashed out with my right foot, kicking her left leg out from under her and making her tumble to the ground beside me. Then I grabbed the gargoyle dagger off my belt, raised it up, and plunged it into her heart, just as Maeven had plunged the blade into Emperia's heart at Myrkvior.

Corvina screamed again, and her power flashed all around us, but it was more bright light than electric burn now, and it quickly faded away to a shower of dim sparks. Corvina sighed, and her eyes went glassy and still. Silence filled my ears, the quiet strange after the continued, thunderous roar of the weather magier's storm—

"No! No, no, no!"

Wexel shoved a Mortan guard out of his way and rushed over to Corvina. I still didn't see Milo anywhere on the terrace.

The captain looked down at the noble lady, agony surging off him in hot, palpable waves. His gaze zipped over to me, and hate erupted in his eyes.

"You bitch!" he hissed. "You killed her!"

Wexel stepped over Corvina's body and lifted his sword high. I raised my hand, but my magic was gone, and I didn't have any way to stop him from killing me—

Wexel flew through the air and hit the ground about twenty feet away.

Leonidas stepped up beside me, his hand still stretched out toward the captain. He had saved me.

My heart lifted, and the storm of emotion roared up inside

me again. Somehow I found the strength to climb to my feet and stagger toward him. Leonidas caught me, just as he had when I'd leaped from the lighthouse. I leaned into him, and he did the same thing to me.

"Leo," I whispered.

"Gemma," he murmured, his beautiful amethyst eyes locking with mine. "Gemma."

I started to tell him just how much I loved him, but Leonidas's lips dropped over mine, cutting off my words. I tangled my fingers in his hair, pulling him closer. That storm of emotion rose up inside me, even stronger than before, and I opened myself up to him and let him *feel* it—let him feel just how much I loved him.

Leonidas's magic wrapped around mine, and heat, passion, and care flowed freely between us, each emotion a string of energy further binding our hearts together. Sometime later, we broke apart, both of us breathing hard, although we kept holding on to each other—

"Leo!" Delmira's frantic voice cut through the air. "Leo!"

We turned around. The princess was still hovering over Maeven, and she waved frantically at us. Leonidas put his arm around my waist, and together, we limped toward them.

By this point, the royal guards from the various kingdoms had beaten back the Dumond fighters, most of whom lay dead on the terrace. Down at the shoreline, the Dumond fighters had also been killed, although the spectators were milling around, shocked looks on their faces, as though they couldn't believe what had happened and how close they had all come to dying. I knew the feeling.

But one person *was* dying—Maeven.

CHAPTER THIRTY-TWO

The Morricone queen was still lying on the terrace. Someone, probably Delmira, had torn the arrow out of Maeven's left shoulder. The wound wasn't a fatal one, but Maeven was sweating and gasping for air like a fish out of water.

Father, Rhea, Zariza, Xenia, Ruri, Tatsuo. They were all gathered around, watching the Mortan queen slowly die. Reiko, Kai, Grimley, Fern, and Lyra were standing off to the side, also staring at Maeven.

"Her wound isn't that bad, but the arrow must have been poisoned," Delmira said in a low, strained tone.

"Amethyst-eye?" Leonidas asked, a bit of hope in his voice.

Delmira shook her head. Leonidas scrubbed a hand over his face, emotions surging off him. Anger. Regret. Sadness. Love. The same emotions also rippled off Delmira.

The princess snapped her fingers at one of the Mortan guards. "Get me a bone master. Right now."

The man flinched at the cold command in her voice and scurried away.

Maeven let out a low, raspy chuckle. "Sorry, my darling, but it's too late for that."

Delmira stared down at her mother, a helpless expression on her face. I couldn't bear to see her suffering, so I looked away, and my gaze landed on my mother's bench. Despite the battle, the silver seat had remained untouched, and the plaque gleamed as though it had been freshly polished. The air flickered, and suddenly, Merilde was perched on the bench, a grave expression on her face. Even stranger, she seemed to be looking directly at me.

I frowned. Had my mother seen this moment with her time magier magic too? The way she had seen Leonidas and me by the river all those years ago? But my own magic was exhausted, just like my body was. So why would I see her now? And what was she trying to tell me, if anything?

Merilde gave me a grim smile. Then the air flickered again and she vanished, as though she had never even been there to start with. Maybe she hadn't been. But I found myself staring at her bench again, focusing on how the liladorn curled around the plaque that bore her name—

Liladorn. Of course.

Maeven's face was deathly pale, even more sweat covered her skin than before, and her breath wheezed in and out in harsh, ragged gasps. Unwanted sympathy pricked my heart. That awful drowning sensation had been the worst part of the fool's bane poison.

I hesitated, wondering if I should actually save Maeven, especially after everything she had done to my family, to *me*.

Orchestrating Uncle Frederich's and Lord Hans's murders at the Seven Spire massacre. Trying to kill Xenia and me that horrible day. Sending turncoat guards to chase Xenia, Alvis, and me through the Spire Mountains afterward. Exposing my true identity at Myrkvior to hang on to her crown. Enacting the Gauntlet to try to further bend me to her scheming will.

Leonidas knelt by his mother's side, clutching her left hand just as tightly as Delmira was holding Maeven's right one. His face had settled back into its usual blank mask, but more anger, regret, and heartache surged off him.

Caring enough about someone else's feelings to put them above your own, no matter what the stakes are or how they might damage you. That's what true love is, Father's voice whispered through my mind.

He was right. True love *was* putting someone else's happiness above your own. Or in my case, my thirst for revenge. And I realized something important about myself—that I loved Leonidas far more than I hated his mother.

So I dropped to my knees and held my hand out to Delmira. "Give me your liladorn dagger."

"What? Why?" she asked.

I looked at Leonidas. "Do you trust me?"

"Always," he said without hesitation. "Give Gemma your dagger."

Delmira eyed me with suspicion, but she plucked the weapon off the ground and passed it over to me. This liladorn dagger was identical to the ones she'd given to Reiko and me, and I was hoping it would help Maeven the same way the vine in my chambers had helped me.

I tightened my grip on the dagger and leaned over the queen.

A humorless smile curved her bloodless lips. "Going . . . to kill me . . . at last . . . Gemma?" she rasped.

"Corvina has already done that. But I might be able to save you—if you want me to."

"What do you mean *if* she wants you to?" Delmira asked.

"Dahlia Sullivan didn't want to be saved. She told Everleigh Blair as much. I'm giving your mother the same choice."

Maeven stared up at me, pain twisting her features. Anger and regret blasted off her, and an image filled my mind—Dahlia gasping for breath and dying from the amethyst-eye poison she'd willingly ingested in the Edelstein Gardens.

A few more seconds ticked by. The image of Dahlia vanished, and Maeven nodded. "I can't . . . die yet. My work . . . isn't . . . finished . . ."

I raised the dagger.

"Gemma?" Delmira asked, worry filling her voice. "Gemma, what are you doing?"

But I ignored the princess, still looking at the queen. Maeven nodded again, so I raised the dagger a little higher.

And then I plunged it into her shoulder.

Maeven screamed as the dagger sank into her shoulder, right in the spot where Corvina's arrow had struck. But I kept going, twisting the blade in deeper and deeper, making her scream again and again. For so many years, I had *longed* to hear her scream, longed to have her at my mercy. Now that I did, part of me was deeply, brutally satisfied at how much pain I was causing her. It was everything I had ever dreamed of and more—so much *more*.

But for as much as I hurt Maeven, equal amounts of pain blasted off Delmira and Leonidas, causing my heart to burn with shame. So I twisted the dagger in a final time, then released it.

I let out a long, tired breath and looked at Delmira. "Shatter it."

She frowned. "What?"

"Shatter the dagger. Break it apart. Force the liladorn blade to split open in the wound. It's the only chance she has."

Delmira blinked at me in surprise, as did Leonidas. The only one who wasn't startled was Maeven, who stared up at me with a mix of wariness and worry.

She knows. She knows about Delmira. Maeven's thought flitted through my mind, but I didn't have the time or energy to examine it right now.

Delmira kept blinking in surprise, but she made no move to do what needed to be done.

"Do you want your mother to die?" I snapped.

"Of course not—"

"Then shatter your fucking blade," I snapped again. "Before the poison reaches her heart, and it's too late."

Delmira stared at me. Then her gaze cut to Leonidas, who nodded. She blew out a breath, took hold of the dagger, and closed her eyes. For several seconds, nothing happened, and I didn't feel so much as a spark of magic emanating off Delmira.

But the longer and tighter she gripped the dagger, the greater the power that rose in her, like water filling up a bone-dry riverbed after years of drought. At first, the magic vanished as quickly as it appeared, but Delmira grabbed hold of more and more of it, as though she were punching through some sort of dam deep inside herself—

The blade shattered in the queen's wound, and the hilt of the dagger broke off in Delmira's hand, making her lurch back. Pale purple liladorn sap spewed up like a geyser, but just as swiftly, the thick, sticky liquid seeped into Maeven's wound.

I leaned forward, clamped my hand on Maeven's shoulder, and used my power to shove the sap even deeper into her body. I drove the sap down, down, down, using it to strangle the poison in the wound, just like the liladorn vines strangled everything they touched.

Maeven screamed, but I ignored her cries and kept going. Finally, when I thought the sap had been absorbed into her body, I released my power and dropped my hand, her blood staining my palm like warm, wet red paint. The queen quit screaming, and her body sagged against the flagstones, but her breath came much easier, and the faintest blush of color returned to her cheeks.

Maeven shuddered out a breath, tears leaking out of her eyes. I stared down at her, anger and revulsion warring with the exhaustion creeping through my body.

Delmira peered at her mother, then at me. "You . . . saved her." Wonder rippled through her voice.

"No, *you* saved her," I replied. "I just showed you how."

Delmira frowned, but I didn't feel like explaining myself right now. Instead, I scooted away from Maeven and sat down on my ass, right there in the middle of the terrace. Leonidas crouched down in front of me and cupped my cheek in his hand. I placed my hand over his, drinking in the warmth of his skin against mine.

"I know how difficult that was for you," he said. "Are you all right?"

"I don't know."

For the second time in two days, I had done the one thing I had vowed to never do.

I have saved Maeven Morricone's cursed life.

Now that most of the Dumond fighters were dead, Father and the other royals took control of things again. The bone masters went through the gardens healing the injured.

Leonidas didn't want to leave me, and I didn't want to leave him, but we both had our respective families and kingdoms to tend to, so we went our separate ways. I could feel his presence in my heart, though. That was enough—for now.

Reiko and Grimley escorted me back to my chambers, so we could all be healed. Then I took a hot bath and went to bed. I didn't wake up until the next morning. Even though I could have stayed in bed for the rest of the day, I got up, dressed, and met with Father, Rhea, and Reiko in the study.

Grimley was also in the study and playing with Violet by the fireplace. Well, the strix was playing, fluttering her wings and running around him, and the gargoyle was growling at her in return. Otto was also here, after having his injuries healed by the bone masters. He was lying by the fireplace, watching Violet and Grimley play.

Violet broke away from Grimley, ran over, and peered up at the other gargoyle. *Mine*, Violet whispered to herself in her singsong voice, then rubbed her head over one of Otto's front paws. The strix cheeped and ran back over to Grimley to continue her game with him.

"Why does she do that?" Otto grumbled.

"I think it means she likes you," Fern piped up from her spot. "Isn't she just the most adorable little thing?"

Otto rolled his eyes, but his lips twitched upward into a small smile. I hid a grin. It was only a matter of time before Violet claimed every gargoyle at the castle as hers and stole all their hearts in the process.

Father cleared his throat, drawing my attention. He was sitting behind his desk, with Rhea behind hers. Reiko and I were seated in nearby chairs.

"I've just received a report," he said. "The Andvarian guards, as well as those from Unger, Ryusama, and Morta, have combed every single inch of the castle, along with the surrounding area."

My hands curled around the chair arms. "And?"

"Milo has vanished, along with Wexel. They apparently slipped out of the gardens and away from the castle in the chaos and confusion."

Disappointment filled me. Of course they had. Sneaky bastards.

"What about Corvina?" Reiko asked.

"Corvina's body was removed from the gardens and given

to the Mortans, as per Maeven's request," Rhea replied. "I have no idea what Maeven plans to do with the weather magier's remains, or why she even wanted them."

"What about the other bodies?" I asked.

"The bodies of the Dumond fighters have been loaded onto wagons to be taken away and burned in a massive bonfire by the Ungers," Rhea replied. "Technically, the Summit isn't over yet, so we are all still bound by Ungerian law, and they often dispose of their enemies by burning them."

I nodded. "And Maeven?"

Father rocked back in his chair and crossed his arms over his chest. "Maeven will live. Apparently, the liladorn sap managed to counteract the fool's bane poison."

"Do you regret my saving her? I know you hate her just as much as I do for everything that she's done to our family."

He sighed. "I *do* hate her, probably more than any of the other royals do, save you and Everleigh Blair. But if our choice is between Maeven and Milo being on the throne, then I will pick Maeven every single time. At least she can be reasoned with. Milo cannot."

"Milo might have fled, but he's not defeated," I warned. "He might have aligned himself with more noble families besides the Dumonds. He might have more men, weapons, and resources that we don't know about."

"Agreed, which is why I've already sent scouts to hunt him down." Anger glittered in my father's eyes. "I've also spoken to Zariza and Ruri. We've all agreed to put a bounty on Milo—one hundred thousand gold crowns to the person who brings us his head."

Reiko let out a low whistle. Even I was startled by the amount. It was literally a king's ransom. Milo might have escaped Caldwell Castle, but every bounty hunter and mercenary in Buchovia would be hot on his trail now—as would I.

Father looked at Rhea, who nodded and got to her feet.

"Come, Reiko," she said. "We're needed in the kitchen. The cook master has a new sweet cake recipe he wants us to try."

The two of them left, tiptoeing past Grimley, Violet, Otto, and Fern, who were all now sleeping around the fireplace.

"There is one final bit of business—the Gauntlet," Father said. "The last challenge was not completed."

My eyes narrowed. "Surely, after everything that happened, Maeven isn't insisting we forfeited the challenge and that she won by default."

Father snorted out a laugh. "No, I don't think even she would be that bold, especially after you saved her from Corvina's poison. I haven't heard a word from Maeven regarding the Gauntlet. Or Xenia either." He paused again. "Leonidas made it through the first two challenges, and he was well on his way to completing the third. But it's your choice, Gemma."

Gauntlet or not, I already knew what I wanted. I'd known ever since Leonidas had come back into my life a few weeks ago in Blauberg, even if I had been too stubborn to admit it before now.

"And what do you think about Leonidas?" I asked.

The decision was mine, but his opinion mattered to me.

Father harrumphed and crossed his arms over his chest again. "The thought of you being involved with a Morricone makes me want to blast everything in this room to pieces with my lightning."

"But?"

He sighed. "But Leonidas obviously cares about you, and he saved you from falling to your death, as well as from being killed by Wexel. So if I *have* to welcome a Morricone into our family, I suppose there are far worse options."

I reached across the desk and squeezed his hand. "Thank you, Father."

He squeezed my hand back. "I love you, Gemma. I just want you to be happy."

I smiled. "Don't worry. I will be."

Father and I discussed a few more things. Then I left the study. Rhea was nowhere in sight, but Reiko was sitting in a chair down the hallway, studying a tray of sweet cakes on a nearby table.

She popped one into her mouth and started chewing. Her nose crinkled with disgust, as did the one of her inner dragon.

"Problems?" I drawled.

"Dire ones," she replied. "Apparently, your cook master thinks dill and cheddar is an acceptable flavor combination."

I stuffed a cake into my own mouth. The herb and cheese made for a delectable treat that was so good I ate two more cakes. "What's the problem? These are delicious."

"Sweet cakes are *sweet cakes*. They should be sweet, *not* savory." Reiko sniffed, as if anything else was unacceptable. Although that didn't stop her from gobbling down another cake as she stood up.

"Will you take a walk with me?" she asked in a more serious voice. "There's something I want you to see."

Curious, I followed her out of the Andvarian wing, through the plaza marketplace, and over to the gardens. Reiko marched down the stairs and veered to the left, where Ruri and Tatsuo were ensconced behind a table, with Kai standing guard like usual. The two dragon morphs were sipping flavored ices and nibbling on refreshments while they watched the castle workers clean up the fallen branches, broken flagstones, and other remaining evidence of the battle.

Reiko stopped in front of the table and bowed, while I dropped into a curtsy.

"What is *she* doing here?" Tatsuo jerked his head at me. "I told you to come alone."

"*Gemma* is the person who saved our lives yesterday." Reiko drew in a deep breath and let it out. "And from now on, I'm going to be working solely for her, for Andvari."

Shock zipped through me. *No.* I sent the thought to her. *Don't give up your family, your kingdom. I know how much they mean to you.*

Reiko looked back at me. *You're a part of my family now too, Gemma. And if my father can't accept that, then he's not the person, the gladiator, the hero, I thought he was.*

Tatsuo's face turned as hard as the flagstones under our feet. "You really think *she* is worth turning your back on your own family? On everything the Yamato name stands for?" He shook his head, clearly disgusted. "After all this time, you still don't know the first thing about loyalty."

Reiko's hands clenched into fists. "Loyalty is not judging your friend, even when she finds out you've been spying on her. Loyalty is trying to warn your friend, even when you lay poisoned and dying. And loyalty is doing everything in your power to save that friend, as well as the people she knows you care about. Gemma did all those things for me—and you too, if you weren't too damn stubborn to admit it."

Tatsuo opened his mouth to keep arguing, but Ruri held up her hand. The queen looked back and forth between Reiko and me. Kai stared at Reiko. His face was serious, but pride filled his eyes.

"Very well," Ruri said. "If that is what you wish, then I release you from all obligations relating to Ryusama."

Reiko exhaled. "Thank you, Your Majesty."

A small smile creased Ruri's face. "Consider it a gift from one cousin to another."

She picked up her goblet again, apparently considering the

matter closed, but I also had some unfinished business with the Ryusamans, so I stepped forward.

"Tell me, Tatsuo, how is your shoulder? I hope I didn't wound you too badly when I threw that crossbow bolt at you in the arena after you tried to kill Leonidas."

Tatsuo opened his mouth again, probably to deny my accusation, but I stared him down, and he cleared his throat.

"My shoulder is fine," he replied in a stiff voice.

I focused on Ruri. "I don't know if Tatsuo tried to kill Leonidas on your orders or not. And frankly, I don't care."

The Ryusaman queen arched an eyebrow. "But?"

"But as of this moment, any attack on Leonidas—or Delmira—is an attack on me, on Andvari." My voice came out even colder than the ice in her goblet. "And we will respond accordingly."

The green dragon on Ruri's hand opened its mouth in a silent roar, black smoke boiling across her skin. I waved my hand, and a sweet cake floated up off the tray in front of her and over to me. I popped it into my mouth, still staring at her.

Ruri considered me for several seconds. "Point taken."

"You will also honor *all* current treaties with Andvari," I continued.

Ruri arched an eyebrow at me again. "Or?"

"Or I will strongly encourage my father to explore new trade opportunities with Morta. I'm sure Maeven would be eager to hear him out, considering I have saved her life twice during the Summit."

"You should have done us all a favor and let the bitch die," Ruri said, her tone cold and clipped.

I shrugged. "Probably. But Maeven is alive, and you have treaties with Andvari. So you have to decide which you want more—Andvari as an ally or pursuing your vendetta against the Morricones."

Ruri considered me for several more seconds, then toasted me with her goblet. "Everyone knows Andvari and Ryusama have long been friends. I see no reason for that to change."

I gave her a thin smile. "Excellent."

I curtsied to Ruri again. Reiko held out her arm to me, and I took it. We started to leave, but a chair scraped back from the table. Reiko froze and slowly turned around, as did I.

Tatsuo was on his feet. He gave his daughter a tight smile, then bowed low to her. "You were magnificent during the battle, Reiko. I had no idea you were even there until you revealed yourself. You are the best spy I have ever seen. Truly."

Reiko's entire face lit up, as did the face of her inner dragon, and she bowed to him in return. "Thank you, Father."

Tatsuo fixed his gaze on me. "Take care of my daughter, Your Highness."

I nodded. "We shall take care of each other."

Still arm in arm, Reiko and I left the gardens together.

CHAPTER THIRTY-THREE

Reiko and I walked back to the plaza in silence.

"Are you okay?" I asked.

"Tatsuo and I have never had the best relationship, but I think he finally understands me a little better," she said. "It might be nothing, but I'm going to hope that it's something."

I slung my arm around her shoulders, hugging her. Reiko hugged me back—

"Reiko," a voice called out. "May I have a word, please?"

We broke apart to find Kai approaching us. He bowed to me, then focused on Reiko, that hungry expression in his eyes again, as though she were a sweet cake he wanted to gobble up.

Reiko lifted her chin. "I don't know what we could possibly have to say to each other. You didn't say much of anything in the arena the other night. But you were just following my father's orders, right? Luring me away so I wouldn't see him try to assassinate Prince Leo?"

Kai shook his head. "Tatsuo suggested that I talk to you, but I didn't know what he was planning. I swear it to you, and to you, Princess Gemma."

His voice rang with sincerity, and the same emotion rippled off him. Reiko looked at me, and I nodded.

"Then why did you want to talk to me?" Reiko asked.

"You know why." Kai stepped closer to her. "I haven't been able to stop thinking about you."

Reiko's eyes widened in surprise—

Gemma, a familiar voice whispered in my mind. I looked over at the library across the plaza.

"Is something wrong?" Reiko asked.

"I need to check on something. I'll let you two talk."

Desperation filled Reiko's face. I winked, and her expression turned into a glower. I walked away, leaving her alone with Kai.

I crossed the plaza and stepped into the library. The building was deserted, so I moved past the tables, chairs, and bookcases until I reached my mother's reading nook.

Maeven was waiting for me there.

The Morricone queen was perched in the chair in front of the low table. I dropped onto the settee opposite her, in the spot where my mother had always sat.

"Gemma." Maeven tilted her head. "Thank you for coming. I wasn't sure you would."

"I'm not sure why I did. Morbid curiosity, I suppose." My gaze roamed over her. "You're looking well. All things considered."

Maeven's face was still pale, and more lines bracketed her eyes and mouth than before, something her makeup couldn't quite hide. But she was still breathing, thanks to me. My stomach soured at the thought.

"Let me guess. You summoned me here to insist on my getting engaged to Leonidas, even though he didn't complete the Gauntlet."

Maeven shook her head. "No. You and Leonidas can make

your own decisions regarding your futures. I won't interfere anymore. I promise."

I wanted to snipe that her promise was about as firm as a piece of parchment in the rain, but I bit back the words.

Maeven straightened, as if bracing herself to do something unpleasant. "Your mother was right."

"What do you mean?"

"The day I came here to poison Merilde, she said that if I spared her life, then I would one day be queen of Morta." Maeven straightened a bit more, as if bracing for another unpleasant confession. "She also told me that if I spared your life, you would one day save mine in return."

My mouth gaped in surprise, even as my mind whirred, thinking about that image of Merilde that I'd seen on the bench in the gardens. She *had* seen that moment play out. I wondered what else my mother had seen involving Maeven and me, and my heart ached that she wasn't here for me to ask.

"I thought Merilde was lying, that she was saying whatever she thought might convince me to spare her life, and yours too," Maeven continued. "But it turns out she was right about that, and a great many other things."

Her gaze dropped to the low table in between us, and her eyes grew dark and distant, as if she was remembering all the secrets my mother had told her.

I hazarded a guess. "Things involving Delmira."

Maeven's gaze snapped back up to mine, anger and worry pinching her face. "I don't know what you think you know, but if you interfere with my daughter, then I'll—"

I cut her off. "I think we're past petty threats at this point, don't you? Face it, Maeven. No matter how delighted each of us would be by the other's death, I won't kill you, and you can't kill me."

Her lips puckered with displeasure, and her sour expression

matched my own mood. Still, we were stuck together, so I might as well make the most of it. Besides, right now, Maeven wasn't my most pressing concern—or my most dangerous enemy.

"Where have Milo and Wexel gone? Where is Milo hiding all the tearstone arrows he's made?"

Maeven's lips puckered again, this time more in thought rather than displeasure. "I don't know."

I studied her carefully, but I didn't get a flicker of deception off her. Still, that didn't mean she wasn't holding something back. "But?"

"But Milo watched me, Maximus, and the other Morricones play our courtly games for years. He's smart enough to have squirreled away money and other resources. He won't give up on his plot to destroy Andvari."

"To kill our gargoyles," I said in a cold, flat voice.

Maeven's mouth gaped, and shock surged off her. For perhaps the first time ever, I had truly stunned her. "How . . . how did you know that?"

"I found some odd burned bits of stone in an old tearstone mine where Milo was conducting some of his *experiments*," I spat out the word. "Then I found a similar burned stone in a book in Milo's workshop on Antheia Island. But they're not just stones—they're *dead gargoyles*. Milo traps the gargoyles with nets, punches his tearstone arrows through their skin, and then tortures the creatures with his lightning magic until they shatter and melt like glass."

Maeven's lips pressed together, but she gave me a single, sharp nod. "How did you figure it out?"

"Leonidas told me how Milo tried to kill a baby gargoyle on Antheia Island when he was younger. Then, yesterday, during the battle in the gardens, Corvina mentioned how Milo had bragged that his tearstone arrows could punch through anything, even a gargoyle's stone skin. That's when I realized what he was really up to." My eyes narrowed. "But it seems you've known about his plot all along, and yet you said nothing to anyone."

"I was curious as to whether he might succeed, and how I might use his invention to my own ends."

"How you could use Milo's arrows so that *you* might finally conquer Andvari."

She shrugged, not at all concerned by my accusation. "I thought I could use Milo's tinkerings in a more . . . skillful way, one that wouldn't bring disaster down on Morta. But I was wrong."

Maeven sighed. "Milo is too much like his father, and Maximus had too strong of a grip on him when he was young. Sometimes, I wish I could go back to the Regalia Games, back to the arena, and kill my brother all over again for how he ruined my son."

"Maximus might have helped him along, but Milo made his own choices, just like we all do—and he's going to suffer the consequences."

"I heard about Dominic's bounty," Maeven said in a toneless voice. "But you're not going to wait for someone else to find Milo."

"No. Too much is at stake. I'm going to find Milo and kill him myself."

Maeven flinched at my cold tone, but she nodded and rose to her feet. "I would expect nothing less from the gargoyle queen."

I also got to my feet. "You called me the gargoyle queen after the Battle of Blauberg. Why do you keep saying that?"

"Merilde didn't tell you?"

I remained silent, and Maeven chuckled. The low, amused sound made me want to force the answer out of her, but I restrained myself. Nothing I could do to the queen would ever compare to the horrors Maximus had inflicted on her over the years.

"How deliciously ironic that Merilde told *me* more about your future than she ever revealed to *you*," Maeven purred.

Frustration spiked through me. "You could just go ahead and tell me."

"And ruin the surprise? Oh, no, Gemma," Maeven purred again. "I wouldn't want to disrupt your mother's grand plans for you." Her face hardened. "Just as you will *not* disrupt my plans for Delmira."

"You need to stop playing games with Delmira. That is an excellent way to lose your daughter."

"I will stop playing games—when Delmira's future is secure," Maeven snapped back. "And not a moment before. Do us both a favor and stay out of my way."

I arched an eyebrow. "And here I thought we had finally moved past petty threats."

Maeven trilled out a laugh, then stepped closer and cupped my face in her hand. Her nails dug into my cheek like talons, but I didn't jerk away.

"My darling Gemma," she purred, "my threats are never, ever *petty.*"

I seized her hand with my magic, and slowly, forcibly peeled her fingers off my face. Maeven stiffened, her hand stuck in midair between us.

I gave her a cold, thin smile. "Neither are mine."

I released her hand, and she staggered back at the unexpected motion. Maeven glared at me, and I looked right back at her. Then the queen lifted her chin, turned around, and swept out of the reading nook.

We would *never* be friends. But for now we were allies, although the cynical part of me wondered how long that would last—and how soon Maeven would try to use, hurt, and manipulate me again.

By the time I left the library, it was midafternoon, but there was one more thing I needed to do today, so I returned to my chambers and opened the secret compartment in my jewelry box. I grabbed the item inside, along with the other necessary supplies, and set my plan into action.

A few hours later, everything was ready, and I once again found myself in the gazebo in the Mortan section of the gardens. Given the gazebo's secluded location, it hadn't sustained any damage from the battle with Corvina and the Dumond fighters.

I stared down at the lake slapping up against the rocks. The moon and stars were out in full force, painting everything a lovely silver, including the patches of fool's bane growing in between the rocks. I shuddered and looked away. I would be quite happy if I never saw those wretched flowers ever again—

"Gemma?"

I turned around. Leonidas was standing in front of me, once again dressed in his black cloak and long riding coat. My gaze roamed over him, but his injuries had also been healed, and he didn't seem to be suffering any ill effects from either the Gauntlet challenge or the battle. A final knot of tension in my heart loosened. I'd known he was okay, had sensed it with my magic, but seeing it with my own eyes somehow made it more real, more certain.

Leonidas stared down at the table. "What is this?"

Three covered silver platters were spaced down the length of the wood, with a single chair sitting in front of them. A wooden music box was also sitting off to the side of the table, with the key already in place to turn it on.

"I can't replicate the second and third challenges of the Gauntlet, but you gave me three gifts in the arena, and I wanted to do the same for you." I pulled out the chair. "If you'll let me."

A grin crept across his face. "I do love getting presents, especially from princesses."

I rolled my eyes at his teasing tone. "These presents aren't from a princess. They're from me. Just Gemma."

"Then that makes them all the more special," he replied in a husky tone.

Leonidas stepped forward and dropped into the chair. I went around to the opposite side of the table.

"First, a gift for your body." I removed the lid on the first platter, revealing a tray piled high with pancakes. "Blackberry pancakes. When we had breakfast at Myrkvior, you said they were one of your favorites. But don't worry. I did not make them myself. Princess Gemma has many talents, but cooking is *not* one of them."

Leonidas perked up, and he grabbed the fork on the platter, cut off a bite of pancake, and ate it. "Mmm. I approve."

"Second, a gift for your mind." I removed the lid on the next platter, revealing a gray envelope.

Leonidas picked up the envelope, removed the engraved paper inside, and read it. *"This letter entitles the bearer to ride on a gargoyle of his choosing at Glitnir palace."*

"You gave me a wonderful gift in Violet. I know it's not quite the same, but I thought you might like to ride on a gargoyle for a change, instead of a strix."

"Lyra will *not* be happy about this." A shy smile spread across his face. "But I have always wanted to ride on a gargoyle."

He'd confessed as much when we'd flown over to Antheia

Island, and I was pleased I could help make his wish come true. Leonidas set the paper on the platter and looked at me again.

"And third, a gift for your heart." I removed the final lid, revealing a silver strix pin with glittering amethyst eyes.

Leonidas frowned. "Is that one of my cloak pins?"

"Yes."

I plucked the pin off the platter, then went around the table and gestured for him to stand up. Leonidas got to his feet, and I carefully slid the needle on the back of the pin through his coat and hooked it together so that it rested right over his heart.

"This is the pin you gave me by the river the day we fought those bandits," I said. "To thank me for saving your life, even though no thanks was necessary."

His eyebrows lifted. "And you kept it all these years?"

"I tucked it away in a hidden compartment in my jewelry box. I could never quite bring myself to throw it away. For a long time, I couldn't figure out why."

"And the reason?"

"Because it would have been like throwing away my own heart," I confessed in a soft voice.

Hot sparks flared in Leonidas's eyes, and he settled his hands on my waist. I stepped into his embrace and rested my hands on his shoulders.

"I know there are still obstacles between us," I said.

"You mean Milo and my mother."

"Among other things."

"Milo will get what's coming to him. So will Wexel," Leonidas growled, a dark promise rippling through his words.

"Yes, they will." My voice was just as dark as his was.

"As for Mother . . ." His voice trailed off. "Why *did* you save her? Why not just let her die? No one would have known."

"*I* would have known. My father always says power without compassion is simply cruelty. He's right about that."

"But after everything Mother has done to your family, to you . . ." Leonidas's voice trailed off again. "Even she couldn't have blamed you for letting her die. And I wouldn't have either."

"I didn't save Maeven for myself—I saved her for you and Delmira. Because she is your mother, and the two of you love her, even if I don't." I hesitated. "And also because I know how very painful it is to lose your mother, even if you don't always agree with or understand the things she's done."

Leonidas's hands tightened around my waist. "You did it for me?"

"There is nothing I wouldn't do for you."

His eyes glittered with heat, and I trailed my fingers down his jaw, drinking in the feel of his skin against my own. After several long, delicious seconds, I forced myself to lower my hand to his shoulder.

"How—how do you feel about me now? After everything that's happened?" I asked. "We haven't always been kind to each other, especially in recent weeks."

A grin creased his face. "Well, you haven't tried to murder me recently, so I'd say we've made considerable progress."

I rolled my eyes at his teasing, then blurted out the words I'd been longing to say ever since he'd stepped into the gazebo. "Come back to Glitnir with me. Please."

He stilled. "But I didn't finish the Gauntlet. You don't have to get engaged to me now."

"I don't care about the Gauntlet or engagements or anything else. I only care about *you*. I love you, Leo." Once again, my tongue kept tripping along, but this time, I did nothing to hold back the words—or my feelings.

"I love you, Leo," I repeated in a louder, clearer, stronger voice. "Part of me has *always* loved you, ever since we were children. I was just too stupid and stubborn to let myself feel it. I'm so sorry about everything I said in the arena dressing room the other night. But I love you, and if you'll let me, then I want to love you the way you deserve to be loved."

I sucked in another breath to keep talking, but his hands tightened around my waist again, and I fell silent.

He remained still for several long, heart-stopping seconds. Then more heat sparked in his eyes, and he captured one of my hands and pressed it to his chest, right over the strix pin. "And you have my heart too, Gemma Ripley. All I care about is being with you, whether it's here or at Glitnir or wherever else life might take us."

I grinned back at him. "I was hoping you would say that."

I tugged my hand out of his, then flicked my fingers. On the far edge of the table, the key slowly turned in the box, and music floated through the air.

Leonidas tilted his head to the side. "That's the same song that was playing the night we danced together at Myrkvior."

"You told me that you remembered everything about our dance. Well, I do too, and I want to finish what we started all those weeks ago."

I held out my hand, and Leonidas captured it in his again and drew me closer.

"I never want to stop dancing with you," he whispered in a low, husky voice.

"Then let's get started," I whispered back, then pressed my lips to his, sealing our new beginning with a kiss, a dance, and all the love in my heart mingling with his.

ACKNOWLEDGMENTS

My heartfelt thanks go out to all the folks who help turn my words into a book.

Thanks go to my agent, Annelise Robey, and my editor, Erika Tsang, for all their helpful advice, support, and encouragement. Thanks to Nancy Inglis, Jeanie Lee, Alivia Lopez, David Pomerico, and everyone else at Harper Voyager and HarperCollins. Thanks also to Lauren Fortgang, Tony Mauro, and Virginia Norey.

Thanks to Amanda Bouchet, Jeffe Kennedy, Gayle Trent, and Rachel Vance for all their help, support, advice, encouragement, and friendship through my ever-evolving writing career.

And finally, a big thanks to all the readers. Knowing that folks read and enjoy my books is truly humbling, and I hope that you all enjoy reading about Gemma, Grimley, and their adventures.

I appreciate you all more than you will ever know.

Happy reading! ☺

Turn the page for a sneak peek at the next book in

THE GARGOYLE QUEEN SERIES

CONQUER THE KINGDOM

Coming Spring 2023

Reiko slid from one shadow to the next, as silent as smoke curling through the air. I crept along behind her, but my boots repeatedly scraped across the flagstones, making far too much noise. If Milo and Wexel were hiding on *The Drowned Man*, then they were certain to hear me coming.

As we neared the ship, I reached out with my magic again. For the first time, I sensed several presences on board, like dim candles flickering in a dark room, but I didn't feel the bright, hot sting of Milo's lightning magic. Perhaps the ship's thick hull and the churning water were blocking my power. Either way, Reiko was right. Finding Milo was worth any risk, so I kept creeping along behind her.

We stepped onto the dock, and a wooden board *creaked* ominously under my weight.

Reiko shot me an annoyed look. "Do you have to be so loud, Gemma? You're tromping around like a gargoyle in a glass shop."

"Sorry, your royal spyness," I sniped back at her. "But some of us aren't as light on our feet as dragons are."

She huffed, as did the dragon on her hand, and moved forward. I let out a breath and followed her, once again trying to be as quiet as possible.

We quickly reached the wide gangplank that led up to the ship's main deck. Reiko raised her eyebrows in a silent question, and I shrugged back. I still didn't sense Milo anywhere nearby.

We'd spent the past few weeks rushing from town to town, chasing down every single rumor that might involve Milo and Wexel. Two days ago, an innkeeper claimed he'd recently hosted a wealthy Mortan noble who was eager to book passage on a ship headed south from the docks here in Allentown.

We'd arrived at the docks several hours ago, closer to midnight than morning. Everyone had already gone to bed, which had made it easy for Reiko and me to break into the harbormaster's office and search for info. According to the records, *The Drowned Man* had sailed into Allentown early yesterday morning, unloaded its passengers and cargo, and taken the rest of the day to resupply. It was supposed to sail back down the Summanus River later today, on a return journey to Fortuna Island, and it was the only vessel currently anchored to the docks that was large enough to accommodate passengers. If the rumors were true, and Milo was planning to escape on *The Drowned Man*, then he was either already on board or he'd have to come here sometime soon.

Either way, this was the closest we'd been to the crown prince in weeks, and I was determined to finally reach out and latch onto the bastard.

Reiko eased up the gangplank and stepped onto the main deck. I followed her, for once managing to be almost as quiet as she was. Weapons in hand, we both glanced around the wide, rectangular deck.

Several barrels filled with arrows were shoved up against

the railing, with longbows standing up against the sides of the fat, round containers. Other barrels featured swords, while a variety of spears, many topped with wicked-looking barbs, were nestled in a net that was dangling from the main mast in the center of the deck. Still more spears gleamed a dull silver in another net that was close to the wheel on the starboard side of the ship.

The plethora of weapons wasn't surprising. Plenty of pirates sailed up and down the Summanus River, boarding ships, murdering sailors, and stealing precious cargo, just as they did on the Cold Salt Sea to the north and the Blue Glass Sea to the south.

"Do you think Milo might be belowdecks?" Reiko whispered, her breath frosting faintly in the chilly air.

I reached out with my magic again, but I still didn't sense his lightning—

Clomp-clomp-clomp-clomp.

Footsteps sounded, and a sixty-something man climbed a set of steps and ambled out onto the deck. Wavy iron-gray hair brushed the tops of his broad shoulders, and his dark brown skin was covered with even darker freckles from years spent in the sun. His eyes were a light golden brown, like the glossy varnish that coated the deck, and a jagged scar curved through one of his bushy gray eyebrows, as though he'd been hooked like a fish at some point in his sailing days.

Despite the early hour, the man's hair was neatly brushed, and the smell of his minty toothpaste overpowered the stench of fish in the air. He was wearing a short, formal sandy-brown jacket, along with a matching tunic, leggings, and boots, and the crest of a man's face with bulging eyes and an open mouth glimmered in gold thread over his heart. The crest matched the wooden masthead and marked him as the ship's captain.

A cutlass with a gold hilt dangled from his brown leather belt, along with a spyglass and a couple of long thin knives. I could easily imagine the captain shedding his jacket, rolling up his tunic sleeves, and gutting the catch of the day with those knives, right along with any sailors who disobeyed him.

The captain yawned and stretched his arms over his head. He glanced up at the sky and grimaced, as if the pretty pink dawn displeased him, then dropped his arms and gazed back down to the deck again.

Reiko jerked her head to the side, asking if I wanted to duck down and hide behind one of the barrels, but I shook my head. I was tired of creeping around, especially since the captain might have the answers—and passengers—we were so desperately seeking.

The captain blinked a couple of times, as if surprised to see us standing on his ship, but a grin slowly spread across his face. "I wasn't expecting visitors this early in the morning. I'm Captain Davies. And who are you two lovely ladies?"

"Armina," I replied, using my middle name the way I always did whenever I was on one of my spy missions. "And this is Resplenda."

Reiko arched an eyebrow, apparently not liking the hasty moniker, but I ignored her chiding glance.

Captain Davies looked us both up and down, his gaze lingering on our breasts and hips. The longer he looked, the wider his grin became. Lust rolled off him in clear, palpable waves, making my stomach churn.

"Have you two ladies come to warm my bed before we set sail? If so, I'll have to give my crew a bonus for their exceptionally good taste." He leered at us both, revealing a mouthful of straight gold-capped teeth.

Reiko growled, and smoke boiled out of the mouth of her inner dragon and skated across her skin. Davies's smile dimmed, then vanished altogether. Anyone with even a lick of common sense was wary of morphs, especially dragons. Plus, Reiko looked like she was one more lascivious comment away from charging across the deck and plunging her sword into his chest.

Davies puckered his lips and let out a loud, ear-splitting whistle that reminded me of a strix's shrill shriek.

I tensed, as did Reiko. For a few seconds, nothing happened, but then more footsteps *clomp-clomp-clomp-clomped*, and a dozen men rushed up the steps and streamed out onto the deck. The men were all wearing dark brown tunics, along with matching leggings and boots, and each one of them was carrying a cutlass. The men spread out across the deck and started leering at us the same way the captain had.

Davies drew his own cutlass and stabbed it at Reiko and me. "What do you want?" he demanded. "If you've come to take my ship, then you're in for a nasty surprise because the crew of *The Drowned Man* never gives up without a fight."

The sailors murmured their agreement and hefted their weapons a little higher.

Reiko growled again, ready to fight, but I slid my dagger back into its scabbard, then held my hands up in a placating gesture.

"We're not here to cause trouble. We just want some information." I reached down and jiggled the small gray velvet bag tied to my belt. "And we're prepared to pay for it."

Davies's eyes brightened at the sight of the bag and the distinctive sound of coins *clink-clink-clinking* together. "What kind of information?"

"I want to know if any Mortans have booked passage on your ship—especially any Mortan nobles."

The captain scratched his chin. "Nope, no nobles have approached me. I only sail down to Fortuna Island and back up here again." He glanced around. "Has anyone approached you lot?"

The sailors all shook their heads, and frustration washed

over me. Milo wasn't here. He had probably *never* been here, and I had wasted yet more time chasing down another rumor that had led me nowhere. I'd thought Milo was heading south, away from both Andvari *and* Morta, but it looked like I had been wrong about that, just like I'd been wrong about so many things lately.

Davies swept his hand out wide, gesturing at the ship. "No Mortans have booked passage, but you two lovely ladies are more than welcome to sail with us. I'm certain we could find a good use for the two of you."

Several sailors leered at us again, and waves of lust rolled off them and slammed into my chest. I resisted the urge to snarl at the men.

"Forget it," Reiko snapped. "We're leaving."

Davies grinned, but cold calculation filled every deep crease and wrinkle on his weathered face. "I can get an excellent price for a pretty little dragon like you at the Fortuna Mint." His gaze flicked to me. "I won't get nearly as much for you, but I'm sure someone would add you to their collection."

My stomach roiled, even as anger scorched through me. Davies and his men weren't simply sailors hauling cargo up and down the river. No, they were pirates—kidnappers—who waylaid innocent people and sold them to the DiLucris, the wealthy, powerful family who ran the Fortuna Mint. The DiLucris traded in all sorts of unlawful things, but they were especially known for their auctions of rare items, which included men, women, and children who were sold to the highest bidders. Supposedly those folks were indentured servants who could earn back their freedom, but really, they were slaves—and used for much, much worse things than just forced labor. Grandfather Heinrich, along with Queen Everleigh Blair of Bellona, had been trying to shut down the DiLucris' auctions for years, although they had never been successful.

Despite the anger still scorching through my body, I glanced at each man in turn, but I didn't see any familiar faces. All of these bastards were the sailors they appeared to be. Still, the fact that Reiko and I had just *happened* to run into pirates was more than a little suspicious.

"Where's Wexel?" I demanded. "Isn't it about time for that weasel to show himself?"

Captain Davies frowned, and his bushy eyebrows drew together, forming a solid gray line across his forehead. "Who's Wexel?"

I opened my mouth to tell him, but he waved his hand.

"Ah, it doesn't matter who sent you here." Another cold, calculating grin creased his face. "But we're going to have a lot of fun with you and your friend before we deliver you both to the DiLucris."

Davies puckered his lips and let out another loud, ear-splitting whistle. The pirates grinned, lifted their weapons, and strode forward.

For once, this didn't appear to be one of Wexel and Milo's traps, but Reiko and I were in grave danger just the same.

ABOUT THE AUTHOR

Neikirk Image Photography

Jennifer Estep is a *New York Times*, *USA Today*, and internationally bestselling author who prowls the streets of her imagination in search of her next fantasy idea.

She is the author of the **Gargoyle Queen**, **Crown of Shards**, **Elemental Assassin**, and other fantasy series. She has written more than forty books, along with numerous novellas and stories.

In her spare time, Jennifer enjoys hanging out with friends and family, doing yoga, and reading fantasy and romance books. She also watches way too much TV and loves all things related to superheroes.

Visit jenniferestep.com or sign up for her newsletter at www.jenniferestep.com/contact-jennifer/newsletter/.

THE CROWN OF SHARDS WORLD

KILL THE QUEEN
A Crown of Shards Novel, Book 1

Gladiator meets *Game of Thrones*: a royal woman becomes a skilled warrior to destroy her murderous cousin, avenge her family, and save her kingdom in this first entry in a dazzling fantasy epic from the *New York Times* and *USA Today* bestselling author of the Elemental Assassin series—an enthralling tale that combines magic, murder, intrigue, adventure, and a hint of romance.

PROTECT THE PRINCE
A Crown of Shards Novel, Book 2

Everleigh Blair might be the new gladiator queen of Bellona, but her problems are far from over.

From a court full of arrogant nobles to an assassination attempt in her own throne room, Evie knows dark forces are at work, making her wonder if she is truly strong enough to be a Winter Queen...

CRUSH THE KING
A Crown of Shards Novel, Book 3

Queen Everleigh Blair of Bellona has survived the mass murder of the royal family, become a fearsome warrior trained by an elite gladiator troupe, and unleashed her ability to destroy magic. After surviving yet another assassination attempt orchestrated by the conniving king of Morta, Evie has had enough. It's time to turn the tables and take the fight to her enemies.

CAPTURE THE CROWN
A Gargoyle Queen Novel

Everyone is trying to capture the crown, but only one queen can sit on the throne ...

Jennifer Estep returns to her Crown of Shards world with an all-new trilogy and a bold new heroine who protects her kingdom from magic, murder, and mayhem by moonlighting as a spy.